Multi-award-winning author [...] novels featuring strong heroines, the heroes who love them and the bad guys who fear them. She called Denver home until she married a Texan without reading the fine print. Now she lives halfway between Houston and Galveston and embraces the humidity. When Leslie's not writing, you might find her camping at a lake, fishing pole in one hand and a book in the other. Visit her at lesliemarshman.com, Facebook.com/lesliemarshmanauthor, Instagram.com/leslie_marshman or @lesliemarshman on Twitter.

Justine Davis lives on Puget Sound in Washington State, watching big ships and the occasional submarine go by and sharing the neighbourhood with assorted wildlife, including a pair of bald eagles, deer, a bear or two, and a tailless raccoon. In the few hours when she's not planning, plotting or writing her next book, her favourite things are photography, knitting her way through a huge yarn stash and driving her restored 1967 Corvette roadster—top down, of course. Connect with Justine on her website, justinedavis.com, at Twitter.com/justine_d_davis or at Facebook.com/justinedaredavis

Discover more at millsandboon.co.uk

RESOLUTE AIM

LESLIE MARSHMAN

OPERATION WITNESS PROTECTION

JUSTINE DAVIS

MILLS & BOON

First Published in Great Britain 2023
by Mills & Boon, an imprint of HarperCollins*Publishers* Ltd
1 London Bridge Street, London, SE1 9GF

www.harpercollins.co.uk

HarperCollins*Publishers*
Macken House, 39/40 Mayor Street Upper,
Dublin 1, D01 C9W8, Ireland

Resolute Aim © 2023 Leslie Marshman
Operation Witness Protection © 2023 Janice Davis Smith

ISBN: 978-0-263-30719-1

0323

MIX
Paper | Supporting responsible forestry
FSC™ C007454
www.fsc.org

This book is produced from independently certified FSC™ paper to ensure responsible forest management.

For more information visit: www.harpercollins.co.uk/green

Printed and Bound in the UK using 100% Renewable Electricity at CPI Group (UK) Ltd, Croydon, CR0 4YY

RESOLUTE AIM

LESLIE MARSHMAN

For my brother, Scott

Here's to laughing at private jokes until we cry, crying over shared grief until the tears stop falling, loving with an unbreakable bond until forever. From M&DFC to M&DOC with love.

Chapter One

Boone County Deputy Noah Reed sat parked just north of town, sighing with pleasure at the first bite of his breakfast sandwich. County patrol, his least-favorite activity, always seemed twice as boring on Mondays.

After leaving a note in the office that he was skipping the morning briefing, he'd grabbed breakfast at the Busy B Café and headed out to enjoy it while it was hot.

He set the cheesy egg-and-bacon delight on the dash and picked up his travel mug of steaming hot, extra-double-strength coffee. It was halfway to his mouth when a deafening explosion caused the mug to slip through his fingers.

Sending up a quick prayer of thanks that the lid was closed and his boys weren't scalded, he fumbled the mug into his cupholder and peered through the windshield. Like the fires of Armageddon, towering plumes of orange and yellow flames surged above the tree line. Black smoke billowed into the cold January sky, bruising the azure dawn. As Noah stomped on the gas pedal, he flipped on his lights and siren, then keyed his mic.

"Helen, this is Noah. We've got an explosion northwest of town in the Rosemont neighborhood." He careened around a corner and followed the smoke to a house engulfed in flames. How many people were trapped inside that inferno?

Powering down his window, he choked on acrid fumes moving in the strong breeze. A cross between the sweet scent of ether and the stench of rotten eggs made his gut churn.

"The 3000 block of Boxwood Lane," he continued, "just west of Barton Road. Requesting backup, along with fire, ambulance and hazmat. Inform everyone that ventilator masks are required. Smells like a meth house. Over."

"Copy. Dispatching fire, ambulance and hazmat to your location." Helen Gibson—the Boone County sheriff's administrative assistant, department dispatcher and de facto mother to all the Reeds—remained as calm and in control as she expected Noah to be. "Sheriff's on her way with backup and masks."

"Copy."

"Noah, you stay sharp."

"Yes, ma'am."

Like a scorching rain, embers showered down on the closest homes, and flaming debris landed in the front yards, igniting small fires in the dry, winter-dead grass. Noah parked several houses away and leaped from his vehicle, his sole mission to make sure everyone was okay. He ran toward the burning home but stopped short as a wall of heat smacked into him. If anyone was in that house, they were beyond his help now.

He turned and took a quick survey of the area. At least a dozen residents, torn from their homes by the explosion, stood across the street like a horde of stunned zombies and watched the conflagration. Noah raced over to them.

"Y'all need to get inside. These fumes you're smelling are dangerous." When they didn't move, he raised his voice and yelled, "Everybody, inside your homes *now*—windows closed! And keep your pets in there with you!"

An older couple started across the street to a house next

door to the destroyed one. Noah ran after them. "You need to stay over there—" he nodded his head toward the direction they'd come and herded them back "—until the fire department says it's safe." He eyed the group who still loitered outside. "Are you friends with anyone out here? Someone you can stay with until the all clear is given?"

A gaunt woman wearing a coat over her nightgown shuffled over to the couple. "Y'all can wait in my house. I'll put on some coffee." She motioned for them to go on in, then turned back to Noah. "Lord have mercy." Her birdlike eyes darted from the destruction across the street to Noah, then to what looked like a decapitated porcelain angel she clutched against her chest. "What is this world coming to?"

After confirming all the residents had retreated inside, Noah turned to her. "Did you see anything happen this morning before the explosion, ma'am?"

"Their comings and goings don't usually start this early." The woman shook her head. "But I'll tell you one thing, don't go getting yourself hurt over the likes of them. Nothin' but druggies in there."

"You know that for a fact?" Noah's gaze swung from the woman to the house and back.

She gave a sharp nod, eyes on the fire. "Everyone on the street knows it. Shady-looking people going in and out at all hours of the night. You learn the signs. It was never like this when the Smiths owned that place, I can tell you that." Finally looking away from the old Smith house, she inclined her head toward Noah, her voice low as if conspiring with him. "At bingo the other night, I heard there's more of them drug houses poppin' up all over the county."

The wind shifted, and Noah grew more concerned about the old woman. "I appreciate your insights, ma'am, but probably best if you head inside now."

She nodded as she shuffled back to her front door, mumbling. "Half my collectibles fell off the shelves while those fools was busy blowin' themselves up. Hmph."

Jogging across the street to where another group of spectators from down the block gathered, he gave them the same warning. "Shelter in place, and do what you can to avoid breathing in that stench. Give the firemen time to put out the flames and contain the chemicals."

They dispersed in a hurry when a new blaze broke out on the roof of the house next door to the main fire. Noah ran to the front door and banged on it. If the owners were inside, they might not realize their home was starting to burn in earnest. When no one answered, he went to the back of the house. There, a wooden shed crackled and sparked, already in flames. He couldn't let anyone inside die on his watch. He banged on the back door, then tried the knob. Again, no answer.

The fire truck sirens, faint a few minutes earlier, now blasted their arrival on Boxwood Lane. As Noah dashed to the front, he slapped at burning pieces of ash that floated down and singed his arms. He sought out Fire Chief Cummings while the men climbed off the trucks and unrolled hoses.

"It's a meth house, based on the odor. I managed to get all the neighbors to shelter in place inside their homes." Pointing to the adjacent homes, Noah said, "But the roof's burning on that blue house next door." Seized by a sudden coughing fit, he bent over, hands on knees. He straightened, still wheezing. "And a shed in the backyard is starting to flame. I banged on the doors but no response. There might be someone in there."

The chief nodded and signaled for two of his men to make

entry and check for occupants. "If you know this is a meth house, why aren't you wearing your ventilator mask?"

At a loss for words, Noah froze, staring at Cummings. He'd screwed up. In his rush to make sure everyone else was okay, he hadn't put his own mask on.

"Well, don't just stand there, son," the chief said, raising his voice through his own ventilator. "Go get it, put it on. Then come back and set up a perimeter, okay?"

Giving him a thumbs-up, Noah sprinted toward his SUV, already getting short of breath. He opened the back and sorted through an equipment box. Blinking against the sting of chemicals, he wiped sweat from his forehead before pulling on the military-grade mask. He made sure it sealed tightly against his skin all the way around. It took him a minute to get used to viewing things through the plastic, but it was a heck of a lot better than going blind. Everyone in the sheriff's department had one and always carried it with them. But it would help if he just remembered to put it on *before* running into toxic fumes.

Grabbing a roll of barricade tape from the box, he headed back to the damaged properties. Though Noah didn't wish a fiery death on anyone, not even bad guys, his blood boiled with excitement. He wanted to be lead on this case. Wanted it so much, it burned in his gut like five-alarm chili. It was only fair—he'd been first on the scene. Besides, he was long overdue to be assigned an investigation to run. He hadn't been a rookie for a few years now, but between his penchant for joking around and being the youngest deputy, he was more often than not treated as one. This was the perfect case for him to show the department that he was more than just a funny guy. That they should be taking him seriously. Especially Sheriff Cassie Reed, his sister.

Speak of the devil. The sheriff's vehicle rolled down the

street toward him, Cassie behind the wheel. Both the sheriff and her passenger already had their ventilators on. Noah approached the lowered passenger window, leaned down and looked into the crystal-blue eyes of a cute brunette with a mess of curls on her head. Granted, the mask hid most of her face, but even so…

She must be the new deputy from San Antonio. The newbie looked past his mask-covered face, casing the scene like a well-honed professional. Impressed on all counts, Noah figured he just might have to reread the HR manual's section on dating coworkers.

"Got everything under control?" Cassie's ventilator muffled her voice.

He nodded. "I'm just about to cordon off the properties involved in the fire for Cummings. I'll meet up with you after you park."

Cassie nodded and continued down the street, followed by another SUV carrying his older brother, Chief Deputy Adam Reed, along with Deputies Sean Cavanaugh and Peter Grant. They must have left Dave Saunders in the office as the on-call deputy, which was fine with Noah. Dave had been a pain to work with since the day he was hired. Cassie thought she'd gotten Dave and his attitude straightened out last year. Cassie thought wrong.

Noah strung the barricade tape, then approached Cummings for an update. "Any sign of victims?"

"Not yet. Still too hot to get in there. But if we find any, they aren't going to be alive."

Scanning the street, Noah asked, "Will the people who live in the neighborhood be all right to stay here, or do they need to be evacuated?"

"They just need to stay inside until we get the fire out." Sweat ran down Cummings's face inside his mask. "We'll monitor the air quality, but they should be fine as long as they don't stand out here and breathe in fumes. If any of them have health conditions, they'll want to take extra measures to avoid inhaling this stuff." He ran through some safety basics and gave Noah an estimation on when it might be safe to enter the building.

Noah gave him another thumbs-up and went off to find Cassie. She stood across the street, talking to Adam and the newbie. They huddled upwind of the fumes, the other deputies in a group close by.

"...second one in less than four months," Cassie said as he approached.

"In my experience, there's never just one or two." Even with her respirator on, the newbie's confident tone came through loud and clear. "Once we have a starting point to investigate, I think we're going to find more of them. Hopefully, in less-populated areas."

Cassie looked at Noah. "What have we got?"

"Everyone needs to avoid contact with these chemicals because they'll burn the skin. Hazmat suits are recommended for anyone staying on the scene." Noah took a deep breath of mask air, regretting the extra onions he'd had on his breakfast sandwich. "No sign of any victims yet. Chief Cummings estimates it may be tomorrow before it's safe enough to send in the hazmat team."

He widened his stance. He'd read somewhere that power poses increased self-confidence.

"As to your point," he said, addressing the new deputy, "you're probably right. One of the residents on the street said she'd heard rumors of meth houses popping up in other parts of the county."

She gave him a slight nod but said nothing.

"Have you started interviewing neighbors yet?" Cassie asked Noah.

Refusing to get defensive, he shook his head. "My main focus was on the safety of everyone in the immediate area. I'd planned to start knocking on doors once that was accomplished." No matter how well he performed on the job, Cassie always managed to find something that made him feel lacking.

Cassie turned to Adam. "Have Sean and Peter stay here with you to control the scene. If any of you go near the house, change into protective hazmat suits." She pointed for emphasis. "And keep your respirators on."

While Cassie issued orders, Noah took a moment to size up the new deputy. A few inches shorter than Cassie's five-nine, she appeared fit and capable. Fingernails short and unpolished. No rings; the only jewelry she wore was a pair of small stud earrings. Her white shirt was pressed, but he was pleased that her black jeans—the pants portion of the department's uniform—didn't hold ironed creases like Cassie's did. Resting her hands on her duty belt with an easy confidence, she kept her head on a constant swivel.

Seeing her next to Cassie, Noah couldn't help but notice the same authoritative ready-for-anything attitude. And he'd bet a six-pack of Lone Star longnecks that she was another by-the-booker, like his sister. That's about all he could tell about the newest member of their department, except for—beyond any doubt—she was definitely no rookie.

When Cassie's conversation with Adam ended, she approached Noah and the newbie. Between her directions to Adam and her somber expression now, he started to doubt her faith in him running this case. He took the bull by the horns.

"Can I speak with you?" Noah asked his sister.

"Wait here," she told the new deputy, then followed him several yards away to a patch of privacy. "What is it?"

"I was first on the scene. Established a perimeter, got the neighbors out of harm's way." Noah's respirator rattled as he inhaled a deep breath. "I want to take lead on this."

Cassie looked him square in the eye, and Noah's hope sank like a stone. Cassie had raised Adam, Noah and his twin brother, Nate, after their free-spirited mother disappeared without a word. He doubted she had an expression he couldn't identify the second it crossed her face, even while wearing a mask. Her brows drew together in a combination of sternness and sympathy. A look he resented.

"I'm tasking Adam with this case. I've got another assignment for you." She glanced over her shoulder, then met his eyes again. "I want you to partner with Deputy Delgado for a while. She knows law enforcement, has plenty of experience—but the way things are done in San Antonio may not be the way we do them around here. Show her the ropes. Get her used to dealing with the folks of Resolute, people who aren't just civilians we protect and serve but are also neighbors and friends."

Noah started to speak, but Cassie held up a finger to stop him.

"A couple of other things," she said. "This isn't some huge drug operation. Just an isolated incident or two of idiots who blew themselves up. So it's not really the big case you want."

"And the second thing?" Noah pressed his lips into a thin line, determined to remain professional.

"I arrived here in time to see you at your car. You didn't follow protocol, Noah." Cassie's voice held an officious tone. "I know you were hurrying to take care of other people, but in a situation like this, you *have* to put your mask on first. You were doing the wrong thing for the right reason, and I get that. But until you're able to stick to protocol, follow the rules, do the right thing no matter the reason—you won't be ready to take lead on an investigation."

During his years with the department, Noah had never been angry with Cassie or envious of his older brother. Now he was both. Angry with Cassie for not believing in him. Envious of Adam for being more respected within the department. These unfamiliar emotions made him disappointed in himself. And the only person who could fix the situation was Noah himself. So he sucked it up and followed his boss back to where the newbie stood, now holding something furry.

"What have you got here?" Noah reached out and pet the rabbit.

"Poor little bunny came hopping over this way from the fire. He looks a little singed and a lot scared."

"Noah, this is Deputy Brianna Delgado. Brianna, Deputy Noah Reed."

Standing in a circle of masked faces, Noah couldn't help himself. He breathed in and out with as much noise as possible. "Brianna, I am your father," he said, mimicking Darth Vader.

"Be serious, Noah," Cassie admonished, no doubt wincing inside her mask.

Probably not the best time or place for a joke, he conceded, but the sharpness of his disappointment had apparently dulled his better judgment. Besides, who didn't love *Star Wars*?

To her credit, the newbie ignored his inanity and stretched out her hand. "Call me Bree." She looked at Cassie. "You, too, Sheriff."

Cassie nodded. "Bree, it is. I'd like you to ride with Noah this week, maybe longer. He'll help get you familiar with the town and the way we do things in Resolute. I'm sure San Antonio operated at a much more hectic pace."

"An all-hands-on-deck for a meth-house explosion first thing in the morning is pretty hectic even in San Antonio. Sure didn't expect this type of excitement here." Bree glanced down at the bunny. "What about my orientation meeting?"

"We can finish that later. You two go ahead, get out of here. Swing by the office first. Helen has your badge and ID, Bree." Cassie's gaze focused on Noah. "Respond to any calls. During down times, show her around town."

"You got it, Sheriff." As frustrated as Noah was, he kept it from his tone. Last thing he wanted was for Bree to wonder why he hadn't been named as officer in charge at the scene. But his use of Cassie's title would let his sister know that he was definitely miffed.

He caught Bree's eye and motioned for her to follow him.

"I'll find the owner quickly." She held up the rabbit.

"There's no telling how long that would take. We'll drop it off at our animal shelter." He started for his vehicle, looking back over his shoulder on the way.

She'd crossed a lawn and was knocking on the front door of a house. When it opened, she showed the occupants the rabbit; they shook their heads, then pointed to a house two doors down.

Noah watched as Bree went to the indicated house. The door opened, a little girl squealed and took the animal, hugging it and burying her face in its fur. Nodding, Bree backed away, then turned and jogged toward him.

As annoyed as he was, the sight of the curvy deputy sporting such a serious frown coaxed a smile from him. She better figure out how to relax, or she'd have a hard time fitting in around here.

"Told you I'd find his owner in a matter of minutes."

He laughed at the satisfaction in her voice. "You got lucky. Probably 'cause you had four rabbit's feet."

As she groaned, he started toward his vehicle again. "Pick up the pace."

All right, then. He hadn't gotten the case and was stuck driving the newbie around. So what? Could be worse. A lot worse. Eventually, his break would come. For now, he'd bide his time, spend the day—no, make that a week or longer—with the cute deputy from San Antonio, who seemed competent, if a little stiff. Well, if anyone could get her to loosen up, it'd be him.

He always could turn a loss into a win.

SOME DAYS, she just couldn't win for losing.

Bree speed-walked to keep up with Noah's long stride as they headed to his vehicle. Aggravating man. His mask made it impossible to tell, but she'd bet her first paycheck he wore a smug grin that she'd love to knock off his face. A drop-dead gorgeous face, from what she saw of it before he'd gotten his mask on. But that wouldn't stop her from walloping him if he got out of line.

Noah Reed was nothing like his sister. Clearly younger than the sheriff, he seemed eager and passionate. Which she liked, but he was also irreverent in an annoying way. Which she didn't. Thank goodness they weren't being partnered longtime. She'd only be stuck with him for a week, maybe less if she could prove herself. After that she'd be glad to be on her own, where no one would be tempted to get up in her business.

She had her reasons for taking this job, for moving to a small town in a small county. Reasons she wasn't prepared to share with anyone. And partners tended to be nosy. *Well, Deputy Reed, you're going to learn real fast that being a loner doesn't mean I'm not a damn good cop.* Interview witnesses, review evidence, track down bad guys—classic policing.

She certainly didn't need some dewy-faced deputy babysitting her, even if he happened to be hot. But so what if he *was* hot? She'd been trained to be observant. Didn't mean she wanted to get involved with him—or anyone else, for that matter. She had enough issues in her life to handle without becoming entangled in someone else's.

Stay frosty.

Once inside the patrol vehicle, doors firmly closed, Bree removed her respirator mask, fastened her seat belt and focused straight ahead. When Noah didn't start the car, she glanced over and found him giving her an easy smile.

"Care to share the joke, or do you plan to sit there all day?"

"There's really no joke. I'd guessed at what you would look like without your mask, and I was wrong." His grin deepened on one side.

Bree lifted her left arm and looked at her watch. "Wow, not even two hours on the job. Gee, Deputy Reed, I think you broke the record for the fastest on-the-job flirting in my career."

His smile disappeared as if it had never been there. "Hey, that's not what I meant. It's like when you hear someone on the radio and imagine what they look like based on their voice. And then you see their face, and it's not what you pictured in your head. I—never mind." Resting his left wrist on the steering wheel, he turned over the engine and put the car into gear and edged around the emergency vehicles.

Running his words through her mind again, Bree acknowledged to herself that she might have overreacted to his comment. In an attempt to restore some equilibrium, she asked, "Where are we off to first? Pretty sure nothing in town can beat this excitement." She waved her hand to indicate the first responders still swarming the street.

"Oh, you'd be surprised. And that's why I'm here to show you the ropes. We have plenty of excitement in good old Resolute. Why, just last week someone let dozens of chickens loose in the city hall during a meeting about repaving the roads." A dimple popped in his right cheek. "Headline the next morning was 'Council Meeting: Nothing but Tar and Feathers.'"

She turned away and smirked to herself. She refused to encourage Noah's odd sense of humor.

"You'd be wrong to think this town has nothing much going on." He glanced away from the road and caught her eye. "Resolute has a way of keeping you on your toes. But not to worry. After a week riding with me, you'll have a good start on learning all of Boone County's dirty little secrets."

Secrets.

Bree looked out her side window, the glass reflecting a deep V between her brows. *This is not what I signed up for.* By resigning from the San Antonio PD and accepting the job in Boone County, she thought she'd traded being on her toes for being a flatfoot. Traded the action of big-city law enforcement for walking a beat in a sleepy little town in South Central Texas. A price she'd willingly pay to keep her badge.

Secrets. She hated them. They had a nasty way of biding their time, then rearing their ugly faces when you least expected them.

She could do without learning Boone County's secrets. She had her own to worry about.

Chapter Two

It was turning into a banner first day. After she and Noah stopped by the justice building to pick up her badge, they were dispatched to the local high school, where a break-in over the weekend had been reported. So much for a slow-paced small-town crime rate.

The downtown shops and businesses of Resolute passed by Bree's window as Noah drove through town. Well-maintained historic homes gave way to shotgun houses on small lots, and as they approached Resolute High, Bree craned her neck to take it all in. "This is a much bigger school than I imagined."

"They built the new additions about five years ago, after they were finally able to buy the surrounding land for the sports fields." Noah's lips twisted to the side. "Would've been nice to have this when I went here."

"Are all the fields just for this one school?"

"Gosh, no. It's a sports complex for the area. Kids who live in the county, or in even smaller towns with no schools, are bused in for classes." Noah parked in front of the main building. "And the fields are used by other schools in the county that don't have facilities to host home games."

As they walked toward the front of the building, Bree checked out the school's entrance, searching for vulnerabilities in Resolute High's security system. A surveillance camera, aimed at the front doors. *Sweet.* That camera would have caught the thieves if they entered this way.

Noah pushed through the front doors and held them open for her.

Unfortunately, no signs of forced entry indicated these doors weren't the thieves' point of entry. Bree checked her watch: quarter past ten in the morning. Except for those with free periods, most of the kids would be in class. She didn't need to speed walk to keep up with Noah. He meandered down the nearly empty main hallway. Maybe taking a walk down memory lane, since he was checking out the glass display cases hanging on the walls. What was he looking at?

Each one contained sports trophies and pictures of the school's star athletes for a given year. He paused at one, and Bree moved closer to read the names. The only player featured for that year was Nathan Reed.

"Relative of yours?" Bree tapped on the glass.

"My twin."

Her eyes narrowed as she looked at Noah, then the pictures in the display case and back to Noah. "You two don't look anything alike."

"Keen observation, Deputy." His mouth pulled into a smirk. "Sure you're not a detective?"

"Hilarious. It's an interrogation method, wise guy. Stating the obvious. Gets suspects to talk."

"So I'm a suspect and my crime is not looking like my twin?" Noah leaned in as if conspiring with her. "We're fraternal, by the way—not identical. But don't tell anyone. Most of the town can't tell us apart." He took a few steps down the hall, then turned back when she didn't follow him. "Come on, newbie. The principal is waiting for us."

But she wasn't done looking at the display case. "Impressive. Football quarterback, baseball pitcher, captain of the basketball team." Bree again glanced at Noah, automatically trying to peel back the layers of this man she'd be working with for the next week. What kind of man was he? Someone she could count on or just another class clown? "Weren't you into sports?"

"I was."

"Then why isn't your picture in there?" Was it her imagination, or did his posture stiffen?

"Only star players for each year are featured, and Nate was the MVP of every sport when we were seniors." The line of his jaw tightened. "If you squint, you can see me just there." He tapped his index finger against the glass case. "In the team pictures with everyone else."

She bent forward until her nose practically touched the glass and peered inside the case. Yep, there he was.

"Come on. Principal's expecting us."

Bree followed, almost growling when his pace once more went into hyperdrive. On purpose? She wouldn't put it past him. Aggravating man. "So your twin—your *fraternal* twin, Nathan—is he also a deputy?" It seemed like half the sheriff's department consisted of Reeds.

"Only one of the four of us who didn't go into law enforcement." Noah stopped at a door marked Principal and knocked.

"Come in," a deep voice bellowed from behind the door, and Noah opened it. "Ah, good, good. You're here." A paunchy older man with a bad comb-over came out from behind his desk and shook their hands. "Seems like a dog's age since I've seen you, Noah."

"I've found it's harder to get sent to the principal's office once you graduate." Noah smirked, then motioned toward Bree. "Mr. Jackson, this is Deputy Brianna Delgado. Today's her first day on the job, but she comes with a lot of experience from the San Antonio PD."

"That so?" Jackson gave her an appraising look, nodded his apparent approval and returned to his chair. "Nice to meet you, Deputy."

"Pleasure is mine, Mr. Jackson." Should've known the principal and Noah would be well acquainted. Everyone in this town probably knew everyone else. Bree assumed an impassive expression as she and Noah took the two visitor chairs. She pulled her notepad and pen from her shirt pocket, ready to question Jackson.

"Been to any of our basketball games this year?" The principal looked at Noah. "Heck of a season so far."

"I've been to a few. Team's looking good." Noah leaned forward in his chair, arms on his knees. "But I made it to every football game. What do you think Armentrout's chances are to get recruited by University of Texas?"

Jackson waved his hand. "He's a shoo-in for the Longhorns. But I know for a fact Texas A&M wants him, and I've heard rumors Baylor will be throwing their hat in the ring."

"Kid's got a bright future, that's for sure." Noah glanced at Bree. When she arched one brow in his direction, he pulled out his own notepad and cleared his throat. "So, Mr. Jackson, what can you tell us about this break-in?"

"All I know is they hit the science, computer and athletic departments. I told the department heads to cobble together lists of whatever they found missing or damaged."

Bree kept her pen poised over her pad. "Mr. Jackson, we'll need to see the footage from your security cameras."

Jackson gave a sardonic laugh. "Which cameras?"

"All of them. I noticed one by the front entrance when we came in, but there were no signs of forced entry." Bree tapped her pen on the paper. "I'm assuming the perps entered another way, so we'll need footage from all exterior doors."

"Oh, we know exactly where they got in. Through the gymnasium door. Tried to pry it open, then broke the glass right out of it."

"Wasn't your alarm company alerted?"

The principal offered a pleasant smile. "Most incidents these days are nothing more than harmless pranks, like what you might expect seniors to get up to right before gradua-tion." He shot Noah a knowing look. "You can find out more about those from this guy here. True, he never broke in—but as I recall, he masterminded most of the pranks during his years here at Resolute High."

"Why, Mr. Jackson, that is so not true," Noah's overly dramatic protest almost made her laugh. "You're making me look bad in front of Deputy Delgado."

That piqued her interest. But stories to ask him about an-other day. She turned to face the principal again. "May I ask what point you're making, sir? About the pranks?"

Jackson stood, apparently ready to shoo them away.

Noah got to his feet, but Bree remained sitting. She'd ob-viously hit a nerve, and she wasn't letting Mr. Jackson off the hook that easily. Keeping kids safe was a big deal to her, and it should be to this man, too.

Jackson must have realized she wasn't ready to leave, be-cause he plopped back into his chair. "We had some budget cuts about four, five years back and decided we could save money by getting rid of the monitored alarm system. Like I said, we typically only have pranks."

Budget cuts that happened right when the athletic fields were purchased. Bree clenched her teeth and her jaw went rigid. *Figures.* She breathed in deeply, nostrils flaring as she struggled to regain her impartiality. But based on the principal's reaction, she failed miserably. Damn her lack of a poker face.

The middle-aged principal sat up straighter, his face coloring red. "It's the school board that makes those kinds of decisions, Deputy, and I make do with what I get. A situation I'm sure is quite similar to your department being at the mercy of Boone County's budget."

His point might be valid, but the decision to save money by sacrificing security wasn't. "We still need the footage from the cameras."

Jackson shrugged. "A while back we had some technical problems with them recording. It's been on our list of things to take care of."

"May I ask how long a while? A couple days? Weeks?"

"I'd say more like a couple years. We've just never had a serious need for them."

"I know. You've only had pranks." She stood. "Thank you for your time, Mr. Jackson." Then to Noah: "Let's go talk to the heads of the departments that were hit." She left the office and walked down the hallway.

After a moment, footsteps followed her. "Hold on, Bree."

She kept walking.

"Delgado, wait."

She stopped and faced Noah.

"Is there something wrong?"

"You tell me." Bree glared at him. "Your school board thinks it's more important to build out the athletic department and fields than to provide security for the school itself, as well as the students." She bet he regretted telling her about the school expansion now.

"Come on. This is Texas. You know—Friday-night football, barbecue, Lone Star Beer." When Bree didn't return his grin, Noah asked, "You *were* born in Texas, weren't you?"

"I was, and I'm for all the Texas traditions." She inhaled a deep breath, then exhaled, accompanied by an internal chant of *You wanted a small town, you got a small town*.

"Look, this is a small county, and the school district doesn't have a budget the size of those in places like San Antonio. Everyone's doing the best they can." Bree opened her mouth, but Noah held up a finger. "And that's another thing that's different from San Antonio, where most people you deal with are strangers. Here, these people are our friends and neighbors. Sometimes for generations. Law enforcement in Resolute is true community policing."

Bree huffed a breath of frustration. "The bottom line is, one of your so-called 'friends' or 'neighbors' now knows how to break into this school. If the principal—no, make that the school board—doesn't stop prioritizing sports over safety and invest in an adequate surveillance system, statistics say the thieves will come back. And frankly, I think your principal back there has more power in this regard than he lets on."

"That man in there—" Noah pointed back toward the office they'd just left "—has been the principal of this school for more than two decades. He's always been trapped within the confines of the school board's budget and always had to rob Peter to pay Paul. I agree, he needs to find money somewhere and reallocate it to school security. But let's give him the benefit of the doubt for now. Maybe he's hit a brick wall with the finances, and the board needs to answer to that."

Bree opened her mouth, a retort on the tip of her tongue. Then she snapped her mouth shut and walked off in the direction she'd been heading. There was no point arguing with someone as stubborn as Noah Reed. Especially since he had some valid points. And some of hers were best kept to herself.

"Where are you going?" he called after her.

"Science department." She picked up her pace. Let him catch up to her for once.

"See you there."

Bree slid to a stop and looked behind her at Noah's retreating back. "Why are you going that way?"

He turned his head around. "'Cause the science department is this way." He and his annoying smug grin made a right turn down another hallway and disappeared.

Muttering a curse, Bree made a U-turn and followed him. *Such* an aggravating man.

NOAH SCOWLED AT the pile of swept-up glass in a corner of the chemistry lab. Wanton vandalism stuck in his craw. A darn shame to waste resources like that.

"As you can see, they broke a lot of glassware." Joan Metcalf, the fortysomething head of the science department, was a barrel-bodied woman with an ample bosom, rosy cheeks and a dimpled grin. This morning, though, her grin was absent as she picked up a jagged shard of glass from the counter and dropped it into a nearby trash can. "But what's on the floor doesn't begin to account for all that's missing. I've asked Mr. Jennings, the chemistry teacher—this is his classroom—to provide me with a complete inventory of the missing items. Should be ready in no time. He's extremely organized."

Noah stepped around shattered beakers and funnels. "Do you have a preliminary idea of what's missing?"

"Well, now, that's the strange thing. Looks like they took a bit of everything. Bunsen burners, mortars and pestles. There's really no rhyme or reason to what was stolen." The department head shrugged. "The biology lab is the same. Dissecting-tool kits, petri dishes, litmus papers… It makes no sense."

"Will the biology teacher also do up an inventory list?" Bree asked.

"Has to. For the insurance claim." Metcalf's brow furrowed. "The physics teacher, too. Neither of their labs have as much damage. Even so, we moved all classes to other rooms so you can dust for fingerprints and whatever else you need to do for your investigation."

Bree glanced around the room, and Noah could see the exact direction of her thoughts. *Don't say it. Don't say it.* "How many classes per day are in each of the science labs, and how many students per class?"

Noah inhaled. *She said it.* Tactful, Bree was not.

"Well, we have…" Joan faltered. "I see what you're getting at, Deputy Delgado. Fingerprints *would* be a challenge."

"Not a challenge. An impossibility."

"But you did the right thing. I only wish more people thought about possible evidence being destroyed." Noah smiled at Joan. "And, of course, it will keep the students from getting cut."

Joan returned his smile. "Thank you. This is the first time since I've been here that anything like this has happened. It's a bit jarring."

"Yes, it can be, and I'm sorry you have to deal with this. Let me ask you, have—"

"Have you or the other teachers had problems with any of the sutdents?" Bree interrupted. "You know, someone who might have wanted to get even for a bad grade or recent discipline?"

"Not that I'm aware of." Joan's vacant gaze drifted toward the ceiling as she seemed to sort through memories. "I know there are students who act up in class or smart-mouth the teachers, but as a department, we try to handle it with humor rather than escalate the situation. Nothing stands out as having warranted this kind of destruction."

"Thank you for your time, and we'd appreciate copies of those lists." Noah handed her one of his cards. "You can email the inventories to the address on there."

Nodding, Joan took the card. "Stay as long you like. As I said, no students will be using this room. But I must get ready for my next class. You know where to go from here?"

"Yes, ma'am, and thank you."

"Please call us if you or the other teachers think of anything that might help." Bree gave her a distracted smile.

Once Joan left, Noah and Bree went into investigative mode. As if they'd been partners for years, they seemed in tune with one another as they worked the room, making notes and taking cell phone pictures of the damage, all the while looking for the smallest shred of evidence that might prove useful.

Finally, Noah closed his notebook and tucked away his cell phone. "Next up, biology lab."

Without a word, Bree returned to the main hall. *Where she'll have to wait for my directions.*

Noah shook his head as she strode away, her gun riding low on her hip. *Oh, man. You're in so much trouble with this one.*

He followed her, forcing his thoughts away from the fascinating view ahead of him. The week couldn't be over fast enough.

Chapter Three

After speaking with the biology and physics teachers, taking more notes and pictures of the damage in their classrooms, Noah led Bree through the maze of hallways to the computer lab.

Back in the day, Ben Irving, now head of the computer science department, had been a classmate of Noah's. A friendly guy, Ben had always entertained with hilarious jokes and stories. At five foot nine and well over two hundred pounds, with eyes that twinkled and a ready smile, he was hard not to like.

"Ben. How's it going?" Noah glanced around the vandalized room. "Other than the obvious."

"Could've been worse." Ben shrugged. "I heard about that explosion. Right in the middle of Rosemont, right? What a crazy world we live in."

"Tell me about it." Noah grimaced. After a moment of considering that crazy world, he managed a smile. "Ben, this is Brianna Delgado, our newest deputy. Bree, Ben Irving. Champion gamer and nerd extraordinaire."

Ben laughed. "Not much time these days for video games, not with a new baby in the house. But you know how it is— once a nerd, always a nerd."

"Nice to meet you, Ben. I happen to have a special fondness for nerds." Bree smiled, and Noah almost gasped. Those upturned lips radiated a genuine warmth that lit up her whole stunning face. "I used to pretty much be one myself."

"Unlike your partner here—" he clapped Noah on the shoulder "—who was forever making fun of my nerd status. But I won't waste your time churning up old stories about what a jerk he was. Here, let me show you what the thieves got up to." Ben pointed to evidence that the burglars had tried to steal some of the laptops. "They probably gave up because of the cable locks we use."

Bree examined one of the locks up close, then got on her knees to look at the underside of the table.

"Those are mighty thin cables." Noah ran his fingers along one of the metal cords. "Seems like they could have just cut it with something."

"It's carbon steel," Ben said. "They'd need bolt cutters to make a dent."

"It also has an anti-shear sleeve around it. Makes it hard for cutters to grab onto the cable." Bree, still kneeling by the table, waved Noah over. "Look underneath. Instead of just looping the cable around the table leg, they've got a round bar soldered to both ends of the table frame."

Noah got down on his knees to examine the setup, distracted by Bree's nearness. Her scent—cool and refreshing, like the air after an early-spring storm—aroused his appetite to taste her, head to toe. *Get a grip, man.*

Ben beamed. "I came up with that idea, and some of the kids from shop class welded the bars to the tables for extra credit."

"Brilliant idea." Bree smiled again, and a ping of annoyance shot through Noah. She had not once favored him with such a smile. But her excitement over the security measure was palatable and contagious. "See, Noah, if they were just wound around the legs, all someone had to do was set the computer on the floor, lift the table and slide the cable off. But with them looped around the bar that's attached, they'd have to take the whole table with them."

"You ought to patent that." Noah stood and reached out a hand to help Bree to her feet, but she rose on her own. Figured.

"Did anyone steal a computer?" Bree asked. "Before the bars were added?"

Ben twisted his mouth to the side and looked away.

"This will be kept confidential, if that's what you're worried about." Noah glanced at Bree, who nodded in agreement.

"Well, yes. Once. That's why I added the bars. A couple of years ago, a student took one of the laptops in exactly the manner you described." Ben gave them a sheepish smile. "When I started teaching here, it amazed me that the administration didn't seem to realize how easy it was to steal a computer. I spoke to Principal Jackson about it, but he said they had no budget. And since there hadn't been any thefts up until that point, he couldn't justify the expense." He looked down at the floor and scoffed. "Okay, so I get it. Kids need textbooks. Teachers need supplies. Money only goes so far. So I took matters into my own hands."

Bree's million-dollar smile morphed from genuine to cynical. "So the theft went unreported?"

Man, she is a tough nut.

If Ben noticed, he didn't seem troubled by her implication. "I couldn't do it. I figured out who had taken it almost immediately. When I confronted the kid, he copped to it right away. Told me he had a part-time job evenings and weekends, and he'd fallen behind in school. His family couldn't afford to buy a computer, so he *borrowed* it."

Now Noah was curious. "Did he return it?"

"Eventually. I let him *borrow* it for a few more days while I refurbished an old one that was gathering dust in our supply closet. When I got it up and running, I signed it out to him for the rest of the year. After that, he stayed on top of his coursework despite having the job. Graduated with honors and earned a full ride to Texas State. Before leaving for San Marcos, he wrote me a note and gave me credit for his success. Man, I've got to tell you—days like that make teaching worthwhile. I still have the note."

Noah watched the judgment on Bree's face soften. *So you're* not *all stone and thorns, are you?* He turned to Ben. "We'll need a few more minutes to look over the area and take some pictures, then we'll be out of your hair."

"Take your time. I'm off to serve time as study hall supervisor."

Noah shook hands with Ben and gave him a card. "If you do find anything missing or damaged, give us a call. And we need to get together one of these days. It's been ages."

"I hope you're serious, because Mary and the kids would love to see you."

"I am."

"Great. I'll have her text you to work out the day and time. And of course, Deputy Delgado, you should join us, too."

"Um, thank you, but—"

Ben held up a forestalling hand. "Save your protests. You'd be doing me a favor. If my wife found out someone new to town wasn't included, she'd have my hide. So I and my hide are not taking no for an answer. Bring your husband or significant other as well. Heck, bring your dog, if you have one. We're all about family-style dining at mi casa. It'll be loud and rambunctious, but you won't find a better cook than my Mary." He patted his paunch affectionately.

Noah watched her waffle. "Oh, come on. I promise to be

on my best behavior." He cocked his head, widened his eyes and blinked enticingly.

And, wonder of wonders, he coaxed one of those dazzling smiles from her.

"Your best behavior, eh?" Bree scoffed. "It'll be nice to finally see that."

Ben burst out laughing, and Bree turned her smile his way. "Thanks, I'd love to come. It'll just be me, though. No significant other, no dog. And only if you call me Bree."

Noah hadn't had time to consider her personal situation before now, but he was a little too glad that she wasn't involved with anyone.

"Done!" Ben exclaimed. "Mary will be the envy of town at being the first to host the new deputy. You've done me a solid, Bree. Now then, let me get your cell number so my wife can text you the details."

Noah had joined Ben and Mary for dinner on numerous occasions, but he couldn't remember ever looking forward to it as much as this time. And he wasn't ashamed to admit, if only to himself, that Bree was the reason.

As Bree and Ben went about exchanging phone numbers, he walked around the computer lab, taking pictures of the minimal damage and fighting a Cheshire cat grin. Every little bit he learned about Bree made him hunger to find out more.

Cell numbers exchanged, Ben left them to finish searching the classroom for clues that might point to the thieves' identities. Noah finally glanced at Bree. "Four down and one to go. Ready to head to the athletic department?"

"Lead on."

As they traversed the building's corridors, Noah glanced at her. "You know, you really won over Ben. And in Resolute, that's a surefire path to good policing."

Her forehead creased, and not in a good way. "Good policing is accomplished through sharp observation, solid reporting and thorough follow-up. In no manual that I've ever read does it say anything about the warm-and-fuzzies."

Seriously? Why couldn't women just accept compliments? He'd never understood it. Cassie was that way, too. It made no sense to him. "Then you haven't read the right manuals."

She looked at him, wild-eyed. "What are you talking about?"

"Just, you know, you seemed to get along better with Ben than with Principal Jackson."

Bree stopped in her tracks. "The difference is that Ben found a way to fix a problem, despite the school's refusal to pay for it. *And* he managed to help a student in need. Whereas the principal just waved away security issues and blamed it on the county."

Noah grudgingly admitted to himself that Bree had a point. A tight budget *was* a sorry excuse for sacrificing security in a school. He made a mental note to check with the rest of the county schools, make sure they weren't in the same position.

They continued to the gym in silence.

"Let me do the talking with this next guy," Noah told her in no uncertain terms.

Bree's tone turned icy. "And why is that, exactly?"

"Because you won't be able to keep your face from showing how you feel about money being spent on sports. Trust me. It would be best if Coach doesn't see that."

"I have no problem with money being spent on sports, unless there's a more important need for it elsewhere."

"Which there always is," Noah countered.

Bree grabbed his arm to slow his furious pace. "Exactly.

Not that it ever matters. But you never answered me—the coach not knowing my opinion would be best for who?"

If ever there was a divide between big-city versus small-town policing, here it was. Plain as the nose on Bree's face. She was just too nearsighted to see it. "It would be best for our investigation. And best for you, if you must know."

"So all this concern of yours is really just for me?" She tapped her chest as she stared at him.

Noah glared. Stubborn, obstinate woman. She wasn't going to let this drop, so fine. She wanted brutal honesty? She'd get it. "Look, our department has a darn-good working relationship with the people of Resolute, and we'd like to keep it that way. Since you're new, you're making a first impression on everyone you meet. If you start ragging on Coach Crawford about how his equipment might not have been stolen if the school had spent more money on security, you will *not* be making a good first impression."

Bree tsked. "I had no plans to rag on anyone, let alone your exalted coach. But let me remind you, he's not a god. He's just one person."

Noah wanted to shake her. "One person who has absolutely nothing to do with the school's budget or how it's allocated. So save your holier-than-thou condemnation. What's even more important for you to understand is that every person who has gone to Resolute High for the past twenty years knows Coach Crawford. The kids love him. The parents love him. And yes, the school board loves him. Why? Because he's not only the basketball coach—he's the director of the entire athletics department. He's responsible for hiring every other coach and assistant coach they have. The buck stops with him, and he wins games. Lots and lots of games. Football, baseball, basketball. You name it, he wins it. Year after year. So trust me when I say that if you tick him off, which you most certainly will with that sour expression on your face, word will spread like lightning. And any chance you have of making friends or succeeding in any kind of meaningful investigation will be harder than finding a black cat in a coal cellar."

It wasn't like him to just lay it out there like that, especially this soon after meeting someone. But if she wanted to last as a deputy in Resolute, she needed to understand the lay of the land. Seemed simple enough to him, but he should have expected her not to take his advice lying down.

"You don't understand what it's like to be a woman in law enforcement."

He rolled his eyes. "Please. I have a sister who's the town sheriff. I beg to disagree."

"In a small town," Bree snapped. "Where half the force is related to her. Not the same thing at all, and don't even bother trying to argue that it is. For most women who carry guns… Well, let me put it this way. I'm used to not making friends. And the few I had didn't last long. So now I just get the job done, as professionally as possible, and call it a day."

"Have you considered balancing your cold aloofness and heated judgment with a little cordiality?"

She clenched her teeth, the muscles in her jaw flexing. "It's been my experience, Deputy Reed, that at the end of the day, people care more about me getting their stolen belongings back or locking up the perp who assaulted them than they do about me being Suzy Sunshine." A shadow of sorrow slid across her face before her features once again hardened.

Without warning, Noah's anger deflated. What had happened to her that made her so harsh? Did he really want to know? Seemed like she had some serious emotional baggage, and that spelled *messy* any way you looked at it. He had his own fish to fry. Why complicate his life?

His gaze lingered on Bree's face, and he knew the answer. Behind her words, behind her fleeting look of melancholy, there was a story. *I want to know that story.* More than anything, he longed to see that smile of hers again. That beautiful, genuine, soul-lifting smile. No matter what it cost.

"Maybe you've just been working in the wrong town." He held open the door that led to the gym. "But I'm still doing the talking."

COACH CRAWFORD'S OFFICE fit Bree's expectations, for the most part. Utilitarian, as everything was in a school, but large and well furnished. A small trophy case on one wall and a mini-fridge next to a couch. Ben Irving was protecting expensive laptops by utilizing shop-class kids, while the athletic department swam in luxuries.

A disapproving scowl tugged at her face, and she made a concerted effort to pull it back to at least a neutral expression. Noah had been right to call her out on that, but it didn't mean she had to like it.

Pasting a smile on her face, she shook Crawford's outstretched hand when Noah made the introductions.

"Nice to meet you, Deputy Delgado." He nodded once to her, then turned a smiling face toward Noah. "And boy, is it good to see you. Resolute High sure got boring after you graduated." Crawford's eyes shifted back to Bree. "You should have seen this guy in school. No matter how bad a day it was, he could cheer everyone up with a joke. He could even break up fights between players on the field with his sense of humor."

Trying to fit in, Bree laughed. But when she glanced at Noah, he seemed more annoyed than affable. A minute ago, he was all but worshipping the coach. What had changed? He hadn't reacted this way when Ben brought up the good old days. Even the principal's comments hadn't bothered him. But almost the first thing all three men had referred to was Noah's jokes. Maybe he was getting tired of being called a jokester.

Noah cleared his throat. "I hear your department got hit during the break-in."

"Yeah, they broke in through the main doors to the gymnasium. Really made a mess."

"Do you have a list of the stolen items?" Bree's pad was already in her hand. "And has anyone been inside the athletics building today other than you?"

"I made an announcement this morning that all classes would be held outside today, so no one other than me has been inside. And I do have a list, but it's a weird one." The coach picked up a paper from his desk. "A few bats, some baseballs and footballs, one tennis racket. Who steals just one racket?" The coach handed her the handwritten list. "Nothing that we can't replace. But since they came in through our door, I figured I'd better report my losses, too."

"What do you mean when you say the stolen items are nothing you can't replace?" Bree asked him. Noah side-eyed her with a warning, but she ignored him.

"They didn't take that much stuff. Hardly a drop in the annual budget for my department."

Drop in the bucket. Annual budget. Bree tried. She clamped her mouth shut. She even rolled her lips in between her teeth. But heaven help her, a sharp retort fought its way to the tip of her tongue, ready to fly.

Noah must have sensed what was about to happen, because he spoke up just in time. "Did you do a thorough inventory of the entire building?" He even shifted his position, completely avoiding her laser-like glare.

The coach nodded. "Checked everything."

Bree hooked her thumbs on her duty belt in a challenging stance. "We'll just do a quick walk-through, see if we notice anything else amiss."

"Help yourselves. If you have any questions, I'll be here for another half hour. Then I have a class."

Before leaving, Bree asked, "Will we need keys to open any doors?"

"Unfortunately, no. They cut every padlock off. Even from the rooms they didn't steal anything from."

With a sharp nod, Bree left the office but paused just outside the door.

"Nice seeing you, Noah." Coach chuckled. "And good luck with your new partner. What was your sister thinking, pairing up Deputy All Business with Deputy Nothing but Fun?"

Noah gave a half-hearted laugh, then joined Bree.

To avoid another argument about sports versus security, she asked, "Do you have particular areas you want to check out?"

"I wonder if there are less-trafficked ones, where we might be able to pull some prints." Noah led the way to a room off a side hall. "This is the laundry room. Coach was in charge of washing all the team uniforms. Said he learned how during his brief stint in the NFL, and apparently there's an art to not destroying them. There might be a baseball or basketball coach who helps, but no one else has ever been allowed in here."

The room held a few huge washing machines and one dryer. An industrial floor polisher sat in one corner.

"Why aren't there more dryers?" Bree asked.

"Uniforms are always hung to dry. Only towels and socks go in the dryer." Noah pointed to a wall of swing-out drying racks.

Bree opened a cabinet door near the sink. "Nothing but

OxiClean, a couple different brands of laundry detergent and some general cleaning supplies."

Noah peered into the storage space, closed the cabinet and moved to another; this one full of clean, folded towels. "I can't imagine anyone breaking into the school to steal stuff and wasting time in here."

Bree nodded in agreement. "Less traffic but nothing worth stealing."

They moved on to the equipment rooms. Each consisted of a sturdy chain-link cage contained within three sides of drywall. The doors, also of metal chain link, were set in the fourth walls of the cages, and the padlocks that had provided security lay on the ground, their shanks cleanly cut.

Noah crouched next to one and, without touching, eyed it more closely. "I'll ask Coach to make sure everyone continues to stay out until we can get someone here to take prints."

"Let's check out the point of entry." Bree turned in a circle. "Where's the gymnasium's front door?"

Noah led her along a side hallway to the front entrance of the building. "This is where people enter and exit for basketball games."

The doorframe itself was damaged near the handle, where the thief had apparently tried to pry it open before resorting to breaking the glass.

"There's not enough glass broken out for a man to go *through* the opening." Noah squatted to examine the broken glass piled up against the base of the door. "They just broke out enough to reach through, unlock the door and waltz on in."

Bree stepped back several feet to take in the overall picture. "That wouldn't have worked."

Noah swiveled around in his crouch, his face screwed up in a questioning glance. "What are you talking about?"

"They could reach in and turn the bolt lock near the handle, but there's another lock at the bottom of the door that can only be unlocked with a key."

Taking a pen from his pocket, Noah moved a piece of glass, revealing the bottom lock. "Son of a gun. Whoever did this had to have access to a key."

Bree nodded. "It had to be an inside job." She considered different scenarios. "If they broke the glass, unlocked the bottom lock and came in, the door would have pushed the glass away. So the thief unlocked the door from the inside, left through it with the stolen property and *then* broke the glass from the outside. Trying to make it look like a break-in."

Noah seemed to process what she said. "You're right. They were just too dumb to think out their whole plan. If they'd just opened the door to push back the broken glass…"

"We still would have noticed the bottom lock."

"*You* still would have noticed it. I didn't even think about it." Noah stood and shoved his hands in his pockets. "Good catch, Delgado."

She shrugged. "I'm just surprised this is the point of entry. With all the money thrown at this department, I'd have thought the gym would be harder to get into than a virgin on her wedding night."

Noah snorted. "Why, Deputy Delgado. I'm surprised by your turn of phrase."

Her mouth kicked up at the corners. "Just been trying to make a good first impression. Now that I'm past that stage with you, I'll let you get to know the real me."

"I'm looking forward to that." A muscle in his jaw twitched. "Let's circle the outside, make sure there aren't any other breaches. As soon as the crime scene techs get here, we'll grab lunch, then I'll drop you at the office for your orientation meeting. The sheriff's leaving for Austin tonight, and I know she wants to see you before she leaves."

"Why's she going to Austin?"

"She's testifying there in a case we closed a while back. She might be gone most of the week."

Bree tried to open a side door that wouldn't budge. She glanced over her shoulder to find Noah sauntering along a few yards behind her. "Can you walk any faster? My stomach hasn't stopped growling since you mentioned lunch."

He quickened his step and passed her. "And here I thought you ran on attitude and opinions."

"Deputy Reed, you haven't seen one ounce of my attitude yet."

"Just one more thing to look forward to, Deputy Delgado." He smiled at her over his shoulder.

"Better be careful what you wish for." She meant it for Noah. But based on her inside tingles brought on by his smile, maybe *she* should keep it in mind, too.

Chapter Four

Noah slid into the red vinyl booth at the Busy B Café, returning several greetings that came his way. In his early twenties, he'd spent four years earning his degree in Houston, the largest city in Texas. Fourth largest in the United States. An enjoyable time for him, but in the end, small-town life and the close ties of family called to him. He returned to Resolute and had never looked back.

The Busy B was already near capacity, boasting a down-home din of conversation and the subtle clinking of cutlery on plates. Though his day had already been full, it wasn't quite noon yet. A bit earlier than Noah normally took lunch, but teased by the savory smells, he was starving.

"What's good here?" Bree studied the laminated menu.

"Everything. And make sure to save room for pie." Noah glanced past her shoulder. Marge, the Busy B's owner, made a beeline for them, coffeepot in hand. "Oh, and get ready."

Bree lowered her menu. "Ready for what?"

"A force of nature."

The *force of nature* was a rotund woman in her sixties with a tight gray perm and expressive caterpillar brows. The squeak of her orthopedic shoes as she shuffled across the black-and-white-checkered linoleum floor halted at their table. "How you folks doing today? No, don't answer that. I can plainly see you're both wrung out. Must've been dealing with that explosion. Heard it was drugs, and maybe some people died in the fire. Terrible thing." She tsked, then pointed to the empty mugs already on the table. "Now, pull them coffee cups a little closer, and let's recharge your batteries."

"Yes, ma'am." Noah complied without hesitation. He'd learned long ago there was zero point in arguing with Marge. In the end, she always had her way.

While she filled his cup, Noah tried to give Bree a look of warning, one that would guide her in dealing with Marge. But she missed it. Bree, it seemed, would have to learn to deal with Marge on her own. Noah sat back to watch the drama unfold.

"No coffee for me, thank you." Bree glanced back at her menu.

"Hon—" Marge set the pot on the table "—scoot your skinny backside over and make room for me."

Bree looked to him for help, but he gave her a small shrug that said, *Too late. You're on your own.*

Marge chuckled, obviously enjoying herself. "Go on, sugar. Scoot. I ain't gonna bite."

Bree slid over, if a bit reluctantly, and Marge squeezed into the booth next to her. "I'm Marge, owner of this fine establishment. And you must be our newest deputy."

"I am." Bree's smile wavered, giving away her discomfort with the personal space violation. "Deputy Brianna Delgado."

Marge frowned. "Well, that won't do. Noah?"

"Bree," he supplied. Marge didn't cotton to formalities.

"Much better. Now, Bree, honey, when I told you to shove your coffee cup closer, I wasn't really asking. First off, it's colder than a well digger's belt buckle since that front blew in, and you need to stay warm. Second, it's clear as a bottle of vodka that you need to add some octane to that tank of yours."

How did one argue with that kind of logic? Bree moved her cup closer, and Marge poured. "Wouldn't hurt to stir in a good amount of sugar. Go on. It's right there."

While Bree reached for a couple of sugar packets, Noah sipped his black coffee. "Marge thinks diabetes is misinformation spread by sugar haters."

Bree smirked as Marge turned to him, brows pushed together in a frown. "It wouldn't hurt you none to have a little sugar, either, Mr. Smarty Pants. Might sweeten that vinegary disposition of yours."

"You know I love you." Noah gave Marge one of his most flirtatious smiles.

"Bah, you scoundrel." Marge winked at him, then turned her attention back to Bree. "Now you understand *one* of the reasons Cassie hired you. That department of hers already has far too much testosterone. You'll balance things out a bit. And for the better, if you ask me."

"Yes, ma'am. Seen that firsthand already." Bree gave Noah a pointed look.

Marge cackled. "Ha! Nailed it. Noah's the one in need of taming most of all."

"I'll do my best." Bree stirred her coffee.

"I'm holding you to that, young lady." Marge gave a motherly pat to Bree's hand, then touched one of her short, dark curls. "Why, aren't you just the cutest thing. So pretty, and like a breath of fresh air. Isn't she a peach, Noah?"

"Oh, yeah. She's a *real* peach." But a peach that doesn't look comfortable being touched.

"Honey." Marge turned back to Bree. "You just gotta ignore this boy when he gets all sarcastic like that. Heaven knows, I did my best with him, but he was motherless." She shook her head and tsked. "Means he's just one step up from a savage with his manners."

"Better not let Cassie catch you finding fault with her child rearing."

"Oh, that poor dear did her best, too. But she was a child herself, and some boys are just too stubborn to corral." Marge patted Bree's hand again. "Now then, little peach, heard you was from San Antonio."

"Born and raised." Bree eased her hand out from under Marge's and reached for the bowl of small creamer pods.

Noah could have sworn she used the motion to cover her annoyance with being touched. And maybe to try to hide the neutral mask that slipped unbidden over her face. *What secrets are you hiding, Brianna Delgado?*

Marge appeared not to notice. "Resolute must be quite the change from all that big-city hullabaloo."

"I thought it would be a quiet town, but today's been pretty exciting."

That produced a contemptuous snort from the older woman. "Reckon so. Imagine, people blowin' themselves up for drugs." Marge shook her head. "So, tell me, what made you decide to leave a big-city police force and come join our little sheriff's department?"

Bree shrugged, almost as if this was nothing more than a casual get-to-know-one-another conversation. But there was something about the set of her spine, the rigidity of her posture that told Noah this was anything but casual for her. Noah would bet money she was definitely hiding something.

"Oh, you know. Little fish. Big pond. Thought I might make a bigger splash in a smaller pond."

"Sound thinking, so long as you know that Resolute's more a puddle than a pond." Chuckling, Marge added, "But it's a beautiful puddle, and we love it. Drug dealers and explosions notwithstanding." Marge reached out to pat her hand again, but Bree must have seen it coming because she lifted her cup. "You'll see. I bet before long, you'll love it here, too."

Bree gave Marge one of her genuine smiles. "I'm sure I will."

"And I don't know about the folks you worked with in San Antonio," Marge went on, "but here, you'll be working with the best of the best."

Bree flashed him an inscrutable look. "Good to know."

Marge waved over Rachel. Wearing a blue polyester server uniform, the waitress hustled up to the table and set a coffee cup in front of her boss. "Need anything else, Marge?"

"Thanks, sweetie, but I'm just getting to know our new deputy while I give these barking dogs of mine a rest. This darling peach is Deputy Bree Delgado. Bree, Rachel Miller. Best waitress, mother and all-around person this side of the Pecos River."

Born in Resolute, Rachel was a thirtyish divorced mother of two and a fixture at the Busy B. She'd had a rough go of it the last year or so, and like the motherless Reed kids, Marge had taken her under her large and loving wing. The younger woman smiled warmly at Bree. "Nice to meet you, and welcome to Resolute."

"Thanks." Bree brandished another genuine smile. "Nice to meet you, too."

"What can I bring you?" Rachel pulled her pad and pencil from her apron pocket.

Noah and Bree gave Rachel their orders, and the nimble waitress took off like a race walker. Between rushing around the diner and having two small kids at home, it was little wonder she stayed beanpole thin.

"She seems very nice." Bree fiddled with another sugar packet but didn't open it.

"And capable." Marge's pleasant demeanor slipped. "You wouldn't know it to look at her, but a little over a year ago—while pregnant with her second child, no less—she caught her no-account drunkard of a husband in bed with another woman. Oh, he was a smooth talker, that one. Fooled us all. But you gotta give Rachel credit. Kicked his sorry butt to the curb and divorced him, just like that." Marge snapped her fingers. "Said she wasn't having nothing to do with a man who had the morals of an alley cat. Takes a strong woman to do that with a toddler at home and a newborn on the way."

"Rachel is definitely that," Noah said.

"What about you?" Marge asked Bree while pouring coffee for herself. Noah grimaced when she stirred in four packets of sugar. "Got a husband? Kids?"

Bree shook her head. "Never married, and no kids." She met Marge's twinkling eyes over the rim of her coffee mug. "And I'm not in the market for either."

"Oh, honey. That's what they all say." Marge's lips curved into a sly smile Noah knew all too well. She'd tossed it around with abandon when Bishop had first rolled into town last summer. As it turned out, Marge had been right about Cassie and Bishop, so there'd be no stopping her now if she aimed to find the perfect match for her "little peach." "Have you found a place to live yet?"

"I'm thinking about renting until I see how things go. For now, I'm staying at Doc's Motor Court." Bree shrugged. "Considering it looks like it was built in the 1950s, it's not bad. The owner suggested I take one of their stand-alone rooms in the back. It's fairly quiet."

"Those *are* the best rooms," Marge said, nodding, "but

you let me know if you have any problems. I'll set Doc straight, make no mistake."

Bree arched a brow. "It's going to take me a while to get used to everyone knowing everyone else. I gather you hold sway over Doc?"

"Why, of course I hold sway over him." Marge snorted. "I'm married to the old coot." Her contagious laughter spread to Bree. Marge leaned in, her voice now a loud whisper. "Hon, the real truth is, I hold sway over darn near everyone in this town 'cause I know all their secrets."

"Oh." Bree's face paled a little, and her cup clinked against the table as she picked it up with an unsteady hand.

Oh yes, Bree Delgado. You're definitely hiding something.

Rachel came back with their meals and was gone in a flash.

"Well, now." Marge smacked the flats of her hands on the table. "Reckon you two have some top secret deputy stuff to discuss, so I'll get back to work myself." She hefted herself from the booth with a groan. "Bree, darling, it was so nice to meet you. And if you ever find yourself in need of a break from that office full of men, come hang out here anytime you like." She headed toward the kitchen.

Noah rested his forearms on the table and smiled at Bree. "Like I said, a force of nature."

"I like her." She picked up her burger and took a bite.

"Hard not to. I tease, but she's good people." Noah shoved a fry into his mouth. "She also knows just about everything that goes on around here. When you're investigating anything, Marge should always be on your list of folks to interview."

"So, the town gossip."

"A gossip with integrity. If you tell her to keep something on the down-low, she will. To the grave."

Bree chewed and swallowed. "Good to know. Any other tips you want to share?"

"I'm sure I'll think of a few. I don't want to overwhelm you on your first day." He laughed when she rolled her eyes.

"Too late for that." Her lips curved into a genuine smile that warmed his insides like the slow burn from fine sipping whiskey. "But I'm sure your intentions were good."

He gave her a sheepish grin. "Didn't want you scurrying back to San Antonio, sorry you ever came here."

"No worries on that score." Bree's smile faded faster than a West Texas sunset dipping below the horizon. She turned her face from him—a sure sign she was lying—and glanced out the café window.

The list of things to learn about her grew, and Noah couldn't help but wonder. Why had she *really* left a promising career in San Antonio to become a deputy in one of the smallest counties in Texas?

His cell phone vibrated in his pocket, interrupting his musings. He checked the number before answering. "What's up, Helen?"

"I called on your phone because I know you're at lunch, and I don't want the whole diner hearing this. You need to get over to the McNultys'. I don't have anyone else available right now."

"Ah, man. Not again. Isn't this like the third time this month?"

"Yes, but this time it was Mrs. Parsons calling. I made her tell me everything that's going on before I'd agree to send a deputy." Noah listened to all the details.

"We're on our way." He ended the call, put away his phone and waved to Rachel. "Need these to go, please." He pointed at their lunches.

"Coming right up." Rachel brought the boxes to the table in record time.

"Thanks." Noah handed her his credit card and packed up his food while she dashed to the register.

Bree pushed her box off to the side, took one last huge bite of her burger and stood. "You don't have to pay for my food, you know."

"I know. I got this meal. You get the next one. Okay?"

She gave a one-shoulder shrug. "Okay."

Noah followed her toward the door, handing Rachel a cash tip and grabbing his card on the way out.

If Bree thought Marge was something, wait till she met the McNultys and Widow Parsons. Boy, oh boy. Their shift was only half over, and already it was turning out to be one heck of a day.

Chapter Five

Bree, stuffed after eating only half her burger, insisted on driving so Noah could finish his on the way. Also, she was already getting tired of riding shotgun. She'd had her own patrol car in San Antonio. Had driven when she wanted to and let her partner drive when she didn't. She had been in control.

But now, even though she had the wheel, she felt like a chauffeur. "Where are we going?"

Between bites, he directed her to a property about twenty minutes outside of town. Not quite a ranch, not even a big farm. Just a lot of land and several outbuildings behind a small wood-frame house.

As she put the car in Park, Noah gave her the lay of the land. "Ray and Ruth McNulty live here." He popped the last fry in his mouth, stuffed his napkin into the carryout container and pointed to another house down the road. "And over there is where Widow Parsons lives. Abby Parsons has been labeled by some people as a redneck trophy bride because she was so much younger than her husband. The kind of woman who always takes pride in her appearance, although I've heard it said she overdresses for every occasion." His mouth kicked up at the corners in a sheepish smile. "Anyway, after her husband died, Ray McNulty offered to help her with home repairs and the more strenuous physical labor needed on her property."

"Let me guess—the widow repaid Ray with her own version of physical labor."

Chuckling, Noah shrugged. "It's been one of the worst-kept secrets around here for a few years."

"The wife…?"

"Ruth."

"Right. So Ruth knows?"

"Yep, though admittedly, she was slow to catch on. But ever since she did, we've been dealing with the McNulty-Parsons feuds on a regular basis."

"*Feuds*, plural? Don't you mean the Ruth-Abby feud?"

"Well, yeah. The women have been at each other's throats for a hot minute. But there's also one heck of a lot of sparring between the two McNultys."

Bree blew out a long-suffering breath. "Why can't men just keep it zipped?" A problem her last boyfriend had had. He just couldn't keep his hands off the badge bunnies. Which was why she'd dumped his sorry butt over a year ago and swore she'd never date another cop. There hadn't been anyone in her life since, and she liked it that way. Uncomplicated. Bree totally got why Rachel threw her loser husband out.

"Hey, no fair generalizing. We're not *all* hound dogs."

"Uh-huh, sure." Bree twisted her mouth to the side. "So, what are we about to walk into?"

"You're gonna love this. Apparently, Ruth got ahold of Ray's cell phone and sent a text asking Abby to meet '*him*.'" He emphasized with air quotes. "Naturally, Ruth made sure to pick a time when she knew Ray wouldn't be home." Noah didn't bother hiding his mirth. He clearly found the whole situation amusing, and Bree wasn't sure what to make of that. As someone who had been hurt by infidelity, it wasn't a situation she normally found funny.

Noah went on. "Okay, here's where it gets good. Do you hear that honking—and maybe an occasional shriek?"

Bree cocked her head. Sure enough. "I do."

"The McNultys raise geese. Mean suckers, geese. At least, the domesticated ones are. Protective of their owners and can get vicious when guarding them against predators. Both real and perceived."

Bree opened the driver's-side door of the patrol car. "And for whatever reason, they think Abby is a predator."

"That they do, and they've got her surrounded on the back patio." Noah got out of the car wearing a devilish smirk. "Tell you what—since I know her, I'll talk to Ruth, try to get her to call off her birds. In the meantime, you see about dispersing the geese and getting Abby off the property."

"Wait. I'm a city girl. What do I know about handling geese?"

"About as much as I do. Just don't make them mad."

"Then why—"

Already closing the distance to the McNultys' front door, Noah shouted one word over his shoulder: "Newbie."

Okay, if that's the way you want to play it, fine. I can handle this.

Patio. Backyard. Bree headed along the side of the house.

I've taken down 250-pound street thugs. What's a few geese? Nothing more than glorified ducks, right? I'll flap my arms around, maybe yell at them, and they'll fly away. Job done.

She hesitated at the back corner of the house. The faint honking and shrieking was louder. She peeked around the corner and sized up the situation lickety-split.

An attractive, fortyish blonde was clearly dressed for a

tête-à-tête in a low-cut, high-hemmed dress, though the fabric was ripped and her hair was askew. Several red welts marred her bare arms and legs; one was maybe bleeding. Hard to tell from this distance, but they all looked painful.

The widow had escaped the reach of her attackers by standing on top of the rickety patio table barefoot, her expensive-looking, shiny red high heels lying on the ground, covered in globs of goose poop. Abby Parsons might be a two-timing redneck trophy wife, but currently she was a hot mess in a terrible fix.

As reported, a flock of maniacal birds surrounded her. No, not a flock—a gaggle. A gaggle of strutting, neck-bobbing, wings a'flapping, honking and hissing, maniacal geese. Alfred Hitchcock couldn't have concocted a better scene.

As the assault continued, accompanied by the widow's occasional shrieks of profanity, poop flew everywhere. Even from Bree's distance, the droppings were like nothing any bird had ever left on her car. These were disgusting.

Bree approached at a snail's pace. "Ma'am, I'm Deputy Delgado of the Boone County Sheriff's Department, and I'm here to help you."

At the sound of Bree's voice, eight black-beaked heads with tiny, malevolent eyes turned their attention her way in unison. For a brief moment of silent hesitation, it seemed the creatures considered whether she was friend or foe.

Streaks of mascara running down her cheeks, the frazzled woman looked up, her relief palpable. "Oh, thank heavens."

The geese did not seem as pleased by Bree's arrival. A couple of the closest birds waddled in her direction, honking and flapping their wings. "That's close enough," Bree warned but was soundly ignored. The two kept coming. *What now?* She called on the strategic principle of the best defense being a good offense.

"Scram!" Waving her arms wide, she ran toward them. Bad idea.

Instead of running away, they hissed, stretched out their wings and charged her, a few of their compatriots joining in.

Bree ran from the patio out onto the grassy yard, the geese hot on her tail. Circling back toward the house, she shouted to the widow, "Why aren't they flying away?"

Ms. Parsons, busy kicking at the geese who were trying to bite her toes, stared at Bree. "Domesticated geese don't fly more than a few feet off the ground." With arms flailing, she managed to keep her balance, roll her eyes and smirk all at the same time. "Where on earth are you from that you don't know that?"

"San—ow!—Anto—get *away* from me!—nio—dammit, stop biting me!" Bree swung her arms behind her, trying to swat at the giant goose that kept ramming his beak into her butt. When she reached the patio, she about-faced and mad-dogged the whole stinking lot of them, making herself as big as possible and yelling at the top of her lungs.

"Stop!" Abby shouted. "That will only make them mad—"

As if Bree needed convincing, the biggest goose rose up from the ground, arched its neck high and clamped down on the closest thing to it: her right breast.

"Son of a..." The intense pain froze the scream rising in her throat. She pushed at the goose until it finally let go of her. More head-bobbing, wing-flapping and honking merged with the flow of expletives leaving Bree's mouth as she rubbed her sore nipple.

The big goose once again started toward her again. "I swear, you try it again and you're mine, mister. After what you did to me, I'll buy you from the McNultys. Don't care what it costs. You're gonna be my dinner *and* my pillow."

Several more birds joined Bree's current aggressor. Forming up like well-trained troops, they spread their wings and stretched their necks.

Then, as a unit, they charged.

Bree turned and ran across the patio. The biggest bird—had to be a male—got in one last painful jab as Bree scrambled up onto the table. Panting, Bree pressed the button on her shoulder mic. "Deputy Reed, this is Deputy Delgado requesting immediate assistance in the backyard."

Noah appeared darn near instantly. Judging by his idiotic grin, he'd been watching the goings-on for some time. Maybe the whole time. Aggravating man.

Bree's eyes narrowed into slits. "You say one word, and I'll pulverize you."

His deep, rich laughter made her feel alive, but she still wanted to kill him. When one of the geese turned and charged him, Bree thought she'd have her revenge. Instead, Noah retreated backward, never taking his eyes off the aggressive bird, and disappeared around the side of the house. The traitor.

Way to have my back, partner.

And darned if the bird didn't halt its pursuit of Noah and return to the patio table.

Glaring down at the stupid bird, Bree derived momentary satisfaction imagining a savory cooked-goose dinner, complete with a sprig of parsley on top of the golden brown feast. "You're this close." She held up her thumb and finger to demonstrate exactly how close. More honking and hissing showed just how unimpressed he was with her threat.

Noah returned a moment later with Ruth in tow. "Come on, Ruth. That's my partner up there on that table. You've had your fun. Now call off your birds."

Abby's hiss rivaled those from the geese. "I swear, Ruth McNulty, I'm going to—"

"Ms. Parsons, what say you hold off with the threats until Mrs. McNulty corrals the geese?" Noah's tone was serious, but he just couldn't hide his amusement.

"Don't see why I should have to." Ruth crossed her arms, looking like a recalcitrant child. "If she wasn't such a husband-stealer who—"

"Ruth!" Noah shouted over the growing din of poultry. "The geese. Now."

With one last glare at the alleged husband-stealer, Ruth walked off in a huff, her beloved gaggle waddling after her. Bree leaped from the table, not even caring at this point about all the goose crap she probably had mashed onto the soles of her shoes. Noah came over and held out a hand to help the disheveled Abby down.

"How'd y'all know to come rescue me?" Abby eyed her shoes, her lip curling in distaste at the goopy decorations left by the geese. "Those are ruined. And they cost a fortune. I ought to make that old biddy pay to replace them."

"Oh, I don't know. They might clean up." Noah glanced at Bree as if she knew the answer. When she shrugged, he added, "And it was Ray who called this in."

Abby's mouth pursed and her nose wrinkled. "That sorry coward. I called him, told him what was going on, and he said *he* was on his way to help me."

Clearly, Ray wanted no part of the cat fight, despite it being a mess of his own making. Bree crossed her arms, wincing when they pressed against her sore breast. Yes, Ray was a coward.

But Abby Parsons was in no way blameless. "You have no grounds to compel Ruth to pay for your shoes, since they were damaged when you trespassed on her property."

Abby glared at Bree. "I did not trespass. I was invited." Then, dismissing her, Abby turned to Noah and batted her lashes. "Would you be so kind as to give me a ride home, Deputy Reed?" Her syrupy southern accent thickened with each word.

Bree rolled her eyes, making sure it was a gesture Noah couldn't miss.

"Sorry, Ms. Parsons, but we've got another call. The geese are corralled, and you're just a short walk down the road."

"How do you expect me to walk all that way barefoot?" It was as if Scarlett O'Hara had been resurrected.

Noah earned brownie points when he didn't fall for the routine. "I don't expect you to walk barefooted, Ms. Parsons. I expect you to put on those shoes."

She looked at them, her eyes wide with horror. "I couldn't possibly."

Bree had had enough. She marched to the back wall of the house and grabbed the hose. She twisted the faucet and, with Noah looking on in bemusement and Abby in disbelief, she squeezed the nozzle, spraying the goop off the shoes from where she stood. To say there was overspray was an understatement. "There. Problem solved."

"Th-they're soaked. My dress is soaked. *I'm* soaked."

"But clean enough for you to get on home all by your little old self." Bree gazed across the property. "And if I were you, I'd get those shoes on and beat feet before Mrs. McNulty comes back with her feathered friends."

Abby tucked loose strands of hair behind her ear in a vain attempt to right her appearance. "What ever happened to 'Protect and Serve'?"

"That's a police motto, ma'am. 'Committed to Excellence' is the promise of the sheriff's department."

"Well, I would hardly call this little episode 'excellence.' I don't imagine anyone would."

Noah hooked his thumbs in his duty belt. "Well, now, I s'pose that's a matter of opinion."

Noah's supportive words filled Bree with an unexpected warmth. But then she checked herself. Why did she care about the validation of a man she'd known for only a matter of hours?

Ms. Parsons, apparently heeding Bree's advice, ceased arguing and took off at a clipped pace, barefoot and bedraggled, her spine rigid with anger, soggy shoes dangling from her hand.

Bree and Noah followed her to the McNultys' front yard and watched to make sure she made it to her front porch before heading back to their cruiser.

"Ooo, doggy. She was madder than a wet hen."

"Is that supposed to be funny?" Bree reached for the car door, pleased Noah was still giving her the wheel.

He slid into the passenger seat. "It was. A little bit funny. Admit it."

"I will not." Bree fished out the keys.

"You could've gone easier on her, you know."

"I could have, but I chose not to. You have a problem with that?"

"Not a bit. Just wondered if that's your general MO when dealing with the shenanigans of infidelity."

"If you're asking if I look the other way, no, I do not. I mostly believe that people who cheat get what they deserve." She cranked the engine.

"For what it's worth, I don't hold with infidelity, either."

"I'm sure your future wife will be very happy to know that, but why are you telling me?"

"You told me your view. Just thought I'd share mine." He scrubbed a hand across his face. "Look, I've had enough of the McNulty-Parsons drama for one day. Let's get out of here."

Bree turned and fixed him with her sternest look. "Not yet. We have unfinished business."

"Seriously?"

"Yeah, seriously. Don't even try to convince me you didn't see those stupid geese attacking me. You made it to the backyard way too fast when I radioed in. You were already at the corner of the house, watching."

Bigger than the Rio Grande, his stupid grin spread across his face again.

"I knew it. You better not have a video of it."

When he didn't deny it, Bree crossed her arms, a habit when angry. She immediately regretted it. "I don't know what hurts more, my backside or my boob."

"We can stop at the store and pick up some goose ointment."

"Oh, you're hilarious."

"For real." Noah erupted in laughter. "It's actually called goose grease. Good for the relief of minor aches and pains."

The man found humor in everything, and it was time for a dose of his own medicine. Leaning toward him and batting her lashes, she drawled as well as Scarlett herself. "Why, you know I'm just a little ol' city girl stuck out here in the big, bad country. Would you be ever so kind, Deputy Reed, as to drop me at the office?" Switching back to her normal voice, she added, "I think I'll see if the sheriff has someone else I can ride with."

"Wow. Already?" His grin still sparkled. "You need to wrangle yourself up a better sense of humor, Delgado."

Bree wore a small smile herself. "And you need to lasso yourself a more mature one, Reed."

She glanced at him, expecting at least a chuckle. Instead,

his grin disappeared, and he turned his head to look out the passenger window. For the life of her, she could not get a read on him. And truth be told, it didn't matter. Forget his good looks. Ignore his soul-deep laughter. Mr. Happy-Go-Lucky wasn't her type.

To banish the aggravating man from her mind, she turned her musings to more important things.

How do I get back to the justice center from here?

And…

How exactly does one care for a goose-bit boob?

Chapter Six

Noah's vehicle idled out front of the justice center while he waited for Bree. She'd lingered after the morning briefing—something about a personal phone call she had to make. Since the explosion and goose shenanigans on Monday, they'd had two days of nothing but mundane calls and minor incidents. Days so tedious that under normal circumstances, eight hours would have felt like twelve. But with Bree riding shotgun, quitting time seemed to butt right up against starting time. He'd actually started to enjoy her company, despite her exasperating stubborn streak and outspoken opinions.

Noah chuckled. When Cassie had assigned him to ride with Bree, his disappointment had been obvious. No doubt she assumed he was still unhappy about it, and he hesitated to correct that misconception.

When Cassie was raising her brothers, she'd been big on learning experiences, character-growth experiences, it'll-be-good-for-you experiences. Last year, when she'd been appointed sheriff, she'd applied those methods at work. As long as Cassie thought Noah didn't want to do something, she'd make him do it for the *experience*. And he might be a jokester, but he was no dummy. If he couldn't work the meth-house explosion, partnering with Bree was the next-best option.

The passenger door opened, and Bree paused. She leaned down, picked up the goose feather Noah had left on her seat and then climbed in. Twirling the feather shaft between her thumb and finger, she cocked one questioning brow at him.

"A memento of our first day together."

Bree snorted. "I hope this came from the goose that goosed me."

He backed out of the parking space. "Besides never yelling at or charging a goose, you should *never* try to pull a feather out of a live one."

"You could have told me about the charging and yelling *before* I had to deal with them," Bree muttered as she buckled her seat belt.

"I told you not to make the geese mad." He fought to keep his face straight as he put the car in Drive.

"Details would have been nice." She bent her head over the feather, inspecting it up close. "It's kind of pretty, the light gray color and then these darker dots making a design toward the tip."

"They're supposed to be lucky, too."

Bree looked at him. "What kind of luck are you hoping for?"

"Oh, I don't know." Noah headed east. "Maybe a little more on-the-job action."

"I see." A small frown formed as she set the feather on the dash. "Monday wasn't enough excitement for one week?"

"You didn't think the last couple of days were boring?" He took his eyes off the road to look at her, but she kept staring straight ahead. "You're not missing the fast pace of your last job?"

"As a matter of fact, I'm not." She crossed her arms. He'd already caught on to that being a sign she was vexed about something or other. "And I doubt I'll be disappointed, since we're just going back to the high school, right?"

"Right." He stopped at one of the few red lights in Resolute and looked at Bree. "I got the forensics report this morning right after our meeting. No viable prints, no evidence collected except broken glass and the cheap padlocks cut off the storage areas in the gym. They compared the tool marks to a variety of possible bolt cutters, and apparently the ones used were as cheap as the locks." The light turned green, and he continued through the intersection. "But based on their findings, you were right—it was an inside job. We need to get a list from Principal Jackson of everyone with a key for that door, or a master key, and then—"

Helen's voice came over the police radio. "Reed and Delgado. What's your location?"

Noah grabbed the radio mic off the dash. "This is Reed. En route to Resolute High."

"Detour immediately to Peake's Sweets and Treats. Major disturbance in process. Subject is not armed but extremely violent. Upon arrival, advise if you need backup."

"On our way." He pulled to the side of the road and checked for traffic, then made a U-turn and sped back the way they'd come, lights and siren running.

"Peake's Sweets and Treats?" Bree asked.

"Ice-cream and candy shop about a block off the town square. Family-owned for generations. Bob Peake retired a few years ago, and now his daughter, Sandy, runs it. She's in her thirties. Super-nice lady, but she doesn't brook any trouble in the store."

The shop sat in the middle of a block of attached stores. Noah braked to a stop directly in front, angled in toward the curb. He killed the lights and siren, and they jumped from the car and approached the shop's windows, evaluating the situation.

"Looks like the place has been trashed. I only see one perp, left side, watching us."

"Several customers at the tables along this wall." She indicated the side closest to the door. "Adults *and* kids."

"And that's Sandy between the perp and the others, swinging a broom at him."

"She's got spunk." Bree stepped back from the window. "Think the back door is unlocked? If it is, we can come at him from both directions."

"No idea. How fast can you run?"

"Fast."

"Go."

In less than a minute, Bree was there and back.

"Locked." She sucked in deep breaths.

"Okay, let's do this." Noah pulled open the front door and walked in, Bree right behind him. "Heard you're having some trouble, Sandy."

"I won't be if you'll hold him so I can whack him." She brandished the broom like a martial arts fighting staff.

The troublemaker was backed up against a wall with the non-business end of the broom. He was emaciated to the point that he resembled a clothed skeleton. Even from several feet away, sores on his face stood out against the pale skin stretched tight across his skull. He definitely *looked* like a meth addict. But that didn't jibe with the apparent sugar craving. That was usually associated with opioids or heroin withdrawal.

"I'm Noah. What's your name?" He took a step closer. Behind him, Bree urged the customers to leave *now*.

The man bounced from foot to foot. Noah estimated the

guy's age to be midtwenties, though he looked older. Hard drugs were definitely not a body's friend.

"His name's Kenny." Sandy still stood nearby, brandishing her broom. "He's been in here before for candy, and I figured he was on heroin or oxy. I've never seen him like this."

"Well, Kenny, looks like you're upset about something." Noah stepped over downed spinner racks and what had to be hundreds of bags of candy, staying alert, ready for anything. As weak as the guy appeared, meth-induced psychosis could make him aggressive. "I'd like to help you work it out, if I can."

"She wouldn't let me have my candy." Kenny waved at Sandy.

"You were sticking your filthy hands in all the bins of loose candy," Sandy said, raising her voice. Her face turned almost as red as her hair. "Then slobbering all over your fingers and sticking them in more bins. I have to throw out my whole inventory thanks to you."

"Sandy," Bree said, "why don't you check on your customers outside while Noah talks to Kenny?"

Sandy cursed under her breath at Kenny but must have listened to Bree, because the front door opened and closed.

"If all you want is candy, we can fill up some bags for you." Noah kept his voice calm. "That sound good?"

Kenny studied the two deputies with dilated eyes, scratched at one of the scabs on his face and then charged Noah.

Raising his arms, Noah took a step back to brace himself. His right ankle rolled to the side, and he glanced down at a bag of monster jawbreakers beneath his foot. At the same moment, Kenny straight-armed him dead center in the chest. Noah's legs tangled in spinner racks that crisscrossed each other on the floor. His backward momentum slammed him into Bree, taking her down with him.

Kenny pointed at them, shrieked something about impostors and ran behind the counter.

"You okay?" Noah asked Bree while disengaging rack hooks that were caught in his clothes.

Pushing herself to her feet, Bree wiped blood from her lower lip, then helped pull Noah up from the floor. She touched the back of her head and winced. "I'll be fine, but Kenny seems to be spiraling."

As he tested his weight on his twisted ankle, Noah watched Kenny. The cash register sat on the counter beside cases filled with truffles and specialty candies. A few feet behind it, a cold case held tubs of ice cream, and next to that sat cones and toppings for sundaes and other icy creations. Having thrown open the cold-case lids, Kenny paced back and forth, shoving his arm down, then raising it with his hand full of ice cream. It melted and ran down his arm as he shoved his fingers into his mouth.

Satisfied his ankle wasn't sprained, Noah signaled for Bree to approach one end of the counter while he headed to the other. Kenny screamed incoherent words at them and faced off with Noah. Bree circled the end of the candy case and picked up speed. But her foot hit a puddle of melted ice cream and she went down, sliding into Kenny's legs like a bowling ball knocking down a seven-ten split.

Facedown in the sticky mess on the floor, Kenny struggled to get up. But Bree held his legs while Noah cuffed the troubled man, who then refused to get up. Unable to get traction in the melted ice cream, they pushed Kenny around the end of the counter and to a relatively clean area. They finally hoisted him to his feet and set him in a booth.

"I don't understand what's happening around here." Noah

studied the wreckage. "Human traffickers and drug dealers last year, now a meth house exploding and an addict destroying the candy store." He shook his head. "What's next?"

"I don't know." Bree shrugged. "But we should probably get him into the car while he can still walk. Hard to say how long ago he used, and I don't feel like carrying his sorry butt if he comes down."

Noah agreed as he grabbed the guy by one arm and Bree got his other.

As they approached the shop's door, Sandy pulled it open from outside and held it for them. They got Kenny into the back seat of their vehicle, locked it up and then returned to the store.

Sandy stood in the center of the shop, hands planted on her hips as she surveyed the destruction of property and loss of inventory. "Thanks, Noah. If y'all hadn't gotten here when you did, *I* might've been the one getting arrested." She scoffed. "What a mess." She picked up a tipped-over rack.

"I know you probably want to jump in and clean up so you can get back to business, but first you need to take pictures." Noah glanced around. "Lots of pictures. Your insurance company will want them for the claim. And if you email them to me, I'll make sure they stay with the file. They'll show the extent of the damage when he goes to court."

Sandy sighed but set the rack back to its overturned position.

"Can I ask how all this started?" Bree asked.

"Well, it started out as a glorious day here in the magical Land of Sweets, with rainbow candies and unicorn farts—" Bree's expression turned incredulous, and Sandy laughed, picking up a bag of Unicorn Farts cotton candy from the floor "—when suddenly, the meth monster breached the moat."

Still looking at the unicorn bag in Sandy's hand, Bree joined in with genuine laughter. It warmed Noah in a way he couldn't describe.

"It was pretty much what I said before. When he came in, he started grabbing loose candy from the bins without using the scoops. I yelled at him, and he came at me." Her mouth twisted into a smirk. "I grabbed the broom and got in a few good smacks with the bristles before I had to turn it around and poke him with the handle."

"Sorry I missed that." Noah laughed.

"I was impressed with your broom-combat skills," Bree said.

"You weren't so bad in the ice-cream wrestling pit, yourself." Sandy nodded toward Bree. "You must be the deputy Cassie was talking about hiring."

Bree stilled and her brows drew together as if she was uneasy at being the hot topic around town. But why?

"Sandy, this is Deputy Bree Delgado. Bree, Sandy Peake. And Bree, you shouldn't be surprised that so many people already know about you. It wasn't exactly a secret we were short a deputy."

"Pleased to meet you, Bree." Sandy beamed at both of them. "You and Noah make a good team."

"Oh, we're not really…" Bree's voice faded away as her cheeks took on a peach hue.

Noah cleared his throat at the awkward moment. Awkward for Bree, at least. *He* hoped they'd remain a team, even after Cassie returned from Austin. "Sandy, after you take the pictures, can you lock up and go over to the station to make a statement about what happened before we got here? Your insurance company is going to want that info, too. I'll add it to my report when I write it up later." He blew out a breath. "Right now we have to haul our friend to the hospital."

Sandy's eyes narrowed. "That jerk better not get off on some lame insanity plea just because he fried his brain with drugs. Not after what he's costing me."

"You do have business insurance, don't you?" Bree asked.

"Oh, sure we do. With a big fat deductible." Sandy rubbed her forehead. "And when Daddy finds out about this…"

"Don't worry—we're arresting Kenny." Noah didn't envy Sandy her situation. "But right now he needs to be cuffed to a hospital bed while they confirm what he's on. We always have to test for drugs and alcohol when we suspect the perp is under the influence. And there's no question with Kenny."

Sandy hmphed but seemed pleased by his words. "You might want to think about hog-tying him for the drive. Even if he crashes from the drugs, the sugar high will probably keep him buzzing for days." She pulled her phone from her pocket and started snapping pictures, muttering words that would make an oil rig roughneck blush.

BREE FIDGETED ON the hard-plastic hospital chair in the emergency room triage. Drumming her fingers on her knees, she waited for toxicology reports on Kenny Schneider—according to the driver's license in his wallet—while Noah handled the hospital paperwork.

With wrists and ankles cuffed to the gurney, Kenny now lay quiet, sedated after still being out of control when they brought him in. Everyone knew the idiot was fried out on meth, but they would need the official findings for the criminal proceedings.

Plus, she had dealt with her fair share of addicts, and she'd bet the family-size M&M's stashed in her go bag that this guy was operating on more than one drug. As soon as his lab work was back, they'd haul his scrawny butt to jail and book him for multiple charges. Including assaulting two deputies.

Bree's body ached from the Sweets and Treats altercation. She must have smacked the floor when Noah slammed into her, based on the throbbing knot on the back of her head and accompanying killer headache. At least her lip had stopped bleeding, but it was tender.

Noah parted the curtains and entered the small space. "Heard anything yet?"

"They must still be running tests. By the way, I hope you're happy that your stupid feather gave you exactly what you wished for." In a mimicking voice she added, "'A little more action. A little excitement.'"

He grinned. "Never doubt the value of a goose feather." His expression sobered. "But seriously, you were impressive today, getting all the customers out safely. Especially the kids."

She dropped her gaze. "Yeah. The kids." Kids lost in the system. Kids needing a chance. Kids risking their lives by being on the streets, in a convenience store at the wrong moment, in a frickin' small-town candy store. When she looked up, she caught Noah studying her with those intense brown eyes of his. When he worked at it—like now—he seemed able to read her mind. She needed to shut that down, immediately. "You also gotta admit, I'd make a mean steer wrangler."

That broke his keen focus on her. "Remind me to take you to the Chute sometime." The corner of his mouth kicked up in a lopsided grin. "Best steaks in the county."

She frowned, confused by his left turn in the conversation. "I think I'm missing the connection between—"

"Help! Someone help me!" A woman's frantic yells brought Bree to her feet.

Noah yanked the curtain back that opened onto the ER lobby, but he and Bree remained where they were as nurses and orderlies ran to meet a woman carrying a child in her arms. A gurney appeared and a nurse helped the woman lay the small boy on it.

"He was playing in front of the house next door. By the grass ditch near the street." The woman sucked in a shaky breath. "Next time I looked, he was lying on the ground. I ran out there and found him having a seizure." Her fingers fluttered near the boy's face. "He threw up and I had to clear his throat."

"Has he had seizures before?" the nurse asked.

"No. Never." Her tears came faster. "I put him in the car and came as fast as I could. But by the time I got here, he was unconscious."

"Is he on any medications?" The nurse had two fingers on the side of the boy's neck as she glanced up.

The boy's mother shook her head.

"Okay, I've got a pulse. Let's get him into triage." The nurse turned back to the woman. "What's his name?"

"Joey. Joseph." She smacked the tears off her cheeks with the back of her hand, the sting seeming to calm her down some. "We call him Joey."

"I've already paged the doctor." Another nurse helped steer the gurney into the space next to their prisoner's.

Bree pulled the privacy curtain between the two beds open partway, and her breath caught as they removed the child's shirt, exposing his thin chest. It barely moved as he struggled for breath. After confirming his throat was clear, one nurse used a manual resuscitator to push air into his lungs as another wrapped a small blood pressure belt around his arm and clamped an oxygen monitor on his finger.

A doctor rushed into the tight space, and one of the nurses addressed the mother: "Ma'am, you should step out and let us work."

Bree had already consoled too many mothers whose

children had overdosed—and stood in for even more who couldn't bother to be around for their kids, even in death. But when this woman's fear-filled eyes met hers, Bree went to her. Putting her arm around the woman's shoulders, she said, "Come stand with us over here." Thankful that the woman shuffled along with her, Bree tried to catch her eye. "What's your name?"

"Cindy."

Noah pulled the side curtain the rest of the way open so she could watch her son as a conversation ensued between the medical staff.

"Did he ingest anything? Come in contact with any contaminants? Cleaning products, maybe?" the doctor asked.

A nurse said, "We don't know."

Exasperated with the nurse, Bree spoke up. "Why on earth would you send his mother, who might be able to answer these questions, out of the room and then stand here unable to tell the doctor what he needs to know?" With her arm still around Cindy's shoulders, Bree moved her a large step closer to her son.

"I… He had a seizure before losing consciousness. He's never had one before." Cindy's voice gained volume. "I don't know if he came in contact with anything or ate anything— but if he did, it wasn't in the house."

Another nurse was cutting off the child's pants after removing his shoes and socks. "He's got what look like burns on his skin. Check his arms."

"They're on both forearms, too."

Everyone leaned in to see.

"He wasn't near any fire." Cindy's voice shook.

"These look like chemical burns. I want blood and urine right now. Complete lab workup." The doctor glanced at Cindy. "Was he playing with anything when you found him?"

"Just his ball." She paused. "There was a backpack near him in the ditch, but I barely noticed it."

Bree gave Cindy's shoulder a comforting squeeze. "Close your eyes and remember the backpack. Was it open or closed?"

"Um, I don't…" Her tear-soaked lashes fluttered shut for a moment before flying open again. "I remember!" Wide pools of blue bored into Bree's eyes. "It was open. There were things lying on the flap. And around it in the ditch."

"What things?" Bree kept her voice soft. "Picture them in your mind."

A frown took over the woman's face, and she closed her eyes again. "Plastic bottles. Funny-shaped papers. I think I saw a glove." Her eyes opened and she pointed at the blue nitrile gloves the medical staff wore. "A glove like those."

Bree signaled Noah to replace her arm with his. She crossed over to where the doctor stood, on the far side of the gurney. "Doctor." He gave her a quizzical look, and she leaned closer to him. "Check for acetone, ethyl alcohol, iodine crystal poisoning—any other chemicals used in meth production. The skin burns may be from opened lithium batteries or drain cleaner, maybe even lye."

The doctor's gaze bounced from Bree to the boy's mother and back. "You think she cooks meth?" he asked, his voice so low Bree barely heard it.

"No. I think someone dumped a backpack full of meth trash in that ditch."

The doctor raised his voice as he looked at the nurses. "Neither one of you leave this boy. Monitor his heart and lungs…"

Bree stopped listening to the doctor as she walked back to Noah and Cindy.

"What did the doctor say?" Cindy grabbed hold of Bree's hand. "Do you know what's wrong with my Joey?"

"I don't, but the doctor and nurses will keep you informed while they run tests. And I'm sure they won't mind you staying with Joey." Behind the woman's back, she poked Noah and motioned for him to move as far away as possible. She edged Cindy into her son's room and started to close the curtain. "I'm sorry, but we have to check on our patient now, and I don't want him to disturb you."

Bree met Noah on the far side of their prisoner's gurney and whispered directly into his ear, "You should call Chief Deputy Reed, suggest he have a hazmat tech collect that backpack and surrounding contents. Since the Austin crime lab covers Boone County, I guess they'll take it there to examine."

Noah raised his brows.

"I've seen this before. Meth cookers are notorious for dumping their toxic trash with no regard for who might happen upon it. Once I heard his mother's description of the backpack's items, I realized that was possibly the case here."

"Just from plastic bottles and weird papers?"

"I'll bet you my certified official *Lone Ranger* silver bullet those papers are coffee filters. They use them to strain their product."

Noah's cheeks puffed as he exhaled. Pulling out his phone, he paused, tapping his finger against its edge.

Bree sensed his frustration but held her tongue. On her first day, she'd noticed how much he wanted to work the meth explosion. He was probably thinking this might be a way into the investigation for him. Just drive to Cindy's and collect the backpack from the ditch as evidence. But instead of grabbing the opportunity, he punched in a speed dial number and followed the chain of command.

Good thing, since she didn't want to be exposed to possible meth toxins if she went with him. Or accused of ignoring protocol by leaving their detainee alone, cuffed to his gurney. Or involved in any high-profile drug-murder investigation. If a child died by meth poisoning, that's exactly what they'd have, and it was something she needed to avoid. Sitting in the hospital with a brain-fried sugar freak seemed the better option for her right now.

Just keep your head down, Delgado. Head down, mouth shut. And you might get out of this mess before your secret is revealed.

Chapter Seven

Bree relaxed after finding out Sean Cavanaugh, the deputy with the military bearing, would maintain the chain of custody on the backpack until a crime tech from Austin arrived to take possession.

Still waiting for the tox screen on Kenny Schneider, she and Noah cooled their heels in the small triage space, sharing a vending machine bag of pork rinds and arguing whether Coke or Dr. Pepper should be the Texas state drink. Once you got past sweet tea, Lone Star beer and top-shelf tequila, that is.

When the blood work came back revealing not only methamphetamine but also traces of heroin in their prisoner's system, they hauled him to the justice building's jail and tucked him away in a cell.

"You want to write up the reports now?" she asked Noah.

"I'm starving, and I was supposed to meet Bishop a half hour ago for lunch."

"Bishop?" Bree asked.

The corners of his mouth curved up in a smile. "My eventual brother-in-law, if my stubborn sister ever agrees to set a date. Meet you back here in an hour? After we finish the reports, we'll need to meet with Adam."

"Works for me."

Under different circumstances, Bree might have enjoyed sitting across from Noah's handsome face and getting to know him better. But considering she had no intention of taking part in the getting-to-know-you's, she was glad to have her lunch hour to herself.

She settled into a booth at the Busy B and opened the *Boone County Bulletin*. Tonight she'd look online for a place to rent, but she'd noticed a stack of *Bulletins* near the diner's front door and figured she'd take a look while she ate. The classified ads included listings for everything from babysitting jobs wanted to crocheted dog clothes for sale. She rolled her eyes at the picture of a poodle in a hooked-yarn dress.

She snapped the paper open to another page and folded it back. She would've been okay with an apartment since she had never planned on staying long. But there was only one complex in, or even near, Resolute. She'd checked out the Oak View Apartments when she met Sheriff Reed for her first interview.

The bulk of the occupants were elderly, living in that undesirable purgatory between their own home and a nursing home. The others seemed to be transient construction workers, living paycheck to paycheck and renting by the month. The building reeked of dead-end despair and end-of-the-road depression.

Which left Bree with only one option. She located the "Houses for Rent" section in the *Bulletin*. With no idea exactly where any of them were located, she drew circles around each possibility with her red pen. She'd look them up later on her map app.

Sensing movement next to her, she looked up to find Rachel holding a tray. She shoved her paper, pen and phone off to the side to make room for her lunch.

"Sorry it took so long. Marge is training a new cook."

Rachel set down Bree's club sandwich and fries. "Looking for anything in particular?" She indicated the paper as she refilled the empty iced-tea glass.

"Right now I'm staying at Doc's, but it's temporary. I'd considered going into an apartment, but there's not much available in that category around here, is there?" With any luck, there were more she didn't know about.

Rachel gave her a smiling shrug. "Not so much, no."

Bree muttered a curse beneath her breath. She still wasn't used to small-town realities. She picked up the *Bulletin*. "I guess that leaves me with renting a house, but I'm not familiar with the layout of the town." She nodded toward the red circles.

"Let me see." Rachel took the paper from her. After skimming through the circled listings, she shook her head. "You don't want any of these. Some of them are way out of town. Others aren't in the best areas. Like this one here." She held the paper in front of Bree and pointed. "That's in an industrial area, mostly warehouses." She inched her nail over to the next column. "And this one is in Flowertop."

"Where's Flowertop?" Bree mumbled around a bite of sandwich.

"A fair drive to the west. You should be able to find something nice a whole lot closer." Rachel set the paper on the table. "Truth is, most things listed in this paper aren't usually worth checking out."

"I thought that might be the case when I saw the basset hound wearing a pink crocheted tutu."

Rachel barked out a laugh. "Some people around here don't have a spare second, and others have too much time on their hands." She lowered her voice. "Or a lack of respect for our four-legged friends."

Nodding her agreement, Bree sighed. "I guess I'll go back to my original plan and look online tonight."

Rachel snapped her fingers. "I may have a solution for you." She pulled her phone from her uniform pocket and fiddled with it as she spoke. "When my ex's parents passed away, I found this Realtor who also flips houses. He bought their house as is and made everything so easy for us. I can give you his name and number. He should know all the properties for sale or rent around Resolute. He's also not too hard on the eyes." She gave Bree a sly smile. "What's your number?"

Bree gave Rachel her number and a moment later the Realtor's info was in her contacts.

"Save my number, too. Give me a call if you want me to come with when you go looking at places. Fair warning—between my hours here, my kids and life in general, I probably won't be able to make it. But I've heard miracles happen. No, wait. That was in a Disney movie, wasn't it?"

"No kids, so I haven't seen a lot of those." Bree smiled. "Thanks for the help. This may save me a lot of time. But please don't tell Marge about the handsome Realtor, or I suspect she'll try to set me up with him."

Rachel laughed again. "You've got our Marge pegged, that's for sure. Don't worry—your secret is safe with me."

It was only a joke, but secrets seemed to be dominating Bree's life these days, and she didn't like it.

Rachel looked toward the front of the cafe. "I'd better get moving before Marge starts looking for me and discovers that you're dying for a date with the Realtor."

Bree's eyes popped open wide. "Oh, you're so bad."

"Sorry. Couldn't help it," Rachel said with an amused smirk.

Chuckling, Bree checked the time on her phone. "Could

you bring me a to-go box? I don't have time to finish my sandwich here, but it's too good to leave behind."

"Be right back." Rachel tucked the tray under one arm and worked her way past the other tables, filling glasses with tea.

A warm happiness swept through Bree that had nothing to do with good food or finding a Realtor. Rachel had bantered with her as if she was someone, um, normal. Not like someone to be wary of, someone who carried a gun. In San Antonio, Bree's only friends had been on the force, and even they hadn't been close. She'd told herself it didn't matter, and for the most part, that was true. The job sustained her. Always had. But just now, the simple exchange with Rachel stirred up a big old pot of "wouldn't that be nice."

I think I just made a friend. So there, Deputy Reed. How was that for finding a black cat in a coal cellar?

AFTER PICKING UP a fried-oyster po' boy and Coke from the Seafood Shack, Noah drove to Bishop Investigations. Business for the private investigator had been steady since Bishop had moved to Resolute from Houston. Helping to solve a human-trafficking case last summer had helped, and word of mouth took it from there.

"Hey, you're late. Wasn't sure you'd make it." Bishop rose from his desk chair and went to his not-so-mini mini-fridge.

"My mundane, on-schedule morning got derailed by a last-minute service call." Noah pulled a visitor chair closer to the desk and made himself comfortable. As he unwrapped his sandwich and spread out the paper to catch drippings, he inhaled a deep breath of fried saltwater ambrosia. "Been working anything interesting lately?"

The disgustingly health-conscious Bishop sat across from him and opened a container of homemade kale salad. Blueberries, chopped apples and chunks of nuts sat on top of it, along with what looked like a pile of bird seed. How he and Cassie managed to coexist was beyond Noah.

"A case over in Houston. Looking for heirs of a very rich, very prolific man. The named heirs in his will want the estate settled before any more offspring are located. I made the mistake of driving there on Tuesday to talk to a possible son, but the guy was an impostor. When he looked like a sure thing, I'd stopped with the background checks and wasted almost two days. Now I'm going to research every possible descendant to death before going back to interview them." He poured something green that Noah hoped was dressing on his salad. "How's the new deputy working out?" Bishop mixed the bowl of salad with his fork.

His mouth filled with a large bite of sandwich, Noah took the opportunity to analyze the week so far. He swallowed. "She's not bad."

"Cassie said she's cute." Bishop's eyes never left Noah's face as he forked kale into his mouth. "That true?"

Noah set his sandwich down and grabbed a napkin to wipe the tartar sauce off his fingers. "Yeah, definitely cute. She has the most amazing eyes, like blue ice. And she's observant. Good at the job."

Taking a long drink of green tea from his clear travel mug, Bishop continued to watch him. "Blue ice, huh? Did you know that's the strongest type? Gets its color and strength from how it's formed with no air bubbles."

"Interesting." Not how the ice formed but how it applied to Bree. Strong.

"So what's on the flip side?" Bishop picked up a piece of walnut with his fingers and popped it into his mouth. "She can't be perfect."

"Oh, trust me, she's not." Noah leaned against his chair back. "She's stubborn as all get-out. And contrary?" He scoffed. "I explain why we do things a certain way here, and she just wants to argue."

"And yet…?"

"I can't stop thinking about her." He wadded up his napkin and tossed it on the desk. "But she won't open up. She has stories she won't tell, secrets she's keeping. It's frustrating."

Bishop shrugged. "So take her to dinner or something. Let her know you're interested in getting to know her." He snapped the lid onto his salad container. "You aren't usually this discombobulated about asking someone out. Even though it hasn't even been a week, sounds like you're developing feelings for her."

"It's not that simple." Noah dropped his head back and groaned at the ceiling. "First off, we work together. Plus, Cassie already thinks I'm a goof-off. I'm trying to up my game on the job to prove myself to her." He looked at Bishop. "Hitting on the new deputy—the only other female in the department besides Cassie—won't win me any points. She'll figure I'm paying more attention to Bree than the job." He blew out a hard breath. "That's really the problem. I have to choose between the job and the girl, and the job's what's always been important to me."

"Sounds like you've got yourself a gen-u-ine conundrum." Bishop tipped back in his chair and rested his boots on the corner of his desk. "Wanna meditate on it?"

Noah summoned as much indignation as he could and crammed it into his reply. "No, I don't want to *meditate* on it, you hippie freak. That's probably why Cassie won't set a wedding date."

"Ha. Guess she hasn't told you she started doing yoga with me." A satisfied smile took over Bishop's face. "You ever hear of couples' yoga? Some of the positions are—"

"I don't need to hear about that." He gathered up his lunch

trash and tossed it in a waste basket. "Anyway, everything I said stays between us, right?"

With a phony frown, Bishop nodded. "Oh, absolutely. I would never tell the person I cherish most in the world any of the dumb stuff her brother shares with me."

"I'm serious, man." Noah pointed a finger at him. "If she thinks—"

"Relax, Noah. I don't tell anyone what you tell me in confidence." He raised his brows. "If I did, I couldn't blackmail you later."

"Funny. Very funny. See y'all Saturday for dinner."

"Yep. Cassie confirmed she'll be home for the weekend. She's not happy about how long the trial is dragging on."

"Can't say I blame her. Doubt I could sit there for a whole week, just to find out I have to do it again next week." Noah opened the office door to leave.

"Don't worry about her being in a bad mood and taking it out on you." Bishop waited until Noah turned around. "I'll make sure she's relaxed several times over before dinner."

"She's my sister, you weirdo. I don't want to hear that stuff." Noah tried to slam the door behind him as a final last word. Instead, he cursed the soft-close hinges for denying him the satisfaction.

On his way back to the office, Noah detoured to the high school and picked up the list of people with access to the school's keys. Once he and Bree were done with the candy-store incident, they could get back to the burglary.

When he walked into the bullpen, he found Bree sitting at his desk, takeout from the Busy B spread out in front of her. "Sorry, but this one's mine." He pointed to the desk where Adam used to sit. "That one's yours."

She looked over at Dave, sitting a couple of places over

from her. "Why didn't you say something when I sat down?" When he only shrugged, Bree rolled her eyes. Then to Noah, "I didn't realize they were assigned." She dropped the french fry she'd been holding onto a paper towel and started to collect her ketchup packets and napkins. "I didn't have time to finish my lunch at the diner. I put my sandwich in the fridge but figured I'd eat the fries before they got too soggy."

"Never mind. Just stay there for now." Noah walked over to what had been Adam's desk. Bree hadn't spent much time in the pen this week, and everyone else was in and out. It made sense she hadn't known each deputy had their own spot. "Go ahead and finish your lunch. I'm going to get started on the candy-store report."

Dave laughed. "Figures you'd let a little thing like her boss you around, Reed."

Almost from Dave's first day, he'd harassed Noah. Cassie had attempted to curb Dave's behavior and stop his constant sniping at everyone else. But Dave got cagier, only heckling the other deputies when she and Adam were out of earshot. It was like dealing with a tiresome school bully, and Noah ignored the taunt, just as he always ignored whatever came out of Dave's mouth. Bree, on the other hand, was on her feet before he'd finished talking.

She stalked across the room and stopped next to Dave, her narrowed eyes glinting. "First of all, it's not appropriate to mock a deputy with seniority over you."

Dave snickered. "And what's second of all, little lady?"

"Don't ever refer to me as a 'thing' again. I'm not a thing *or* a little lady to you. I'm your coworker. A deputy. And you'll refer to me as such."

Noah sat in his chair and watched, a smile plastered on his face. Dave was about to make things so much worse for himself.

"Or what?" The confident sneer he usually reserved for Noah appeared.

She leaned over his desk. "Or one of two things can happen." Noah was pleased to see Dave flinch as Bree held up a finger inches away from his face. "One, I'll punch those pearly whites of yours down your throat, hold your nose and watch you choke."

"I'd like to see you try."

Bree went on as if he hadn't spoken. "Or two, I inform our boss—the by-the-book, forward-thinking female sheriff—about your misogynistic attitude and lack of respect toward your fellow officers."

Dave's look turned mutinous.

"Now, I've only been here a week, so I don't know you very well, but I'd say it's a crapshoot on which would be more painful." The hand in front of Dave's face curled into a fist. "But you look like a man whose head could take a licking better than his pride, so why don't I call this one for you?" In a flash, Bree adjusted her feet and cocked her arm back, her chest turned in such a way that showed she knew exactly how to put her body behind a forceful right hook.

Dave realized it, too, because he raised his arms in front of his face. Not to fight, but to protect said pearly whites.

Noah jumped to his feet, closed the space between them and grabbed her arm. "Bree, as much as I hate to, I can't let you do that. You have an unfair advantage over poor old Dave. The rest of us have noticed that he hides from physical confrontations, so I doubt this would be a fair match. And as sorry an excuse for a deputy as he may be, Cassie doesn't have time to find another new one right now."

Her arm relaxed and she turned to Noah, her eyes now sparkling with amusement. "I understand. I'd hate to have Cassie upset with me during my very first week."

She returned to Noah's desk, packed up her lunch and re-located to what was now her own.

"She's a psychopath," Dave whispered to Noah, loud enough for her to hear.

"You better believe it," Bree stage-whispered back, staring at Dave with disturbingly wide eyes and an evil grin.

Noah left the room until he could control his laughter. Then he got back to work, trying to focus on the report he needed to type up instead of on Bree. The more time he spent with her, the more she fascinated him. When he first met her, he'd found her pretty. Or was it cute?

Could a woman be both? Because in Noah's estimation, Bree was.

Pretty as a peach, as Marge had noted. Cute in the way she tried to avoid attention, had a quick-draw temper when coming to someone's defense, and in the way she daintily dipped each french fry in ketchup exactly three times before she ate it.

But after spending just a few days with her, Noah pegged her as being made up of so much more. And he was hooked. Already, he spent way too much time obsessing about learning her likes and dislikes, her past, her dreams—and yes, her secrets, too.

And then there was the growing obsession to have her under him, naked and thrashing with need. He gave a mental shrug. No sense in denying it, especially to himself.

Unfortunately, she was wound tighter than an eight-day clock, and he was stuck trying to figure her out while on the job, bit by arduous bit. Because no matter how intrigued he was by Brianna Delgado, priority one for him was to be taken seriously. To be given cases to work on his own.

So while he might desire the only female deputy in the

Boone County Sheriff's Department, dating Bree wouldn't help his cause. Knowing Cassie, probably just the opposite.

As he finished adding Sandy's statement, as well as the pictures she'd emailed, to their report, Bree came to his desk with a printed-out summary of what had happened at the hospital with the young boy.

"I checked in with the nurses' station, and they confirmed he was definitely exposed to toxins related to meth. They don't know the full extent of his internal injuries, but the prognosis isn't good. Apparently, he absorbed a near-lethal amount for someone his size, but he's a fighter. Hanging on by a thread." Bree's face, her whole stance, radiated rage. Might have included some residual anger left over from her confrontation with Dave, but probably not. She was definitely a champion of the underdogs.

Noah, also angry on behalf of the child as well as his mom, swallowed the sudden lump in this throat. "It makes me sick every time I remember his small body on that gurney." He rose, and they headed for Adam's office. "If I were his father, I'd be tempted to find the creeps who dumped that trash and leave *them* lying in the ditch."

Bree nodded. "Too many kids start out life at a disadvantage. And then even ones like this little boy, with loving parents and a decent home, get hurt or kidnapped or fall in with a bad crowd." Somehow, she found a smile. A sad one, but still…a smile. "All we can do is find the bastards who did this and shut them down."

Noah knocked on Adam's door. Six months ago, Adam didn't even have a door. Or an office. He'd sat at the desk in the corner of the bullpen with the rest of the deputies. But stick the word *chief* in front of *deputy*, and the new title came with a door prize.

"Come in." Adam looked up from his computer, his usual

serious expression in place. "Heard you two have had quite the day, huh?"

"Yep, and still plenty of it left." Noah pulled out a visitor's chair for Bree before taking the other one. "Report's filed on the Sweets and Treats incident, and the culprit is in our detox cell."

Adam frowned. "We don't have a detox cell."

"We do now." Noah chuckled.

Adam turned his gaze to Bree. "And how's your first week going?"

"Unexpectedly exhilarating." She reached across the desk and handed Adam the summary on the toxic exposure. "This was everything we saw and heard at the hospital, from the moment the boy came in until we left. While we waited for our detainee's blood work, we had ample time to speak with the child's mother."

"And?"

"We have a high degree of confidence that his family has no connection to the drugs or trash. The boy is an only child, his father's a roughneck on a drilling rig off the coast and the mother is a stay-at-home mom. The next-door neighbors, who own the property where the child was playing, are an older couple who attend the same church as our victim's family." Bree paused, started to say something, then closed her mouth.

Adam gave her a warm smile. "Go ahead, Deputy. What's on your mind?"

"It's unusual for meth cookers to dump their toxic trash near their own house, sir, unless they just throw it in the backyard. The usual MO for them is to take a drive somewhere and toss it out the window so it won't be connected to them."

Noah sat back, impressed with Bree's knowledge. But

what really caught his attention was the way she presented the information to Adam: with deference to her superiors, her words succinct—to the point—and not one wisecrack. Bet no one questioned *her* seriousness on the job.

Well, okay then. If he wanted his siblings to see him in the same way, he'd need to take a page from her playbook.

Adam glanced down at the paper he was holding, then back at Bree. "Did you work a lot of drug cases in San Antonio?"

"A fair number, yes, sir. We also had extensive training in dealing with people high on different drugs as well as handling meth-house scenarios." She paused and gulped a breath of air, as if fortifying herself for the rest. "The lingering toxicity inside the building, possibility of explosions—pretty much anything that could happen."

"Sounds like you have more knowledge about meth than our entire department combined. Do me a favor. As soon as you two join the drug investigation, speak to Helen and get on the schedule for the morning briefing." His brother's rarely seen smile flickered to life again. "I'd appreciate it if you'd spend—oh, I don't know—about fifteen or twenty minutes sharing your knowledge with the rest of the department."

A hesitant smile appeared on her face. "Yes, sir. Whatever I can do to help."

"Outstanding." Adam stood. "Our sheriff was right, as usual. You're going to become an excellent addition to our department, and particularly to this investigation, as it seems the case just keeps on getting bigger."

A slow burn crawled through Noah. A petty sensation that he hated but couldn't stop. He hadn't been assigned to the case, even though he was first on the scene. Now Bree, a deputy here for exactly—he glanced at his watch—three days, five hours and twenty minutes was being hailed as the be-all and end-all of the department.

Adam glanced at Noah. "You two will still be riding together until the sheriff returns, and we need to get the high school burglary wrapped up. After that, I'd like you both on the meth case with me."

Shocked by his brother's announcement, then deeply ashamed of his thoughts just moments earlier, Noah maintained a serious expression. While he couldn't bring himself to address Adam as *sir*, he could at least show his brother the proper respect due someone in his position.

Noah stood, biting his tongue against any protests, wisecracks or even one harmless little joke. "We're on it, sir."

Dang if that "sir" didn't just slip on out. And it didn't taste nearly as bitter as he'd expected it would. The faint nod of approval he received from Adam in return made it worth it.

Hell, he'd call Adam *sir* all day long and twice on Sunday for a chance to run his own investigation, as long as Bree was at his side.

Chapter Eight

Bree speed-walked back to the bullpen, relieved when she found Dave Saunders gone. She'd had enough of him today, and she and Noah had a lot to do. Under the best of circumstances, an investigation could be slow, laborious work, but even more so in Resolute. The one thing they'd planned on doing today was the one thing still not done.

Bree checked her watch. "We better get going if we want the list of people who have keys to the high school."

Noah pulled a folded sheet of paper from his back pocket. Wearing a triumphant grin, he held it up. "We don't need to. I stopped by the school on my way back from lunch and picked it up."

"I thought we'd planned to interview anyone still at the school while we were there." Bree struggled to keep her voice free of exasperation.

"That *was* the plan. But then something Bishop said about a case he's working got me thinking. It makes more sense to check the backgrounds of all our suspects before we talk to them."

Infected by Noah's exuberance, Bree's irritation sloughed away. In some ways he was still like a rookie: excited about every discovery, proud of every good idea.

She nodded her approval. "We might catch them in a lie from the get-go."

"Yeah, and less back-and-forth." Noah planted himself at his desk.

She rolled a chair over from another desk and sat next to him. He spread the paper open, and they both leaned over it, almost knocking heads. Before Bree could pull back, Noah turned. They were face-to-face. Noses almost touching. His dark, penetrating eyes locked with hers. The magnetic force captivated her, filling her with a torrent of sensual energy.

Get a grip, girl. Before she made a complete jerk of herself, Bree summoned a Herculean amount of willpower and pulled her gaze from his. An almost impossible task when she inhaled his faint earthy scent of cedar and eucalyptus.

Noah shifted in his chair and cleared his throat.

He's not unaffected, either. That mollified her. Somewhat.

"Okay, this is everyone who was issued a master key to the school." Noah tapped the paper.

Focus on the list of names. "That's a pretty short list."

"According to Principal Jackson, the teachers don't get a master key—just one for their classroom. If they have to get into the school after hours, it's arranged ahead of time for someone to meet them and let them in. In an emergency, either Jackson or a custodian needs to be called to unlock the main door, then walk them back out and lock up behind them."

"So administrators and custodians, then." Still distracted by his close proximity, Bree pushed away from the desk to put some real estate between them.

Noah added to the distance by leaning back in his chair and crossing his arms over his chest. "Well, administration-wise, there's just the principal who has the master key. Then there are the three custodians and the maintenance man. The vice principals and other admin staff don't have master keys. We'll ignore the principal for obvious reasons."

Bree jerked upright in her chair. "Whoa, whoa, whoa. Just because he's been there forever and you respect him, doesn't mean we shouldn't look into him."

"And normally, you'd be absolutely right. But the weekend of the break-in, he and Mrs. Jackson were in Houston, visiting their grandkids." Noah's eyes sparked with humor. "We still need to verify that, of course, but I think it's a safe bet that he's not our guy."

As much as Bree wanted to wipe the smug smile from his face, she found herself amused. And that wasn't her style. What was it about Noah Reed that turned her ordered existence upside down? "You could have led with that."

"Where's the fun in that?" He tapped his finger by the next names on the list. "So that leaves the head custodian, his assistant and the guy who polishes the floors. The floor polisher fills in as needed if one of the first two are out. Plus, the maintenance man."

"I thought you said the teachers don't have keys." Bree pointed to the last grouping of names. "I clearly see Coach Crawford's name. I'm assuming the rest are the athletic department staff. What gives?" Even Bree didn't miss the acid in her question. Nothing like blatant school favoritism to cool her ardor.

Noah gave her a quick look. He'd noticed her attitude change. "Between nighttime basketball games in the gym, extra innings in baseball and football games on weekends, the coaches need access around the clock. Didn't make sense for them to pay a custodian to be on constant call. We'll take a look at the coaching staff, but I think we should leave them for last."

Bree narrowed her eyes. How many times had she railed

against the inequity of it all? "Interesting." Sarcasm dripped from the word. The push and pull between athletics and education was anything *but* interesting. It was shameful. "Less than a thousand kids total at the school, and that department has five coaches. Poor Ben Irving uses bandages and spit to hold on to... What? Thousand-dollar laptops? But the athletic department—"

"Before you completely dog Resolute High's coaching staff, between the five of them, they cover every competitive sport Resolute participates in, either as a head coach or an assistant. Three of them, including Coach Crawford, also teach other subjects like history and math. The other two, in addition to coaching, teach phys ed." Noah's smile had disappeared.

She held up her hands in surrender. "Just forget it."

"I don't get what your problem is with our sports program."

"It's not *Resolute's* program. It's sports programs in general. You know how it is. In bigger school districts, at least in Texas, it's common for a huge slice of the budget to go toward sports. I've seen some high schools that have football-coaching staffs almost as big as NFL teams."

For once, Noah remained silent. Allowing her to make her point? Or too angry to speak? Whatever he was thinking, she needed to soften the rhetoric. "I just think more money should go to academic and outreach programs for under-resourced kids. I'm not saying sports in school aren't important. They are. But equally important is keeping kids who don't participate in sports off the streets and out of trouble. Keeping them busy with community projects. Teaching them how to navigate the parts of life after high school that they don't learn about *in* high school." Bree massaged her forehead. "The schools do as much as they can with the money allocated toward programs like that. But it's usually not enough."

Noah uncrossed his arms and straightened in his chair. "So what's the solution? You're fighting a losing battle in the 'God, family and football' state."

"Believe me, I know. That's why I started a youth program through my precinct in San Antonio." *And this is where I need to shut up.* She closed her eyes, took a deep breath and got herself under control. To protect her secret, she'd sworn to keep to herself at the new job—and here she was, blowing that big time. At this rate, how long before she revealed more than just her personal opinions? "Look, we need to focus on the investigation here. So, the principal's not a suspect. Why leave the coaches for later?"

Like a desperate man, Noah seemed to leap at the change in topics. "Because Crawford reported the break-in. Besides, why steal equipment he has access to all the time? Same for the other coaches. Like I said, we'll check them all out, of course, but—"

"Could they be throwing us off with the sports equipment, while what they really wanted was something from one of the other departments?"

"Possibly. That's one of the angles we need to look at."

"But you like the cleaning crew for this? More than anyone else?"

Noah shook his head. "No, not really. For the same reason. They already have access. Why stage a break-in?" His gaze drifted away from her for a moment. "I've known most of these men for a long time. I know you're going to say I'm biased, but I just don't think they look good for this. However, we'll still start with them."

"Do you have the final inventory list yet?" Bree asked, satisfied with Noah's game plan.

Noah scrolled through his work emails. "Yeah. Here it is. I'm forwarding it to you."

Leaving the borrowed chair at Noah's desk, Bree crossed over to the far corner and logged in to her work computer. "Okay, I've got it."

Bree scrolled through the inventory, comparing it to the preliminary list they'd received earlier from the principal. The list of missing sports equipment hadn't changed, and still nothing was missing from the computer lab. From the science department, the list of missing or broken items had become longer and more detailed. The number of beakers and funnels, stirring rods and petri dishes was updated. Boxes of slides, a drying oven, Bunsen burners and two microscopes. As the science teacher had said, no rhyme or reason.

Bree returned to the empty chair next to Noah. "Okay, it makes sense that the coaches wouldn't have attempted to steal anything from the computer lab, since they all have their own work computers." To be absolutely sure, they'd confirmed that with Coach Crawford on Monday.

Noah nodded. "Even if one of the coaching staff wanted a laptop not issued by the school, to watch porn or access the dark web, it would've been easier to just pick up a cheap or used one somewhere."

"We also have to consider that a key could have been swiped and copied, then the original returned. Or someone on the list could have lost theirs and borrowed someone else's to make a copy without reporting it." From her back pocket, Bree pulled out a small notebook and began writing.

The list of names. The list of missing items. Leads to follow. Her personal impressions. Anything she could think of, because sometimes when there were a million facts to consider, you forgot the details.

A quick glance in Noah's direction showed that he was

making notes, too, but on his computer. Her mouth twitched as she noted how old-school she was when building a case compared to him. And then she noted other things about him. How he tapped one finger against his lips while he stared at his monitor. How his fingers flew over the keys when he typed. How—*Stop it. Stay focused.*

Her mind churned. Not to mention her libido. "Let's split the list. I'll find out what I can on the head custodian and his assistant. You can have the other two."

Without looking up, Noah nodded.

Bree started with the head custodian, Bill "Rusty" Nails.

Bree snorted. Rusty Nails? Poor guy. *Bet he was teased to no end when he was a kid.* She opened the background-check program.

Along with the list of names, Principal Jackson had also sent basic employee information. Based on his picture, fifty-six-year-old Rusty had no doubt acquired his nickname due to his full head of reddish-orange hair. He'd worked at Resolute High for almost forty years, ever since he'd graduated from the school himself. Married, he and his wife had three children who were now out-of-the-house married adults with kids themselves. No police record for him, not so much as a parking ticket.

Jack Williams, the assistant custodian, was a different story. Twenty-six years old and single, he'd worked with Nails for the last seven years. His juvenile record was sealed, but the fact that he had one meant nothing good. One, two—no, *four*—public-intoxication arrests and a handful of drunk-and-disorderly charges since turning twenty-one, the latest just a few months ago. One of these involved misdemeanor-assault charges.

A real charmer. Definitely someone who might run afoul of the law for more than just swilling his booze and getting physical. She put a star next to his name and looked up from her computer. "You familiar with this guy, Jack Williams?"

"We've hauled him in a time or two. Not the sharpest crayon in the box—and I'm talking the big box, 152 colors and a sharpener." Noah spread his arms wide to exaggerate the box size. "By the time he starts getting into fights, he's usually so drunk he just swings and follows his fist around into a cowboy pirouette."

"What on earth is a 'cowboy pirouette'?"

"Like the kind in ballet, except the guy is drunk as a skunk, misses his target and his momentum carries him around and down. Oh, and he's wearing jeans and boots instead of tights and those shoes that make you stand on your toes."

"You mean pointe shoes?"

Noah's eyes widened in surprise. "*You* know what they're called?"

"What? You think a cop can't like things like the ballet or opera?"

Noah's face screwed up. "You like *opera*?"

"Hell no." Bree laughed. "But I do enjoy the ballet."

"Good luck with that in Resolute." Noah stretched his arms above his head. "You ready? I've got enough on the maintenance man and the night guy who does floors to start with."

Bree glanced at her watch. "I'm ready, but it's three forty-five, and school will be letting out around now. It'll be hard to talk to any of them privately. Besides, we might learn more if they let us into their homes."

"Works for me." Noah yawned. "I need a little downtime. Meet you in the parking lot at six?"

"See you then."

He gathered up his personal belongings and headed out.

For half a minute, while he was still in sight, Bree allowed herself to enjoy the view. Handsome face, dreamy eyes, ripped physique—not to mention a winning smile. Throw in an offbeat sense of humor and his enjoyment of the smallest things in life, and Bree knew she was in trouble.

Get out of my head, Noah Reed. But he was like a tick that had burrowed under her skin.

In the past, whenever Bree had found herself on an emotional roller coaster, she could always fall back on the job. The job was her saving grace. The job was everything. Heck, the job was the reason she was here. For all that Noah called to her on so many levels, it was well past time she remembered that protecting her job would always be the most important thing to her.

And to do that, keeping things professional with Noah and laying low in general were imperative. Now Adam's voice popped into her head, asking her to speak at a morning briefing about drugs.

Stellar job you're doing of keeping off everyone's radar, Bree.

She pulled up the reports that Noah had run on the maintenance man and the third custodian. Both were older men. Both had been with the Boone County School District for decades and at Resolute High for at least fifteen years. She printed out everything on all four men and went to the break room. Opening the fridge, she retrieved the half sandwich she'd saved from lunch, grabbed a can of Diet Coke from the vending machine and began rereading everything.

After all, forewarned was forearmed. Especially since she couldn't trust herself to pull her actual firearm. *Yet.*

NOAH PARKED IN front of the justice center's steps at 6:00 p.m. on the dot. The last streaks of an orange-and-purple sky disappeared below the western horizon, and he was pleased to find Bree already waiting. He believed in punctuality, one of the few characteristics he shared with his big sister.

Bree's dark blue Ford F-150, an older model, sat in the next space with its windows fogged over. She locked the vehicle and slid into his passenger seat, bringing with her a blast of icy air unusual for the area, even in January. A chill raced through Noah, and he cranked up the heat.

Bree adjusted the collar on her heavy jacket before buckling herself in. "Am I imagining things, or is it colder this winter?"

"Seems every winter's colder than the last one." Noah backed out of the parking space and headed east, past downtown businesses and historic homes. "Rusty Nails first?"

"That name," Bree said, a smile behind the words. "Sure, why not? Seems best to begin at the top, especially since you think he's a long shot to be our guy. Would be great to start crossing names off the list." She flipped open the file folder on her lap. "I brought a printout of our background checks on everyone. Rusty lives on Baker Street."

"Whoa, Delgado, you didn't have to kill a tree. We can always pull it up again on here." Noah laughed, determined to keep things light as he tapped the computer in his department vehicle. Despite the obvious heat that existed between them, their relationship needed to stay strictly professional if he wanted to impress Cassie and change his reputation in the department. "You do have mobile-data terminals in San Antonio, don't you?"

"Ha ha ha. Yes, we have MDTs. It's just that I absorb more when I read a hard copy." She waved the thin folder at him. "Besides, it would've been a pretty small sapling if this tiny stack killed it."

He'd been admiring her attention to detail since her first

day on the job. Her head always on a swivel, taking in everything. Asking questions if she didn't already know the answer, getting confirmation if she did. And apparently, she didn't just read their investigative reports and background checks—she *studied* them. Her career path seemed to point toward a detective in the making. Which made her decision to come to Resolute all the more curious.

They came to a neighborhood of modest clapboard houses with yards of winter-brown grass and bare trees, except for the live oaks. The sidewalks were empty, no doubt the frigid air and thoughts of dinner driving people inside. "What's the house number?" Noah glanced across the console at Bree.

Her profile leaned more toward cute than pretty, with her pert nose and short, loose curls going every which way. "2725 Baker." She hadn't referred to her file; she'd already memorized it.

He parked in front of the Nailses' home and switched off the engine.

Bree turned to him. "Ready?"

Her blue eyes sparkled, most likely with the thrill of the hunt. Definitely not from some burning desire for him. Oh, he was no idiot. She was attracted to him on the surface, but it didn't go any further than that. Instead of appreciating humor in the day-to-day, she was dead serious about pretty much everything, especially her career. As he should be.

Deputy Brianna Delgado might help him solve cases and prove himself worthy on the job. But *Bree* was a powerful distraction who teased and enticed him, like the glint off a fishing lure hiding sharp, dangerous hooks.

He took a deep breath. "Ready." And he was.

Chapter Nine

Thank goodness for the frosty air outside. Bree, burning up from sitting so close to Noah, sucked in deep breaths of it. Just when it seemed she had her overactive libido in check, he gave her a look or a smile that shot her control to smithereens. And the explosive aftermath left her happy, optimistic and grinning like a fool for no obvious reason.

This reaction to a man had never happened to her before, and it bothered her to no end. The return of the sheriff and the end of her partnering with Noah couldn't happen soon enough for her peace of mind.

"Good grief. Come on in out of the cold." Rusty held his front door open. He didn't seem surprised by their unannounced visit. Or he was just the type who enjoyed drop-in guests.

Her frozen cheeks tingled when she walked into the Nailses' overheated home. The small, cozy living room was immaculate, the only exception a pile of crocheted something-or-other on one corner of the couch, its dangling yarn leading to a basket of multicolored skeins. An inviting, easy place that reminded Bree of her beloved grandmother. Yet another unexpected tug on her emotional heartstrings.

I'm a mess.

"Take off your coats and sit a spell." Rusty waved at the

other end of the couch as he took the well-used recliner and muted the news program he'd been watching. The hair responsible for his moniker was more white than red these days. What was left of it, anyway. Lean and well-groomed, he wore nice slacks and a heavy plaid flannel shirt.

Bree and Noah removed their jackets and hung them on the coatrack near the front door as Rusty hollered, "Iris? Come on out here and offer these deputies something to warm their bellies." He chuckled. "I don't know about you folks, but my bones don't take to the cold so much these days."

Mrs. Nails hustled into the living room from the kitchen, wiping her hands on a dish towel. "Gracious. You two look frozen stiff. I was just washing up the dinner dishes, but let me get some coffee on. Or perhaps you'd like hot tea?" Her appearance was opposite that of her husband's in almost every way. Tiny, round and with a darkish stain down the front of her blouse, she seemed as friendly as her affable spouse.

"Coffee would be great." Noah sat on the empty end of the couch.

"Let me help." Bree followed the woman into a tidy kitchen. Dinner dishes sat in the drying rack on the Formica countertop. A row of small plants lined the sill of a window over the sink. Like the front room, it was cozy without being cluttered, an easy thing to happen in a small home. Bree ought to know. Her mother had been a borderline hoarder, and to this day, Bree detested clutter.

Besides discovering the Nails were neatniks, Bree found that everything in their home was comfortably worn. No new purchases, no apparent ill-gotten gains from a burglary windfall. Bree also noticed nothing that would indicate a love of science, so no need to steal petri dishes and Bunsen burners. No sports equipment tagged with Resolute High's name, either. Not that any of that would be sitting out in plain sight if they *did* have it. But Noah's assessment that Rusty was not their perp seemed to be on target.

Mrs. Nails loaded the coffee maker, pulled out two mugs and then planted her backside against the counter while they waited for the coffee to brew. "What's your name, dear?"

"Bree."

"Well, Bree, you didn't need to help me, but I really do appreciate the company." She pointed to the living room, where her husband was head-to-head with Noah, reminiscing about the days when Noah ran the hallways as a student. "The old coot watches the news every night at this time and then again at ten, as if something monumental will pop up in the few hours between broadcasts. The man is like clockwork. In fact, I'd venture to say he hasn't missed a newscast in over twenty years. If not for my crocheting, I think I might have lost my mind ages ago." She leveled the criticism with a smile and obvious affection.

Bree said nothing. It had been her experience that people revealed all types of things when given a receptive audience and free rein. Mrs. Nails went on blathering away, either unaware or unconcerned that her husband was a potential person of interest in the school break-in.

"So, Bree, you must be the new deputy brought in to fill the opening. I suppose you heard all about the ambush of the former sheriff." She gave Noah a sympathetic look. "Noah's father. So sad. Wallace Reed was such a wonderful man. Practically raised those kids on his own after their mother up and disappeared without a word. Just a tragic death. I don't think a single one of them has come to terms with his loss yet."

Whoa. Bree had heard about the former sheriff being

killed in the line of duty. And of course, the last name tied him to half the department. But no one ever mentioned him, and she'd failed to regard the deceased man as a father they still grieved. She'd just learned more about the Reed family in three minutes with Mrs. Nails than in almost a week of working with Noah.

So, I'm not the only one with demons haunting my past.

When the coffee was done, Mrs. Nails loaded the mugs, along with cream and sugar, onto a tray and returned to the living room with Bree in tow. She handed Noah a mug, then one to Bree. "Help yourself to the coffee fixings." She sat opposite Noah on the far end of the couch and picked up her crocheting.

Noah, Bree had noted, drank his coffee black. She added in some cream to hers, glad Marge of the Busy B wasn't around to insist she add sugar. *Ah, this was heaven.* The coffee was hot, smooth and pleasantly bitter on her tongue. Choosing an accent chair, Bree sat and placed her mug on the side-table coaster, then pulled out her notebook and pen to take notes.

"Well, let's get on with the reason you're here," Mr. Nails insisted once they'd had time enough for several warming sips.

From joking and laughing, Noah went into serious mode, which he seemed able to do at the drop of a hat. "You know about the break-in at the high school, right?" He took another sip of his coffee, then found a place to rest his mug.

"'Course I know about the break-in. Had to get the window replaced in the gym door." The custodian shook his head. "Like those darn kids don't make enough work for us already."

"What makes you think it was kids?" Noah crossed one ankle over the opposite knee in a relaxed pose. It was a casual move, probably a habit, but the way his thigh muscles bunched almost made her mouth water. How in tarnation did he manage to pull off that degree of sexy with absolutely no effort whatsoever? *So* aggravating. "Have you heard anything about who it might have been?"

"No one's talking about it, but who else could it be but kids? Probably figured the mess would be enough to get them a day off of school." He huffed. "You got any leads?"

"Nothing substantial. We wanted to get your opinion about something." Noah sipped more coffee. "Any chance someone could have gotten hold of a key to the school, used it to get in?"

A frown creased Rusty's forehead, and he took his time before answering. "Well, now that you mention it, there was something hinky about the way that door looked. Can't quite put my finger on it." His expression cleared. "Besides, if someone already had a key, why not use it instead of *breaking* in?"

"That's what we're trying to figure out." He uncrossed his leg and leaned toward Rusty. "You think there's a chance any of your crew lost their key? Or loaned a copy to someone?"

The custodian's face turned as red as his hair must have been once upon a time. "Are you accusing—"

"No, I'm not accusing anyone of anything." Noah held up his hands in a calm-down gesture. "We have to explore every possibility, rule out everyone we can in order to narrow our list of suspects."

After a tense moment, Rusty gave a sharp nod. "Fair enough. You've got a job to do, same as everyone else. But I vouch for my men."

Noah and Rusty stood, and the two women followed suit. Mrs. Nails had kept her nose buried in her crocheting the entire time, but her hook flew through those stitches at top speed when her husband's voice rose. They moved to the front door as a foursome, everyone smiling and the two men shaking hands.

"I'd like to ask a favor, Rusty." Noah handed Bree her jacket and shrugged into his own. "Please don't mention our talk to anyone at the school. Not even your own crew."

Rusty waved his hand. "Don't worry—mum's the word. Right, Iris?" He gave his wife a stern eye, apparently trying to nip gossip in the bud.

She rolled her eyes. "My lips are sealed."

As Noah opened the front door, Bree leaned toward Iris. "I love your needlework. I've never had a knack for it, but I know the skill and patience it takes."

"Oh, thank you, dear. So nice of you to say. I'd be happy to teach you, if you have the time and inclination. It's much easier than it looks." The older woman patted Bree's arm. "Feel free to stop over anytime. I'd love the company."

Bree thanked her as she left, stopping just short of committing to crochet lessons. But she didn't completely rule it out. For however long it took her to work through her hesitation about drawing her piece, she'd need something to occupy her free time. Crocheting was as good as anything. Something to remind her of her grandmother. Something she could do alone.

After the warmth of the Nailses' home, the outside cold was especially brutal. Bree pulled up the collar on her jacket. Noah rubbed his hands together for warmth as they jogged to the SUV. "You did good in there."

As she opened the passenger-side door, Bree shot him a look that said he better tread carefully. "What do you mean?"

Noah climbed in. "I mean, I believe you've just gone forty or so minutes without making anyone mad."

Bree slammed her door shut and reached over to turn on

the heater—not that it would do any good until the engine warmed up. "Give me a sec. I'm sure I can change that in no time."

"Hot to cold, cold to hot. Hell of a skill set you've got there, Delgado."

You have no idea, Reed. No idea at all.

WHILE WAITING FOR the SUV to warm up, Noah lifted the file folder from Bree's lap and flipped it open. "We can catch the janitor who polishes the floors later, at the school, since he works nights. Let's save him for last." He rifled through the papers. "Maintenance guy or assistant custodian next?"

"The maintenance man has been working there almost as long as Rusty. Seems odd that one of the long-timers would suddenly do something like this." She leaned across the console and scanned the paper in Noah's hand. "I vote we talk to Ed Charleston, head of maintenance."

She tipped her head to meet his eyes, her curls releasing a scent that brought images of palm trees and beaches. Coconut. Citrus. A tropical flower he could picture but had no name for. Her lips, close enough to kiss, parted slightly. He just needed to lean in a fraction of an inch—

In one swift move, Bree straightened and was back on her side of the console as if nothing had almost happened. Noah released a silent sigh of frustration. With any luck, his sister would decide Bree was ready to solo sooner than later. Then he'd be rid of the constant temptation that tortured him when he was with her. Not just her physical attraction but a bone-deep hankering to know everything about her.

He glanced at Ed's address, handed the file back to Bree and pulled away from the curb. Just a few blocks away from the Nailses' residence, Noah parked in front of another older home. This entire neighborhood featured small houses with neat yards.

Bree, silent during the short drive, paused with her fingers on the door handle. "Want to do the talking again?"

"Sure. But when we visit Jack Williams after Ed, I think we should both question him. I've arrested him several times and he doesn't know you, so double-teaming him might knock him off balance."

He could tell by how her lips tried to twitch into a smile that Bree liked this plan.

They climbed out and started up the walk. Before Noah could ring the bell, a porch light came on and the front door opened.

A large, square man stood in the entry, wearing a belligerent frown. "Wondered how long before you got around to asking us questions. Might as well come in." Ed Charleston stepped back and held the door for them.

"'Us'?" Noah asked, and by the rise of her brow, he knew Bree's curiosity was also piqued.

"*Us*, as in maintenance-and-cleaning crew. If anything goes missing or gets broken, it's always us who get blamed."

Once they were inside, out of the cold, Noah shook Ed's hand. "We're not just interviewing the cleaning and maintenance employees."

"Came to us first, though, didn't you?" Although his hostility was evident, he was keeping it in check. But if this man had any information, Noah doubted he'd be sharing it.

Bree suddenly leaned forward, a ridiculous, toothy grin on her face. "Hi there. I'm Deputy Delgado. My partner has absolutely no manners—but then, Marge over at the Busy B warned me about that. Do you know Marge?"

Ed laughed, a bit strained, but a laugh. "Everybody knows Marge. Here, let me take your jacket."

"Thanks, Mr. Charleston."

"Since we're about to talk all personal-like, call me Ed."

She gave the man a warm smile. "So, Ed, you were expecting us?"

Leading the way into a living room that smelled of cooked cabbage and spicy sausage, Ed motioned for them to sit on the couch. "It only makes sense you'd be talking to people at the school, employees and students. And like I said, we're usually first." He ran a weathered hand across his gray-stubbled chin. "Though that whole break-in is a mite curious, if you ask me."

"How so?" Noah welcomed new thoughts about the case.

"Looked amateur. Which would lead you to think it was a kid, or kids." He tapped a calloused finger against his chin. "Seems to me that kids would only be interested in gym equipment, once they found out that Irving's computers weren't worth the effort." He chuckled. "Gotta hand it to old Ben. But I had to ask myself, if it was kids, why mess with the other departments? Could've just been random vandalism, I suppose, like kids sometimes get up to. But then I got to wondering—where were the dirty words in spray paint? The empty beer cans? You know, things like that? Unless…"

"Yes?" Bree prompted after a few seconds of silence.

Always pushing, Noah noted. She never just let the information flow. Not always a bad thing. Not always a good thing, either.

"Well, unless they were trying to mislead you. You know, trying to cover up something else. Can't figure out what that would be, mind you, but I was wondering."

"That's one possibility we're considering," Noah said. "You think there's any chance someone got their hands on one of the school keys?" He stopped short of suggesting ways it might have happened, curious to see what Ed might come up with.

The older man settled against the back of his chair and gave Noah a shrewd look. "Clued in on that, did you? No one could have come in that gym door without the bottom lock being unlocked."

Noah nodded. "Yep, we caught that right away." He ignored Bree's smirk at the word *we*.

"Well, I can't speak for anyone else, but I have possession of my key to the school. You're welcome to compare my fingerprints to any at the crime scene—but since me and the custodians touch just about every surface in the place on the regular, not sure it'll help." As he spoke, he dug out a key ring from his pocket. He unclipped the chain it was attached to from his belt, sorted through the many keys and passed the ring to Bree, sitting closest to him.

She took it by the key he'd been holding, examined it closely and then passed it to Noah.

It was similar to most keys he'd seen, other than the etched warning not to duplicate. "If one of these did get lost, whoever found it wouldn't have a clue as to what it opened. But I doubt you misplace *your* keys very often." Noah held up the chain. "I don't know how you relax at home with all this still attached to your pants."

"After a while, you get so used to it, you feel naked with it off." Ed chuckled. "'Less of course, you *are* naked."

Chuckling along with Ed, Bree asked, "Do you have any thoughts on who might've broken in?"

If he was a betting man—and he was—Noah would have placed money on Bree getting offended by this joke. And he would've lost. This easygoing demeanor of hers was a far cry from her usual approach, but it, as well as her keen powers of observation, could only help solve the case. Even if the extent of her flirtatious behavior rankled him a bit.

Ed shook his head. "I do have thoughts on who *wouldn't* have. For us older guys—Rusty, Bud and me—if we wanted something enough to steal it, we'd just slip it out of the school with our tools or in a bucket or something. Now, I'm not saying we'd actually do that. I'm just saying none of us got the energy to go about it like a burglary. We spend our weekends drinkin' beer, watchin' football and restin' up for the following week."

"You didn't include Jack Williams in that group." Noah kept a sharp eye on Ed's expression.

"Well, now, Jack's a mite younger, and I don't know him very well." He paused as if considering how to explain further. "Hasn't been at the high school long. I'd hate to think Rusty's pup had anything to do with it, but I can't vouch for him like I can Rusty and Bud."

Bree pulled her brows together in a look of confusion. "'Pup'?"

"His assistant." Ed snickered. "That kid follows him around like a puppy from the pound. Has since they hired him. If he don't start takin' on some responsibilities, I doubt he's long for the scintillating world of janitorial work."

Bree snorted, then tried to cover it up with a cough.

Ed pretended to be offended. "I'll have you know I learn a new word every day, young lady. I just open the dictionary, close my eyes and point. *Scintillating* happened to be yesterday's word." His lips fought to contain a smile; then he and Bree gave in to laughter.

As it tapered off, Ed wiped his eyes. "Whoo-ee! I can't remember the last time I had a good laugh with a pretty lady. Y'all need to come question me more often."

Instead of taking his head off for calling her a lady, like she nearly had Dave's, Bree smiled. "Aren't you sweet."

Her tone was still syrupy enough to cause a toothache, and Noah rose, shaking his head at both of them.

"Well, I may not be the pretty one, but maybe we can all just meet up for beers instead."

Standing, Ed shook his hand. "Got yourself a deal, Noah." He turned to shake Bree's as she joined the men. "And by the way, Deputy Delgado, welcome to Resolute."

"Thank you, Mr.—"

The older man held up a finger as if to scold her. "I told you to forget that *mister* nonsense."

"Thank you, Ed. And I'm Bree."

Noah handed him a card. "If you think of anything else or hear something, give me a call, okay?"

"Will do." The man pocketed the card, his keys jangling as he did so. "And after you two solve this case, call me for that beer."

"You're on." Noah handed Bree's jacket to her and put on his own. Once they were outside, she gave him a questioning look. He waited until they were back in the car.

"He seems nice." Her pleasant expression from a moment ago had faded into one of concentration. "But you know him better than I do." She shivered and wrapped her arms around her body. "What do you think?"

"What he said made a lot of sense." Noah glanced at the dash clock. "We still have time to talk to Williams—and at this point, he sounds like our most interesting person of interest." He grinned.

"Seriously? Is that what passes for wit these days?"

Slightly miffed that he didn't garner the same reaction that Ed had from his jokes, Noah cranked up the heater. "You're just jealous you didn't say it first."

Bree scoffed. "As if." She dropped her head back against the seat. "And speaking of jealousy, what the heck was your deal in there?"

"*My* deal?" Noah buckled his seat belt.

Bree snapped hers in place as well. "Half the time I was talking to him, you were either rolling your eyes or glaring at me."

Noah batted his eyelashes; then, in a breathy falsetto voice, he said, "Hi there, Ed, you big old cutie pie. I'm Bree. Blink, blink, blink. Why, you are so terribly funny. Blink, blink, blink." He ended with a high-pitched giggle.

Bree's mouth hung open. "You were antagonizing him to the point that I thought he'd kick us out. Stop sounding like a jealous boyfriend. I was simply getting information in a different way."

A jealous *boyfriend*? Not in this lifetime. Plus, he'd never had a jealous bone in his body. "Just didn't think you had it in you to be so phony."

"Lots of things you don't know about me." Bree snapped her mouth shut and went all starch and vinegar. She stretched out her arm and tapped a finger against her watch. "Let's go. Time's a-wastin'."

Aaand she was back. The woman he'd already grown used to. The one he liked as a colleague. *Just* as a colleague. *The fool doth protest too much, methinks.*

Leave it to his brain to misquote Shakespeare.

Chapter Ten

It didn't surprise Bree when Noah pulled into the parking lot of the Oak View Apartments, a place where she'd considered renting. Jack Williams was an assistant custodian in a rural county school district with a tight budget. Unless he wanted to live with his parents, an apartment here might be all he could afford.

On the wall outside the main door to the building, a list of names identified the buzzer for each apartment. Bree grabbed Noah's arm to stop him from pushing Williams's bell.

"Let's try this first." She pushed the buzzer labeled Manager. Instead of asking who it was through the intercom, the door release clicked, and Bree grabbed the handle. "This way, we don't risk Williams leaving by the back door." She entered the tiny foyer and started up the stairs.

"How'd you know there was a back door?" Noah followed on her heels, making her self-conscious of his view.

"At one time, I thought I might rent here." She reached the first landing and continued up the next set of stairs. "Until I saw the vacant apartment. Pretty small and kind of gross."

"Yeah, that could change your mind."

Reaching the top floor, Bree started down the hallway, checking apartment numbers as she went. When they reached Williams's, she motioned for Noah to stand to the side. Music blasted from inside. Scrunching down a little so only her face would show in the peephole, she knocked.

Footsteps approached, then retreated. The music disappeared and a moment later, the door opened, with Williams leaning forward with a black eye and a crooked smile. The smile only lasted a second, until he eyed her badge. "Oh hell, no!" Scrambling backward, he tried to slam the door.

Bree had often been called petite, but her feet never had. She considered them a welcome counterbalance to her also-not-petite boobage. She blocked the door with one foot, and Noah helped her push it open.

"You're hurting my feelings, Jack. Makes me think you're not happy to see me." Noah paused at the threshold, Bree next to him. "Now, we can talk to you from here, if that's what you'd prefer." He leaned back and looked down the hall in both directions, then faced Jack again. "'Course, we'll probably cover more topics than we'd planned on. I sure hope none of your neighbors gets the wrong idea about the extent to which you're helping us on a very important case."

"Come on, man. I haven't done anything." His swollen eye, the only thing marring his handsome face, said otherwise. He threw his arms up in the air. "Fine. Come in."

Noah walked in. "That wasn't so hard, was it?"

Bree closed the door and leaned against it. "How'd you get the shiner?"

Jack gave Noah a sideways glance. "Hit myself in the face with my mop at work."

"I'd admire you for wanting to look stupid instead of guilty, *if* I bought that." Noah sat on what looked like a thrift-store couch and waved toward the mismatched chair. "Have a seat. We just want to ask you a few questions."

"Said every cop who ever arrested me." Jack dropped into the chair.

"Well, yeah, since I'm the cop who usually arrests you." Noah shrugged. "What can I say? Habits are hard to break."

Bree walked over to the only other chair, a wooden one at a small table. "Where were you Friday night?"

Raking both hands through his dark hair, he said, "I swear I didn't get in a fight."

"Not what I asked you." Bree turned the chair around and sat backward on it. For some reason, it bothered men when she did that. Made them more defensive.

"I was at the Dead End until it closed. Playing pool."

Bree gave Noah a questioning glance.

"It's a bar." Then to Jack: "After that?"

"I was here. Sleeping it off." Jack scowled at them. "And again, I didn't get in a fight."

"Were you with anyone?" Bree already had her pad and pen in her hand. When Jack nodded, she said, "We're gonna need her name. Or his."

He started to rise, so she raised her hands. "Hey. No judgment here."

"It was a woman. And I'm not telling you her name." He blew out a sigh. "She's married, and her husband will kill me if he finds out."

"For a second there, I thought you were protecting her honor." Bree blew out a heavy sigh of her own. "Why don't we cut to the chase. Give us the play-by-play of your whole weekend, from leaving work on Friday to back at work Monday morning."

Jack flopped back in his chair and began a boring, detailed description of his every move during the sixty hours in question. She and Noah listened until the end without interrupting.

"I was wrong, Deputy Delgado." Noah yawned. "Apparently, our most interesting person of interest isn't interesting after all."

"Only if we're expected to believe that a good-looking, charismatic man like Mr. Williams has such a limited social life." Bree winked at Noah.

But he obviously didn't appreciate her attempt to provoke Jack. Instead, Noah's mouth compressed into a hard line, and the skin around his eyes tightened.

What was his problem? He was the one who'd suggested she help throw Williams off balance. Between this and accusing her of being a flirt earlier...did he honestly think she was flirting *now*?

The room had been silent for less than a minute, but it seemed much longer to Bree. She met Jack's eyes. "I'm sure you heard about the recent break-in at the high school."

"That's what this is about?" He jumped to his feet. "I had nothing to do with that."

"Then who did you loan your school key to?" Noah stood and assumed a challenging pose.

"I don't loan my key to anyone. It's not allowed." Jack's face turned red.

In what? Anger, indignation or frustration at being caught?

"So all of a sudden, you're a rule follower?" Noah asked.

"When it comes to my job, you're damn right. I need that job."

"You have quite the history of shoplifting." Bree rose from her chair as she sensed the conversation coming to a close. "It's not that far-fetched to think you've graduated to burglary."

"How did you know that? Those files were sealed."

"They still are." She stepped closer to Jack. "But you just told me. Oldest trick in the book, and they still fall for it every time."

Noah stepped between them. "How 'bout you let us search your apartment while we're here. As an act of good faith since you say you don't have any of the stolen items."

"How 'bout you come back with a warrant?" Jack's hands squeezed into fists. "Now get out."

Noah held his hands in front of him. "Okay, okay. We're leaving—but know if we have to come back with a warrant, we're going to be *very* thorough."

"Take your best shot."

"Don't be stupid and try to move anything out of your apartment. Someone will be watching you until we come back."

"Get *out*!"

The door slammed behind them with finality. But final only for now. She'd be back, with Noah in tow, and Jack better hope they didn't turn up anything. She never had liked wasting her time.

Noah walked behind her in the narrow hallway. "Based on the interviews, our buddy Jack looks the most promising so far. Everyone else has been cooperating."

"Unless one of the other guys was lying. And we can't forget the coaching staff. Still need to work up backgrounds on them." She glanced over her shoulder and stopped Noah when he opened his mouth to speak. "Look, I know they're a lower priority. But I'm a check-off-all-the-boxes kinda girl."

"I promise we'll get to everyone on the list." He aimed a mischievous smile her way. "But while we're on the subject of Jack, I'm pretty sure you're mistaken about who the good-looking, charismatic one was in there."

Ah, there it was. He'd thought she was flirting and got his man feelings hurt. At least he approached the subject with humor now. Bree turned around and walked backward down the hall, peering at Noah with her head tipped to the side. "Hmm. I suppose it might've been the bad lighting."

"I'm proud of you, Delgado. Takes a big person to admit when they're wrong."

Bree groaned with frustration, then faced forward again before reaching the stairs. Noah *was* the best-looking, most charismatic man she'd met in a long time.

But she wasn't about to let *him* know that.

"You're so full of it," she tossed over her shoulder.

"If you mean full of charm, charisma and a boatload of magnetism, then yes I am."

"You just go ahead and think whatever makes you feel better about yourself, Reed."

"Always do, Delgado. Always do."

NOAH PULLED INTO the Resolute High parking lot closest to the gym and checked his watch. "It's seven forty-five, on the dot."

"What's going on at this hour?" Bree looked around at the half-full lot and brightly lit building.

"Coach always runs late practice sessions the night before varsity basketball games."

When they approached the door, a young assistant basketball coach unlocked it and let them in.

"Evening, Noah. Ma'am."

"Hi, Isaac. This is Deputy Delgado."

"My pleasure, ma'am. Principal Jackson said you'd be stopping by. I'd almost given up on you."

"Had a few other stops to make first." Noah checked out the court, where the team ran drills. "How much longer will you be here?"

"At least half an hour. Maybe longer." He led the way along the perimeter of the room to the corridor door leading to the main building. Unlocking it, he pushed it open and held it for them to pass through. "Think you'll need more time than that?"

"Half an hour should be plenty. But just in case, can we borrow your key to let ourselves out? I can get it back to you first thing in the morning."

Isaac paused and, as if making a life-altering decision, gazed at Noah's badge while his fingers twirled the key. When he finally made eye contact, he shrugged. "I'm sorry, I can't do that, even if you *are* the law. Especially since the break-in."

"Good answer." Noah clapped him on the shoulder. "You hear about anyone else with a key loaning it out?"

"Or maybe losing theirs?" Bree joined the conversation.

The man shook his head. "We all have to be able to open up and lock up, just in case. If someone lost their key, they'd have to get another one from Coach. And he likes to announce it when people screw up. You know, kinda like a drill sergeant who embarrasses his men in front of the whole platoon?"

Bree was scribbling in her notebook. Without even looking up, she asked, "Couldn't they just have a duplicate made?"

"Nope. The school keys are restricted." The assistant coach smiled. "And I know this for a fact. When I first started here, I was so terrified of losing mine, I tried to get a copy made. The local places wouldn't touch it, so I drove all the way to a locksmith in Victoria. They took one look at it and refused, too."

"So what happens when someone does lose a key?" Bree stood ready to take more notes, pen tip touching paper.

"A request is sent to the school district, and they order a new one from the manufacturer. A serial number is on each key, and they keep records of who's assigned each one." Isaac scrunched up his face in thought. "As far as loaning a key to someone, I haven't heard anything."

"Gotcha," Noah said. "See you here in about thirty minutes."

"Me and my key will be waiting."

The door clicked closed behind them, and the bolt lock slid into place. Noah and Bree moved at a fast pace down the hallway and into the main building. As they turned a corner, heading deeper into the school, their boot heels thumped out a rhythm on the linoleum floors until challenged by the hum of a floor scrubber. Noah stuck his arm out to the side to stop Bree. "Hear that?"

"I think it's coming from that way." She pointed ahead and to the left, leading him through the hallways.

Three minutes passed, then four. No floor scrubber. Noah could still hear the darn machine humming, so where the heck was the man pushing it around? He picked up the pace and zipped past Bree. "Hurry up, slowpoke. We're losing time, and I don't want to get locked in here."

"Slow down, will you? It's been a long day, and I'm too tired to keep running after you. If we do get locked in, you have Coach Crawford's number. You can just call him."

He hated it when anyone thought of something that he should have. But with Bree, it sat differently on him. He would have to prove his worth to his siblings, but with her— well, he just wanted her to *know* he was on the ball.

"Hopefully, we'll finish up in no time, so it won't matter." Noah looked over his shoulder to find Bree gaining on him. "If we can just find our guy."

They reached the end of another hallway, rounded another corner and there he was: the janitor, swinging the floor buffer from side to side as he worked his way toward them. But when he glanced up, instead of the older man Noah knew, a young guy—late teens, early twenties—stared at him. Maybe five foot ten and skinny as a rail, he wore ripped jeans and a Rolling Stones classic tongue T-shirt, a hoodie and sneakers. No mistaking him for Bud.

For a split second, the kid's eyes darted back and forth as if debating what to do. Noah instantly pegged him as a runner. And sure enough, he ditched the machine and blazed a path down a side hall. Taking off after him, Noah saw a blur from the corner of his eye. He glanced that direction only to find Bree leaving him in her dust.

She must've gotten a second wind, 'cause that girl could flat out run. He sped up, determined to pass her, but she managed at least two strides to each of his longer ones. She finally slid to a stop at a hallway intersection, breathing hard and waving her hands.

"I'm lost. And I can't hear him running anymore." Bree stomped her foot. "I could've caught him, but this school is a doggone maze."

"Let's try to catch him outside." Noah motioned for her to follow him, and he raced back to the gym. Pounding on the door for it to be unlocked, he cursed the seconds ticking away.

"That was fast." The assistant coach held the door open, almost getting run over in the process.

"Come on." Bree grabbed the poor guy by his arm and dragged him to the exit. "Hurry up. Unlock it."

Isaac crouched at the bottom of the door. "I'm going as fast as I can." He dropped the key ring, then had to find the right key again.

"I see headlights in the parking lot." Noah slammed his fist against the door.

"It's open. Go. Go." The assistant coach stepped to the side, almost cowering.

Noah sprinted toward the white Toyota sedan as it pulled forward out of the first row of cars. It turned right, and as Noah closed the distance, the kid looked out the side window, his terror-filled face focused on Noah's. Speeding past the curved sidewalk, the kid raced for the exit at the back of the lot. Noah cut through rows trying to keep up, but he was no match for a V-6 engine.

The moment the kid knew he was in the clear, he celebrated with an impressive backward skid-and-spin maneuver that Noah had seen in every *Fast & Furious* film, disappearing in a stinking cloud of burnt rubber and exhaust.

"Son of a—"

"Hey!" Bree slid to a stop at his side, bending at the waist and resting her hands on her knees, breathing almost as heavily as Noah. "Get his plate?"

"84N, but that was all. Should earn us a few hits when we plug it into the system."

Coach jogged up to them in the parking lot. "Who the heck was that?"

Noah turned and gave the coach a penetrating look. "So, as far as you know, the school hasn't hired a new floor polisher?"

"What? Are you kidding? No way Bud would ever give up that job. He'd be lost without it. Told me so himself on more than one occasion." Coach tipped his head to the side. "Are you saying that kid was in the building, buffing the floors?"

Before he could answer, Bree asked, "Do you usually see the janitor when he does the floors?"

Coach took a few beats to consider the question. "You know, I used to see Bud pretty frequently, depending on my schedule and which part of the building he started in. But now that I think about it, I haven't seen him at all in the past week or so."

Something about this whole scenario with the kid didn't sit right with Noah. "You didn't recognize him? The kid?"

Coach shook his head. "Only saw him for a second when he ran past the exit door, outside of the building. But there was something vaguely familiar about him. Maybe the way he ran. I don't know, but it's right here somewhere." He tapped the side of his head. "Just out of reach."

Noah rubbed at the stubble on his cheek. "If you think of it, be sure to let us know."

"Of course."

"Thanks, Coach. And good luck with the game tomorrow."

"You'll be there, right?" Coach looked from Noah to Bree. "You should come, too. You ain't seen Texas varsity b-ball until you've seen the Resolute Roughnecks play."

She glanced up at Noah instead of Coach. "Ah, well, I'd certainly hate to miss that."

"Great. See y'all there. And good luck. Hope you find that guy."

"Oh, we'll find him." Excitement filled Noah's chest because he had a pretty good idea where to look now. Together, with Bree, they'd find the kid and solve the case.

It seemed ridiculous to be putting this much energy, this many hours, into such a petty crime. But he'd been assigned to it, and when Cassie returned, she'd learn how professional he'd been. How he'd followed protocol. By then, he'd have joined Adam's team, investigating the meth-house explosion. And after that, maybe—just maybe—he would finally be given his own case to run.

He was so close to reaching his goal, he could almost savor the sweet taste of success.

Bree reached out and touched his hand. "You know something, don't you?"

Her touch had been light, soft. Anyone else might have thought they'd imagined it. Not him. The hairs on his arms stood on end, and a chill raced through him that had nothing to do with the frigid weather. She stood so close, her breaths fogged the air he breathed, and her scent intoxicated him.

Lord, he wanted her. Not just her body. He wanted *all* of her. But he couldn't have her, and he needed to get that through his head once and for all.

"I know where our next stop is." He gave her his half grin that seemed to aggravate her so much. "Let's go."

BACK IN THE SUV, Bree massaged the back of her neck. "Hey, look, I'm all about chasing down a good lead, but it's past eight. You sure this overtime is approved?" Maybe, if they'd been working the meth house. But a school break-in?

Noah turned into a neighborhood. He must have a notion about who tonight's mystery floor buffer was. Something flickered in her mind, gone before she could grab hold of it.

"So, about that. How ticked off would you be if I unofficially told you that officially we're off the clock?"

"Dude, you are so going to owe me for this." Irritated at getting conned, she drummed her fingers on the armrest. "I'm thinking a Wagyu-steak dinner with all the trimmings. And of course, a top-shelf whiskey."

"Of course." That lopsided grin of his was back. "You drive a hard bargain, Delgado, but you got yourself a deal. Be the perfect time to introduce you to the Chute. Not sure they have Wagyu, but they've got the best steaks in Texas."

"Yeah, yeah, I heard all about the Chute and how you Reeds like to initiate newcomers there." She sighed in exasperation. "I'm willing to go there for food and drink, but don't think for one minute you're getting me on that mechanical bull. And, Noah?"

"Yeah?"

"Before you play fast and loose with my free time again, you'll ask me, right?"

His grin disappeared as he glanced at her. "I should have this time."

"Yes, you should have. Lucky for you, I'm the forgiving sort." Bree craned her neck, looking down the street they were on. A few streetlights were out, making it difficult to orient herself. "Isn't this the same neighborhood where Rusty lives?"

"Good eye, newbie. Yeah, Rusty lives a few blocks that way." He hooked his thumb toward the passenger window. "Getting your bearings, eh?"

"Trying." Having lived in San Antonio her entire life, Bree could traverse it blindfolded. Although being geographically challenged around here hadn't been an issue yet, she'd hate to get lost on a call. "But the streets run at an angle inside Resolute, so once I pass the town limits, I have to recalibrate."

"And that's why we love our GPS." Noah slowed, then parked at the curb in front of a small, dark house and turned to face Bree. "Want me to fill you in?"

"Sorry, Reed." She tapped her head, much like Coach had done. "This brain is just way too fast for you."

"So enlighten me, Delgado."

"We went to the school to interview Bud, the floor polisher. Someone else was cleaning the floors, obviously on behalf of Bud. We're now parked in front of Bud's house to find out why he wasn't at the school, why he gave his key to someone else and who that someone was." She gave him a knowing smile. "Can we please stop wasting time now and get this night over with?"

"Don't blame me if you're smarter than you look." Noah opened his door.

"At least I can play the cute-but-dumb card when I need to." She met him on the sidewalk. "You know, when I have to hide my brilliance so as to avoid offending someone."

Holding up a finger, he stammered a couple of times. "This conversation will be continued later."

When she laughed, he headed up the front walkway with those ridiculously long strides of his. So *aggravating*.

"What's Bud like?" she asked before they knocked.

Noah shrugged. "He's, well, a different sort of person."

"'A different sort,' huh? Care to explain?"

"He has obsessive-compulsive disorder to some degree. He's also got social anxiety. Introvert to the max. He usually gets along fine with people he knows, but that's why he loves his job so much. He works nights—he'd never be able to be a daytime custodian in a high school."

Noah knocked four times and waited. When no one responded, he knocked four times again. The television voices they'd heard through the door cut off, and eventually a man Bree assumed was Bud Jenkins appeared. Midfifties maybe, a little taller than her, and stocky.

"Noah." Bud's infectious grin stretched across his face. He glanced sideways at Bree, then took a step back.

"Bud, this is Bree. She's our new deputy and works with me."

Bud nodded, glanced from her to the floor and back a few times, then kept his eyes downcast. And just stood there.

Noah poked her arm and indicated she should go on in. With Noah following, she led the way into an immaculate living room furnished with a retro '70s vibe. Yellows and greens. Gold shag carpet on the floor. Everything seemed worn and faded, but not a speck of dust or an item out of place.

"Okay if I sit on the couch?" she asked Noah.

He nodded, and they sat at opposite ends, Noah closest to a recliner. The sound of the front door being locked and unlocked, over and over, drifted in. Bree's stomach tightened, unable to imagine the impact OCD could have on someone's life.

The noise finally stopped, and with a shy smile and no eye contact, Bud crossed the room with an uneven gait and plopped into a well-used recliner.

Noah leaned forward, forearms on his knees. "I noticed you're limping, Bud. Did you hurt your leg?"

With his eyes occasionally darting to Bree, the older man focused on Noah. "Eh, it's sciatica. Hurts all the way down to my toes. Flared up a week or so back, and some days I can barely stand."

"Is that why you aren't at work tonight?" Bree asked.

He tapped a rhythm on the recliner's arms but didn't answer.

Guess I should let Noah handle this.

"I get it. It's hard to do all that walking if it hurts to even move." Noah leaned back on the couch. "You get someone else to do the floors for you?"

Sighing, Bud nodded. "My sister's oldest boy, Sammy. Told him I'd pay him, and he was glad for the money."

"Why didn't you just call in sick and let the school bring in a replacement until you felt better?"

"Last time my sciatica got bad, that's exactly what I did." Bud scratched his balding head. "Principal Jackson told me I couldn't be out that long again. And I just can't lose my job."

"By any chance, did you give Sammy your master key to the school?"

Bud's gaze dropped to the floor faster than a copperhead's strike.

"He probably needed it to get in, right?"

"Yeah. But I told him to be careful with it. And he's been doing a good job, he says." Bud raised his eyes, brows drawn together. "Something must have happened, or you wouldn't be here."

Bree couldn't take her eyes off Noah. Besides his lop-sided smile and ridiculous jokes, he was just flat-out good with people.

"We just need to talk to Sammy. Someone broke into the school, and we're hoping he saw something that will help us."

"Am I going to lose my job?"

"I don't think so, Bud. I'll talk to Jackson myself if it's necessary."

That seemed to appease him. After collecting a bit more information and reassuring Bud again that everything would be all right, Bree and Noah left.

Back in the truck, they each made notes: Noah on the MDT, Bree in her notebook.

She sneaked a glimpse of his profile while he typed. As much as she hated to admit it, she hadn't been this hot for anyone in way too long. Her ex had been handsome, but his lack of morals, ethics and compassion finally revealed his true repulsiveness.

Noah was the full package. But she had too much on the line to risk taking things any further. No matter how appealing the fantasy, reality was seldom as rosy.

Shoring up her emotional fortitude, she looked up from her notes. "I see now why the sheriff wanted me to ride with you. This small-town, community policing thing is more complicated than I expected."

"You're catching on quick." Noah deepened his voice. "However, for now you are but the learner. I am still the master."

"The master of evil." She laughed at his shocked look. "What? You think you're the only *Star Wars* fan in this town?"

He clasped his hands over his heart. "Don't toy with me, Delgado. Because I seriously think I love you right now." Chuckling, he pulled away from the curb.

Bree chuckled, too. She had to because it was a joke. Just another one of Noah Reed's lame, stupid jokes. So why had this one strummed a chord deep within her? Notes of happy promises joined with tones of painful loss, the poignant tune enough to make her cry.

But tears of joy? Or heartbreak?

Chapter Eleven

In the daily briefing the next morning, Noah assumed his usual position—feet up and ankles crossed on a vacant chair next to him, arms folded across his chest. He didn't mind the meetings. But once Deputy Dave got started on his daily manifesto of detailed *in*actions, imagined slights and unwanted opinions, Noah lost his patience. And today he'd been running late, so his infusion of extra-strong Busy B coffee still sat on a warming burner of the diner's Bunn-O-Matic brewer. It almost brought a tear to his eye.

He glanced a few chairs down to Bree, as he did in every meeting. Frequently. She'd gone from sitting erect and taking notes while Adam spoke to slumped in her chair, pen lying on her closed notebook. She caught Noah looking, and with a thumb hooked in Dave's direction, she smirked and rolled her baby blues until the color disappeared.

Good to know the newbie still didn't think much of Dave.

By the time the meeting ended and they reached Noah's SUV, the air had warmed enough to toss their jackets in the back seat. They swung by the Busy B for to-go orders but had to wait for Marge to brew another batch of Noah's special strength.

"Next time you're runnin' late, you better call me, or I'm gonna scrape that swill into a cup and make you eat it."

Marge played musical burners with the coffee servers to open up a brewer space.

"Sorry, Marge. Would've been here in time, except Dave started talking and—"

"Say no more. I don't know where that man got the idea anyone wants to hear what he has to say." She hollered into the kitchen for the cook to hurry up. "Not much I dislike more than training a new cook. And this one?" She shook her head. "Just pitiful."

Noah peered through the pass-through at a twentysomething working the grill. "Where's Gus? He finally have enough of your cranky moods and quit?"

Marge smacked Noah with a menu. "The old man's fallin' apart. Had shoulder surgery and needs at least a month to recover. Probably longer." She leaned in toward Noah and Bree. "To be honest, I think Gus's wife got the short end of the stick. She has to stay home and rehab him."

Marge cackled, which got Bree laughing, which Noah approved of. It was a big, loud laugh. A nice laugh. A laugh he wanted to hear more often.

Marge pointed toward the kitchen. "But in the meantime, I'm stuck with Dumb or Dumber. Haven't decided which yet."

"Well, if it helps, my lunch here yesterday was excellent," Bree said.

"Club sandwich with fries?" When Bree nodded, Marge poked at her own chest, "That's 'cause I made it. Genius boy in there was out back on one of his many breaks. Claims the gas fumes irritate his asthma. More like the fumes he inhales on his own time."

When the extra-strong coffee had dripped its last drip, Marge filled Noah's travel mug and handed Bree a large to-go cup with regular strength. She pushed a bag against his chest that held breakfast sandwiches, based on the aroma.

"You two skedaddle. Breakfast's on me. Your sweet faces and laughter mean more than money this morning."

Noah gave Marge a peck on the cheek; then he and Bree left. They chowed down while taking Highway 111 north toward I-10. Adam had assigned them county-wide patrol duty all day but shortened it to a half shift when he'd learned about their burglary lead. With any luck, they'd close the high school case this afternoon and be ready for something new come Monday.

"Thanks again for agreeing to hold off on the search for Sammy until today." Bree sipped her coffee. "Last night, I was so exhausted, I barely managed to undress before I passed out in bed."

"Uh, sure." He stopped speaking, his attention wandering to a naked Deputy Delgado. He shifted uncomfortably, trying to bring his attention, as well as everything else, back to its original focus. "We'll track him down this afternoon."

Bud's sister's house had been their last stop the previous night, where they learned Sammy *didn't* live there. According to his mom, he crashed with friends, and his two younger brothers should know who. Noah had asked nicely, Bree had questioned more firmly, and the boys' mother had threatened life and limb before the two teens gave up the friends' names. They'd make those rounds when they got back.

As it edged past noon, Noah zigzagged back toward Resolute on two-lane blacktops. They pulled over a total of two cars, with Bree handling both stops. She wrote one speeding ticket, gave a warning for not signaling a turn and seemed completely at ease for the first time all week.

Her attitude baffled Noah. Nobody in the department enjoyed traffic patrol. It was boring. At least, he'd always thought so, and he couldn't imagine someone from a large urban environment not feeling the same way. But apparently, he'd been wrong.

Might be that she was an introvert and sought the solitude of patrol duty. She'd mentioned being used to not having friends, so maybe she was accustomed to going solo. Then again, perhaps solitude provided a barrier to shield her secrets.

Still several miles northwest of town, they came upon skid marks leading to a car on the side of the road. As they rolled up on the vehicle, Noah assessed the man bending over the open trunk.

Even in small towns, traffic stops came with an element of danger from the environment, the weather or oncoming traffic. None of that was an issue here. Or from driver hostility. The man straightened and gave them an inscrutable look.

"Stay sharp. Looks like a blowout, but you never know." Noah turned on his flashers and parked behind the old Chevy Impala. The man looked to be in his thirties and, based on the size of his biceps, someone who worked out on a regular basis. He also had what seemed like a nervous tic, bending his head to the side as if popping his neck.

Noah got an uneasy vibe and wasn't comfortable having Bree handle this stop.

Okay, maybe it was blatant sexism, especially since she had big-city experience, but he didn't care. His father had raised him and his brothers to be both respectful and protective of the fairer sex, and he wasn't about to change his spots to save anyone's sensibilities over the issue. Even hers.

"Run the plates," he said to Bree as he climbed out of the SUV, surprised when she raised no objection.

Noah walked up on the man with outward casualness. His hands rested easily on his duty belt in a nonthreatening posture, but one that would allow him to quickly draw his gun should the need arise. "Need any help?"

The man's mouth tightened into a thin line. "No thanks, Officer. Just digging out my jack. But I appreciate the offer."

Based on his dirty T-shirt and torn jeans, Noah would have guessed the guy had already changed his flat. But examining the trunk's interior, it looked like the man took care of himself about as well as he took care of his car.

What looked like a pile of rags, but might have been more of his wardrobe, was balled up in one corner next to a dirt-encrusted cooler. Fast-food bags, wrappers and cups filled an old cardboard box and spilled over onto the floor. Two plastic milk crates held cleaning supplies, everything from window cleaner, drain cleaner and laundry detergent to toilet-bowl cleaner, dish soap and bleach. A lot of supplies for someone who clearly wasn't a neatnik.

The driver followed Noah's gaze and forced an insincere chuckle. "Yeah, I need to clean it out one of these days."

"Heck, my brother's trunk looks ten times worse than that." Noah smiled as he told the lie, wanting to put the man at ease. "You from around here?"

He leaned against the back of his car and crossed his arms, and that's when Noah's radar started pinging. This guy was trying too hard to appear unaffected.

"McAllen. But I just rented a house up near Hudsonville."

"Hudsonville is a real nice place. You'll like it there."

Bree approached in time to catch the end of the conversation. She gave Noah a small nod, which meant nothing had come back on the plates. Still, he couldn't shake the feeling that something was hinky.

Bree moved into a backup position several paces from Noah. She must've ridden with a partner before, because she did it smoothly and automatically.

"Moving to Hudsonville for work?" She took her own casual peek into the trunk, though her right hand rested at her hip, near her service weapon.

The man nodded. "Heard about an offshore oil rig that might have some openings."

While Bree talked to the man, Noah had made a nonchalant circle of the Impala. Back at the trunk, he said, "Your inspection sticker and tags are expired. I need to see your license and proof of insurance."

"Ah, man. You gonna ticket me right when I'm about to get my act together? I'm already going to have to buy a new tire. You know how much tires cost these days?" He reached into his back pocket, pulled out his wallet and handed Noah the documents.

He's cooperating and he's not belligerent, so why do I feel that I'm missing something?

"Jason Watson. Crescent Drive in McAllen. Your insurance is up to date, which is the reason I'm not going to ticket you." Noah handed the license and the insurance card back to him.

"Thanks, man. I appreciate that."

"I'm not going to ticket you, Mr. Watson," Noah repeated, "but when you change your address on your license, which must be done within the next thirty days, you need to bring your vehicle up to date on its inspection and tags."

"You got it, man. First thing. I swear." He seemed sincere for the first time.

"If you're sure you don't want a hand, we'll let you get back to it."

Jason nodded as he returned his wallet to his back pocket. "Have a good day, Officers. And thanks again."

Once back in their SUV, Noah activated the MDT and entered the house number on Crescent Drive that he'd memorized from the license. Bree had run the plates; now Noah would run the man. "What kind of vibe did you get from him?"

"I think he was lying about his job. Hudsonville seems a bit far from the coast for an offshore job he didn't even have yet." Bree pulled out her notebook. "So what set off *your* alarm bells?"

"And here I thought I was being so subtle."

"You were, but you have your tells."

"Remind me to never play poker with you." He chuckled, then grew serious again. "I can't say what bothered me about the guy. Just a hunch."

"Hunches are right more often than not."

Noah agreed. "I sure didn't like the looks he gave you."

"It's nothing I haven't seen a thousand times before. Part contempt, part lust." Bree looked up from her notebook. "Most of the time, guys like him decide a chick with a gun's not worth the hassle."

Most of the time. *What about the rest of the time?* A muscle-bound guy that size would have no problem taking down Bree. Of course, as she pointed out, Bree did carry a gun. But then again, maybe Jason Watson of McAllen, Texas, did, too. They hadn't searched his car. No cause.

The results on Mr. Watson came back. "Not even a parking ticket." Noah put the SUV in gear, pulled around the Impala and continued down the road. "What did you think about all those cleaning supplies in his trunk? Not exactly bomb-making materials, but it seemed strange, considering how filthy he was."

Bree closed her notebook and mechanically tucked it between her thigh and the car seat, leaving the little wire spiral sticking out. "What I noticed was everything in his trunk looked like it had been there for ages, but the cleaning supplies looked new."

"I didn't pick up on that, but you're right. Maybe he bought them to deep clean his new place in Hudsonville."

"Maybe, but…"

"But what?"

"For one thing, he had dirt under his fingernails and his hair was greasy. I doubt he's bathed in over a week. Seems hard to believe such a smelly, grungy guy is going to care if his windows are dirty or his countertops need wiping down."

A loud, gurgling rumble interrupted their conversation, and Bree laughed. "By the sounds coming from your stomach, I'd say it's lunchtime. Let's grab some chow and then go find Sammy."

"You're on." Noah took the next right turn and headed back to the highway. "It'd be nice if we could wrap up the school burglary by quitting time. Give us something to look forward to come Monday morning."

"You're talking about the meth-house case, aren't you?"

Noah shot her a high-octane smile. "Yes, I am."

Bree gave him a half smile in return, then turned her head and looked out her side window.

"Hi, Ms. Gibson. How's your day going?" Bree asked as they passed Helen's desk in the lobby.

"Can't get much better than a slow Friday afternoon with everyone out of the office." The petite woman, whose hair was turning gray, smiled at her. "And for heaven's sake, call me Helen. We're mostly only formal in front of outsiders."

"Well, I sort of am an outsider. I've only been here—"

"Doesn't matter." Helen waved her hand. "Once you're working with us, you're family."

"God help her." Noah smirked. "Where is everybody?"

Helen checked her calendar where she kept track of all the office comings and goings. "Dave and Pete took over patrol for you two, and Adam and Shawn responded to a domestic dispute." Looking at Bree, she added, "One of our regular couples, south of town. They're usually past the point of reason by the time a neighbor calls us."

"We need to run a few searches, then we'll be out of your hair, too." Noah winked at her.

Bree laughed when Helen winked back.

In the bullpen, Bree copied the list of Sammy's friends from her notebook and gave it to Noah.

"I'll start from the top." He settled into his chair and tapped on his keyboard.

"Fine. I'll work my way up from the bottom." Walking to her desk, she looked over her shoulder at him. "Betcha I make it through more than you do."

"You're on." He typed faster. "What's the wager?"

"Hmm, I think I'll tell you after I win."

"In your dreams." He chuckled.

They pulled up names, searched for addresses, ages, records.

Bree liked her notes on paper, but she researched faster than most cops could turn on their computer. In less than ten minutes, she let out a whoop. "Five done, which means I win." She gave Noah her sweetest smile. "Would you like me to help you with your four?"

"Nice, Delgado. Hanging around with me is improving your sense of humor." He tapped a key and the printer whirred.

She picked up both hers and Noah's printouts and strutted to his desk. "And guess what's even better?"

"I'm sure you're about to tell me."

She waved the papers at him. "I've got an address for one of them."

Noah stood and read over her shoulder. "Oak View Apartments. Let's go."

Before they could take a step, his desk phone rang. He grabbed the receiver and listened to whoever was on the other end of the call for what seemed like a full minute before saying, "We'll take it." He dropped the handset in its cradle, a concerned frown on his face.

"What's wrong?"

"Have you got your notes from our talk with Bud and his sister last night?"

She retrieved her notebook and gave it to him without a word.

"Give me a second." He flipped through the pages, then cupped a hand loosely over his mouth.

As he handed the notebook back to Bree, a picture of Sammy slipped out from between two pages. His mother had made them promise to return it. He picked it up from the floor and gave it to Bree.

She'd been patient long enough. "What's going on?"

"I think Sammy is dead."

NOAH FILLED HER in on the way. A couple of kids playing by the railroad tracks east of town had seen a body. Male, young adult, dark hair. The general clothing description sounded similar to what Sammy had been wearing at the school the previous evening. Especially the T-shirt with the big red tongue.

"You think this somehow ties back to the burglary?" Bree asked.

"Could be coincidence, but—"

"I don't believe in coincidence." She crossed her arms.

"Neither do I. But I didn't see a single thing on the list of stolen items that would be worth killing for."

She tapped a finger against her chin. "What if we didn't get a complete list?"

Noah glanced at her. "You think someone's holding out on us?"

"More like something hasn't been missed yet. Something expensive." She shrugged. "We don't even know if it's Sammy yet."

"We'll know soon enough." Noah cut the lights and siren and turned onto a dirt service road running parallel to the tracks. They bumped along until he sighted a smaller dirt path leading into some woods.

He parked and climbed out, waiting for Bree, who grabbed crime scene tape and extra gloves. The body lay in a small clearing surrounded by trees and bushes.

It was Sammy.

The clothes he'd been wearing when they chased him through the school matched what was on the body. But it was his face, the same face as in the picture his mother had given them, that left no doubt.

"Looks like he was strangled." Bree indicated the bruising around his throat. "Maybe if we'd kept looking for him last night, this wouldn't have happened."

"Woulda, coulda, shoulda. No point thinking that way." He pulled his phone from his pocket and dialed. "Helen, can you call the justice of the peace, tell him we need a body declared? Then contact Austin, ask them to send a crime scene team and a wagon."

As he put his phone away, Bree asked, "Y'all use a JP for death declarations?"

"Yep. Small-town life and all." He looked back at the body and grimaced. "Man, some days I hate this job."

Bree considered the area. "His car isn't around. He didn't come here on his own."

"He probably came with his killer." Noah studied the crime scene. "Or was just dumped here." He walked around the edge of the clearing, peering into the trees.

"What are you looking for?"

"I thought I heard something." He stopped moving and listened again. A rustling in the bushes made the hair on the back of his neck stand up. He spun toward the sound, pulling his gun.

Bree moved closer, her eyes huge. As usual, her head was on a swivel, but she had no weapon in her hand. Noah caught her attention, pointed to his gun and then to hers. She stared at him briefly, then indicated she'd circle around behind the rustling.

Why hadn't she drawn her gun?

He went in the opposite direction, planning to meet her halfway. Then they could push whoever was out there in toward the clearing. As he rounded a large tree, an odd sound began, along with more frantic movement. And then he saw it.

A female javelina with two babies. The mother, snorting and sniffing, found his scent and went into baby-protection mode. Noah raised his gun, intent on killing her before she went after him with her razor-sharp tusks.

And suddenly, Bree was by his side. Letting loose with a blood-curdling scream, she raised her arms above her head and threw a large rock toward the animal. The mama and babies took off deeper into the woods.

Noah gaped at Bree. "What the hell was that about?"

"Javelina usually run from loud noises, especially if you throw things at them." Her forehead creased. "You never learned that when you were a kid?"

"You know that's not what I mean." He narrowed his eyes at her. "Why didn't you pull your gun as soon as we heard the noise? It could've been Sammy's killer for all you knew."

She stayed mum and avoided his eyes. Like she was hiding something.

"I'm serious, Bree." It took every ounce of his control to not yell at her. "I want to know what's going on with you. Before everyone else shows up."

She lifted her head and squared her shoulders as if readying herself for battle. But when she spoke, her voice was almost a whisper. "I can't fire my gun."

"What?" Her words made no sense.

She stared him straight in the eye and repeated it, louder this time. "I can't fire my gun. I can't draw it, I can't fire it." She gnawed at her bottom lip.

"Physically?" Was that her secret? She was losing strength in her muscles or something? "Like, what? Arthritis in your hand?"

"Nothing like that." She combed both hands through her hair, leaving it tousled. "A while back, I shot someone. I was on duty, he had a gun pointed at me. It was a clean shoot." This last came out as if by rote. A memorized explanation, defending herself. "I haven't been able to pull it since."

"And Cassie knows this?" His by-the-book, rule-following sister had allowed this?

"No one knows. Except you, now." She dropped her gaze and kicked at the loose dirt.

He glared at her. "Does this have anything to do with why you quit your job and came here?"

Bree found a tree to lean against. "I did all the regular stuff after the shooting. Desk duty while they investigated it, which didn't take long. Saw the department shrink, who said I was fine. *Everyone* said I was fine. Ready to go back out."

She crossed her arms and seemed to fold in on herself. "But I couldn't report the gun…problem. They'd pull me from patrol, and that's what I live for. It's what I *am*. A patrol cop."

"So you decide to put everyone else at risk instead? Hell, Bree. You can get your partner killed if you don't have their back." He paced in front of her, fury pouring out of him. "You just put *my* life in danger. If that animal had been someone with a gun sneaking up on us… I can't believe you did this."

"I'm sorry, Noah. I truly am. I thought Resolute was a small town with little to no crime." She raised her hands, then dropped them. "I figured I could work through my problem while I'm here. Go to a gun range, practice. And I *can*. I know I can turn this around. I just need a little time."

He stopped pacing and stared at her. "You know I have to tell Cassie about this, right?" The past several days replayed behind his eyes. She'd impressed him with her powers of observation. Her attention to detail. And the whole time, she'd just been boondoggling him. Him and the whole damn town.

"Please, Noah, I'm begging you. Give me a chance, and I won't disappoint you." She pushed off the tree. "Please?"

"You've *already* disappointed me. I gave you way too much credit as a law enforcement officer." A bitter taste filled his mouth. "You played us all for fools, didn't you? Cassie, Adam, the whole country-bumpkin lot of us, right?"

She jerked her head back as if he'd slapped her. "I never thought you were a fool. None of you. That's not what… I didn't mean to…" Her tears flowed freely, and she spun away from him, her shoulders shaking in silent sobs.

Fighting the urge to comfort her, he crossed over to the far side of the clearing. "I can't promise anything right now."

His heart and his mind and his gut all threw down, each

intent on winning this fight. He'd never experienced so many physical reactions at one time. Anger… when his father was murdered. Confusion…when his mother disappeared without a word. Care and compassion to this extent for a woman… this was a new one.

He sighed. "But I'll think about it."

Still facing away from him, she nodded her head.

He'd been right. Bree definitely had a secret. And now he had to decide what to do about it. As a responsible member of the department, he should report this to Cassie. If he didn't, would he ever be the deputy he was striving to become? And if he did, would he ever be the man he hoped to be?

He didn't want Bree to get fired. He didn't want her to leave Resolute. Because somehow, in less than a week, he was already falling in love with her.

Chapter Twelve

Despondent, Bree crawled out of bed Saturday morning and checked the time. Her appointment to look at rentals with the Realtor, Seth Whitlock, was in just over an hour. She straggled into the bathroom and gasped when she glanced in the mirror. Her sleepless night of worry and regret showed in the puffy, bruised crescents beneath her eyes.

Noah knew her secret. The sheriff, home for the weekend, would know soon enough. And Bree would be right back in the same situation she'd tried so hard to avoid.

She turned on the shower and stepped in, the cold water hitting her skin like icy needles. As if doing penance, she stood with her arms out to her sides, her face upturned beneath the frigid cascade.

Being a cop was who she was. She knew nothing else, wanted nothing else. She should have informed the SAPD brass the minute she knew she couldn't draw her gun. But that would've meant riding a desk, maybe for the rest of her career. And she'd heard the stories. Street cops didn't do well with desk duty. Some resigned. Some retired. Some ate their gun.

She'd chosen option number one, resigning—but with her secret intact, escaping to a place where she could work through her phobia with no one the wiser. Once she accomplished that, she'd return to San Antonio, or maybe check out Dallas, Fort Worth, Houston.

But she'd sure picked the wrong place to escape to.

It had been late when the last vehicle pulled away from the crime scene last night. And to say the ride back to the office to get her truck was awkward was laughable. Unless absolutely necessary, Noah hadn't looked at her or spoken to her the entire time.

She'd offered to go with him to notify Sammy's mother and brothers, as well as his Uncle Bud. But he declined, saying he'd prefer to do it alone. Which translated to: he didn't want to spend any more time with her. Or he no longer trusted her to work on the case.

As she dressed, Bree considered canceling. What was the point of looking at houses if she wouldn't be here long enough to rent one? But in the end, getting out of her motel room—and her troubled mind—won out.

When a knock sounded on her door, she paused just long enough to plaster on a smile. No reason this guy should have to suffer with a moody client.

"Hi. You must be Seth." She gazed up into eyes so dark, they appeared black. Flawless three-day stubble on his cheeks, black hair styled with care. His chiseled jaw and cheekbones made him perfect for modeling jobs, especially men's cologne or expensive suits.

Rachel had said he was good looking, and that was an understatement. But definitely not anyone Bree would be interested in. She gravitated to the rough-and-tumble type, jeans and boots, not afraid to get dirty. This guy probably showered three times a day.

"And you're Bree?" He flashed a white smile. "Ready to look at some houses?"

"Absolutely." She locked the door behind her and followed him to his car.

As they drove around Resolute, he made charming small talk, and Bree chastised herself for judging him based on his looks. She still wasn't interested, but Seth *was* a pleasant diversion from her dilemma.

"Rachel told me you flip homes?" Bree waited for Seth to remove the lock box from the front door of a cute yellow two-bedroom house. "Is this one of them?"

He opened the door and ushered Bree inside. "No, no. I don't have any flips available at the present time. A couple who moved closer to their kids and grandkids rent this one out. According to the property manager, it just became vacant last week."

Bree took the tour, which didn't take long. It was small, but she liked it. Close to work. Cozy inside, eclectic outside with flower boxes on the windowsills and a pink front door. A one-car detached garage sat off to the side, at the back of the lot with a long driveway leading to it. Definitely an improvement over the Oak View Apartments.

By midafternoon, she'd seen several more rentals, was starving and still liked the pink front door house best. When Seth dropped her back at the motel, she thanked him for his time.

"I know which one I want, but I'd like to take the weekend to think about it." *And wait until Monday to see if I even have a job.*

"Of course. Just give me a call when you decide."

Inside her room, she flopped onto the bed and stared at the ceiling. *When I decide. Not sure* I *get to make* this *decision.*

Noah had mentioned that since the sheriff would be home this weekend, they had a family dinner planned for tonight. She glanced at her watch. He'd probably wait until after the meal to tell Cassie about Bree's *problem*. No point in ruining a nice meal.

Then again, there was a chance he wouldn't say anything.

Yeah, right. Noah was so focused on following protocol, of course he'd tell her.

Bree rolled over and rested her head on her pillow.

And he should tell her. Because her selfish, ignorant decision could have had dire consequences. Because one day, they'd respond to a situation where words wouldn't resolve it. Where a physical altercation wouldn't end with the guy in cuffs. Where a civilian's life, another deputy's life—*her* life—might depend on the one thing she was incapable of doing: drawing her service weapon.

The oppressive weight of guilt over that possibility threatened to flatten her. She couldn't live with herself if people who depended on her were hurt or killed because she froze.

If Noah doesn't tell Sheriff Reed, I'll tell her myself.

NOAH LINED UP four shot glasses and grabbed a couple of limes. "Nate, what time did Bishop say they'd be here?"

"He was kind of vague." Noah's twin filled one of the small glasses with top-shelf tequila. By the time the limes were in wedges, Nate had tossed his first shot. "He said he'd have Cassie here before the food was ready, 'glowing like a candle flame.' No clue what he meant."

Noah scooped the limes into a bowl and gave his brother a doubtful look. "Seriously, dude. How long has it been since you've been with a woman?"

Nate met his eyes. "Oh. Got it." He shrugged. "Bishop's a dweeb. No one wants to hear that stuff about their sister."

Just then, a blast of cold air blew through the house. The front door slammed, and a minute later, Cassie and Bishop walked into the kitchen.

"I bring you pecan pie." Cassie set one of the Busy B's delicious pies on the counter, tossed her purse and jacket onto a chair in the living room, and bellied up to the shot glasses.

Nate filled the four glasses while Noah handed out lime wedges. The saltshaker sat front and center. Bishop didn't drink, so he poured himself a glass of iced tea while the Reed siblings each licked one hand, sprinkled salt on it and took hold of their glasses.

Adam started the toast with the first word, followed by Cassie, Noah and Nate; then they all shouted the last word together: *"Arriba, abajo, al centro, pa'dentro. Salud!"* They licked their hands, tossed their shots and sucked their limes.

"Y'all ought to take that show on the road." Bishop leaned against a cabinet, shaking his head at the family he was about to marry into.

"That chili smells pretty darn good, Adam." Cassie tried to sneak by him to sample it, but he chased her out of the kitchen.

Working like a well-oiled machine, Noah grabbed a tray of toppings from the fridge while his twin carried a cast-iron pan of jalapeño cornbread, and Adam brought the pot of simmering Texas chili to the dining room table. Adam ladled chili into bowls, and the rest of the Reeds passed the toppings and cornbread.

Meanwhile, Bishop sat quietly, his hands folded on his plate in front of him. Noah and Nate started spooning chili into their mouths. Cassie glanced across the table at Bishop, then glared at Adam.

"Where the heck is Bishop's dadgum dinner?"

Adam slapped his forehead. "Oh no, I forgot. He doesn't eat meat."

"Still," Bishop said with a smirk.

"I am so sorry. Let me go see what I can scrounge up for

you." Adam disappeared into the kitchen, returning a minute later with a small cast-iron pot. He set it on Bishop's plate and removed the lid with a flourish. "Ta-da."

Noah leaned over to see the contents. "Looks kinda like chili."

"So here's what I did." Adam returned to his chair at the head of the table. "As you all know, Texas chili doesn't have beans. So I took all the beans some ignorant non-Texan would've dumped in my mouthwatering chuck-roast chili and made Bishop his own little dainty pot of vegetarian chili. With no beer."

"Thanks, Adam. Very thoughtful of you." Bishop took a taste, his eyes grew wide and his forehead broke out in sweat.

"Even if it doesn't have beef, you gotta know it's gonna be spicy." Cassie winked at him.

"His might be a little hotter than ours." At Cassie's raised brow, Adam added, "I couldn't get the flavor in there with meat, so I added extra chilies."

"*Ours* has beer in it, right?" Nate waited for Adam's nod before eating more.

Noah poked his spoon in the air toward Bishop's food. "You can*not* call that chili, Adam. It's bad enough when people put beans in chili. But *all* beans? *No* beef? Uh-uh. That's not chili."

Bishop drained his iced tea and went back to the kitchen for more.

Adam glanced at Cassie as he scooped shredded cheese into his bowl. "How's the trial going?"

She swallowed a mouthful of cornbread. "I think it's going well, but I'm not supposed to talk about it. And even if I could, I couldn't." She took a sip of beer. "I can't be in the courtroom until they call me to testify. I've been sitting on a hard bench for a week, trying to catch snippets of gossip."

"You think they'll wrap it up soon?" Noah hoped they wouldn't. He needed more time to think things through.

"For all I know, I could be there another week. I thought it would be within a few days." She shrugged. "What's been happening around here?"

"Well, a meth head trashed Sweets and Treats," Adam said.

"What?" Cassie set her spoon down. "Is Sandy all right?"

"She's fine. Deputies Reed and Delgado tackled the guy and brought him in."

"Really?" She smiled across the table at Noah.

"You don't have to sound so surprised," Noah teased.

Adam continued, "Yeah, they're quite the dynamic duo. While they had that guy at the hospital for his blood test, a mother brought in her young son, unresponsive. They were the ones who figured out he'd been exposed to toxic meth trash."

"Well, actually, Bree figured it out," Noah mumbled. *Just have to be honest, don't you?*

"What on earth is going on around here with meth?" Cassie asked.

"We're working on it." Adam leaned back in his chair and drank some beer. "Delgado knows a lot about drugs from her time on the SAPD, so when she and Noah wrap up the high school break-in case, they'll be joining my investigation."

Nate brought another round of cold beers for everyone but Bishop.

"Thanks, Nate." Cassie caught Noah's eye. "That break-in sounded pretty minor. If Adam needs you two, why don't you just hold off on the burglary for now. There's a good chance it'll never get solved, anyway."

Noah pushed the chili around in his bowl. "You assigned me to that case. And I'm working it until it's done."

She frowned at him. "Come on, Noah. Don't waste any more time—"

"They're not wasting time, sis." Adam grimaced. "They just about had it wrapped up, and then their lead suspect was found murdered."

Cassie's mouth dropped open.

"So now they're working a murder investigation, which in the end might solve the burglary."

"Noah and Bree are working the murder?" Cassie's brows rose almost to her hairline.

"Yes, they are." Adam reached for another piece of cornbread. "Noah's been doing a great job, and I'm convinced he's ready for a big case. Especially since it developed from the one he was already working." He grinned at Noah. "He's been like a dog with a bone this week."

"I'm glad to hear that." She turned to Noah. "Sounds like you and Bree are working well together."

Bishop scoffed, then pretended he'd choked on a pepper. Cassie's gaze bounced between them before landing on Noah. "Is there something I should know about you and Deputy Delgado?"

Noah shoved a spoonful of chili in his mouth and shook his head. His brothers laughed. His sister didn't.

"Is working with her going to be a problem?" Cassie scowled at him. "Because you need to stay focused on the job, not her."

"Lighten up, Cassie. I was just teasing him." Bishop shrugged. "Didn't mean to rile things up."

She set her napkin on the table and sighed. "I'm sorry. It's been a long, frustrating week." To Noah: "I know Adam's proud of you, and so am I. I asked you to step it up, and you obviously have." She rose, rounded the table and kissed him on the cheek.

"Thanks, sis."

"I haven't seen the new deputy yet, but I've heard she's cute." Nate gave his twin a mischievous smile. "What say you, bro?"

"Don't go stirring things up again, Nate." Adam stood and picked up the pot of chili. "While I'm putting this in the fridge, why don't you clear the table."

"I'll cut the pie." Cassie started for the kitchen.

Noah should help Nate clear. That was the deal. Adam cooked, they cleaned up. But instead, he remained at the table, pondering his dilemma.

Adam's confidence and Cassie's approval filled him with pride. At the same time, his dinner was burning a hole in his stomach, and not from the hot chili peppers. It wasn't in his nature to be deceitful, and the Reeds didn't lie to one another. But wasn't keeping quiet about Bree's secret a lie of omission? He didn't know what to do, and for once in his life, he didn't want to make an impulsive decision.

After fresh pie and hot coffee, Cassie and Bishop left, claiming exhaustion. Noah figured their excuse was close to the truth, since they'd most likely be spending the rest of the weekend in bed. Adam headed out for his cabin, one of a few separate buildings on the Reed property. Noah and Nate went into the kitchen to start doing the dishes.

"Seriously, what's this Bree like?" Nate rinsed off a plate and handed it to Noah.

"No leaks?" Their code for keeping their mouths shut. Like a pinkie swear for grown men who happened to be twins.

"No leaks."

"She's fascinating." Noah set the dry plate on the counter and took another one from Nate. "And you heard right. She's cute. And pretty. And smart. Riding with her this week has been great. But you heard Cassie—focus on the job, not Bree." His smile disappeared. "Nate, you have no idea how hard it is to be with her all day and know nothing can happen between us."

"Dude, life's short. Follow your passion. Whether it's a place, a job or a woman, you have to go for it, or you'll always regret it."

"Sounds like you've been hanging out with Bishop a little too much lately." Noah snapped him with the dish towel.

After they finished in the kitchen, Nate went upstairs to play a video game. Noah poured himself a small glass of sipping tequila and wandered into the living room. Sitting in his dad's leather recliner, he took Nate's advice to heart.

A week ago, he was already following his passion: the job, pure and simple. Now he was torn between that and another, unexpected passion. A cute one with dark messy curls and crystal-blue eyes.

Which one should he follow?

Chapter Thirteen

A woodpecker hammered at Bree's head until she peeled back one eyelid and checked the clock. Seven thirty. On Sunday morning. The noise continued, but farther away. Someone at her door. Doc hadn't mentioned any early-Sunday maid service.

After Seth dropped her off at the motel yesterday, she'd summoned enough energy to pick up some take-out from a burger joint in town. She would have preferred one of Marge's, but Bree wasn't up to talking to anyone at the Busy B.

On the way back, she'd stopped at a liquor store for a bottle of wine. Just one glass to calm her had turned into just one bottle to forget the mess her life was becoming.

Crawling out of bed, she shuffled to the door and peeked through the peephole. Nothing but a wide expanse of T-shirt material. She closed her eyes, took a deep breath and opened the door.

"Morning, sunshine." Noah's voice ricocheted in her head, stirring up remnants of the wine hangover.

With one eye closed against the rising sun, she squinted at him with the other. "What are you doing here?"

"Not a morning person?" He held a bag in one hand and

a coffee carrier—with two large, steaming paper cups—in the other. "I brought breakfast."

She reached for one of the coffee cups, popped it out of the holder and closed the door in his face. After burning her tongue on the bitter brew, Bree took a quick shower, dried her hair, and dressed in jeans and a pink long-sleeve button-down. With any luck, he'd be gone when she checked.

She had *no* luck. When she opened the door again, he stood leaning against the SUV's hood, a half-eaten breakfast sandwich in one hand, coffee in the other.

"Good thing you were fast." He tossed the bag at her. "I was going to eat yours if you weren't ready by the time I finished this one." He grinned, then took another bite.

Her stomach didn't want food, but her hangover did. "Come on in. It's too cold out here." She led the way into her room and sat on her bed, leaving the uncomfortable desk chair for Noah.

Peering into the bag, she inhaled the glorious scent of grease, bacon, fried egg and cheese. As much as she wanted to just stick her head in the bag and breathe until he went away, she might as well find out her fate.

"What time do I meet with the sheriff?" Bree took a bite of her food, then reached for her coffee on the nightstand. She couldn't quite bring herself to look him in the eye.

"No idea. She thinks the trial may run another week."

"What do I do in the meantime?" Pulling her feet beneath her, she sat cross-legged and leaned against the headboard. "Desk duty? Or watch daytime TV in here, waiting for her to return and fire me?" She picked at the paper wrapper around her sandwich. "Why doesn't she just do it now, instead of making me wait?"

"I didn't tell her." Noah took a long sip of coffee, watching her over the rim of his cup. "Yet."

Bree's sandwich fell into her lap. "Why not?"

"I'll explain when we get where we're going." He stood and waited by the door. "Come on, let's go. Get your shoes on. You'll need a light jacket. It's cool this morning but supposed to be warm later."

Having no idea what was going on, she pushed her feet into her boots and grabbed a jacket. "Anything else?"

"Your gun and extra ammo."

She stopped in her tracks and stared at him. "Why?"

"You'll see." He paused, then added, "And you better make that *lots* of extra ammo."

There would be no point in asking him more questions, so she grabbed her gun and a canvas bag for her boxes of ammo.

Two minutes later, Bree put on her sunglasses as they drove east. She'd lost track of the roads and turns, and just enjoyed the scenery flashing past her window. After bumping over a cattle guard, they drove down a long gravel drive and stopped in front of a rustic two-story house.

"Welcome to Casa de Reed. I'll be right back." Noah left the vehicle running and dashed into the house, returning a moment later with two coolers. He stashed them in back, slid behind the wheel and they were off again.

"This is *your* house?" It seemed too big for a single person.

"My family's. Nate and I live there. Adam has his own cabin by the north end of the creek." He took a one-lane dirt road that branched off the large parking area.

"What about the sheriff?" *I'm not nosy, I'm curious.*

"She and Bishop live together in Cassie's house in town."

"Bishop's an odd first name." She held on to the grab handle as they bumped across a washboard section of road. "What's his last name?"

"Bishop."

Another one of his dumb jokes? *Okay, I'll play.* "So he's Bishop Bishop."

"Nope. Just Bishop." He glanced at her, lopsided grin in place. "His first name's Tyler, but everyone calls him Bishop. Something to do with when he was a kid."

A few minutes later, Noah parked in a wooded area and got out.

Bree followed suit, inspecting the area. "You're going to make me shoot tree trunks?"

"Close, but no cigar." He set up a wooden TV tray near a tree, then put a computer case on it. "Come on." He waved for her to follow him.

She tromped along behind him and his aggravatingly long legs. "Does all this property belong to your family?"

"Yep. My dad bought it and built the house before he even asked my mom to marry him. She was artistic, loved nature, and he wanted to present her with a place she'd never want to leave."

Bree smiled. "And they got married." She loved a good happily ever after.

"They did indeed. They got married. Had four kids. And then she left."

She caught up to Noah and put her hand on his arm to slow him down. "I'm so sorry."

He lifted one shoulder. "Thanks, but it was a long time ago."

"How old were you?" Her heart hurt just thinking about four children being abandoned by their mother.

"Nate and I were eight. Adam was ten, Cassie eleven." Noah leaned against a tree. "Cassie got the short end of the deal. Dad worked a lot, so she basically raised us. Along with plenty of advice from Helen and a shoulder to cry on in Marge."

Bree stepped closer, rested her hands against his chest. "It amazes me how some people are such survivors. Instead of wallowing in self-pity, y'all just kept on going." She looked up into his warm brown eyes, captivated by the passion they held. "You're one hell of a man, Noah Reed."

"And you're one fascinating woman, Brianna Delgado."

She studied his mouth, the way the very corners curled up, even when he wasn't smiling. She'd thought about kissing that mouth more times than she'd admit, even to herself. But taking that first step—the one that could lead to so many others or to no more at all—was a complicated one.

Noah lifted a hand to her temple, his fingers brushing her curls in a way that was almost erotic. She closed her eyes and luxuriated in the sensation, trying to stay with it instead of wondering where his fingers would touch her next.

His other hand went to her waist, paused a moment and then slid to the small of her back. It remained there, holding her with just the smallest amount of pressure, as if to keep her from floating away from him.

There was no longer a reason to push him away. He knew her secrets. He knew things about her she'd never told him, because he'd watched her, studied her, *learned* her.

She opened her eyes to find him staring at her with an intensity that took hold of her entire being. His mouth was so close. And she knew. She was ready for that first step, to see if it would be the beginning of them or the end.

He cupped the back of her head with one hand and met her lips in a kiss that brought her to her toes. She leaned into him, delighting in every inch pressed against her—from the hard planes of his chest to his sculpted abs to his muscular thighs.

Sliding her arms around his neck, she hugged him closer to her still, if that were even possible. When the pleasure flowing through her body went far beyond their kiss, she pulled back, gasping for air. She rested her head against his chest until her breathing had slowed.

"I wasn't sure you…" he said, caressing her hair.

"I was." She straightened and smiled at him. "It was just so…"

"Complicated."

"Yes. But not so much, anymore."

THEY SAT ON a log, Noah's arm around her shoulders. He was trying to hold on to the kiss, the feelings, the sensations. But they'd come here for a reason, and he was determined to help Bree pull her gun.

"Tell me about what happened the day you shot that guy."

Bree leaned away and glared at him. "Wow. Talk about a mood killer."

He hugged her against him again. "That's what this day is supposed to be about. Getting you to where you can shoot again." He kissed her forehead. "But I want to understand the whole situation first."

"You want the short version or the long version?"

"Might as well take the long."

"When I was a kid, I started to get into trouble. A cop gave me a choice—get arrested or join the youth program hosted by his precinct." She snuggled a little closer. "I joined the program, it worked and I never forgot that cop. Fast forward, I'm a cop, I start a program through *my* precinct. One day, this kid walks in, says he's trying to keep his brothers from forcing him into a gang. He joined the youth program and stuck with it. Seventeen years old, college scholarships lined up, the world at his feet."

She stopped talking and scrunched her eyes closed. Her bottom lip trembled.

"What is it?"

Bree kept her eyes shut. "And I killed him."

He tried to wrap his other arm around her to console her, but she wouldn't let him.

"Just let me get this over with." She explained about the call she and her partner had answered for a jewelry-store alarm. Three men came out of the store—dark clothes, ski masks. They split up when they saw the patrol car. Her partner went after one; she chased the other two.

"When the two men suddenly stopped and turned toward me, they both had guns. One raised his at me, and I shot him. The other man hesitated, looked at the guy on the ground and then back at me. His gun was waving all over the place. He wouldn't drop it no matter how many times I told him to, and when the muzzle pointed at my chest, I did what I had to do." She paused, taking a deep breath. "When I pulled up their masks, I saw that the second guy was my kid from the program. Found out later that his brothers had threatened him to make him take part in the burglary. I *know* he didn't want to do it, because he was afraid of guns. Didn't know the first thing about them."

"Was his loaded?" He brushed a curl off her cheek.

Bree nodded. "But it doesn't make it any easier."

"And you haven't been able to shoot since then?"

"Every time I look at a target, I see his face. I can't even get it out of the holster."

"Well, why don't we fix that?" He kissed the top of her head, pulled her to her feet and showed Bree why they'd come out to this isolated spot.

"What the..." Her mouth hung open.

"My dad wanted a shooting range on the property so he could teach us how to handle guns properly. But just plain old targets were too boring for him. Instead, he built this."

"A Hogan's Alley?" She walked from one life-size wooden

cutout to the next, touching them in wonder. An old lady with groceries, a bad guy with a gun, a girl on her bike. And on it went.

"Before any of us could even start the process to become deputies, we had to ace the course ten times in a row. One miss, the ten-count started over."

"How do they work? Do you have to pull a rope or a lever on each one as I go through?"

"Originally, that's what he had planned. But Nate happens to be a computer genius. He moved up from video games to hacking and working on motherboards. I can't even explain the mechanics of it, but all I have to do is start the program. He's got them timed on some sort of continuous circuit, so once it starts, it runs by itself."

"This is unbelievable." She seemed lost in thought for a moment, then said in a soft voice, "Thank you for helping me. I hope I can do it."

The look of gratitude on her face reinforced his decision not to tell Cassie. And he hoped he'd never have to.

"Here's the deal. I'll walk behind you, keeping track of your hits and misses. You've got one week to ace this course."

Her face paled. "Ten times in a row?"

"No. Just once." He gave her a stern look. Both of their jobs might be on the line if she screwed this up. "One time through with no misses to prove to me, and to yourself, that you can have your partner's six when it counts."

The anxiety on her face morphed into determination. "Let's do this."

BREE DISASSEMBLED, reassembled and loaded her gun. Noah had moved the computer closer to the start of the course and carried extra ammunition for her.

"Tell me when you're ready, then I'll start the program."

She nodded, too nervous to speak. She kept wiping her sweaty hands on her jeans. "Let me practice drawing first."

"Okay. This is all on your schedule."

She shook out her arms, held her right hand near her gun and bent over with her hands on her knees. She was pretty sure her heart had stopped beating for a second there. Inhaling through her nose, she straightened.

Noah touched her shoulder and she jumped, some sort of squawk leaving her mouth.

"I'm sorry, I didn't mean to do that."

"Aren't you supposed to be back there with the computer?" She pointed behind him.

"In theory. But I don't need to be there until you're ready to start the course, and right now you can't draw your gun." His smile was sympathetic. "How about I stay up here and see if I can help you get over the first obstacle."

Bree tipped her head back, blinking fast enough to create a breeze. She was not about to cry because she couldn't pull her gun. Even if she *was* embarrassed, panicked and about to throw up.

Noah put his hands on the back of her neck and gently tipped her head down. "We both already know the problem, right? So why don't we both work on it?"

Nodding, she gave her cheeks a quick swipe just in case and shook out her arms again. "Do we have water in those coolers?"

Chuckling, Noah turned around and went to fetch not just a bottle of water but the whole cooler.

After a few sips, Bree was ready. She turned toward the course, and Noah stood directly behind her. So close, she felt his breath on her neck. It tickled. *Focus, Bree.* She brought her hand close to her holster. And froze. Then Noah's hand wrapped around hers, barely touching it. When she didn't

move, he applied a gentle pressure, directing her hand closer
to the gun.

"Take as long as you need."

His words in her ear acted as a spark. She touched the
handle, then wrapped her fingers around it. As Noah took
his hand away, Bree lifted the gun from her holster.

She put the gun back, turned around and hugged him.
"Thank you," she whispered.

She practiced drawing it several more times, then worked
her way to holding it in a two-hand stance.

"You know what?" Noah said. "Instead of starting with
the course, let's try a plain old bullseye target."

"You think that'll be any easier?"

"You know this is all in your head, right?" He tipped her
chin up so she looked him in the eye. "But the mind is powerful. So we need to catch it off guard."

"I'm not sure how to do that. Every time I think I'm making progress, I start hyperventilating again."

"Trust me." He retrieved an adjustable target stand from
his truck and clipped a paper target to the two narrow side
boards. After placing it in front of a small dirt hill that would
catch the bullets, he moved Bree until she was facing it from
a fair distance away. "Take your gun out of its holster and
assume a two-hand stance."

When she was in position, he said, "Okay, that's just a
piece of paper, right?"

She rolled her eyes. "Yes, it's just a piece of paper."

"It's a piece of paper that you can't hurt and it can't hurt
you, so just shoot it."

Holding the gun in front of her, she aimed at the center
of the target. Her hands trembled and her chest started to
tighten. She placed a finger on the trigger and pulled.

Noah hauled her in for a bear hug. "Did I hit it?" Bree asked, still shaking.

"It doesn't matter. You shot your gun, and that's the only thing that does. Come on, let's take a break and have something to eat."

After spreading out a blanket for the picnic lunch Noah had brought, they ate and relaxed for a while, soaking in the sunshine amid a comfortable silence. Then they started another round of practice, continuing until Bree began to shake from the mental and physical exertion.

"Why don't we call it quits for today?" Noah said. "You must be exhausted."

"But I haven't even tried the course. If I quit now, I'll never make it through within a week." Her voice rose in panic.

"Let's set aside the time frame for now. You're making progress." He took her by the hand and led her to the blanket. "I've got some beers in the cooler. Want one?"

Bree collapsed into a sitting position. "That sounds good."

Bringing over two cold bottles, Noah sat beside her. "Here's to a day well spent."

"I'll drink to that." She'd been running on adrenaline, her emotions a roller coaster for most of the day. The icy liquid slid down her parched throat, instantly relaxing her. She leaned against Noah, and somehow the bottle disappeared from her hand and then he was kissing her. He held her, like he'd held her all day—supporting her, helping her overcome the biggest obstacle she'd ever faced. He cared enough to help make her whole again.

"I'm feeling a little more confident about my gun," she said when their lips finally separated. "But I can't quite put the moves together yet. Each thing is a separate, teeny, tiny step." She traced his lower lip with her finger. "Just like our first kiss."

WITH HIS ARM around her shoulders Bree lay back on the blanket, bringing him with her. He propped himself on one elbow and studied her face as if memorizing it. She would normally blush under such intense scrutiny, drop her gaze or look away. Instead, she reveled in being seen by Noah. She placed her palm against his cheek, shivering as her fingertips slid across its raspy stubble.

He kissed the corner of her mouth, her jaw, her throat, and she arched her neck, lost in desire. He fumbled with the buttons on her shirt with one hand, his lips never leaving her skin.

Threading her fingers through his hair, she gasped when her shirt began to fall open and his kisses followed his fingers all the way down to her belt buckle.

As the late afternoon's cooling air grazed the burning trail, she shivered. From the sensation. From anticipation.

Too impatient to wait any longer, Bree sat up, tugging her shirt free from her jeans. Noah gave her a knowing smile while her arms slipped from the sleeves and her bra followed. Then his smile vanished, replaced with an expression she'd never seen from him before and which made her shiver, her already hard nipples turning almost painful under the weight of his perusal.

But his gaze wasn't enough. She wanted his hands on her. On *all* of her. After pulling off her boots she stood and unbuckled her belt, meeting his eyes the entire time. Noah rose and toed off his own boots, then paused to watch her unzip her jeans, push them down her legs and step out of them.

In just her panties, she took one step closer and stopped

inches in front of him. Her need to touch his body overrode all else and she pulled the hem of his T-shirt up. He took it from her hands and tugged it over his head, then tossed it on the blanket.

Where it fell, Bree didn't know or care. She was too laser-focused on Noah's well-defined chest and chiseled six-pack. Not overly bulked-up. Just toned and muscular. She licked her lips, reaching out with her fingertips to explore. As her hands moved lower he sucked in a loud breath, then released it on a shaky one. She inhaled the scent of his soap mixed with clean sweat and fresh air, growing lightheaded at the intoxicating combination.

With unsteady fingers she unbuckled his belt while searching his face for…what? A sign of regret for what he'd started?

But no. His warm brown eyes pulled her into their depths. He lowered his mouth to hers in a kiss that told her he regretted nothing. Then he unbuttoned his jeans and by the time Bree tucked her thumbs into her panties and slid them to the ground, Noah stood naked, his desire for her obvious.

She dropped to her knees, taking him in her mouth, teasing him. He held on to her shoulders, his grip tightening when her lips and tongue moved faster. Just as he tensed, he pulled out of her mouth and eased her down on the blanket to return the favor.

As his tongue and fingers worked their magic on her, Bree grabbed fistfuls of the blanket and arched her back, moaning as she came. Sailing on an orgasm afterglow, the faint sound of crinkling plastic drifted to her. Then Noah was entering her. Filling her. Making her feel like she'd found her new home.

WITH EACH THRUST, Noah felt Bree tighten around him. She'd driven him crazy with her mouth, but he belonged inside of her. Belonged *to* her. He'd been searching for respect at work, but what he'd really been aching for was a place of acceptance, a connection to someone, a home for his heart. And he'd found all that in Bree.

She was clawing at his back, calling his name. And every expectation anyone ever had of him faded in the moment, his mind and heart solely fixed on satisfying this woman. *His* woman.

Noah hooked one of her legs over his shoulder and thrust even deeper, making Bree come again. The pull of her around him, her fingers digging into his shoulders, set off his own orgasm.

This time they drifted back to awareness together, serenaded by the sounds of nature, cloaked by the lowering sun that filtered through the trees. And later they lay wrapped in the blanket, snuggled together while exchanging lazy kisses and tidbits of their lives until long after the warmth of the day had dwindled.

Chapter Fourteen

When Bree's alarm went off early Monday morning, she bounced out of bed, glad to be alive. What a difference a day—and Noah Reed—made.

She'd crawled into bed last night after a long, hot shower to soothe her aching muscles. She hadn't made it through Hogan's Alley a single time, but her anxiety and panic and adrenaline had left her body hurting. And then there were the good aches in other parts of her body. Those, she didn't mind.

Driving to the Busy B, she caught sight of herself in her rearview mirror. She sucked in her cheeks to get rid of the permanent smile on her face. The one that would alert the whole world that she'd had sex, it had been good and she wanted more. But each time her cheeks popped back out, the smile reappeared.

The whole world will just have to be jealous.

And the whole world began with Marge the moment Bree walked in the door.

"Morning, my little peach."

"Hi, Marge. How are you doing this morning?"

Marge peered at her and grinned. "Apparently, nowhere near as good as you are." She winked at Bree. "You must have had a fine and dandy weekend."

Trying not to care that her cheeks were burning, Bree shrugged. "It was okay."

"Well, I have a feeling Noah's weekend was okay, too, 'cause he's waiting in the back booth for you with the same silly grin on his face."

Her laugh followed Bree down the aisle. And Marge had been right. Noah sat with his back to the wall, watching her approach. And if her smile matched his smile, they'd be in big trouble at the morning briefing.

"Hi." She slid into the seat across from him.

"Hi." His eyes sparkled. "You look happy."

"You don't look so down in the dumps, yourself." She laughed.

"Sleep well?" Noah opened his menu and scanned it.

"Best in months." She dropped her gaze to her menu, cursing the butterflies in her stomach.

"Good morning, y'all." Rachel filled Bree's cup and topped off Noah's. "Ready to order?"

They gave her their requests, and before she left, Rachel said, "Sorry I couldn't go with you Saturday, Bree. Did you see anything you liked?"

Bree fought the urge to smirk when Noah did. "I did. A cute two-bedroom with a pink front door."

"Great. I'm glad Seth could help. Did you sign the lease?"

"Not yet. I'll do it later this week."

"Let me know when you're ready to move in. I'll come over to help." Rachel joined the smirk party. "And forget my kids there when I go home."

After Rachel left, Noah gave Bree a curious look. "You're renting a house?"

Bree nodded. "I looked at some Saturday. But I wasn't sure I'd be staying in town, so I held off on the lease."

"You'd leave Resolute if Cassie fired you?"

"I had no other reason to stay." She sipped her coffee.

His right eye twitched, a quick movement she almost missed.

"I see." He tapped one finger against his upper lip, a habit she was beginning to recognize.

"As of Saturday, I had no other reason to stay." She dropped her gaze, then looked at him from beneath her lashes. "As of Sunday, I have a great reason to stay, whether I get fired or not." *But please, God, don't let me get fired.*

The look of relief on his face zapped her heart like a defibrillator.

By the time they finished breakfast, they had a game plan for the day. Bree read it back from her notebook.

"After the department meeting, we'll get the forensics report on Sammy, assuming they're done by now. Then talk to his friends, see what they know."

"Or at least, what they'll tell us, which will probably be nothing." Noah leaned back in the booth.

She snapped her notebook closed. "Then maybe you should let me question his friends."

"You think *you* can get more info out of them than I can?"

"I guess we'll see, won't we?" She winked at him. "Care to make it a wager?"

"Darn right I do." His excitement was palpable. "If I win, you have to spend the night with me."

"And if you lose, *you* have to spend the night with *me*."

"You drive a hard bargain, Delgado."

"As do you, Reed. As do you."

AFTER THE MORNING MEETING, Noah went straight to his desk and checked his computer. "Still no forensics report on Sammy."

"Then I guess it's time to go find the boys and win a bet." Bree gave him a teasing smile.

He shook his finger at her. "No fair flirting."

She hooked her thumbs in her duty belt. "A deputy's gotta do what a deputy's gotta do." She turned and sashayed out of the bullpen.

Noah grabbed his jacket and rushed after her. He'd probably lose the bet, so he might as well enjoy the sashaying.

They drove to Oak View Apartments first, hoping to catch the friend who was renting there. With only parents' addresses for the other boys, they could easily waste the whole day running everyone down.

"This place is giving me definite déjà vu vibes." Bree peeked in her notebook one last time and stuck it in her pocket. "Just follow my lead." She got out of the vehicle and headed for the building.

She buzzed the manager to get in, like she had last time; and once again, it worked. She marched down the first-floor hall to apartment 116 and listened. "Voices. More than one here." She knocked.

A male voice came through the door. "Who is it?"

"Boone County Deputies Reed and Delgado," Noah answered.

"Hang on."

They waited about a minute before Bree pounded on the door again.

"I'm coming."

Locks disengaged, the door swung in and Noah stared at the new cook from the Busy B.

"Are you Lee Hayes?" Bree asked and waited for him to reluctantly nod. "Can we come in? We need to ask you a few questions."

Hayes's eyes ping-ponged between Noah and Bree. "What's it about?"

"Sammy Jenkins."

Hayes opened the door and let them come in. Three other men who looked to be in their early twenties were lounging on a couch and on the floor, playing a video game with the sound muted. Bree had each one identify himself.

Noah addressed them as a group. "Y'all know Sammy, right?" When they nodded in unison, he asked, "You heard what happened to him?"

A few mumbled responses, including from Hayes, indicated they had.

"We're following a lead that he's the one who broke into the high school." Bree looked at each of them, one at a time. "Is that true?"

"Yeah, he told us he did it." One of the guys on the floor spoke up. "Didn't sound like he got anything worthwhile, though. Pretty stupid, if you ask me."

"*Why* did he break in?" Noah asked.

"He never said." The kid on the couch lifted a beer can from the wobbly end table and drank.

Noah looked to the two still sitting on the floor. "Did he break into other places? Was this a regular thing for him?"

The only one who'd yet to utter a word shook his head. "Had to be the first time or we would've heard about it."

"Yeah. If he was proud of something, he always told us." This from the couch potato. "Like working for his uncle. No one was supposed to know, but he trusted us. Said he was making good money."

Hayes hadn't said a word since letting them in.

Bree faced him directly. "You knew he broke in?" Another nod from Hayes. "What else do you know about him?"

He shrugged and developed a sudden interest in the carpet.

"How's it working out at the Busy B?" Noah asked.

Hayes's head snapped up. "How do you know I work there?"

"Saw you the other day. Marge said you take a lot of breaks." Noah towered over him and used that to his advantage. "Marge is a good person. I hope she decides to keep you."

"Hey, man. I really need that job."

"That's between you and her. I just don't want to hear about you giving her any grief."

Bree turned back to the others. "Does anyone else have *any* information that might help us find the person who killed Sammy?" No one made a peep. "We're not interested in getting y'all in trouble. We just want justice for your friend."

"Thank you for speaking with us, Lee. If you think of anything else, call us." Noah gave him a card on their way out the door. "*Anything.*"

"I CAN'T FOR the life of me figure out why anyone would kill Sammy." Back in the bullpen, Bree pulled the extra chair up to Noah's desk but paced around it instead of sitting. "Do you think it had anything to do with the break-in?"

Signing in on his computer, he shrugged. "Seems unlikely, since nothing that valuable was taken."

"That we know of." Bree stopped moving. "We never finished that discussion about how maybe something wasn't included on the list of stolen items."

Noah gave her a doubtful look. "If something was worth killing him for, why wasn't it worth reporting?"

Bree snapped her fingers. "What if it was something illegal?"

Again with the skeptical looks. "Like maybe a stolen piece

of art, hanging on a teacher's wall?" He snorted and went back to his computer.

Bree sat and pondered the feasibility of her idea while Noah continued to tap on his computer keyboard.

"Finally!" He pumped his fist. "We've got the forensics on Sammy." He scanned his monitor for a moment, then read the information out loud.

"We already knew he was asphyxiated. But the autopsy indicates repeated strangulation attempts with a narrow piece of cloth. Hair and fiber's not back yet, but the marks and bruises are similar to those made by a man's tie." He skimmed parts of it further. "The repeated strangulation indicates the possibility of torture. Cutting off the air supply until the victim is almost dead, then releasing the pressure, reviving the vic and repeating."

"Maybe the killer wanted an answer and Sammy wouldn't tell him." Bree twisted a curl around her finger. "The fact that he was strangled instead of shot or stabbed makes it more personal."

"Could be the killer didn't have another weapon. Had to make do with what he had."

Bree nodded. "Or he didn't want to get bloody. Hard to explain to the family when you get home."

Reading more of the report, Noah said, "Holy sh… Listen to this. They found traces of meth on Sammy. Not like he used but was exposed to it. They found it on his fingers and inside his mouth."

"Maybe it got on his hand, then he touched a finger to his tongue. Like he wanted to taste it?" Bree pulled her notebook from her pocket. "Does it say if the meth contributed to his death?"

Noah ran his finger across his monitor screen, reading

under his breath. "No. The report indicates it was diluted, so probably liquid meth."

Bree tapped her lip, then realized she was copying Noah's quirk and stopped. "Curiouser and curiouser."

Noah logged off and stood. "Do you have the phone number of Sammy's friend, Lee Hayes? The guy who works at the diner?"

She found it in her notes and read it to him as he punched in the numbers.

"Lee? Deputy Reed here. Are you still at home? We've got one more question for you. Okay. See you in ten." Noah ended the call. "He's at the diner. I want to ask him what he knows about Sammy and meth."

They made it to the diner in less than five minutes and waited out back in the alley. Lee finally pushed through the door, sat on an overturned five-gallon bucket and looked up at them.

"You and Sammy ever do meth?" Noah asked.

Lee's shocked expression seemed genuine. "I don't do meth. Smoke a little weed but nothing harder."

Bree took up a position next to Noah. "What about Sammy? Did he use drugs?"

His eyes flicked away. "I don't know, man."

"I think you do." Bree swung her boot against the bucket. "And this is your last chance to keep this here in the alley. Keep lying, we're taking you in for a proper interview."

Hayes blew out a breath. "I never saw him do any, okay? But I know he was friends with a guy who cooks meth."

Bree flipped open her notebook.

"Name?"

"He never told me his name. But he bummed a ride from me once when his car was in the shop and he couldn't borrow his mom's." Hayes looked up at them like a puppy hoping for a treat if he sat up and begged. "I think the guy lives on Mulberry. Sammy had me drop him at the intersection of Mulberry and Sunset. He headed up Mulberry, but I drove away so I don't know for sure where he went. He could have doubled back to the intersection and gone a different direction after I left. Maybe that guy knows who killed Sammy."

Chapter Fifteen

"Somewhere on Mulberry." Noah scoffed. "He *thinks* somewhere on Mulberry."

They sat in front of the justice center, SUV idling, trying to decide what to do next.

"Well, it's more information than we had." Bree checked her notes. "And he did narrow it down with the cross street."

Bree had suggested driving around on Mulberry, see if anything caught their eye. But they couldn't knock on every door and ask if there was a meth lab in the house.

"Let's go in, run the property records for that section of Mulberry. Maybe we'll recognize a name." He turned off the vehicle and looked over at her. "If we come up empty-handed, we can always pick up Hayes when his shift is over. Drive him up there and see if he can pick out the exact house."

Bree nodded and they headed back inside.

Helen caught them before they made it past her desk. "I swear, this town's going crazy. Adam's tied up with another case, and he wants you two to handle a call that just came in." She handed Noah the information.

After he read it, he passed it to Bree.

"Another murder? Good grief. How many do you usually have in a year?"

Helen and Noah exchanged a look.

"We're reaching our max, and it's only January." The older woman studied Bree. "Seems like things have really picked up around here since you hit town."

Noah fought a smile as Bree narrowed her eyes at Helen.

"This isn't my fault. Don't even try to blame this on me. Nope. Uh-uh." Bree spun around, marched across the lobby and out the door.

"I better go, or I'll be stuck riding shotgun." Noah jogged after her.

The GPS directed them to an area southeast of town. Bree, as usual, had her head on a swivel, and caught Noah off guard when she gasped.

"That was Mulberry Street." Excitement made her talk faster. "When we're done with the body, we can check it out. I mean, we're already out here, so we might as well. Right?"

"Right." He figured it would be easier to humor her. But cruise around for the rest of the day, looking for a random meth house? Over his dead body. *Bad choice of words.*

After a few more turns, he parked on the shoulder of a narrow road. They exited the vehicle into a warm day with no breeze. Noah checked his coordinates again, then led the way to a grassy culvert and looked down.

The deceased lay partially on his side, his blank eyes staring at the cloud-free sky. Noah and Bree stood there, not speaking, staring down at Jason Watson from McAllen, Texas.

BREE LEANED AGAINST their SUV, waiting for the crime scene techs to finish up. The justice of the peace had already declared Watson dead, then left in search of more pleasant JP duties. Noah was talking to a CSI named Brett, whom he knew. And Bree raked her brain like the sand in a zen garden, searching for any elusive detail she might've missed when they'd stopped to help the victim with his flat tire.

Noah joined her as the body was loaded into the medical examiner's van.

"This may not be a murder," he said. "My buddy Brett said there's no obvious signs of external trauma. But it did look like an overdose. We won't know for sure until the autopsy, but I'd prefer the OD scenario than another killer running around Resolute."

"Maybe this guy and Sammy are connected, and the same person killed them both."

"For now, let's just focus on Sammy. You wanted to go find his meth friend on Mulberry, right?"

"I thought you didn't want to."

"This call went faster than I thought it would. Might as well look while we're here."

She tried to appear nonchalant, like she didn't care one way or the other. But she had a feeling they'd find something if they just kept looking.

"Want to drive?"

Her shock must have shown on her face, because Noah laughed at her reaction. But he had the same reaction as hers when she refused.

"I want to pay attention to everything while you do the driving." She hopped into the passenger seat.

Noah nodded. "Probably for the best. The way your head swivels around, you'd probably hit a tree."

"Funny." She powered down her window. "Just drive."

He backtracked to the intersection Hayes had mentioned, then crept along Mulberry. Bree practically hung out her window, taking note of everything she saw.

They passed the fourth house, and she'd turned to say something to Noah but instead yelled, "Stop!"

Slamming on the brakes, Noah looked around. Bree pointed behind his head, and he twisted around to get a better view.

"See it? Way back along the side of that green house? Isn't that Watson's Impala?"

Noah made a U-turn, stopped at the curb and they got out. Pulling out her small notebook, Bree compared the license plate number on this car to the one from last week with the flat tire.

"Same car, all right." She slipped her notebook back in her pocket. "Didn't Watson say he was moving near Hudsonville?"

Nodding, Noah circled the car and peered in each window. "We need to get a warrant to search the car."

"You think he lied about where he was moving to?"

"Either that, or he was visiting whoever lives here." Noah glanced at the house. "We should knock, see if anyone's inside."

Bree wrinkled her nose as they walked back to the front porch. "This place smells...methy. I wonder if this is where Sammy's cooker friend lives, and Watson somehow learned he could score meth here. But that'd be quite the coincidence."

"Watson didn't look or act like an addict. I think he *is* the cooker." Noah knocked on the door and called out, "Boone County Sheriff's Department. Open up."

Lowering his voice, he continued to Bree: "And either he killed Sammy, or he knew who did."

"I'm betting he didn't do it. I think whoever did also killed Watson to tie up a loose end." Bree pounded on the door and repeated Noah's loud announcement to open up.

She stepped around a camping chair, set up next to a TV-tray table holding a coffee can filled with cigarette butts, and approached a large picture window. Curtains covered most of the glass, but in the center where they should have met, the two pieces of cloth fell away from each other. And through that gap Bree had a view across an almost-empty living room and straight into the kitchen.

"Hey, take a look." She stepped aside so Noah could view the scene. "If that's not a meth-cooker's dream kitchen, I don't know what is."

Noah moved away from the window, pulling Bree with him. "We had reason to knock because the deceased's car is on the premises. And the window next to the front door offered plain view of illegal equipment, including what looks like a drying oven similar to that taken from the high school chemistry room."

"And the odor of meth cooking was in plain smell, which usually holds up with associated items found in plain view." Bree smiled, satisfied with their findings. "Cover me while I check the other windows." Staying alert, Bree rounded the house and crept up to a window. Making sure Noah had her six, she tried to peek inside. The window was completely blacked out.

They circled the house; all the windows except the one in the front were the same. They approached the back door and listened. No sounds inside.

Bree tried the handle. Locked. "Wait a minute." She ran to their vehicle, retrieved their masks and returned, then handed one to Noah before she put on hers.

Once his was fastened tightly, Noah motioned her away and put his shoulder to the door. He threw his weight against it, and it swung in.

They walked into a small kitchen, cluttered with equipment and materials for cooking meth. After a look around from where they stood, they backed out and moved a good distance away. Noah called Adam, told him what they'd found.

Adam made it in less than fifteen minutes. After poking his head in the back door, he joined Bree and Noah by the back fence, an expression of amazement on his face. He made a call, and after disconnecting said, "Austin's sending the hazmat crew. Fill me in."

Noah explained about Watson, the OD and their previous encounter with him when he had the blowout.

Bree jumped in with the rest. "One of Sammy's friends told us Sammy knew a guy in this area who cooked meth. We were cruising around, trying to find the cooker's house, when we saw Watson's car."

"Impressive job. Both of you." Adam nodded his approval. "I guess y'all wound up on the meth investigation sooner than planned."

"I'm not one hundred percent sure if Sammy's death and the meth investigation are connected, but they definitely intersect." Noah tapped his lip. "I feel like we're still missing something. Hayes said Sammy didn't do meth."

"I have faith we'll solve it soon." Adam clapped Noah on the shoulder. "You okay with taking charge here and waiting for hazmat? I've got a meeting with the mayor that I already canceled once."

Noah nodded. "No problem. We've got this."

After Adam had left, Bree turned to Noah. "Something's been tickling my memories since we found Watson. And it tickled harder when I went in there." She pointed at the house.

"When the hazmat team gets he—"

Bree didn't wait for him to finish. She picked up her mask and slipped it over her head.

"Bree, you can't go back in there."

"It'll only be for a second." She adjusted it, donned gloves, and ignored Noah's protests as she headed for the back door.

She went right to it and was back by Noah's side in seconds. She set the object at a distance from where they stood, pulled off her gloves and mask, and smiled in triumph.

"Laundry detergent." He didn't sound excited.

"Remember the cleaning supplies in the Impala's trunk? One of these bottles was in there."

Noah still didn't seem to make the connection.

She gave his brain a prod. "Remember the different brands of detergent in the gym's laundry room? Two of them were this brand." She peeled off her gloves, pulled out her phone and googled away before holding the screen toward Noah. "Which is only sold in Mexico."

Emotions flashed across his face: Confusion as he tried to make sense of it all. Realization about the soap bottles. Rage, most likely from a betrayal by his beloved Coach.

Chapter Sixteen

When Noah shuffled past Helen's desk Tuesday morning, her reaction to his disheveled appearance came as no surprise. Monday had been another long one, and he'd spent most of the night trying to put together the puzzle pieces of Coach, meth and murder.

"Good grief, Noah. Did you sleep under a park bench?"

"Good morning to you, too, Helen."

"If you're sick, you shouldn't have come in." Helen always had been able to scold and sympathize at the same time.

He scrubbed his hands across his bristly face. "I'm not sick. Just didn't sleep well."

"Hmph. At least you don't stink of alcohol."

"Gee, thanks." Since Cassie was still out of town, he went the long way through the building, stopping in her private bathroom to splash cold water on his face and finger-comb his hair. At least his clothes were clean, even if his shirt was wrinkled.

Looking a little better, he made his way to the briefing room and sat in the back row. He didn't want to talk to anyone this morning. Well, anyone except Bree.

The meeting was short, with Adam catching up the others on the new dead body and additional meth lab. Noah told

Bree to meet him in Cassie's office. He wanted privacy for their discussion.

She showed up with two large notebooks, two large coffees and one large hug. The hug revived him more than the cold water had and more than the coffee would. They sat at Cassie's desk, the office door locked, and he began.

"We need to look at every possible angle on this thing before we take one more step." He downed half his coffee. "If we make a move on Coach and we're wrong about him, we'll both be leaving town on the next train."

Bree opened one of the notebooks and folded back the cover. "What did Adam say about it?"

"I haven't told him. I haven't told anyone." He leaned back in Cassie's executive chair. Their dad's chair before her. "What you have to understand, Bree, no one's going to accept our allegations at face value. I meant it when I told you before that everyone in Resolute loves Coach. We can't barrel in there and arrest him without any evidence."

She nodded. "Then we wait until everything's back from forensics. There has to be something they'll find. And then we'll have him."

He loved her for not arguing with him this morning.

"Let's start, shall we?" She handed him the other notebook.

While he jotted words and thoughts all over the page, Bree made orderly paragraphs and lists. They reviewed everything they knew for sure, beginning with bottles of the same off-brand laundry detergent—only sold south of the border—found in Coach's room, Watson's trunk and the newest meth house.

Bree looked up from her notes. "We don't know if the bottles contain meth. We don't know if the meth-house bottle was the same one from the trunk or an additional one."

"We have no proof that the bottles in the gym belong to Coach." Noah rubbed a spot above his eye where a headache was forming. "Anyone else with access to that area could have put them there. Including the burglar, who may or may not have been Sammy."

"As far as the connection between Sammy and Watson, we only have Hayes's statement that Sammy knew an unnamed meth cooker in the vicinity of Mulberry and Sunset." Bree sighed. "But we have Watson's car at the meth house, and hopefully we'll soon have his prints inside the house."

"But in the meantime we're assuming everything based on logic, which is the wrong way to investigate. Any lawyer worth his degree would drive a car straight through our case." Noah dropped his pen on the desk in frustration. "And I'll bet you my left nu…arm that there aren't any laundry-detergent bottles in the gym anymore. At least, not that brand. Which means Coach is free and clear."

In a low voice, Bree sang, *"Heeere she comes to save the daaay,"* while she fiddled with her phone. She rounded the desk with a self-satisfied smile on her face and thrust her phone in front of him.

Noah stared at a picture of everything that was in that gym cabinet the day they investigated the break-in. Including two bottles of their off-brand detergent.

"It doesn't prove our case, but it proves the bottles were there, and when." She pointed to the time stamp on the photo. "Told you I like to dot my i's and cross my t's."

Noah glanced at the locked door, then picked Bree up and kissed her like he'd never stop.

When Bree got her breath back, she said, "It still doesn't prove they're Coach's, but it proves they were there."

An hour later, Cassie's desk phone rang. Noah had told Helen where he'd be working, so he answered it.

"Forensics on line two."

Brett, a forensic investigator he'd met on a case last year, greeted him. "I'm sending you the reports, and you should have them within half an hour. But I know this is time sensitive, so I figured I'd give you a few of the results by phone."

Noah punched the speaker button and set down the receiver. "Bree's here, too, Brett. I put you on speaker."

"Okay. Before I forget, the autopsy report isn't completed yet, but they did run a tox screen on Watson. It was a meth overdose, like we thought."

"Okay."

"But highly unlikely it was accidental."

"You think he killed himself on purpose with meth?" Bree asked.

"He died from a large dose of one hundred percent pure meth. Uncut." After a dramatic pause, Brett added, "Your guy was murdered."

Noah glanced at Bree, pretty sure his expression looked as surprised as hers.

"We also found contusions on his abdomen. We didn't see them at the crime scene because they were covered by his clothes, but they're large. We think the killer was kneeling on Watson's torso to hold him down while he injected him." A thread of excitement ran through Brett's voice. "But get this: the vic tried to fight back. We found quite a bit of flesh and blood under the fingernails of his right hand. Even had some under his thumbnail."

Noah couldn't believe their luck. "Tell me you got a DNA hit through CODIS." If the forensics team found a match in the Combined DNA Index System, this murder investigation would take a giant leap forward.

"Sorry, no hits. But at least we've got it and can test any suspects against it." Brett chuckled. "All you have to do is find someone with four parallel scrapes that are scabbed over. Easy peasy, right?"

"Right." Noah rolled his eyes. "Should have this case wrapped up within the hour."

"Maybe, now that you're working with Bree." This time Brett let loose with full-on laughter. "Anyway, I've got a little more info for you. The laundry-detergent bottle tested positive for meth. Apparently, mega-labs in Mexico make huge quantities of meth, but it's hard to get it across the border in its original form. So they put it into cleaned bottles of any sort and bring it across as liquid meth. Then the cookers on our side extract it from the liquid, dry it out and it's back to crystal."

"Wow." Noah already knew that, and from the bored look on Bree's face, so did she, but Brett liked to explain things.

"Next thing, we got fingerprints from the bottle. We ran them and got hits on a Samuel Jenkins; a Charles Crawford; and your dead body, Jason Watson."

Bree did a jump that made her look like a cheerleader for a law enforcement school. "That's it. That ties Sammy, Coach Crawford and Watson together with the bottle."

Noah was having a hard time containing his enthusiasm, himself. This was what they needed. But he had a question.

"Hey, Brett, where did the matches come from on Jenkins and Crawford?"

"Hold on for a sec. Okay, I've got it here. Samuel Jenkins. He was arrested at age nineteen for drag racing in Victoria County."

Well, that explained the tricky car maneuvers in the school parking lot.

"And Charles Crawford did a two-year stint in the army, starting at age eighteen."

"Thanks. I was just curious."

"No problem. And for the last fun fact, we got into Watson's phone. One incoming number was from a cell phone belonging to Cora Jenkins. So I'm guessing Mom paid for Sammy's phone." Brett chuckled. "There were also calls to and from a couple of burner phones. We don't have exact locations for them, but we tracked one to Resolute and one to Victoria. Both phones were purchased at the same store in Victoria."

"I didn't realize burners could be traced that well," Noah said.

"Well, we could only narrow it down to the cities. But it'll help in court if you happen to find the burners, especially in the possession of your bad guy."

"I appreciate the call. See you next time a body drops."

"See ya then."

"Do you realize what this means?" Bree paced circles around the desk.

"It means we've got a man to arrest. But first..." He grabbed her as she walked by and kissed her, leaning her back over his arm. When he righted her, she gasped for air.

"What was that for?" She fanned her face.

"That was for nothing. For everything. For being you. For helping me. For—"

Laughing, Bree said, "Okay, okay." She wrapped her arms around him. "Save the rest of the reasons for later." She tipped her head back until she met his eyes. "If you get my drift."

He leaned forward and kissed the tip of her cute little nose.

Her expression became thoughtful. "Noah? How do you feel about all of this with Crawford?" She patted his chest with the flat of her hand. "In here."

I feel mad, disappointed, betrayed...

"Not very good, but—"

"No, I mean, are you sure you want to be the arresting officer? You thought so highly of him, and he was your coach. Won't it be hard for you?"

"Community policing, remember? It's not always fun, but it's the job." He gave her a soft kiss on her forehead. "Let's go get a bad guy."

At 11:00 a.m., the basketball court was full of kids practicing their free throws when Noah strode past them, Bree at his side. Perhaps it was their posture, backs straight and shoulders set. Or maybe the Stetsons, which they rarely wore. But the laughter and joking faded away until the gym was silent. From the corner of his eye, Noah saw mouths hang open, eyes go wide.

He knocked once on the closed door of Coach Charles Crawford, then opened it without being invited in. They stopped at his desk, hands on duty belts. He wasn't sure about Bree, but Noah enjoyed watching the man's smile disappear, replaced by confusion.

"Hey, Noah. What's going on?"

"Charles Crawford, you are under arrest for possession and distribution of methamphetamine." Noah circled around the coach, who'd jumped to his feet, and placed cuffs on his wrists while Bree read him his rights.

Noah's vehicle sat double-parked in front, and they'd entered through the main school building. Bree had asked him if he didn't want to use the gymnasium door and keep it low-key. But Crawford's embarrassment didn't concern Noah. Meth in Resolute concerned him. Exploding houses concerned him. Murdered young men concerned him.

The ride back to the office was quiet. Other than a few feeble protestations from the back seat that they had the wrong guy, no one spoke.

They put him in the cell next to Kenny, the candy-store destroyer.

"You ready?" Bree asked Noah.

"As I'll ever be."

They walked past the bullpen and knocked on Adam's door.

Chapter Seventeen

"Helen, I might be back a little late from lunch." Bree stopped at the older woman's desk, digging through her purse for her sunglasses. The cold snap had broken, the days now sunny and clear.

"Don't you worry about that. Half the office seems to forget their watches on Fridays." She cocked her head to the side. "Doing anything fun, I hope?"

"I'm signing a lease for a rental house. I want to get the paperwork done today so I can move in this weekend."

"I'm so happy things are working out and you're planning on staying." She leaned in. "I always hesitate to get attached to people, in case they wind up leaving. It's so difficult to say goodbye after you've become friends."

Bree grinned. "Well, I'm staying, so if you want to be friends…" She spread her arms wide.

"I'll take you up on that, Bree." Helen's phone rang, and as she picked up the receiver, she waved Bree toward the door and whispered, "Go get that house."

Driving through town in her own truck, she hadn't wanted to take an official vehicle for a personal errand, Bree practically vibrated with excitement. Life was good. She had her job. She had Noah. And now she'd have a house.

But dang, this week was one for the record books. Adam

had been livid about their arrest of Crawford. Once they'd laid everything out for him, he was only livid that he hadn't been informed in advance. But livid was livid when it was the boss.

Next week would be busy, too. They hadn't charged Crawford with murder yet, so that was on the agenda. It was easy for her to lay out a scenario where Sammy stole Crawford's meth and the coach killed the kid to get it back. But had he also committed the OD murder? Was he the only one involved, or were there others? Hard to believe the coach was top of the Boone County meth pyramid.

Enough! No more thinking about work until she was back in the office this afternoon. She lowered the window and let her hair dance in the breeze.

Turning the corner onto what was about to become *her* street, she noticed her Realtor's car parked in the driveway right in front of the garage. Seth was leaning into his open trunk and as Bree pulled in behind him, he looked over his shoulder, waved at her and turned his attention back to the trunk.

She joined him at his car. "Hi, Seth. Thanks again for working your schedule around mine."

He turned around, a binder thick with papers in his hand and a big smile on his face. The trunk lid fell from his fingers, and his smile faltered for a second. And then, as if it hadn't happened, the smile was back.

"Hello, Bree." He gave her a quick once-over. "I had no idea you're a deputy."

"Oh, that's right. We looked at houses on the weekend, and I wasn't wearing my uniform." She shrugged. "I'm on my lunch break today. I hope this won't take more than an hour."

"Nowhere near that long. A few signatures and you'll be back to keeping our streets safe."

He led the way through the house and spread out the paperwork on the kitchen island.

"Do you live in Resolute, Seth?"

"Me? No." He shook his head as he sorted through the leases and addendums in his folder.

"Well, I hope you didn't have to make a long trip today just for this."

"Here you are. One copy to sign, one to keep. After the owners sign, I'll forward you a copy of the fully processed document."

"That will be perfect." She started to read the lease, but part of her mind was wondering why he didn't want to tell her where he lived.

"It's a standard lease agreement for the state of Texas."

Bree glanced up from beneath her lashes. "Mm-hmm." As she continued to read, Seth seemed to fidget more. A couple of times, she caught him looking at her with a cryptic expression on his face.

She turned to the second legal page of small print.

"Would you like to take that with you, read it over this weekend? We can meet again Monday for the signatures."

"Oh, no. I'm anxious to move in." She smiled. "But I do read contracts." *Especially when the other guy appears hopeful that I don't.*

The contract read like the ones she'd signed in the past, so she signed both copies and leaned over the deep island to hand one to Seth.

He slipped it back into the folder and pulled out another form. "This is the lease application. We don't usually bother with them unless someone is serious about renting. It's more of a formality, just to have on file. The owners don't have to approve you or anything."

He pushed it across the slab of granite, and the paper apparently hit a slick area. It shot toward her, Seth's hand still holding it down. His arm stretched out beyond the cuff of his long-sleeved shirt and Bree's eyes locked onto a row of four angry-looking scabs. The place where they started was farther up his arm, still hidden beneath the pale blue cloth of his shirt. But they ended just above his wrist bone.

Fighting the urge to glance at his face, Bree picked up the paper and pretended to read it. But the words and phrases flowing through her mind were: the killer was scratched, four parallel scabs, I need backup and how the hell did my Realtor end up being the killer?

She noticed a section on the application requesting personal information. She patted her pants pockets and lied. "I must have left my phone in the truck. I keep all this info in an electronic file. I'll be back in a sec."

He nodded as though glad she was wrapping things up. But as she trotted to her car, her radar was already way past sending her *Danger! Danger!* messages.

She pulled her phone from her pocket as she walked between the two vehicles. Just before she dialed, she noticed his trunk lid hadn't latched when it slipped from his hand. She gave a quick glance toward the house; no windows along the wall facing her. Turning back, she opened the trunk. Two plastic bins of files and paperwork. An umbrella. And, partially covered by a bath towel, a box holding four jugs of off-brand laundry detergent, only produced south of the border.

Bree gasped and dropped the lid.

Does he know that I know?

She froze. A sense of something. Not a sound. Not a smell. The hair on the back of her neck stood on end. She reached for her gun and started to turn when her head exploded, blasting bright white light and colors and pain in every direction until nothing was left. And then, like a black hole in space, the nothingness sucked all the light and colors and pain and her into it, leaving just one final thought:

He knows.

BREE AWOKE IN the dark and assessed her situation. Pitch black, but no blindfold. The space itself was dark. A gag. Crunchy cloth in her mouth. Tape on her lips, pulling her skin. Sweet, rusty scent. Blood. Wet in her nose. Dried in the hair that was crusted to her cheek. Her head throbbed so much, she wanted to exchange it for a new one. Her ankles were tied together. Her wrists, too, behind her. She had no sense of time, of place.

But if she planned on living, it was time to leave.

Her extremities tingled from lack of circulation when she moved. She was on her side, so she tried stretching her legs out. Her boots hit a wall or some other obstruction while her knees were still bent. She wiggled her bound arms and body in the other direction, almost screaming in agony when her shoulder threatened to dislocate.

She could stretch full length moving that way, but the empty space was narrow. Rolling onto her back, she lifted her knees in a rocking move, gaining momentum. When her butt cleared the floor, she pushed her hands down and managed to get them past her butt and hooked under her knees before she blacked out again from pain.

NOAH LEANED INTO Adam's office doorway. "You seen Bree lately?"

"No." A frown crinkled Adam's forehead. "I thought she was working with you on the murders."

"She was, this morning. But she took off for lunch, and I haven't seen her since." He wandered into the office and took a seat. "She's not answering her phone, either."

Adam picked up his phone and pushed a button. "Helen, have you heard from Bree?" He listened, thanked her and hung up.

"She said Bree left at noon and was going to sign the lease for a rental house during her lunch hour."

Noah looked at his watch. "That was three hours ago."

"You think she decided to celebrate and just didn't come back?"

"She wouldn't do that." He stood, a growing panic taking over. "I'm going to go look for her." He left without waiting for Adam's approval.

At the bullpen's door, he asked if anyone had heard from Bree. A chorus of no's. Did anyone know where the house was that she was renting. More no's.

He stopped at Helen's desk and waited for her to get off a call. "Did Bree tell you where the house she's renting is?"

"No. But she was so excited about it."

The phone rang again and as Helen answered it, Noah left. In his vehicle, he called Doc's Motor Court and repeated his questions. Doc knew nothing, said her car wasn't there, but he rang Bree's room. No answer. Noah's anxiety grew.

He drove to the Busy B and double-parked by the back door. He passed Lee Hayes at the grill and found Marge by the front register. She hadn't talked to Bree lately, hadn't a clue.

Rachel squeezed past him with order tickets for Lee. "What's going on, Noah? You look like your dog died and your truck ran away with your girlfriend."

"Not the time, Rachel." Helen touched Noah's arm. "He's worried."

"I can't find Bree. Did she tell you anything about the house she's renting?"

"Yeah." Rachel yelled for Lee to grab her tickets, then

pulled out her phone. "She said it was yellow and had a pink front door. I got the idea it was somewhere over near where Cassie and Bishop live." She held her phone in the center of the three of them. "It's on speaker. I'm calling Seth, the Realtor she used. He can give me the exact address."

When it went to voice mail, she ended the call.

Noah was already moving. "Thanks. I'll let you know when I find her."

He raced back to his SUV and started driving toward Cassie's while calling her cell. Straight to voice mail.

Dammit, Bree, where are you? A band was tightening across his chest. He didn't have time for a heart attack.

It's not a heart attack, you fool. You're in love with her.

He *was* in love with her, and he'd never even told her.

Noah punched Bishop's speed dial.

"Hey, Noah. What's up?"

"Do you recall seeing a house anywhere in your neighborhood that's yellow with a pink front door?"

"Yeah, it's one street north, two blocks west of us. Why?"

"Thanks. I'll call you back."

In less than two minutes, he'd parked in the street behind Bree's truck and pounded on the pink front door. There weren't any other vehicles near the house. Maybe her Realtor took her out for lunch and she lost track of time.

Nope. Something's wrong. I can feel it.

He drew his gun and kicked the locked door open.

"Bree!" he called.

No answer.

Noah cleared each room, continuing to yell her name. In the last room he checked, a small back bedroom—obviously empty—he paused. He'd looked in every room, opened every door except one. Fighting down panic, he walked toward the closet. Double folding doors, the knobs locked together with zip ties.

"Bree!" The door shook, and a muffled groan followed.

Noah holstered his gun and pulled his tactical knife. After slicing through the ties, he yanked the doors off their tracks. "Bree." He dropped to his knees and cradled her, pulling her into the room. He hardly recognized her with her face covered in dried blood, bruises and duct tape. But those eyes... He'd know those eyes anywhere.

He removed the tape with care not to rip her lips, murmuring to her the entire time, "I've got you, baby. I've got you." The rag followed the tape.

"Hur-ry. Coming back. Hands." Her voice cracked with each syllable.

Bent over her, he sliced through the zip tie on one wrist and was reaching for the other when she moaned an ungodly sound. He sat back on his knees and glanced at her face for no more than a second. Her eyes were wider than seemed possible, and as they bounced from him to behind him she wiggled her brows. The moan grew louder.

Thank God they could read each other's signals. He slipped the knife into her free hand, pulled his gun and spun to face the monster who had done this to his Bree.

The man launched himself across the room and landed on Noah. They both fell to the floor near Bree, swinging fists at each other. Noah forced his way up to his feet until the two men leaned against each other like two evenly matched grizzlies fighting for dominance.

Noah surged forward and pushed the other man against a wall. He realized his gun was no longer in his hand just as the stranger headbutted him. Swinging away from the man, Noah spotted Bree struggling to cut herself loose. His gun lay on the floor next to her.

Damn. Wish I'd spent more time at the gun range with her.

The man charged him from the side, slamming Noah across the room. Noah kicked back with a foot, landing a hard boot heel to the guy's crotch. The man folded over in front of Noah, who grabbed his opponent's ears and followed up with a knee to his face.

Blood streamed from the man's face and Noah continued to pummel him. Then the monster within the man awoke once more. He wrapped his hands around Noah's throat and roared, blood and spittle spraying. Noah fought to loosen the man's fingers that were cutting off his air. He tried to force the man's arms apart to break the suffocating grip. He stretched his arms toward the man's face in an attempt to gouge out his eyes. Nothing worked.

Noah's lungs burned. His vision grew cloudy. Dizziness overcame him.

I'm dying. Bree doesn't know I love her and now it's too late to tell her. But I can hear her voice. So soft, so far away, calling my name. Bree...

"Noah!"

Not so far away now. And definitely not soft.

Bree screamed, "Noah! Boot! Drop!"

Somehow, through the fog in his mind and despite the cryptic message, he understood. Noah swung his leg forward as hard as he could. Too close to hit the man with his boot, he put all his energy into his shin this time. And when his shin bone connected to the man's, uh, man bone, the fingers around Noah's neck loosened. The man pulled a gun from his suit coat pocket. Noah dropped flat on the floor. And Bree shot the monster.

"GOOD MORNING, HELEN." Bree set a pastry bag with a prune Danish on her desk.

"Thank you, sweetie." She opened the bag and pulled out the sticky little pastry. "Who told you these are my favorite?"

"Must have been a little birdie." She gave Helen a wink and headed for the bullpen.

"Oh, wait. I don't think you've heard." Helen set the pastry on the bag and licked her fingers. "They got Crawford to roll."

"What?" Seth Whitlock, curse his black soul, had survived Bree's gunshot. And that turned out to be a good thing. With Crawford and Whitlock both locked up, there was a better chance of getting one of them to roll on the other.

"According to what I heard, as soon as Coach found out he could wind up in prison with Whitlock, he sang like a canary."

"Awesome news, Helen. Thanks for telling me."

Helen waved a hand, her mouth already filled with sweet prune delight.

Bree set her stuff on her desk in the corner, where she now spent most of her time. *Coulda been worse.* Even though she'd proved she could draw her gun, when Cassie had returned from Austin, Bree held true to her word. She told the sheriff the whole story and awaited her fate.

Luckily for her, Sheriff Reed valued integrity and didn't fire her. Her punishment? Desk duty until she was cleared by a shrink and passed the Texas Police Academy firearms test. Small price to pay to stay in law enforcement, stay in Resolute, stay with Noah.

The aroma of Busy B coffee reached her, and she looked toward the door with anticipation. She just couldn't get enough of Marge's coffee. Or the deliveryman.

"Good morning." Noah set the coffee on her desk, took a quick glance around and locked lips with her.

Bree batted at his shoulder. She didn't need to worry about more reasons to get fired. "We can't do that in the office."

"Relax. I checked with Helen when I came in. We're the only ones here right now."

"Hear anything about the program?"

"Adam's meeting with the county council today. It's a slow progress." When she'd confessed to Cassie, her story included her youth program as well as her desire to start one in here. Impressed with the idea and initiative, the sheriff had started the ball rolling to create one for Boone County.

He gave her a smug smile. "I'm not supposed to tell you this yet, but my resourceful sister contacted a friend of hers from college. Sara Adams is a judge in Austin now. She came from an extremely wealthy family and inherited the whole fortune. And I guess judges make pretty good money, so Sara's philanthropic to the max."

Bree's excitement rose.

"When Cassie reached out to her about your program idea, Sara couldn't wait to jump on board. She told Cassie she'd make up whatever difference there is between what we need and what the council approves."

"Are you kidding? That's amazing. Your sister's amazing. Her friend is amazing. I just hope the council approves it."

"Don't worry. I'm sure if there are any speed bumps, Cassie and Adam will double-team the council and make the program happen."

"I hope so. By the way, I heard Crawford rolled." She took the coffee container with a large B on the side from the holder and opened the lid. "Helen told me."

"I wanted to tell you, but that's okay." He waggled his brows. "I've got all the details."

"Do tell." Bree followed him to his desk and dragged over the extra chair.

"According to Crawford, Whitlock was the local manager for this area. His boss's boss is in the cartel in Mexico." He drank coffee and turned on his computer. "Crawford was one of Whitlock's liaisons. He received deliveries and stored them, then dispersed them to the local cookers."

"Why on earth did he store them in the gym?"

"They had a routine set up. Whitlock would come to the gym on a prearranged day, at night when no one else would be there—but it wouldn't be suspicious for Crawford to work late. The coach also knew there were no working security cameras at the school."

Bree shook her head in disgust. "How convenient for him."

"He said at first he'd planned to move them. But they blended in with all of his laundry supplies, and it made him more nervous driving around with several bottles in his trunk. When he dispersed them, he only took one at a time and met the cookers in a private spot not far from the school."

"Are there a lot more cookers in the county?"

"Unfortunately, yes. But Crawford provided a list of all of them that he knew about. So unless we've got a few lone wolves out there, we should be able to collect the bunch."

"If they haven't all already moved far, far away." She reached over and straightened Noah's collar. "What about Sammy?"

"Guessing about parts of this, but Crawford thinks Jason Watson might have watched him leaving the school for one of their meets. Jason knew Sammy was doing the floors for Bud and told Sammy if he could grab a bottle, he'd cook it for the two of them. He most likely told Sammy to check in the science department for a drying oven."

Bree's mouth dropped open. "That was on the final inventory list."

Noah nodded. "So Sammy trashed the rooms and stole

other stuff so the oven wouldn't stand out. And he faked the break-in so it wasn't obvious a key was used."

"But he wasn't smart enough to figure the back door situation." She sighed. "I'm almost afraid to ask who killed Sammy."

"Crawford. You and I actually put Sammy in his crosshairs. He said until the night we went to the school to talk to Bud, he had no clue who'd stolen his stuff. But when he found out the person we were chasing had been buffing the floors, and when he'd finally—" Noah tapped his head "—remembered what was vaguely familiar about him, it all fell into place."

"Are you going to tell me, or do I have to hurt you?"

Noah smiled his lopsided grin at her.

"What?"

"You just make me smile."

Damn, she loved this man. She hadn't wanted to. She'd tried not to. And she'd failed in the most fabulous way. The solitude she'd always craved now seemed impossible to endure, and she could only hope Noah felt the same way about her.

"Before Sammy dropped out of school, he was on the track team and had a distinctive running form. And since Crawford was responsible for the missing meth, he tortured Sammy until he told him Jason had it."

"Please don't tell me Crawford killed Jason, too."

"That was Whitlock, as far as Crawford knows. Said he'd told Whitlock everything up through who had possession of the meth, and Whitlock said he'd take it from there."

"You believe him?"

"I think so. It's up to the courts now." He looked around the bullpen. "I wish you were out there with me instead of riding a desk."

"Me too. But I will be, soon enough. And once I'm back in that car with you, don't think you're ever getting rid of me again."

"Like I would ever want to." Noah wrapped his arms around her and pulled her onto his lap. "You do know how much I love you, don't you?"

"I might. But it's still nice to hear."

"Then get used to it 'cause you'll be hearing it every day for the rest of your life."

Bree snuggled against him. "I love *you*."

"I know."

She punched him in the shoulder. "You do remember how that scene ended for Han Solo, right?"

Noah smiled his lopsided grin and kissed her.

Epilogue

"This girl needs no more champagne." Noah laughed as Bree danced around her living room. To help celebrate her release from a month of desk duty *and* her move into the new house, Noah had planned a party for her. And Cassie decided to add another reason to celebrate.

The entire sheriff's department, Marge, Doc, Nate—the whole gang was here. Casual dress was mandatory, except for Bree. Noah had managed to find a prisoner's uniform for the occasion.

When the music paused and Bree stopped dancing, Marge called across the room, "If I'd known horizontal stripes were so flattering, I'd be wearing them."

Bree pivoted like a model, rocking the prison stripes. The lightweight chain around her ankle, connected to a small soft ball, swung with each pose.

Adam sidled up to Noah. "She's a good sport for wearing the chain."

The zip ties she'd been cuffed with by Whitlock had cut deeply into her ankles and wrists, leaving noticeable scars.

"I know." He shrugged. "I left it up to her."

Helen carried a tray of appetizers from the kitchen and got stuck in a bottleneck next to Marge. Each woman's mouth set in stubborn lines, and they looked in opposite directions.

"What's up with that?" Bree appeared at Noah's side.

"What?" He pulled his best *what? where?* look.

She tipped her head toward Marge and Helen. "I've never seen either one of them ever look that angry."

Tapping his lip, he went with the first thing that popped into his mind. Actually, it had been on his mind all evening, so it didn't have to pop. He pulled her into a hug. "Do you know how hot you are in that uniform?"

"Nice try. What's going on between them?"

"We're not supposed to speak of it. Those that did, learned to never speak of it again."

Bree crossed her arms over her chest.

"Okay, okay." He pulled her to a quiet corner and whispered in her ear, "It's the oldest family feud Resolute's ever seen."

Bree gave him her questioning brow, the one he'd learned required an explanation or he'd have no rest.

"Helen Gibson and Marge Dawson are sisters."

"Get out!" Bree pushed him, and everyone in the room looked.

"Nothing to see here, folks. Carry on." He pushed his mouth against her ear again. "Do you understand 'do not speak of it'?"

Bree nodded with an adorable grin. "Why is it a secret? Why don't they talk?"

She'd never let him save the rest for later. "Marge stole Doc from Helen back when they were maybe eighteen or twenty. Something like that. Helen's never forgiven her."

Bree turned to him, leaning toward him from the waist, knees bent slightly. Her eyes were wide as dinner plates, her mouth open in an even bigger O. She looked like a bunny-slope skier who'd just hit a jump on a black run. He couldn't open his mouth without laughing, so he just held his finger against it in the universal sign for *keep your trap shut*.

He kept her in the corner until they could both compose themselves. "About that costume," he said. "Think you could leave it on after everyone goes home?"

"I think that can be arranged." She gave him her sexiest smile. "But now that I don't have any secrets of my own, I want to know *all* of Resolute's."

"Bree?" Cassie waved her over to the other side of the room.

"Hold that thought." She kissed him and disappeared into the crowd.

Noah moseyed over in the same direction, stopping at a table of filled champagne flutes. Helen called out for everyone to get a glass but not drink yet. Easier said than done with this crowd.

When everyone was quiet and holding a glass, Cassie stepped to the front of the room.

"I'm glad we all can be here tonight to celebrate Deputy Bree Delgado's release from desk-duty prison, as well as her move into this beautiful home."

Everyone cheered. A few tried to applaud, but…full champagne glasses.

"However, we're also here to celebrate another significant event."

"You and Bish are finally tying the knot?" Nate grinned as the whole room laughed.

"Very funny, little brother." Cassie's green eyes met Noah's, and the sisterly love in them almost made him cry. She motioned him up there, next to her. As he joined Cassie, Bree stepped to his side.

"I'd like you all to drink to the engagement of my brother

Noah Reed and my soon-to-be sister-in-law, Brianna Delgado."

Noah retrieved Bree's diamond ring that he'd been hiding in his pocket until the announcement. He slipped it on her finger and they raised a glass to each other as their friends and family cheered, drank and applauded *after* they set down their glasses. Noah pulled her into his arms again.

"I was thinking," he said, "maybe after the party's over, we could head out to my place. Have a little competition at Hogan's Alley."

The corner of her mouth kicked up in a sly smile. "Bet I can get a higher score out there than you, Deputy. Even dressed like a prisoner."

He nuzzled her ear. Man, he loved this woman. "You're on."

* * * * *

OPERATION WITNESS PROTECTION

JUSTINE DAVIS

Chapter One

All I wanted was a cup of coffee.

That refrain went through Case McMillan's head as he got out of his truck, but his eyes were fastened on the struggle several yards in front of him. There was only one light in the alley behind the convenience store, so as the two figures wrestled they moved in and out of its halo like some kind of angry-dance light show.

A couple of drunk guys? Gang clash? Big bully versus kid?

From here he couldn't see details, but his gut already knew before they staggered into the light again. Before he saw the shape of the much smaller figure, or the ski-glove-sized hand over her mouth.

He swore under his breath. If it had only been one of his first three guesses, he could have—maybe—walked away. Gone in, gotten his coffee and been out of here before it eventually broke up or someone called the cops.

He managed not to swear again at the last part of that thought. Barely.

But he couldn't deny what he was seeing. This was a big man grappling with a woman half his size. A woman who, despite the fact she had no chance against the sheer bulk, kept fighting.

Damn.

He broke into a run even as he called himself a fool for doing it.

He had only the four seconds it took him to cover the distance to plan. To take in the surroundings and assess what he had at hand. Then he had to jettison the plan when the faint gleam from that overhead light skittered along metal. The barrel of the weapon in the man's hand.

A gun was jammed under the woman's chin.

He grabbed his keys out of his jacket pocket. Threw them as hard as he could. Hit his target, the metal trash can next to the back door of the store. The loud, harsh clang did the job. The man's head jerked around to see what had suddenly happened behind him. The gun moved with him. Away from the woman. Just enough.

When he turned back Case was on top of him. He caught the hand with the gun. Clamped his fingers down and shoved upward hard and fast. The man yelled in pain and surprise. And even in the dim light he saw the man's dark eyes widen as he looked upward; the guy might be twice the weight of his victim, but Case had at least four inches on him. And the man's weight was soft, Case could tell that, too. As he looked up, shifting the position of the thick, long, heavy beard, Case got a glimpse of a ring of tattoos on his neck.

The guy twisted away. Hung on to the gun but shoved the woman aside. She hit the back wall of the store hard. Out of the corner of his eye Case saw her slump down to the ground in the half-circle of light. He stepped between them. The man spun and started to run. That instant felt like an eon to Case, because the instinct to pursue the bad guy kicked in. He quashed it, vehemently, using whatever he had. In this case, what he had was a victim down, because she hadn't gotten up.

He let the man go, swearing out loud this time.

He crossed the distance to the downed woman in two strides. He knelt, relieved that she was moving now, pushing herself upright. But he was certain she'd hit her head on that solid wall, so he put a hand out to slow her until he knew if she was truly hurt. She jerked away, and he pulled back instantly. At least she was aware enough to react.

"It's okay," he said reassuringly. "He's gone."

She looked up then. He could see her eyes were blue, and that the fear in them was rapidly fading. But more than that, they focused on him with a look he hadn't expected. Not just gratitude, not even trust, but…as if she knew him.

But he'd never seen her before. He would have remembered. Because she was attractive in that cute sort of way he'd always been a sucker for. Those big blue eyes, the long, wavy hair an almost blond shade of sandy brown he'd bet got streaky in the summer. She was a little thin, though, which along with her stature—if she was over five-two he'd be surprised—had made the attack even more one-sided.

When she didn't speak, he asked, "Are you all right? Your head hit the wall, didn't it? I'll call the paramedics—"

"No!"

She sounded horrified at the thought. He was nearly as horrified by the other call he needed to make, to the police. But it went totally against the grain to force her, the victim, to make the call that needed to be made.

"You need to report this," he said.

Her voice calmer now, she went on. "No, don't. I don't want…anyone else involved. I'm very grateful to you for stopping him, and for staying with me but…no, I just can't."

For staying with her? Had she somehow sensed the urge he'd crushed down, the urge to go after her attacker?

It's not your job anymore.

The phrase that had become a mantra ricocheted through

his mind yet again. He shoved it, and the subject, aside. Her condition was more important now.

"You should still get checked out. I can take you to the emergency room, or an urgent care."

"No, no, I think I'm fine. I saw stars for a second, but only a second."

"Dizziness?"

She considered that for a moment, then shook her head. Then smiled, as if that in itself had been a test and she'd passed. "No, no dizziness. Just that first moment of stars." She lifted a hand to touch the back of her head. A delicate chain with a couple charms on it—a bird that looked like an eagle, and a second he couldn't tell—slide down her arm as she raised it. "It's only a tiny bit sore."

She moved as if to get up, but he put a hand out to stop her. This time she didn't recoil.

"Let's just be sure. What's your name?"

She hesitated, then said only, "Terri." He didn't hold the hesitancy or lack of last name against her; it was only wise.

"Do you know where you are?"

She grimaced. "Behind the store I stopped into, to get warm." He'd noticed she had on only a sweater, not enough for this unseasonably chilly night. "Stupid me. Or lousy timing."

His brow furrowed. "Are you saying this started inside?"

Her brow furrowed in turn. "You didn't see?"

"I was just pulling in when I saw you here in the alley."

She started to shudder, then her jaw tightened as she suppressed it. That she still had the strength to do even that amazed him.

"He robbed the store. And beat up the clerk."

He went still. This time a string of oaths rammed through his mind, although he didn't voice any of them even under his breath. "You saw it?"

She nodded, a bit shakily, as if that shudder she'd suppressed was still trying to grip her. "Please," she said, her voice dropping to a whisper, "let me get up. I have to get out of here. The clerk will call the cops, and I don't want to be here when they arrive."

Suspicion bit deep. Had she been involved? Was what he'd witnessed not an attack on an innocent bystander but a falling out among crime partners?

It's not your job anymore.

Still, he couldn't stop himself from asking, "Were you his diversion? To keep the clerk distracted?"

She looked at him blankly. "What?"

"Did you disagree on the split of the take? Is that what happened back here?"

"What?" she repeated, still blankly.

"He had a mask, pulled down around his neck."

"Yes. I saw him like that outside, through the window, before. But when he came in, he had the mask over his face."

"But he'd pulled it down again when he met up with you out here. Because it didn't matter anymore?"

"I don't understand what—"

She broke off as comprehension dawned on her face. Her eyes widened with obvious shock. And maybe he was a fool—okay, probably—but he believed it was genuine. She'd had no idea what he was talking about.

She scrambled to her feet. He straightened up himself. She'd had no trouble standing, but she wobbled slightly once she got upright. Instinctively he reached out to steady her. Felt her shakiness as if a connection had been established at the touch.

She sounded utterly broken when she said, "You think I was part of what happened in there?"

"Not anymore." And against every self-protective instinct he had, he put his arms around her. Just to keep steadying her, he told himself. She was still trembling. Aftermath could be hell. "I just wonder why you're so desperate to avoid the police."

"Nothing to do with that robbery," she said. She looked up at him. "Please, you have to believe—"

"I said I did." He did, even if he wasn't quite sure why he was so certain, beyond a gut feeling. It might not be his job anymore, but his gut was still well trained.

"Then I can go?"

It sounded like she was asking his permission. As if he still wore the uniform. He again shook off the odd sensation that she somehow knew.

She felt unsteady enough that he wasn't thrilled with the idea of letting her walk off alone. Hell, he felt a little unsteady himself, at the simple idea of letting the witness to a robbery and assault leave the scene. And that irritated him. This time he stopped the mantra before it fully formed, and focused on the more urgent matter at hand.

"Is there someone at home, who'll be there? In case that bump on the head turns into something worse later?"

Her brow furrowed. "No, I don't live here. I used to, but I'm just visiting, staying in a motel—" She caught herself, as if she regretted saying even that much. "No," she repeated.

"You shouldn't be alone. Not with a possible head injury."

"I'm fine."

"Now. Sometimes it takes time for problems to show up. You need to be with someone who will watch, wake you up every hour or two and make sure you're still okay."

"I…" She shivered again in his arms. Then, her voice low and shaky, she said, "I don't have anyone like that." She paused, lowered her gaze. And barely audibly, she murmured, "I don't have anyone."

The protector inside kicked him hard and fast. Apparently not even betrayal could kill it completely. He closed his eyes for a moment, letting out a compressed breath. Even knowing he was going to regret this, he said it. "Yeah, you do."

"Who?"

He sighed. "Me."

Chapter Two

Terri Johnson—whose not quite genuine ID currently bore the name of Terri Jones—wondered if she'd hit her head a little harder than she'd thought. How else had she ended up here, in the apartment of a total stranger, settled in to spend the night?

A total stranger who yet somehow felt familiar. Not that she actually knew him, of course. She knew she didn't, and not just because she hadn't set foot here, in the area around Puget Sound where she'd grown up, for over nine years. No, she knew because she would never have forgotten meeting a man like this, the proverbial tall, dark and handsome. He had to be six feet or better, with dark, sleek hair with a couple of strands that kicked forward over his brow in that way she'd always liked. And those eyes had to be the most amazing she'd ever seen. Hazel, she supposed, gold around the pupil shifting to a lovely green farther out. Yes, definitely tall, dark and handsome.

And strong. No doubting that, and the robber had realized it immediately. So he'd cut and run rather than try to take on someone who, unlike her, was bigger and tougher than himself.

It was much easier to assess all this in the aftermath. At the time she'd been too frightened to think clearly. Who wouldn't be, with a gun barrel jammed under your chin and a man trying to drag you out of sight so he could kill you? She'd realized in the moment that her rescuer appeared that he was big enough and strong enough to do it. That was about all she'd had time to process before the robber had slammed her into that wall.

She'd gotten a strange feeling then, a sense that the man who'd saved her life had been torn between staying with her and chasing down her attacker. She couldn't say how she knew. It wasn't just the tension in him; she would have expected that, but something about the way he looked down the alley after the escaping robber. His instinct was to go after him. She was as certain of that as she was absurdly grateful when he'd decided to stay with her instead.

Of course, he was probably regretting that now, since he'd acquired an unwanted guest.

Yet he'd been unfailingly kind, even gentle. In fact, for such a big, powerful guy, he'd been as gentle as…as…

As her brother had been.

She bit back the old pain that threatened to well up again. She pulled the blanket he'd put over her up around her shoulders, although she wasn't really cold. Not on the outside, anyway.

Some people told her it was time for her to get over it, or that she should be past it by now. How did you ever get past the death of the one person who had always stood between you and malevolence? The one person who had sheltered you, tried to protect you, to keep that malevolence from drowning you even as he also bore the burden of it?

She didn't know how, and wasn't certain she wanted to know. Wouldn't it deny the relationship she and her brother had had, wouldn't it belittle his memory to pretend she'd forgotten, no longer cared, didn't get those horrible jabs of grief when she thought of him? She had progressed, no longer broke down and became nonfunctional when she thought of him, and that was as good as she ever expected to get.

Terri only knew she'd fallen asleep when he woke her.

"Hey." A gentle nudge of her shoulder.

"Wha—?" She sleepily opened her eyes. Damn, he was even more gorgeous than she remembered. Those eyes…

"Talk to me for a minute."

I'd much rather listen. What a voice. All low and rough and rumbly...

"You awake?"

"I am now." She looked away to avoid saying something stupid.

"What's your name?"

She looked back at him. "Terri Jo—Jones."

Wake up—you almost blew that.

She tried to think if she'd done any damage giving him that last name. No, she decided, it was too common. Which was why she'd picked it, of course. And for all she knew he'd checked her ID while she'd slept, so best to go with it. The ID that so far had held up, and now had seven years of living under the name to back it up. Not that anyone would be looking for her. No one cared, and the people who should care were no doubt as glad to be rid of her as they had been ten years ago to be rid of her brother.

All the while her brain was churning with thoughts and unwanted memories, she was trying not to notice him quite so much. Not notice how broad his chest was, how powerful his arms and how flat his waist, now that he was wearing only a T-shirt and jeans. That fit…beautifully.

"What's your mother's name?" he asked.

Her mouth twisted. Well, that certainly changed the mood. "Mud?" she suggested. "Witch? Something that rhymes with?"

This time he blinked. She thought, even in the dim light, she saw one corner of his mouth twitch. "That bad?"

"Worse," she said flatly.

She had long ago decided some people simply should not be parents. Or in their case, they should simply have themselves cloned, since they were the only people they approved of, and anyone who strayed outside their narrow lines was to be condemned and cast out. She had merely saved them the trouble by leaving on her own.

And as far as she knew, they'd never even looked for her. She'd put some distance between them quickly, just in case, and had spent her eighteenth birthday in a friendly little town in Oregon. She'd wondered, for a while, if they might have at least reported her missing, but a stop at the public library and a quick search turned up nothing. And she'd decided it didn't matter and never looked again. Because she wasn't going back, never wanted to see them again.

She hadn't searched for anything on her brother. She didn't want to know how it had happened. She'd lived with the fear of losing him from the moment he'd first deployed, and that was bad enough; she didn't want to carry around the details of the reality.

Her mind dodged the thought with the agility of long practice and, brow furrowed, she asked, "But you don't know her name, so how would you know if I answered that right?"

He smiled then. How unfair was it that on top of everything else, he had such a great smile? "That you figured that out tells me your brain's working fine. Go back to sleep."

Her brow didn't unfurrow. "Are you really going to get up every hour and do this? What about you getting some sleep?"

"I'm fine, Terri." Him using her name gave her an inner jolt. But she didn't have time to dwell on that as he went on. "I'm used to grabbing sleep when I can."

Why?

All sorts of speculation ran through her mind. Did he simply work nights, or was it something more? On call? Did he work at a hospital? That might explain his reaction to her hitting her head. She didn't think he was a paramedic or anything official, or he wouldn't have let her beg off on the trip to the ER. Or maybe he was—

"We'll do every hour a couple more times, then go longer, if you seem all right."

"I'm fine," she assured him. "Not even a headache, just that sore spot."

She glanced around the apartment again. It was small, but clean and tidy. And impersonal. The only things she noticed that showed someone lived here were the jacket he'd hung on a hook by the door, a couple of books on the table where she'd set her purse and the TV remote control beside them.

"Where...is this place?" she asked. "I'm afraid I wasn't paying much attention earlier to where we were going."

"Edmonds. Only about three miles from where you were."

"North of Seattle?"

He nodded. "That where you live? Seattle?"

She shook her head, sharply and almost involuntarily. Her first thought was to be glad she experienced no dizziness or other reaction. Her second, after seeing his considering look, was what she might have betrayed by that reaction.

"I'm sorry. I won't tell you that. So maybe it would be best if I leave now."

"Not until we're sure you're okay. Did you have a car parked back at that store?"

"No."

"That makes things easier, then." She looked at him, puzzled. He shrugged. "Abandoned car at a crime scene? Always suspicious."

The puzzled look became a stare. The way he'd said that,

the terms, the phrasing… It didn't seem possible. Surely he wouldn't have not only let her but helped her leave that crime scene, as he'd put it? But why would he even think about that, in those words?

"Are you a cop?" she demanded.

His jaw visibly tightened. "Not anymore."

She flashed back to those blurry moments when she'd sensed he was torn between chasing after the robber and staying to help her. She guessed she had the explanation for that, now. She wasn't sure what made her ask, maybe the pain in his eyes. Those distinctive eyes.

"Why?"

He drew back slightly. "I'm sorry. I won't tell you that."

She felt her face flush as he echoed her own refusal right back at her. "Fair enough," she said after a moment. "I had that coming."

He straightened up then. Tall wasn't the word for it; he seemed to tower over where she lay on his couch.

He started to turn. "Wait, I don't even know your name." Her own fault, she hadn't even thought to ask. All she'd cared about at the time was how safe he made her feel. But she'd given him hers, albeit not the one she'd been born with, so he couldn't counter with another refusal.

After a brief moment, he answered. "Case McMillan."

She managed not to chuckle out loud. "A cop named Case?"

His wry expression told her he'd explained this before. "I was named for my grandfather, but my mom thought Casey was too old-fashioned so they dropped the *y*. Now go back to sleep."

She watched him walk away, feeling a bit ungrateful as her gaze focused on the way he moved, the way he looked in those jeans, especially that taut, trim backside.

She thought of how he'd tried, when they'd first arrived

at the small apartment, to convince her to take his bed while he crashed out here. She'd taken one look at the size of the couch and his six-foot-plus frame and refused, firmly. Later it registered with her that he only would have done that if he slept alone. She told herself it mattered because she didn't want to cause any trouble, or embarrassingly run into someone outside the bathroom.

She tried to imagine the kind of woman a man like this would be with. He could have his pick, obviously, so maybe it was a different one every night. She mentally shoved aside the idea, knowing it wasn't true. He reminded her too much of her brother, not in looks but in that solid, strong core, both physically and mentally. He might not have any shortage of offers, but she was certain that he didn't jump any woman willing.

Why was she even thinking about it? All that mattered right now was that she was safe. The memory of that evil man's remote, dark eyes, the cold metal of a gun barrel digging into her flesh, the pounding of her heartbeat in her chest, the careening chaos of her mind facing the likelihood of being blown out of existence in the next second, would never leave her. She'd fought, yes, but she was under no illusion that she could have stopped it, not when her assailant was so much bigger, and twice her weight.

Something Case had said earlier, about the mask, came back to her…*he'd pulled it down again when he met up with you… Because it didn't matter anymore?*

She realized the last sentence was absolute truth. It hadn't bothered the robber that she'd seen his face, because he'd fully intended to kill her.

But she'd survived, thanks to Case McMillan.

And she had to admit, it was nice to have someone looking

out for her; she'd been on her own for a long time now. Surely she couldn't be blamed for enjoying it, for just one night?

She fell back asleep, telling herself to stop linking him and enjoyment in the same thought.

Chapter Three

He hadn't meant to snoop.

Case crouched beside the couch where she was sleeping soundly, looking at the scattering of items that had spilled from the purse on the floor. He hadn't knocked it over; it had been on the end table but was now toppled. Perhaps she'd done it, hitting it inadvertently when she'd shifted position. Seemed logical, since she was lying on her side now, one arm folded under her head, that hand actually touching the table.

He'd only intended to put the contents back and right the bag. But then he'd seen the notebook and envelopes. Two rather battered envelopes tucked in the center of the small paper book, each addressed in the same hand, oddly a half cursive, half printed combination like his own. Addressed, but unstamped and unsent to the same man at a military address.

I don't have anyone.

She'd said it so sadly it wrenched at his heart, so quietly he knew he wasn't supposed to have heard it.

But who was this man she'd been writing to? Was he an ex? And if so, whose idea had the ex part been? Or was it worse? Was she one of those left behind by a hero?

What the hell does that matter, McMillan? It's no difference to you.

He slipped the envelopes back to where they'd been, between the pages of the notebook. A notebook that served as a journal or diary of some sort. With entries to the same man the letters were addressed to. The phrase at the top of the page the envelopes had been marking caught his eye.

Anything I ever knew about kindness and love came from you.

Feeling like a trespasser, he shut the notebook and shoved it back into the bag, and set the bag upright on the floor. He stayed there for a moment, studying her. She looked at peace now, the tension gone, the horrible fear no longer showing in her face.

Her lovely face.

He couldn't deny that. She was lovely, even more so now that the panic had ebbed away. He felt a familiar sort of satisfaction about that, something he'd often experienced as an officer, when he'd helped someone. But there was an unfamiliar side to this as well, something that tugged at a place so deeply buried he rarely heard from it.

And it worked out so well the last time...

He quashed the bitter thought, knowing it accomplished nothing. Besides, that disaster had been born out of his own stupidity, the only word he had for believing in Jill. He should have known better. If he had, maybe only part of his life would have crumbled around him.

He crushed that thought, too, wryly acknowledging he was doing more avoiding thinking than thinking. He went to where he'd originally intended, the kitchen to set up the coffee maker; the broken sleep tonight, with the timer he'd set to make sure he checked on her regularly, was starting to register and he was going to need the caffeine earlier than usual.

Once that timer was set, he went back to his bedroom, yawning. He picked up his phone from the nightstand and reset the timer. He sat on the bed, reaching out to put the phone back down. And stopped, the device still in his hand. Sat staring at it, trying to resist. But just as the urge to protect hadn't been killed by betrayal, apparently neither had the investigator in him.

He started a search on the name on the envelopes. Quickly realized it was going to take a deeper dive. He got up and went to the table that served as a desk, and booted up his laptop. He opened the browser, called up his favorite search engine and typed in the name.

Teague Johnson.

He wasn't particularly optimistic, given the last name was second only to Smith in commonality. He soon realized that Teague often being a last name didn't help either, so he went back and restricted it to those names in that order.

He checked entries for a while—including lists of military casualties—thinking he should have left well enough alone. She'd be gone in a few hours and he'd never see her again. Never have to look into those big blue eyes that somehow held a lifetime of weariness and hurt in her young face.

He'd try one more thing, narrowing down the search to this area, recalling she'd said she used to live here. Then he'd quit sticking his nose in where it didn't belong, something she surely wouldn't thank him for. Not that she'd ever know, since she'd be gone as soon as the sun was fully up, most likely.

Then again, maybe not. She'd witnessed an armed robbery, and there had no doubt been security cameras in that store. And while the robber had been hidden behind a full face mask, she had not. He knew what he'd do, if he'd been the officer on the case; he'd track her down.

And if he'd been the robber, he might just want to do the same.

But he wasn't—either, thankfully—and since she was

only visiting, hopefully she'd be long gone before the robber had a chance to look for her.

And again he had to stop the inborn instinct to urge her to go to the police, to give them the information she had on the bad guy. He wondered again why she was so determined not to. Was she in more trouble than being in the wrong place at the wrong time? Did she have some reason not to want to deal with the police? A criminal record, or maybe even a warrant out for her?

Not your job anymore, McMillan. Not after they tossed you out on your ear for doing it.

With effort he turned his gaze back to his laptop. One last entry remained on this page of search results, and he resolved it would be his last as well. He nearly shut it without reading, seeing only a post on a personal blog, but something about the title stopped him. "To Those Who Saved Us."

He scanned the entry on what was apparently a blog about one family's fight against a county government that had attempted to seize property that had been in their family for generations, and do it by various underhanded or threatening means.

I can't go into detail because it's confidential, but I also can't close out this blog without saying thank you a thousand times to the people who defended us, stood up for us and made it all happen. So here's to the Foxworth Foundation, and in particular their operative Teague Johnson, who fought Goliath for us and won. To anyone who is ever in that kind of trouble, if you're the little guy up against impossible odds, if big power or money or both are arrayed against you, if you know you're in the right but have run out of options, know there is help out there.

Foxworth. He knew the name, as many in the area did. And not just from the big scandal involving the governor a while back. As a cop he'd come across them a time or two, not directly but via hearsay, sometimes from both sides of whatever they were involved in. He remembered thinking that the caliber of the people who hated them was a pretty good measure of who they were.

But could this be the Teague Johnson she'd been writing to? Obviously this man wasn't in the military, but those letters had looked old, as if she'd been carrying them around for a long time. Maybe he had been?

If so, what was her connection to the man? Was he that ex he'd thought of when he'd seen those letters, lover or husband? Or current, but estranged? Current, but merely separated for some reason? She wore no ring—so sue him, he'd noticed—but that wasn't really proof. Was he the man behind that bracelet she wore, and so frequently touched?

He realized with a little jolt that his focus had shifted entirely to that last string of questions. As if what this man was to her, what their connection was, had somehow become more important than who he actually was. And a hum began in the back of his mind, one he hadn't heard much from since taking off the badge for the last time. The hum that warned him he was heading into danger-ous territory.

He slapped the laptop shut, stood and crossed the room in two long strides, spinning in the same movement and let-ting himself fall onto the bed. With an effort he shoved the thoughts out of his mind, knowing he needed to get what sleep he could. Although why he worried about function-ing tomorrow he wasn't quite sure. It wasn't like he had a job to go to.

When the timer went off again a bare half hour later, he sat up groggily. Hard to believe he was the guy who used to pull off double shifts easily, barely getting sleepy on the graveyard segment. He rubbed at his eyes as he swung his legs over the side of the bed, stood and headed once more for the living room.

If she was still coherent he'd leave her be after this time; it was nearly morning anyway. If she was still fine when she woke up on her own, then he'd count his self-inflicted job done. She would be on her way, and he could go back to his own miserable life, such as it was.

She was coherent, but a little edgy, probably from the interrupted sleep. He ran through the string of questions, promising her it was the last time before morning. She seemed to relax at that. He wasn't sure if that was what impelled him to do it, but just as she was about to drift off again he asked quietly, "Who's Teague?"

Her eyes snapped open. He bit back the urge to explain, that he'd seen the letters, letting the question hang there, the silence grow. Experience had taught him sometimes the best way to get an answer was to ask and then shut up. Why this was so important to him he wasn't sure. Wasn't sure he wanted to know.

She turned on her side, putting her back to him.

Guess you've truly lost the knack, McMillan.

And then, just as he was about to stand and leave her in peace, she answered him. Quietly, barely audible.

"He was my brother."

Only then did it hit him how much he'd been expecting her to say, "My husband." And the fact that she hadn't gave him a kick of relief that in turn set off not just a warning hum, but a siren.

He stood abruptly, backing up a step. This woman was dangerous. To him, anyway.

He didn't answer her. Couldn't risk saying something stupid, something he didn't want to say, had no business saying. Like asking her out to breakfast, or at least for her phone number. He was in no position for anything like that.

It wasn't until he was back in his own—empty—bed that the full import of what she'd said hit him.

He *was* my brother.

Chapter Four

Terri supposed her rescuer's quiet question had triggered the dream. In the decade that had passed she had managed to cram it into a compartment of her brain that was fairly solid, the images only escaping now and then. Usually when she was excessively tired, or sick or...

Or had nearly been murdered in an alley?

She sat up on the couch. Judging by the light coming through the window it was a sunny morning. Still, she kept the blanket wrapped around her. It seemed almost unreal now, but the sore spot on the back of her head and a couple of other twinges told her it had been all too real.

Who's Teague?

The dream's core was consistent, it was only the trappings that changed. The surroundings ranged anywhere from their backyard as kids to a sand dune in a place she'd never been, the circumstances anything from climbing the big maple tree in the backyard to sand giving way under their feet. But whatever and wherever, the nightmare part never changed. Teague always slipping away from her.

And their parents, cheering about it. Just as they had when she'd overheard them that awful day.

So it's happened. He's dead, blown to bits. Her mother's

cold, satisfied voice, even in memory, still had the power to chill her.

Just as you said he'd end up. Her father, on the other hand, had sounded merely flat.

We're rid of his stupid wrong-think now. I told them we didn't want a funeral. To just put him wherever they do that kind of thing. I'd hate to have to pretend to grieve.

She wrapped her arms around herself, trying to stop the shaking that wanted to seize her, as it always did at that too-vivid memory of a conversation she hadn't been meant to hear. The conversation that had shattered her world in many more ways than one.

She knew they had hated that Teague joined the military. How could she not, given the many arguments that had echoed off the walls at night, after she'd been sent to bed? But until then she hadn't realized they hated him, too. This made her feel stupid, because she should have realized long ago, after all the times they'd warned her against ever taking any advice from him. No, in her family the only advice worth following was theirs, which they'd made demandingly clear.

They'd just never realized that in her own way, she was as much of a rebel as her brother.

She'd always known her parents weren't the loving kind that many of her friends had. Sometimes she wondered why her parents had had children at all, since they didn't seem to like either of theirs very much.

She sighed, shoving away thoughts that still had no answers. She was more adept at dealing with it now than she had been the day she'd gotten home early after a school event was cancelled, found her parents not just unexpectedly home but having the conversation that had shattered her world and frozen her spirit with its cold lack of feeling. Her beloved big brother, killed in action in a faraway place, and they were glad about it. He had embarrassed them among their circle of like-minded friends, and they were glad to be shed of him.

Teague was *dead*, and they were happy about it.

She'd left that night and never looked back. Nor had she ever been tempted in the slightest to return to the house she'd grown up in, even now, when she was within easy reach. She didn't know if her parents were alive or dead, and she didn't care much either way. They'd killed that in her that day. She couldn't spend another moment under the same roof with people who could be glad their son was dead, simply because he believed differently than they did. Because he believed in something more than self-interest, believed in fairness and truth and that they were worth fighting for.

The shivers broke free, and she had to stifle the moan of remembered pain that rose to her lips.

Don't let them turn you into them, Terri.

Teague's words to her as he'd hugged her before he'd shipped out that last time were etched into her mind like an epitaph on a headstone.

She thought again about finding out where he was buried and going there. After ten years she should be strong enough, steady enough to do that, shouldn't she? She'd lasted all that time, including a couple of very rough years she'd barely survived, before she'd regained her determination. Then she'd gotten her GED, even did a couple of years in a community college, learned enough to get a job in an office and had ended up helping manage it a few years later, thanks to the trust of her boss, Mr. Gibson.

She'd done that, so surely she could face the fact of her brother's death by visiting his grave, wherever it might be? She was strong enough to acknowledge he was gone, to look at his name on some official record at least, if not on a headstone, wasn't she? She could, finally, say goodbye?

She wasn't that emotional, spiraling-out-of-control teenager she'd been anymore.

So why did she feel so utterly empty inside? So empty she'd come back here, to the home turf she'd fled, as if the place where her life had changed forever held some kind of answer to that emptiness.

And look how that worked out for you. You'd be dead if not for...him.

Another man with the strength and courage and will to fight for others.

CURIOSITY WAS GOING to be the death of him.

Case leaned back in his chair and stared at the laptop screen, determined to convince himself that only curiosity had driven him to search further. Curiosity because there wasn't a trace of a Teague Johnson of the right age that he could find in the public records of military deaths in service. That was what had driven him to keep looking, not the aching sadness that fairly radiated off the woman in his living room right now.

And certainly not the woman herself.

No, she hadn't been the impetus for continuing the search, not at all. It was simply that curiosity, and the fact that as a cop, he never had been able to let go of a case until it was solved. The detective division used to roll their eyes when they saw him coming, and finally had taken to making copies of cases they'd resolved that had his name on them as the reporting officer, and forwarding them to him. He'd never been sure if they were saving him the trouble or themselves the interruptions, but he suspected the latter. They'd eased up when he'd told them he had no interest in their job. He preferred being out on the street, doing what he'd signed up to do.

And look where that got you...

He shoved aside the old, worn thought. He'd turned over a big, slimy rock and found much worse underneath. Had exposed some nasty corruption to the light of day. He'd done the right thing. If the powers that be and the system didn't agree, then obviously they no longer wanted done what he'd signed up to do. And if he couldn't—wouldn't—play by their new rules, he was better off gone.

Even if he estimated that by the end of the year he'd be dead broke.

Not for the first time he considered leaving, going somewhere where his name hadn't been in the news so blaringly for so long, and starting over. He certainly had nothing—no one, anyway—holding him here. Jill, his not so loving wife, had bailed on him the moment the thing blew up, and had filed for divorce barely a month later. She didn't care about the right thing; she only cared that he'd gone against people of such influence, and she didn't want to go down with him.

So yeah, he could move. But no such thing as strictly local news existed anymore, so the whole case was available to anyone who bothered to look. As any new employer would. Besides, he loved this part of the country, and certain people aside, it was where he wanted to stay.

Just the thought that he might have no choice irritated him, and for distraction he sat forward and reached for the laptop again. There had been only the one connection he'd found so far, and it couldn't hurt to probe a little further, to discard the possibility if nothing else. Because it nagged at him, that there was no death record, that she and presumably her brother had grown up here and there happened to be someone with that name working for an organization in the region.

It only took a moment to find the Foxworth Foundation's website. Not that it was much help; there were no names mentioned other than the siblings who started the foundation, Charlaine and Quinn Foxworth. He would have thought it consisted only of them except for the posts from individuals and families thanking them, the only place where other names were mentioned.

The website was even pretty vague about what they did. The only clue he really found was in the "About" section, where the inspiration for the foundation was explained by the story of a convicted terrorist responsible for hundreds of deaths who was released to go home because of some back room political deal. Their parents had been among those killed, leaving the Foxworths orphaned at young ages and helpless to fight what happened, and it had shaped their life path. They took the insurance money left by their slaughtered parents and had built the Foxworth Foundation solely to fight that feeling of helplessness in others. If you were an honest innocent who had fought hard but been up against impossible odds or immovable objects—or bureaucracies—you were the person Foxworth wanted to fight for.

Maybe I should have gone to them, back then.

That was how he referred to that time when by doing that right thing he'd brought his world crumbling down around him. Back then. He didn't really have another name for it. Back then. Before. How many people had moments like that in their lives, where one simple, honest act had destroyed nearly everything? Probably a lot. He couldn't be alone in this kind of situation, or places like this Foxworth wouldn't exist, would they?

He looked for more on the website, but there was amazingly little, considering just about anybody who lived in the region had heard the name. There was no real PR, no trumpeting of success, no advertising, not even a list of the kind of things they did.

Don't get involved.

The self-issued warning rang loudly in his head, but then

he almost laughed. If he could live by that maxim, he would have just left Terri to her fate last night. And no matter what life had done to him, no matter what doing the right thing back then had brought down on him, he clearly was not capable of that.

He stared at the home page of the website, at the logo of the organization whose reason for existence was so simple, yet so nonspecific.

So here's to the Foxworth Foundation, and in particular their operative Teague Johnson, who fought Goliath for us and won.

The words he'd read stuck in his mind, and in the end prodded him into pulling out his phone. He dialed the number on the screen.

To his surprise, the very Quinn Foxworth shown on the website answered. His deep voice had that undertone of authority he'd once respected, until he'd found too many of them were as slimy as that rock he'd turned over.

And he was about as unhelpful as the website when it came to parting with information about this foundation he supposedly ran. At least, he was until Case cut to the chase with the crux of the situation.

"I've gathered from other sources that you have someone named Teague Johnson working for you."

"Have you," Foxworth said flatly, neither confirming nor denying.

"Was he in the service? The Marines, specifically?"

Case didn't think he mistook the slight note of wariness that came into the man's voice. He'd had enough practice in recognizing it, before. "What is it you're looking for, Mr. McMillan?"

He should have thought about how to condense this before he'd called. But he slogged ahead. "A man by that name from this area who was reportedly killed in action overseas, ten years ago. But I couldn't find anything in the public military death records that matched. And I came across the name in a blog post about your foundation. I know it's a long shot, but I figured it was worth a try."

"You have reason to believe the report of his death is an exaggeration?"

Case found himself smiling slightly at the old Mark Twain joke. "More hoping it was, I guess."

"You knew him?"

"Not me, no. I…encountered a woman last night, who also grew up around here, who had a brother with that name."

He knew he hadn't mistaken the bare second of silence before the man spoke again. Or the sudden tension, although masked, in his voice.

"You're saying you met a woman who says she had a brother named Teague Johnson, that she thinks is dead?"

"Yes."

"What's her name?"

He hesitated, but in the end went with his gut and decided to tell the man what he knew. This was the guy who'd helped take down a murderously corrupt politician, after all. One Case had personally loathed.

"Terri Jones. At least, that's what she's going by now."

"Terri."

"Yes."

"Jones, but you have doubts?"

"She kind of stumbled when she first said it. Then when I saw the name of Teague Johnson on some old letters she'd written, I wondered if maybe that's what she'd almost said."

"Letters? To a brother she thinks dead?"

"I get the feeling they were very close. She writes in a journal now, but the entries are still addressed to him."

Again a slight pause. "You're being very open with a guy you just called on the phone."

"I've had to judge people on less. And you do have a Teague Johnson working for you."

"You sound very certain, given I haven't confirmed that."

"You sort of did. You wouldn't have taken so long on a cold call if it wasn't true."

"Mr. McMillan, I think you'd better bring her to us."

Chapter Five

Terri was half-convinced maybe her brain truly had been scrambled last night. How else could this be happening? Maybe it wasn't really happening. Maybe she was unconscious, still lying in that alley, and this was all a product of a wishful imagination. Or maybe she was dying, maybe the robber really had shot her, and this was how her brain was making it bearable.

Maybe you're already dead, and this is heaven. With you getting all you've ever wanted, and delivered by a man who could surely be an angel, if you believed in the strong, brave, handsome type.

But everything felt too real, from the morning chill in the air as they'd left his place and walked to his truck, to the feel of her nails digging into her palms because her fists were clenched so tightly.

Teague, alive?

Impossible. She knew what she'd heard, that night that had put an end to life as she'd known it. That had cast her into a life without mooring, without a center, aimless and lost. The only good to come out of it was that she'd finally broken free of the cruel detachment and rigid doctrine that ran the house that had never really been a home for either of them.

I promise, sis, that as soon as you turn eighteen I'll get you out of there. You just have to hang on and be strong until then.

'She'd never forgotten the last words he'd ever spoken to her, in the last video call they'd had. She'd clung to those words just as she'd clung to the last time he'd promised her in person. He'd been her hope, her beacon in the darkness… before the news had come that had extinguished that hope and light forever.

For the first time Teague had broken a promise to her. And it had taken him dying to cause it.

Yet now, here she was, with a man cut from the same cloth, a man she'd only met last night, heading toward someplace she'd never been. Toward a beacon of hope she was afraid to even acknowledge, because she knew it couldn't be true. If someone else had told her they were doing what she was about to do, she would have thought them crazy, or worse, suicidal.

But they wouldn't have what Case McMillan had told her ringing in their ears.

It had been unsettling enough when he'd revealed he'd done a little investigating. But the rest…

Once more she internally stomped down on the hope that wanted to rise. One thing she'd learned in life was that hope was a wasted effort. She'd thought her capacity for it had died that night, but now, foolishly, it wanted to rise again. Even Case knew the truth of that, because his first words to her had been a warning.

Don't get your hopes up, but…

"Why did you do this? This…investigating?" she finally asked, giving up picking at the breakfast muffin he'd gotten for her to eat on the way. Another thoughtful gesture that she suspected he would never have done for himself. They were sitting in line for the next ferry across the sound, to where he'd told her they were going. The last time she'd been on one of the famous state ferries wasn't a pleasant memory, given she'd spent some time peering over the railing and wondering what it would feel like to drown, while her mother ranted on her topic of the moment.

He dodged the question by turning it back on her. "Why didn't you?"

She frowned. "Because I heard our parents after they got the news, saying he was dead. And that they were glad to be rid of him."

She bit her lip; she hadn't meant to let out that last part. And the shocked look he gave her made her regret it even more; she didn't like sharing her ugly parentage with strangers.

Except he didn't seem like a stranger. She wondered if this was what Teague had meant when he'd talked about how the bonds built quickly between his brothers in arms.

Belatedly it occurred to her to wonder if he was one of them. He'd been free to do this on a weekday, after all. And before he could say anything about what she'd let slip she asked, "What do you do now? Work, I mean?"

As a diversion, that went better than she'd expected. He let out a compressed, rather sour chuckle. "At the moment, nothing."

He did not seem like the kind of man who was content doing nothing. "But you used to be a cop?"

He gave her a sideways glance. Then, with a tinge of bitterness, he said, "I was."

"I gather you're not happy about the past tense?"

"Let's just say it wasn't voluntary."

Her stomach knotted. Had he been crooked? She couldn't imagine it, but then chastised herself for thinking she knew a man she'd met all of ten hours ago. Had he killed someone, the wrong someone? She couldn't picture that, either. Finally she just asked.

"What happened?"

She didn't think he was going to answer, and she opened her mouth to apologize for prying, but in that moment he did answer.

"I arrested a guy with too many friends in high places."

Now that didn't surprise her at all. "And those friends made you pay." He gave her a sideways glance again, as if he was surprised. She shrugged. "I came from a family of influence peddlers. I know how nasty they are."

"You…and your brother."

"Yes. He escaped by joining the military, much to their horror and dismay. And he was going to rescue me, as soon I was legally old enough to leave."

"Rescue? Sounds like the situation was pretty dire."

"What else would you call it when people nearly do a dance of delight when they find out their only son is dead, because his choice to serve his country went against their own opinions?"

The cars ahead of them finally began to move as the loading began, but Case didn't look away from her as he said, "I have a list of things I'd call it, none of them fit for polite company."

For some reason that struck her funny. "Polite?" she asked, scanning the cab of the pickup as if looking for another passenger.

He chuckled, and the one-sided smile that accompanied the light, amused sound did strange things to her insides. She wondered what he'd look like if he ever grinned. Or laughed. Just her imaginings took her breath away.

Fortunately, before she had to think of something to say, it was their turn to move ahead and onto the big white-and-green ferryboat and he had to look away. She said no when he asked if she wanted to get out of the car once the ferry was underway. She said it was the cold, but in truth she was afraid. Afraid to get out of the car, as if that would mean this would all vanish, including the very, very thin chance that there was anything to this, this possibility that Teague...

She couldn't even finish the thought. She had to assume this was a wild goose chase. Case had been right about that warning not to get her hopes up, because she wasn't sure she could deal with the aftermath when it was all proven to be a mistake.

"If this turns out to be nothing, are you going to be all right?"

Startled, her gaze shot from the spot on the truck's dash she'd been staring at to his face. She supposed when he'd been a cop he'd learned to assess people and that on occasion his life had depended on it.

"I'm trying not to let the idea take root," she said.

He nodded. "Good plan. Until you know for sure."

She told herself she already knew for sure, but she didn't say it. The man was being nice enough—more than nice, he was going way out of his way—already, it would not be right on her part to say she thought this was a waste of time and effort that would accomplish nothing but drag the old pain back to the surface.

She picked again at the muffin, even taking a bite or two this time. It was good, she just wasn't hungry. Her stomach was churning a bit, with nerves, anticipation, and fear all rolled into one. She stared out the window at the water, at the container ship heading south over there, the small fishing boat hugging the shoreline there, and the sailboat, under power not sail on this calm morning, heading north. As she often did, she found herself making up stories for each, who they were, what they were doing or carrying, and what they would go home to when they were done.

Or wondering if they had a home to go to. She'd spent

enough time without one herself to still think about what it had been like.

They were nearly across the sound before he spoke again, this time very gently, "Will you tell me why you were so desperate to avoid the police?"

The question didn't just startle her out of her memories, it scared her—was he thinking he should dump her on the cops?—which sharpened her voice. "Why? Thinking I could be your ticket back in?"

He drew back sharply. His brow furrowed deeply, and she knew her wisecracking response had been far off the mark. "What are you talking about?"

She drew in a long, deep breath and let it out slowly. "Sorry. Teague always said when I got scared I turned into a smartass."

His index finger tapped the steering wheel lightly. "And me asking that question scared you?" She shrugged. "I'm not a cop anymore," he reminded her.

"My brother used to say once a Marine, always a Marine. I figured that sort of held for cops, too."

He let out an odd sort of compressed breath. "So did I, once."

Something in his voice, some pain that seemed an echo of her own, made her answer. "When I first took off, after…that night I heard our parents practically rejoicing that Teague was dead, I had a rough couple of years, until I got my feet under me. I…stole some clothes from a donation bin. And some food from…a store like the one last night. And I… got caught. The police were called. I got away before they arrived, but there were video cameras, so they could have found me."

He was giving her that assessing look again. "And after that?"

"I spent my last money on a bus ticket out of here. When

I felt far enough away, I settled. Got my GED. Eventually got a job. Didn't pay much at first, but a room came with it. And I stayed, worked my way up. Tried to live in a way that would have made my brother proud."

"Sounds like you did."

That made her brave enough to say, "I swear, I never stole anything again." Somehow having him believe that seemed crucial.

"Okay."

"You believe me?" Surely it couldn't be that easy?

His mouth twisted upward at one corner. "One of the things about not being a cop anymore is I don't have to be suspicious all the time, or assume everyone is lying to me."

Her curiosity sparked. "But what if they are?"

He shrugged, turning his head to look up front, watching the deckhands work as they docked. "Then the only one who gets hurt is me."

As they drove off the ferry she stared at him, at his profile, wondering what kind of mindset it took, what mentality to prefer being hurt yourself rather than perhaps misjudging and having others be hurt. There truly was a protector mentality, she'd known that from her brother. She just hadn't encountered it in many others. But this man had it, she had no doubt. Perhaps that was what she'd recognized, why she'd trusted him almost instantly last night.

That realization threatened to turn her thoughts down the path she was trying to avoid, the path of hope that it was possibly true, that her brother was alive. So hastily, as he adroitly anticipated the offloading lanes narrowing from two to one, she said, "You seem to know your way around here."

He didn't look at her, but kept his eyes on the stream of cars ahead and behind as the ferry continued to unload. "I like it over here. Been thinking about moving."

She looked around at the few blocks of little town they

were passing through, found it quaint and as appealing as its name, Redwood Cove. It felt like a different world. No wonder the locals here called the city just "the other side."

"It's nice," she said. "Seems more peaceful already."

"I think it is. But then, compared to the city…"

"Anything is?"

"Pretty much."

Another silence as they drove. Odd, silence didn't usually bother her, but riding with him in a confined space made her nervous. Nervous in ways she didn't recognize.

Once they were out of the little town, they made a turn onto a smaller road that headed away from civilization, or so it seemed. She saw unmarked driveways, and little side roads with no signs to indicate a name; apparently if you didn't know right where you were going out here, you were on your own.

Case seemed to know. They'd been on the small road a few minutes when she noticed him glance down at the dash and start to slow. The odometer, she guessed. This Foxworth person must have given him pretty exact directions.

He made a right turn onto an unlabeled gravel drive which wound its way through thick evergreens.

"This is their office?" she asked, noticing the lack of any kind of signage.

"Headquarters, he said. And it's about as obvious as their online presence." He'd told her they were beyond subtle, that he'd found more people talking about them than they talked about themselves.

"And they're here on a Sunday?"

"He said they would be."

After the second curve she caught a bit of a shine from the morning sun striking through the trees. Not a reflection exactly, more of a…shinier shade of the same green.

When they rounded the last turn into a wider gravel parking area, she realized the sun had been hitting the big green three-story building; the siding had a bit of a sheen to it that had caught the light. Farther on was a second building, only a single story but a tall one, that looked like storage or a huge garage or maybe both. But what held her gaze rested between the two structures. A large square of concrete with markings painted on it, and sitting on it…a helicopter.

She glanced at Case, who was staring at the helicopter as well.

"Who are these people?" she asked.

"Not what I expected," he admitted.

He parked near what appeared to be the front entry, a large wooden door painted the same green as the walls. She looked toward the other side of the building and saw a huge open space, sprinkled with colorful flowers, even some lingering, late-season daffodils. On the far side the trees began again, tall evergreens, maples, and she thought she even saw one of her favorites, a red-barked madrone. She'd missed these trees more than she'd ever realized until she'd come back.

Case released his seat belt and turned to look at her.

"You ready for this?"

"I won't be crushed, if that's what you mean. I fully expect this to be just a coincidence of names."

He nodded, then opened the driver's door. For all her bravado in the words, she sat still for a moment, steadying her nerves. And then he was there, opening her door for her. She looked at him with some surprise at the gentlemanly gesture, but couldn't help the smile that curved her mouth.

Before her feet hit the ground a noise came from the building. She looked just as the big door swung open.

And then she saw the dog. She froze, staring. Fairly large, a black-and-reddish-brown combination.

Head down and tail up, it headed right for them at a dead run.

Chapter Six

Case watched the dog, ready, but not particularly concerned. He'd learned a lot about canine body language, both from animals he'd encountered on the job and the police K9s he'd worked with, and this one just seemed alert and maybe a little excited at a visitor. A glance at Terri told him she was a little more wary, but he didn't get a fear vibe from her.

And then the dog skidded to a halt about a yard away. He glanced at Case, just long enough for him to register the intensity of the animal's dark eyes, which caught some of the gold of the sun's rays. But then he zeroed in on Terri, intently, looking as if she was some creature he'd never encountered before.

I hear ya, dog.

And then, oddly, the dog sat, right where he was, still staring at Terri. His head was cocked slightly sideways as he studied her. If a dog could look puzzled, this one did. He almost looked as if he'd thought he knew the visitor, but once he'd gotten closer realized he didn't.

The door into the big building opened again, and a couple stepped out. The man was about Case's own height of six feet, powerful looking, and had that air of easy confidence Case knew meant he could handle himself. The woman beside him was about a half a foot shorter, trim and graceful, with hair that reflected the morning sun and lit up with shades of red and gold.

But the thing he noticed most was how they moved together, as if an unbreakable unit. Two people meant to be, as if together they were greater than the sum of the two individuals. It was the kind of connection he'd hoped to find someday, thought he'd had with Jill, but now had pretty much decided it wasn't in the cards for him, not anymore.

As they started toward them Case could see that the man was assessing them both. Or rather all three of them, since he seemed to be noting the dog—his dog?—as well, and how he was staring at Terri. The woman, on the other hand, seemed to be focused on Terri, and the closer she got the more her eyes widened. In…recognition? Did she look like her brother, and that was what the woman was seeing? Could this really be more than just a shot in the dark?

And then the dog moved, walking over to Terri, nuzzling her hand gently. In what seemed to be an instinctive reaction, she put that hand on the dog's head. And suddenly Terri was smiling, her hand moving now as she stroked the animal's fur. It was such an instantaneous change, as if touching the dog—or more accurately the dog touching her—had wrought some sort of inner shift in her, calming her.

"Hi, there," she said, bending slightly toward the animal, and looking into its eyes. She was smiling now, a lovely, genuine smile, as if at least for the moment the trauma of last night was forgotten.

Nice work, dog.

"Quinn Foxworth," the man said, "and this is my wife, Hayley."

"Case McMillan," he said, more to the woman since the man knew this from their phone conversation.

Terri hadn't spoken yet, she seemed too enraptured by the dog. But then the animal did another odd thing. He turned around, sat practically on Terri's feet, and looked up at his owners. Stared at them really, with an intense expression he could only liken to the police K9s he'd known.

"Got it, boy," Quinn said to the dog. And then, with a glance at Case before he went back to Terri, who had straightened now, he added, "That is Cutter."

Her smile held as she faced the two Foxworths. "He's a sweetheart."

"Among other things," Quinn said, his tone dry, but holding a very obvious respect for his canine companion.

"I think he knows," Hayley Foxworth said softly, her eyes warm and welcoming. "That you're connected to Teague, I mean."

And Case once again wondered if this could all be true, if Terri looked so much like her brother that she was immediately recognizable to those who knew him. Wondered if indeed she was going to get her miracle, and he was still alive.

Then he saw Quinn very gently touch his wife's arm before he said to them, "Come on inside. We have some talking to do."

The moment they started toward the building the dog raced ahead. Case watched with amusement as he raised up on his hind legs and batted at the large square button beside the door and it swung open.

"Handy," he said.

Quinn looked at him as they walked. "You have no idea." He sounded equal parts amused and proud, but with a touch of as close to amazement as Case guessed the man ever got.

They stepped into an entry clearly designed for the northwest, a tile floor complete with a drain beneath a rack for coats and jackets and boots. There was also a small basket of clean towels, handy for those times when you got caught without a hat or hood.

The rest of the interior was a surprise. He'd expected an

office sort of environment, but instead it was a welcoming open space that could be the great room of any home. The gas fireplace on one wall was turned on, casting a nice warmth into the room and the seating area around it. Beyond that was a compact but efficient-looking kitchen. A stairway went up along the back wall, and in the corner to the right of that were a couple of interior doors, one closed, one open and apparently leading to a bathroom.

"Coffee's on," Quinn said as Hayley led them to the area in front of the fireplace where there were armchairs, a long couch and a large square coffee table that held an open laptop computer and a couple remote controls. The blue-and-green area rug beneath the furniture added color and personality to the spot, finishing off the homelike air.

"Fair warning though," Hayley added with a smile, "he made it, so it's a bit strong."

"Sounds just right," Case said, barely managing not to rub at his gritty eyes.

"No, thank you," Terri said. "I'm too wound up already."

"Of course," Hayley said understandingly. "Quinn, if you'll get Case a mug, then we'll get started."

"Started?" Terri asked, stopping the pacing she'd begun, her every step watched alertly by the dog, who was sitting nearly in her path.

"How do you like it?" Quinn asked.

"Straight," Case said, and gratefully accepted the mug of coffee Quinn quickly poured.

"Shall we sit down?" Hayley suggested gently.

"I don't think I can," Terri said, turning to face Hayley. "I have to know. Is it true? Is it really…is he…"

She stopped, biting her lip so fiercely Case thought it was a wonder she didn't start bleeding. Instinctively he went to her, gently took her arm. She resisted for a moment, but then the dog nudged her knee with his nose, and she gave in. He felt a shiver go through her, so he led her to the end of the couch closest to the fire. She sank down on it, seeming to accept the idea she didn't have the strength to stay on her feet.

To his surprise the dog—Cutter, he remembered—nudged his knee in turn, as if urging him to sit down beside her. And it occurred to him that, despite his rather intense curiosity to find out, she might prefer to have this discussion in private. So instead he crouched down in front of her, and she met his gaze.

"I can leave, if you'd rather."

"Leave?" She sounded startled enough that it gave him an unexpected jab of pleasure.

"This is very personal. And could be…life-changing."

She reached out then, and took his hand. The jab of pleasure was harder this time. "Stay. If it wasn't for you, if you hadn't been there last night, I wouldn't have a life to change."

Case knew he hadn't imagined the sudden shift in the tenor of the room. Hayley Foxworth's gaze had shifted to him, and her husband was looking at him even more assessingly. They hadn't gotten into exactly how he'd encountered Terri last night.

Terri seemed to sense it too, because she looked at Quinn. "He saved my life last night. He took care of me, after, even though I'm a complete stranger to him. And he's the one who searched you out. If there's…" She swallowed visibly, then went on. "If there's anything to this, he's earned the right to hear it."

Quinn nodded, but he was looking at Case, as if he'd had a speculation confirmed. "Thought I'd judged you correctly," he said, in a tone that matched Case's guess on his thoughts.

"Right place, right time," he said with a shrug.

"And right man," Hayley said quietly. He wasn't able to shrug off the undeniable approval in the woman's tone, and in the warmth of her smile, quite so easily.

And Terri was still holding his hand. So when Cutter nudged him again, he sat down beside her. However this turned out, she might need the moral support. And the grateful look she gave him made him certain it was the right decision, even if the sensation that went through him at the close contact was unsettling.

"Let's look at what we've got here," Quinn said briskly. "First, a little honesty. Is Jones your real name?"

She hesitated. Looked at Case. He couldn't stop himself; he reached out and touched her cheek with the back of his fingers. "You have to decide. From everything I've seen, they do good things, help people."

"Then why can't they be honest first?" she asked, with a flash of what he guessed would be her normal spirit had she not been so drained over the last twelve hours.

"Fair point," he said, looking at Quinn.

"Yes," the man agreed, surprising him. "But we also have people to protect. Sometimes in helping out the little guy, we tick off some big guys."

Case let out a sharp, short laugh. "Been there, done that."

Quinn gave him a steady look, then turned back to Terri. "It's your call."

Then Hayley, in that same quiet, gentle tone, said "It's Johnson, isn't it? Your true last name."

Terri looked at the other woman. Still hesitated. Case glanced at Quinn, half expecting him to show some upset with the way his wife had stepped in. There was nothing of the sort. He was ceding control to her easily, with that kind of faith and trust he'd only ever seen with his own parents.

"I can see him in you," Hayley said, even more quietly.

And then Cutter, who'd been sitting on Terri's other side, watching with a rather startling focus, leaned against her and put his head down on her knee. She lifted a hand to pet him, and again she seemed to change, not to relax exactly, but to lose some of that high-pitched tension.

And it tilted the scale. "Yes," Terri said suddenly. "It's Johnson. My brother's name was Teague."

"Any objection to a DNA test?" Quinn asked, rather casually. "For Teague's sake?"

"Of course not."

"So why the name change?"

It came pouring out then, the full story he hadn't yet heard but had sensed, of a brave, loving brother who had been an anchor, sanity in a family devoid of the kind of love Case had always known. A brother who died serving his country, and the icily cold parents who hadn't grieved but had welcomed his death. And of the little sister who had adored him, idolized him and upon overhearing their relief at being finally rid of him hadn't been able to get away from them fast enough.

At that point Terri had gotten to her feet and begun to pace, as if she simply had to move. He thought he understood. He felt a churning sort of nausea in his gut. Wished he'd not downed half that mug of coffee in a rush. He wondered if her parents were still alive, because he'd like to hunt them down and…and…he wasn't sure what. Even if this was a dead end, even if their Teague wasn't her Teague, he wanted to find those monsters and make them face their own evil.

"So you've been on your own since then?" Quinn asked, much more gently than he'd spoken before, and Case knew the horrible story had gotten to him as well.

She nodded, wiping at her eyes, at the tears that had welled up as she spoke of the one person in her life who had truly loved her, and the cold dismissal of his death by the ones who should have been grieving the most.

"I couldn't go back to them. Ever. I know it's awful to hate your own parents, but I do. I loathe them, for who they are, for how they made us feel. They should never have had us—they should never have had children at all."

"And yet," Hayley, whose eyes were suspiciously bright, said, "we're glad they did." Case saw her glance at her husband. Quinn nodded, and picked up one of the remotes from the coffee table as his wife went on. "We're glad they did because if they hadn't, we wouldn't have one of our absolutely best people."

The screen above the fireplace came to life. He and Terri reflexively looked at it. He heard her suck in a gasping breath as an image appeared. It was a man, smiling, strong looking, confident, with short hair, masculine jaw, broad shoulders, and light blue eyes.

Terri's eyes. Same color, same shape. Terri's hair, the exact same sandy brown shade. And the smile, captured in a light-hearted moment, was so very like the smile Terri had worn when she had first touched Cutter.

He looked from the image on the screen to Terri's face. Tears were pouring over her cheeks now, unheeded as she stared at the picture. The picture that so resembled her.

The picture of the alive and well brother she'd mourned for a decade.

Chapter Seven

"I don't understand."

Terri barely managed to get the words out. Her knees had given out first, then her entire body, and only Case's strong arms catching her had enabled her to sit down rather than fall. She felt almost numb, and her brain seemed to have shorted out.

"When he first came to work for us, Teague told me there'd been a mix-up, on his last deployment. A last-minute change in the lineup, as it were, so the initial reports listed him as KIA. It was corrected very soon after, but sadly not before your parents had been notified." Quinn's mouth twisted. "Sadly for you, I mean. Not them."

She seized on his last words, because at least they made sense to her. "They were *glad*." She couldn't help the bitterness in her voice, even after all this time. "I couldn't spend another day there. I didn't care if I died, too—I had to get away from them. Whenever I hear the word evil, it's them I think of."

Hayley spoke then, her voice still that soothing, kind thing. "Just her, now. Your father's gone, Terri."

"He's dead?" She wanted to shout, but managed to say a satisfied, "Good." Then, with disgust, she added, "It figures she'd still be alive. She's just too mean to die. Ice-cold, self-centered and self-righteous. Our father just took it. And took it, he never really fought her." She drew in a deep breath. "He didn't used to be that way. When I was little, I remember him, smiling, laughing, playing with us…but she ate that out of him like acid."

"Teague told us he nearly drank himself to death, a couple of years after you left. He doesn't have any contact with your mother anymore."

A sudden punch of awareness hit her, as if on some level her brain had still been functioning, processing. And had finally arrived. Teague *doesn't* have any contact…

He was alive.

Her brother was alive.

She looked back to the image on the screen. He didn't look that much different from when she'd last seen him, same haircut, same broad shoulders she'd leaned on so often. But his eyes…they were still that same blue she'd shared with him, a gift from grandparents they'd never known. As a kid she'd been happy their eyes were different from their parents, because the less she was like them the better.

But his eyes in this photograph were touched with something else, the same sort of thing she saw in Case's eyes, not quite sadness, just the look of having seen too much.

But he was alive.

The image blurred as tears began again, and this time she didn't try to wipe them away. And without thinking, she sought out Case's warmth beside her. And when she leaned against him, he put a strong arm around her without question.

"He's really alive," she whispered. Her fingers crept down to the delicate bracelet around her wrist, the one Teague had given her, with a promise to add a charm to it every year. The one thing she'd never even considered selling or pawning, because she would die before she gave it up.

"He is," Quinn said.

"And he never stopped looking for you, Terri. Never stopped thinking about you," Hayley added.

"I...ran pretty far. But I never, ever stopped thinking about him, either." Case tightened his arm slightly, giving her a sort of one-armed hug. It surprised her, how much strength that simple gesture gave her. And her voice was steadier when she finally asked, "Where is he?"

The Foxworths exchanged glances. Fear suddenly shot through her. They had only said he was alive, not that he was alive and well. The man in that picture looked both, but... had he been hurt? Wounded? Had he come home but in a wheelchair or something?

As if he'd sensed her fear, Case's arm tightened around her again. And it calmed her, and she knew she didn't care if he'd come home in one piece, as long as he was home and alive. "It's all right. As long as he's alive, I can take anything else."

"He's fine," Quinn assured her, as if he'd guessed where her mind had gone.

"Better than fine," Hayley said with a smile. "He's on his honeymoon."

Her eyes widened. "He got married?"

"He did." Hayley's expression was warmly sympathetic now. "I'm sorry, you just missed it. The wedding was here, in the meadow, last week. And I assure you, he and Laney are crazy about each other."

At the mention of that new name, Cutter's head came up and he gave a happy yip. She realized that she'd been stroking the dog's soft fur this entire time. Between Case holding her on one side and the dog's seeming knack for comfort on the other, she was a lot steadier than she might have been.

"Yeah, dog," Quinn said wryly, "we know. It was all your doing."

Terri shifted her gaze to him; he did not seem a man given to flights of fancy. "It was?"

Hayley laughed. "Quinn hates to admit it, but yes, it was. Laney's a groomer, and that guy—" she nodded at the dog "—managed to get himself filthy every other day for...well, as long as it took."

"And you managing to be too busy to pick him up every time and making Teague go had nothing to do with it," Quinn said blandly.

"I help where I can," Hayley said blithely. She looked back at Terri, and the earnestness in her voice was utterly sincere. "They were meant to be, Terri. I promise you. And...he made a toast to you, at the wedding. That wherever you were, he loved you, and that he'd never give up looking."

That quickly had her eyes swimming again.

"And Laney corrected him," Quinn said, his brusque voice softer again. "Said that *they* would never stop looking."

The tears kept flowing and Case's arm remained tightened around her in support.

"Sounds like he's still the brother you remember," he said to her softly.

"Teague would never change. He's too strong." She couldn't describe the joy it gave her to refer to him in the present tense.

"He is that," Quinn agreed, and even though she'd just met the man, Terri knew that was quite an accolade.

"But you," Hayley said, sounding delighted, "are going to turn him to mush. What a wedding present you're going to be!"

Finally coming out of the stunned haze, her brain kicked into gear. "When? Where did they go?"

"They went to San Diego, and they're due back next Sunday," Hayley said. She gave her husband a sideways glance. "And you're going to revoke that permission to take extra time if they want it, and tell him he has to come right back on schedule."

Quinn lifted a brow at her. "And I suppose I'm not going to tell him why?"

"Don't you want to see his face when he sees her for the first time and realizes?"

Quinn's mouth quirked into a crooked grin. "Indeed I do."

They loved him, Terri realized. These Foxworths loved her brother, and were delighting in the thought of a coming reunion. Which only confirmed what they'd said, Teague had never forgotten about her.

"So where have you been?" Hayley asked. "Since you escaped, I mean."

Terri liked that she put it that way. And she felt safe in answering. "A lot of places. Oregon, to start, but it was too close so I didn't stay long. Then Colorado, but I didn't last long there. First place I stayed was Iowa. I got my GED there, and a couple of different office jobs. I ended up in a little town called Boone, working for an air-conditioning contractor. He was a really nice guy. His wife ran the office. I helped her. His sons worked with him. It was a family business. A real, normal family." And it had been her first taste of that.

"That must have been a nice change for you," Quinn said.

"It was. I stayed until he retired last month."

"And that's when you decided to come back here?" Case asked.

"Yes. He gave me a lovely bonus when he sold the business, enough to hold me for a while. I thought I was strong enough now. I wanted to find out where Teague was buried—" It hit her then, belatedly. Her eyes widened, and remorse flooded her. "If I'd come back sooner, if I hadn't been such a coward, afraid to face them again—"

"Whoa," Case said, touching her cheek in that sweet way he had before. "Don't go there. You didn't know, so why would you have? Not like you have good memories of the place. Or that they deserved to ever see you again."

"But if I had—"

"Living with would haves, could haves and should haves will drive you crazy," Case said, with a certainty that told her he had some familiarity with the idea. "Just savor the now. You got your biggest wish, Terri. Grab it and hold on."

She looked straight at him, and she had not just a feeling, but more of a certainty that he knew exactly how it felt to be the one who didn't get that big wish, and to live with those would, could and should haves. It was strange; he now knew so much about her, but she knew so little about him. Except what really matters. That he's a good, solid man, just like Teague was.

Like Teague *is*!

Joy flooded her and she knew Case was right. She needed to grab it and hold on, and revel in the fact that the biggest, most impossible wish of her life had actually come true.

Chapter Eight

Hayley Foxworth seemed bent on making sure Terri celebrated. She ordered a couple of huge pizzas, some luscious desserts from a local bakery, and brought out a bottle of champagne.

Her eyes a bit reddened now from crying, Terri thanked the Foxworths, saying to them she'd never known this kind of welcome before.

"We're your family now," Hayley said firmly.

"Better them than those evil misfits," Case muttered. And that got him a smile. But then what Hayley had said about family dug at him. He had no place here, really. He'd found these people, yes, and gotten her here, but now his part was over. He should just quietly slip out and leave her to it, to enjoy finally finding what she'd been deprived of in her life.

He set his champagne glass down on the counter. He could drive, he'd only had a couple of swallows, and it took a heck of a lot more to put a guy his size under. He knew that, because he'd tried, in the beginning, only to find no amount of alcohol helped.

"I'll leave you to enjoy it," he said, the gruffness of his voice surprising him almost as much as the fact that Cutter, suddenly on his feet again, was standing between him and the door, blocking him. Those intense, gold-flecked eyes were fastened on him, and it was surprisingly disconcerting.

Terri quickly stepped up to face him. "No, don't, please."

"You have a lot to catch up on, questions only they can answer, and you don't need me for that."

Cutter made a low sound, half whine, half growl, that sounded oddly like a protest.

Terri spoke hurriedly. "If you want to go, of course, you've done so much already. But please, please don't feel you should go, or that I don't want you to stay." She reached out and put a hand on his chest. His heart kicked, and he could only hope she hadn't felt it. "I meant what I said before—I wouldn't be here if not for you."

"I'd like to hear that part of the story," Quinn said. "Stay."

It wasn't an order, because the man had no authority over him. But it was spoken by someone clearly used to giving orders. And no doubt having them promptly obeyed.

Case eyed him a little warily. "Police or military?"

Quinn smiled. "Army."

"Army Ranger," Hayley added, proudly.

Case sighed. "Should have known."

Quinn gave him a considering look. "And you?"

He supposed he should be grateful the man didn't recognize his name. "Police. Once."

Case was glad Quinn didn't pursue it, but merely asked, "So how did you two connect?"

"Yes," Hayley added. "Sit back down and tell us. It has to be an interesting story."

Case glanced at Terri, who looked cautious once more. Cutter shifted again, now leaning against Terri's leg until she reached out and stroked his head. And again Case could see some of the tension fade from her expression.

"Sit with me," she said to him, and took the same spot on the couch as before. Case thought about taking a seat closer to the door—he still wasn't convinced he shouldn't leave—but the dog stared up at him still, and it suddenly didn't seem worth fighting. So he sat.

Terri looked at Case, smiled slightly and nodded, giving him the go-ahead to tell the story. Still, he kept his answer as vague as possible. "I happened along last night as she was having a little trouble with a guy in an alley behind a convenience store over in the city."

"He had a gun and would have killed me," Terri said bluntly. "Case saved my life."

"I see," Quinn said, as if he saw a lot more than the simple words declared.

"And then he took care of me," Terri went on. "I hit my head when the guy pushed me away and ran, and Case took me home with him and checked on me every hour until morning."

"And found us," Hayley said, studying Case with a knowing smile that hinted she'd expected no less. Which was odd, since she'd only just met him. And then there was the way their dog was looking at him as Terri petted him. That steady, intense gaze was almost unnerving.

"Rabbit hole of the internet," he said, shrugging it off.

"But you made the effort. And you helped a stranger in trouble," Hayley said.

"Who turned out to be someone very, very important to Foxworth," Quinn added. "We owe you."

Case shook his head. "I just did what—"

"What very few people would have done," Hayley said, cutting off his protest. "So if you ever need help we can give, you have it."

He didn't know what to say, so merely shrugged. There was nothing they or anyone else could do for him. His law enforcement career was over, and he should probably be glad about that, the way things were going. But he wasn't. Because he hadn't left on his own terms. He'd been forced out, by a wave of corruption and purchased influence.

Quinn looked steadily at Terri for a moment, then asked, "Did you know the man in the alley?"

She shook her head sharply, as if just the memory made her shiver. And rightfully so, she had come close to dying next to that trash can. "No. I just went into the store for a few minutes, and then he came in and—"

She stopped abruptly, her eyes darting away from Quinn, and Case realized she'd almost told them what had really happened last night. It took more determination than he ever would have expected for him to leave it to her to tell the whole story or not.

It's not your job anymore.

His jaw tightened as he gritted his teeth in the effort to leave it alone. Quinn's assessing gaze shifted from Terri to him, then back.

"There's something you should know about Foxworth, Terri," he said. "We help people who have been wronged, either by powerful people or by circumstance. People who through no fault of their own have landed in a tough spot and tried to battle their way out, but the forces against them are too powerful. People who are in the right but don't have the resources we do to fight back."

Case remembered the description on the website of how the Foxworth Foundation had begun. And he felt a burst of admiration for how Quinn and his sister had taken the tragedy that had orphaned them and built it into an operation capable of finding justice for innocent victims at very high levels. Case had been in the midst of his own career chaos at the time, but he still remembered his amazement that someone had actually taken down that crooked, murderous governor.

Terri was staring at Quinn, but when Hayley spoke quietly she shifted her gaze. "And Foxworth takes care of its own, Terri. You're part of this family now, because Teague is one of us. Whatever it is, you have us in your corner. And we have a lot of resources, things that—" she gave Case a glance with those bright green eyes "—official organizations don't have."

"I… I don't know…"

"I know it's hard to trust strangers, so don't," Hayley said. "Trust your brother. Trust his judgment. He's been with us, heart and soul, for years now."

Cutter gave a low whine and nudged Terri's hand with his nose. Almost like he was adding his own "Trust us," To the chorus. Or more likely he just sensed her distress and was trying to ease it, as he had before. Dogs were good that way.

"Let us help," Quinn said, in a voice gentler than Case would have thought the man could manage. "Whatever it is."

With that the Foxworths tactfully withdrew to the kitchen, giving Terri time and space to decide. Case watched her, saw her brow furrow as she tried to decide. He stayed silent; this wasn't his business. But then, to his surprise, she turned to look at him, the question clear in her eyes and expression.

Should I trust them?

She barely knew him but was asking for his advice? He'd already told her everything he knew about Foxworth. So she had to be wanting his opinion of the Foxworths themselves. Was she implying she trusted his judgment, even though they'd just met them?

Hell, she only met you last night…

He understood then, she felt she owed him for stepping up last night in that alley. It was only natural to trust someone you believed had saved your life, but for all she knew he was a lousy judge of people. He wasn't sure that wouldn't be right, given how long it had taken him to realize how deep the rot had gone behind the badge he'd once worn with such pride.

But now she studied him like he held all the answers she needed.

"I've already told you all I know about them," he finally said. "But the only bad things I saw about them have come from people or institutions they've stopped or beaten. And all the praise comes from...just ordinary folks. The ones who say they had nowhere else to turn."

"So you think I should trust them?"

He'd given advice to strangers before, when asked, when he was wearing the badge. Part of the job. But he'd always been careful not to tell them what to do, just tried to help them see the best path for their situation. So why was he finding this so hard?

Because she doesn't feel like a stranger, even though she should?

In the end, he went with his gut. "I think," he said slowly, "you should do what she—" he nodded at Hayley "—said. Trust your brother."

"Teague," Terri whispered. He could tell by the wonder and the tiny shake in her voice that she still wasn't used to saying it about someone who was alive.

He felt a slight qualm when she clearly took his words to heart, and proceeded to pour out her entire story to the Foxworths. But he quashed it, because everything he'd heard about her brother so far made him believe in what he'd said. And if a man like Teague Johnson believed in Foxworth that much, then he wasn't going to try and stop the man's sister from following his lead. Especially when her joy was overflowing, so much that he couldn't stop his own smile. Seeing this change from the terrified woman last night was worth whatever he'd done to help.

And so, unless and until proven otherwise, Foxworth had his trust, too.

Chapter Nine

Terri hadn't smiled this much in years. Maybe ever. Her cheeks hurt, but she didn't care. Even the Foxworth dog seemed to realize she didn't need his comfort anymore. It was truly strange, though, how simply petting the animal gave her reassurance. He provided a sense of ease she'd never known.

Sort of like how she'd felt safe with Case, safer than she had in the ten years since she'd left her old life, and her childhood, behind.

She listened with rapt attention as Hayley told the story of how Teague and Laney had met, how the groomer's concern over her best friend's situation had led them to a case that was worse than Laney had even feared. But thanks to her unfailing loyalty, Teague's determination and Foxworth help, it had all been resolved.

And her brother had found the love of his life.

She wiped at her eyes again, thinking she hadn't cried this much since the first morning after she'd run, when it had finally and inescapably hit her that she'd lost her only champion in life.

He's alive!

Cutter, from where he'd curled up on the bed beside the fire, suddenly sat up and let out a bark—or rather an odd, almost musical combination of barks. He was looking toward the back of the room, at a door that apparently led to the back meadow she had seen when they'd arrived, and where Hayley had mentioned Teague's—and in fact, their own—wedding had taken place.

"And I think we'll be having another one soon," Hayley had said. "You'll meet Liam and Ria later, I'm sure."

But now Hayley just smiled, and Quinn remarked, "Rafe must have gotten curious."

"Or restless," Hayley said.

"Another Foxworth guy?" Case asked.

"The scariest one," Hayley said, but so cheerfully Terri thought she must be joking.

But when the back door opened and dark-haired man stepped in, she wasn't so sure. He was as tall as Case, but leaner. Rangier. And where Case's eyes were that intriguing mix of gold and green, this man's were the color of the Northwest sky on a stormy day. But they both had the sort of shadows that only a rough life could give a person. The kind of shadows Teague had begun to develop, after his first deployment. Case's had no doubt come from his days as a police officer. And she had an odd sense of security, knowing she was in the company of people who would see to whatever needed to be done.

Cutter went over and greeted the man happily, tail wagging. Terri heard him say "Hey, buddy," softly as he bent to stroke the dog's head. He continued into the main room. She saw him nod at the Foxworths. He turned, his brows lowering a fraction when he saw Teague's photo on the screen. She thought she saw something change again in his expression when he saw Case. As if he was assessing somehow. *Friend or foe?* The phrase popped into her head, perhaps sillily.

But then those stormy gray eyes locked on to her. She had only a split second to realize she would not want to ever be on the wrong side of this man before those eyes widened. And she couldn't doubt that it was in recognition.

The newcomer's head snapped back around to stare at Quinn who smiled. "Rafe Crawford, meet Case McMillan." His voice went from brisk to a softer tone that matched the smile. "And yes. At last."

Rafe looked back at her. And said, in a shocked tone she suspected was beyond rare for him, "Terri? Teague's Terri?"

She glanced at the image on the screen, her smile widening once more, because she couldn't seem to do anything else. Then she looked back at the man named Rafe. "Yes," she said simply.

He muttered something inaudible. Then, "How did you end up here?"

Quinn gave him the bare bones of what had happened last night, much more concisely than she'd been able to. He ended with, "The bottom line is that she's thought all these years that Teague was dead. KIA."

Rafe drew back slightly. Looked at her, with a new gentleness in his fierce gaze. "Does Teague know yet?"

"Which brings us to the big question of the day," Hayley said, walking over to sit in the chair opposite Terri. "I know we joked about it before, but it's really your decision to make, Terri. Do you want us to contact him now, tell him? Or wait until you're face to face?"

Just the thought of being face to face with her living, breathing childhood hero gave her such a jolt of happiness it nearly made her shudder under its force. She had to calm herself, to think.

"Wait," she finally said, although it was difficult. "It will be hard for me, but I don't want to take any attention away from his honeymoon. And I don't want to start out with... his wife upset with me."

His wife. Teague's wife. Living, breathing Teague's wife.

"Laney would understand," Hayley assured her. "She knows what you mean to him."

"I have to admit I wasn't joking," Quinn put in, "I'd like to see his face the first time he sees you. It takes a lot to put him off his stride, but I'm guessing walking in on you unexpectedly would do it."

"It'll put him on the floor," Rafe said, and he sounded like he'd enjoy the sight as well.

Teague had good friends here. The kind of friends he deserved. The kind that were as close, or in their case even closer than family.

"I'm so glad he found you," she said, although it was hard to get the words out past the tightness in her throat.

"We're the lucky ones," Hayley said. "He's not only one of our best people, he's a good friend."

"Liam know yet?" Rafe asked.

"Not yet. You can call him," Hayley replied. She shifted her gaze to Terri. "That is, if you're all right with that. We've all been part of Teague's search, because we know how important it is—has been," she corrected with a smile, "to him. And he's important to us."

"That's fine," Terri said, wishing she could find the words to express how happy she was that Teague had landed here, among these people.

"And sometime," Case, who had been quiet through this all, "maybe you'll explain how you managed to disappear so thoroughly. That takes some doing."

She shrugged. "I dumped the name because I hated it. The man who gave it to me and the woman who shared it most of all. I got fake ID, and used it to get some real pieces of ID. I went only to places I'd never been and had no connection to, and never mentioned…here. And I never looked back, not even in internet searches. I didn't want any connection at all to…them, or that life."

"Efficient," Quinn said.

"Then why were you so worried about the police last night?" Case asked.

"Because…all that happened, what I did—" she'd skimmed over her earliest days, when she'd had to steal to eat, in her story to the Foxworths "—if they had pictures of me, stealing food…"

"Somehow I don't think grabbing some food and taking some clothes that had already been donated landed you very high on the most wanted list," Case said with a crooked grin that eased her worry over that aspect of her story. "Especially ten years on. You're way outside the statute of limitations."

"If you want, later, we can see about making sure you're clear on that point," Quinn said briskly. "But for now, let's just get you settled."

"Settled?"

"Yes," Hayley said. "Are you staying with Case?"

Her pulse took a little leap. That sounded so lovely that warning bells went off in her mind. "I…no. He was just helping me, after last night." She slid him a sideways glance, and could not read his expression at all. Mainly because he didn't seem to be wearing one—his face was utterly emotionless.

She looked back at Quinn. "I have a room at a motel on Highway 99, near the store where it happened. Or at least I did," she added, with a touch of alarm. "I just realized I only paid through last night, and now it's past checkout time."

"We'll take care of that," Quinn said in that same brisk tone. "Which place?"

She mentioned the name, apologized that she didn't know the phone number. Before she could say any more, Rafe said, "On it," and started up the stairs at the back of the room. She noticed then that his gait going up was a little uneven, although it didn't seem to slow him down any.

"We'll make sure they hold your things," Hayley assured her.

"Thank you. I don't have all that much, but…it's all there."

"I should have thought of that before we headed over here," Case said, sounding genuinely regretful.

"Why would you?" she asked.

"There was a time I would have," he muttered. "Guess I'm already out of the habit of thinking of all the possibilities."

Terri saw Quinn's gaze shift to Case, studying him. She knew some people would assume he was an ex-cop because he was the proverbial bad apple, or had done something terrible. But then she supposed some people, like her mother, would think upsetting the apple cart of influence was just that, terrible.

"We'll get your things so you can stay here on this side and be here when Teague gets home," Hayley said. "The question is, where? Teague and Laney have a place closer to town, a guest house they're renting for now. But it's small, just one bedroom."

"I couldn't," Terri protested. "Not move in on them like this, when they're newlyweds."

Hayley nodded in understanding, and not showing a bit of surprise at her reaction. She simply went on. "There's a bedroom and bath in the back here, but that's for clients, and you're family. So you'd better come stay with us. Our place isn't too far, and we have a nice guest suite. You could—"

"Your house?" she asked, startled. "But you barely know me."

"We know what's important. You're Teague's sister. That's what matters." She grinned. "Besides, if you're there we get to use boss privilege and make Teague and Laney come over for dinner as soon as they get back, so you don't have to wait any longer than you already have."

Terri couldn't help laughing, that joy bubbling up again. Hayley still grinned as she looked at Quinn. "I'll do all the rest, if you'll do your ribs." She looked back at Terri. "He does the best barbecued ribs on the planet."

"You only say that to talk me into cooking."

"Yep."

Terri felt her eyes begin to sting again. This was the kind of lighthearted, loving teasing she'd never seen growing up. Her mother was too cold, too judgmental for it, and her father had gone along. She'd always suspected it was because her mother had simply worn him down and it was easier, but the reason didn't really matter anymore.

In fact, nothing they'd said or believed had mattered from the day they'd told Teague if he went ahead with his plan to join the military they wanted nothing more to do with him. She had never forgotten the way her big brother had stood up tall and straight, facing down not Father but the one with the true power, Mother, and said simply, "Good."

She'd almost cheered aloud from the stairway, where she'd been hiding to listen after Teague had told her he was going to tell them. Even though it meant she'd be left alone with them, she'd been so happy to see that moment she didn't care.

And now here she was, listening to her living brother's friends and colleagues planning a dinner for his return, with her present, welcomed into their home...

"I'd say your life just took a big turn for the better," Case said, giving her shoulders another squeeze.

Then he pulled his arm from around her, removing the steady, warm support. She hadn't truly been conscious of how much she'd needed that until it was gone. He was pulling away completely now. And she didn't like it. At all.

She shifted on the couch to look at him straight on. "A life I wouldn't have if not for you. And do not just shrug that off, please," she added when she saw the movement of his shoulders begin. "I would have died without ever knowing my brother was still alive, if you hadn't been there. And been who you are."

"She has," Quinn said, "a very good point."

"Yes," Hayley agreed. "And Teague would have spent the rest of his life searching, never knowing what had really happened to her. So you in essence saved two lives last night, Mr. McMillan."

Case looked as if he was at a loss for words. Before he could find any, there was the sound of footsteps on the stairs. Rapid ones, and a moment later Rafe was back in the main room.

"That convenience store," he said, not wasting time on any preamble, "was it down the street from the motel?"

"Yes," she said. "Just a couple of blocks. I didn't realize how chilly it was outside and I—"

Rafe shook his head, cutting her off. "You said the guy who grabbed you robbed the store and beat up the clerk?"

Something about the way the man spoke told her not to take offense at his brusqueness. "Yes."

Rafe looked at Quinn. Something clearly shifted, Quinn must have read something in Rafe's intimidating gaze, for even from here she could sense the change in him, his sudden alert tension.

And then Rafe said it.

"The clerk died this morning."

Instantly Case was back, both arms around her now, even as her brain struggled to process. She could feel the tension in him, as if the words had been a blow. Even Cutter was on his feet, as if the animal had detected a sudden change in the atmosphere.

"That's awful," she said. "He was very nice to me, and that robber beat him for no reason—he was handing over the money."

She shivered, leaning into Case once more. Cutter was back at her side, leaning into her, offering that strange comfort he'd given before. She saw Case shift his gaze to Quinn, who looked as grim as Case did.

Quinn looked at Rafe. "Liam?"

"On his way."

"Have him go pick up Terri's things. She shouldn't go back there."

Rafe only nodded, but Terri frowned. The entire tenor of the room truly had shifted, Rafe and Quinn communicating more than they were saying, and Case seemed to be on the same wavelength. She suppressed another shiver, at the change of mood as well as the sad fact of an innocent man's death.

"She'd better stay here at HQ," Quinn said. Rafe nodded again. Even Cutter yipped as if in approval.

"Here?" she asked, puzzled, still thinking about the poor man behind the counter, wondering if he'd had a wife, maybe kids.

"Better security. Nobody's getting past our systems here, and even if that was possible, nobody's getting past Rafe, or him," Quinn said, nodding at Cutter.

"Should we call Brett?" Hayley asked.

"Probably. He'll have access to info we might need, including if they've identified the suspect."

"The robber?" Terri asked, wondering who this Brett person was and worried she wasn't quite keeping up.

"He's not a robber anymore," Case said grimly. "He's a murderer."

The word sent a chill through Terri. She gave a sharp shake of her head. "Maybe he didn't mean to do it. He might not even know the poor man died. I can just go get my things and—"

"That's not the point." Case touched her cheek gently. "He killed a man, Terri. And you saw him do it. You're the only witness."

Chapter Ten

Terri stared at him. Case realized she was having trouble processing all this. The Foxworth crew, on the other hand, had jumped on everything so quickly he had to reassess what he'd thought they did; they were clearly more than just some do-gooder, moral support operation. But then, he'd suspected that from the moment he'd seen the helicopter.

Visible distress swept over Terri, and he guessed she'd finally realized the import of what had happened. As he'd suspected, she'd been focused on the death of the innocent clerk, not the ramifications of her own situation, and having been the only one to see it happen.

"The police are going to want Terri, so we'd better call Gavin, too," Hayley said. "To protect her."

"I'll protect her." The words were out before Case even thought about it. He told himself it was only natural, that once he'd involved himself he was in it until she was safe. That things had suddenly taken an unexpected turn and they were dealing with a killer didn't change that. Besides, he had the experience; he'd worked protection details before. Although he wasn't altogether sure Quinn Foxworth hadn't seen more and worse.

Quinn held his gaze for a moment, then nodded. And Case thought he saw approval in the man's look before he explained, "She meant in a legal sense. Gavin's our legal consultant. He'll see that she's treated fairly, both as a witness and in regard to anything in the past."

"A...witness," Terri said shakily. "You mean like in court? Testifying?" She looked from Quinn to Case. And with a sudden revival of spirit asked, "Was anyone going to consult *me* about this?"

For a moment no one spoke. Case glanced at Quinn, who looked a bit disconcerted, something he guessed didn't happen often. Hayley looked worried, but was focused on Terri, as if concerned they'd inadvertently hurt her.

Finally Case said, very quietly, "I agreed you had the right not to pursue this when it was just you being grabbed in that alley. But this...this changes everything."

"I think we assumed you wouldn't want to let the guy get away with it," Hayley said, also quietly.

She let out a harsh little laugh. "You don't know me—why would you assume that?"

"Because we know your brother," Quinn said. "And he would always do the right thing."

Case felt a shudder ripple through her. "Yes," she said. "Yes, he would. But he was—is a stronger person than I am."

Even as she caught herself on the past tense she'd been so accustomed to using, he sensed her steady herself. He thought something had occurred to her, something that had shifted her thoughts. Maybe even changed her mind.

She drew herself up and met Quinn's gaze. "I came back here because I told myself I was through running away. I hadn't planned on having to make such a...public declaration, but you're right. I don't want him to get away with this."

It took Case a moment to realize that what he felt at her pronouncement was pride. He was proud of her. Or at least, he admired her. After what she'd been through, facing near-certain death in that alley, to go from wanting nothing more than putting it behind her to taking a stand like this, that was worthy of admiration.

Yes, definitely admiration, not pride. There was a certain…possessiveness in being proud of someone. There had to be a connection for that, and he didn't have one to her, beyond that right time, right place link.

"Good for you," he said, glad he'd sorted that out in his head.

The Foxworths, and Rafe, had already sprung into action. Each of them was on the phone in seconds. They'd gotten to their feet and put some space between them to avoid background chatter on the calls. Not sure what else to do, he walked out and refilled his coffee mug, and this time brought one back to Terri after she'd said yes to the offer.

"They seem…practiced at this," Terri said when he handed her the mug and sat down. He thought about sitting somewhere else, but Cutter seemed to be in the way and it seemed rude to push the Foxworth dog aside when they were doing so much to help.

"They do," Case agreed as he resumed his old seat. "I think there's more to the Foxworth Foundation than I ever realized."

"You said they were well-known here."

He nodded, and told her what little he knew about their part in the whole governor scandal. "I was a bit…involved in my own mess at the time, so I wasn't paying as much attention as I normally would."

"Sounds like a lot of cages got rattled about then. The governor goes down, and you take down some scummy power broker."

"Who walked away clean," he said sourly.

"Not clean," she corrected. "That will always dog him." She leaned down toward Cutter, attached to her since they'd arrived, and nuzzled his nose. "No offense, sweetie."

Case found himself watching her not just with interest, but with surprise. Once she'd decided, the fear and worry had fallen away and determination took over.

"When you make up your mind, you really make up your mind," he said.

She looked up at him. He saw the change there, too, in her face, in those eyes so like the man's in that photograph. And even as he thought about the resemblance, she spoke again of the man who had so shaped her life.

"I've spent over a decade thinking the brother I so loved was dead. Thinking there was no one who cared or who I cared about, so it didn't matter what I did. But now I know he's alive…"

"You want to do what he would do?"

"What's right," she said. "Now I have to make him proud of me."

"Terri, he's going to be so glad you're alive and here, nothing else is going to matter."

"It will to me," she said firmly.

He shook his head with no small amount of wonder. She clearly had her feet back under her now; she was like a different woman. But he should have known. She'd been tough enough to survive being on her own before she was even out of high school, and you didn't do that without a lot of grit and determination.

It was a few minutes before the Foxworth operatives—he wasn't sure what else to call them, and the way they worked supported the term—reported back.

"Liam's on the way to the motel," Rafe said. He looked at Terri. "They have your cell number at the desk?" She nodded. "They'll likely be calling then, for an okay for him to pick up your stuff."

Terri nodded again.

"Brett's going to find out what he can on the case," Hayley

said, then looked at Terri and Case as she explained. "Brett Dunbar, a detective with our sheriff's department here, and a good friend who's helped us out before."

Case's brow furrowed. He knew that name, didn't he? "Dunbar," he said slowly, trying to remember. "Isn't he the guy who—"

"Spearheaded taking down our not so illustrious governor, yes," Quinn said.

He didn't remember much of the outside world from that time, but he'd apparently noted the name of the deputy involved. That was the level of law enforcement they worked with? His assessment of Foxworths' resources and reach went up another notch.

"Speaking of truly illustrious, did you reach Gavin?" Hayley asked her husband.

"Katie's away at a library conference this week, so he's available. He'll be here shortly." Quinn's mouth quirked. "I think he was glad about the call."

"Of course he was. He misses her," Hayley said with obvious satisfaction. "I'm expecting an announcement any day now. One of Cutter's biggest successes," she added with a grin at her dog, who was still glued to Terri. At Case's curious look, Hayley laughed. "Another of his skills, but that's for later."

Terri was still petting the dog, whose eyes were half-shut now, as if he'd finally relaxed enough to enjoy her stroking.

I don't think I'd find it relaxing.

Case jerked his mind off that path, and instead fixed on the crazy but less unsettling thought that the animal had sensed when she'd leveled off and found that determination. Decided that idea wasn't much saner, so reached for his coffee again.

"So who's this illustrious Gavin of yours?" Terri asked, even managing a steady smile now as she added apologetically, "I was a little out of it when you mentioned him before."

"Our advisor on legal matters," Quinn said. "Gavin de Marco."

Case nearly choked on his half-swallowed coffee.

"Gavin de Marco?" he said when he could speak, knowing he was gaping at the man but unable to stop. "Your legal advisor is Gavin de Marco?"

"The one and only," Quinn said. Then, lifting a brow, he asked, "I gather the name's not unfamiliar?"

"Who doesn't know that name?" One of the most famous defense attorneys in the world—who had also mystified that world by suddenly dropping off the map—was working for an operation like Foxworth? Here, in this quiet little place, so far from the halls of power he used to walk? No wonder it had never occurred to him when Quinn had said the before.

"Even I've heard that name," Terri said. "And I don't pay attention to such things."

"I saw him in action once," Case said. "I was at the courthouse for something, there was a crowd around the main courtroom. When I heard it was because de Marco was the defense attorney, I couldn't resist. I only watched for a few minutes, but it was long enough to see him take apart the major pillar of the case."

"And how did that make you feel?"

He only shrugged. "He was right. Turned out the witness was lying, trying to get payback for some perceived insult. Broke the guy down right there on the stand and the entire case fell apart. It was genius—even I could see that. I always wondered why he sort of vanished."

"He had his reasons. Ones you could relate to, I suspect."

"Oh?" He held Quinn's gaze, wondering exactly how much he knew. Because he had been accused of the same thing, lying under oath.

"We'll get to that later," Quinn said. "Right now, let's get Terri settled in and start gathering the data we need to deal with her situation. I'll start doing a bit of research until Liam gets here, and he can take over, since he's our resident nerd. Between him and Brett we'll get what we need."

The man headed up the stairs Rafe had gone up before. Case supposed what served as an actual office must be up there, because Rafe had silently vanished.

"I'll make sure the room's ready," Hayley said. "Terri, why don't you make up a shopping list of anything else you might need. Oh, and check the kitchen to see what you might want that we don't have on hand."

She turned and headed to the back corner of the room where Case had seen the two doorways.

"They seem very...efficient," Terri said.

"Yes." *They seem like they've been through something like this before. More than once.*

Case had just decided that he wanted to dig up and read some of the reports he'd missed when the governor's scandal had erupted, when Terri stood up. Automatically, so did he.Then she spoke, very quietly.

"Thank you. Again."

He snapped out of his speculation on exactly who and what Foxworth was. Because she had said that with a tone of finality. As if his part in this was done, and she was giving him a final thank-you...and saying goodbye.

But his part was done. She was in good hands now. Foxworth clearly had the resources and knowledge to deal with the situation, and from the way they had spoken about her brother, he suspected they would go to any lengths to help her. So he was, indeed, done.

So why didn't he just say "No problem," and leave? Yes, he'd vowed to Quinn that he'd see to her safety, but that was before he'd quite realized the extent of those resources. They were obviously much better equipped to protect her than he was. Now, anyway. Now that his career as any kind of a protector had blown up in his face.

He tried for a light tone. "Kicking me out?"

She looked appalled enough that it soothed him, which in turn embarrassed him; he really was far too touchy still about what he'd lost. It was over and done, but every time he thought he'd moved on something happened to remind him he had not.

"Of course not! I just assumed you'd want to be done with this. It's not like you're...responsible for me, because you saved my life."

"What if I feel like I am?"

"You don't have to feel like that."

His mouth twisted wryly. "I don't seem to have much choice in the matter."

She just looked at him for a long, silent moment. Then, softly said, "Those people that let you go were fools."

His throat tightened. It wasn't that he hadn't heard the sentiment before. He had, from a few friends. At least, he had before it had been made clear that anyone who defended him was risking their own career. He didn't blame the ones who had clammed up then. He didn't want to carry the guilt of costing them their jobs on top of losing his own.

But somehow coming from her, it felt...different.

She just feels like she owes you. That's all.

That was the logical answer.

The problem was, when it came to her, his logic seemed to fly out the window.

"You're welcome to stay as well," Hayley said.

Case had been so focused on Terri that he hadn't even heard the other woman come up behind him. Something that never would have happened, before. It startled him enough that he spun around to look at her.

"I got the idea you feel you're invested in this now. Seeing that Terri stays safe."

He didn't want to admit to that much, so just said, "I don't feel like I can just walk away." He turned back to Terri then. "Unless you want me to."

He thought he saw her cheeks pinken slightly. "No. No, I don't, not at all. The opposite, in fact. But you've already done so much—I thought you'd want to."

She said it all with enough emphasis that it eased whatever this churning in his gut was. And he was able to smile at her and tease a little when he answered, "Now that I know the story, I'd kind of like to be there when your brother sees you for the first time. And for that to happen, I need to be sure you stay alive and well."

"You've certainly earned that right," Hayley said. "And it can't hurt to have another capable guard around, eh, Cutter?"

Case realized the dog, who had stayed glued to Terri's side, was now sitting at her feet but staring up at him. And again there was something so intense in that amber-flecked gaze that he found it difficult to hold.

He's a dog. You've stared down killers, and you can't look at a dog?

And then the animal got up and crossed over to him. He nudged his hand, in the way he'd done with Terri. And he understood why she'd immediately started to pet him; it just seemed the thing to do.

When his fingers stroked the soft fur he knew. Or at least, knew what he assumed Terri had felt, that had so quickly calmed her. A sort of warmth, but not just that. A comforting reassurance that all would turn out as it should.

Which had to be the craziest thing he'd thought since his life had blown up and he'd foolishly expected the department he'd given his life to, to have his back. The craziest thing since his faith in the rightness of the world had vanished.

"Hey, dog," he said, not sure what else to say.

"He makes you feel better, doesn't he?" Terri asked.

"Sounds crazy, but…yeah."

"One of his major talents," Hayley said cheerfully. "Has been ever since he turned up on my doorstep when I needed him most." Case gave her a questioning look. "Right after my mother died. He held me together. And then, of course, he found Quinn for me."

Case blinked. "He what?"

She laughed, and the atmosphere lightened. "Long story. So if you want to hear it, you'd better stay. That couch isn't too bad to sleep on, for a night or two. By then we should have a much better idea where things stand. And you're about Quinn's size, so we'll get you some clothes to borrow, and pick up whatever else you need."

And that easily, Case found the decision made, even as he wondered exactly how it had happened. But the dog nudged him again, and as he instinctively scratched behind one ear, it didn't seem to matter.

It just seemed right.

Chapter Eleven

He was going to stay.

Terri could breathe easier, only then realizing how keyed up she'd been, afraid he'd walk out that door and she would never see him again. She supposed it was a holdover from what he'd done. It seemed only natural that you'd want to... cling to the person who saved your life, didn't it?

Hayley walked over to Terri and gave her a rather fierce hug.

"I don't want to lose sight amid all this of how delighted we are that you're here, alive and well. Just thinking of how Teague's going to feel makes us all happy."

Teague. In just a few days, her brother would be here. Her brother, alive, not dead and buried in some grave she'd never visited or even known the location of, because it hurt too much.

She shivered, but this time with some of that delight Hayley mentioned. "Thank you," she said. "Thank you for being his friends, not just who he works for." She almost giggled, the strangest feeling she'd had in years. "I'm still not used to talking about him that way."

"You'll get used to it," Hayley said with a final squeeze. "He's one of the most alive guys I know."

Terri resisted glancing at Case. He, too, was intensely

alive, but he was also wounded in a way she understood all too well. Understood because she'd been living with a similar wound for ten years. The wound of having your very foundation, the reason you were who you were, the support you'd thought would always be there, ripped away from you.

And yet there had been enough of that original man left that he'd risked his own life to save that of a woman he didn't even know. Just because it was the kind of man he was.

Some time later Cutter, who had been lolling with apparent contentment on his bed beside the fire, suddenly scrambled to his feet, letting out a staccato, two-note bark.

"There's Liam," Hayley said.

"How do you know?" Terri asked, thinking not only that it could be anyone, but that she hadn't even heard a vehicle yet.

Hayley nodded toward Cutter. "That's his bark."

She remembered the different way the dog had barked when Rafe had been heading toward the back door. She laughed. "What, everyone has their own bark?"

"Exactly," Hayley said blithely, as if it was the most normal thing in the world to have a dog who differentiated between arrivals long before they actually arrived.

"Handy," Case said. Then, eyeing the dog, he said, "He looks like a long-haired version of a police K9 I worked with."

"That's the consensus," Quinn said, having come back downstairs in time to hear Case's words. "We've not had his ancestry checked out because it doesn't really matter. He's the best at what he does, and he does a lot."

"Indeed he does," Hayley said, and something hot and loving flashed between the couple when they glanced at each other as their dog trotted over to the front door.

Terri could hear the sound of tires on gravel now, slowing first, then stopping. She stood. Cutter rose and batted at the door pad and it swung open. The dog raced out.

"Liam'll be in with your things shortly," Quinn said. "Rafe's out working on Igor, so they'll probably talk for a minute."

"But only a minute," Hayley said with a smile. "It is Rafe, after all."

"Igor?" Case asked. "Let me guess, the helicopter?"

Quinn grimaced, but Hayley's smile became a grin. "Exactly. Liam's doing. He's got nicknames for everything."

"Why Igor?" Terri asked, thinking of a character in an old horror movie.

"Sikorsky," Case answered. "The guy who pretty much invented modern helicopters."

She laughed. She had the feeling she'd like this Liam. The door swung back open and Cutter dashed in. Terri heard footsteps on the walkway outside, fast ones, as if the person was about to break into a run.

Cutter was just inside the door, looking back, his paws dancing impatiently on the tile entry. "I'm comin', dawg," the newcomer drawled from outside, and she remembered Hayley saying he was from Texas.

A man stepped inside, carrying a familiar backpack and suitcase. It suddenly and belatedly occurred to her that this total stranger had gathered up her things, probably including the already worn underwear she'd had in a laundry bag. At least the rest had still been packed.

She barely had time to notice he was leanly built, a bit shorter than Case, with hair almost the same sandy brown as her own at the base, before he spotted her. He stopped dead, staring. She felt she should say hello or something, but couldn't find the words. And then a wide, wonderfully warm grin spread across his face. He dropped the bags and ran the rest of the way, halting a bare two feet away as he stared at her with eyes that were a light golden shade of brown.

"It's really you! Damn, you two look alike."

This present-tense reminder put an echoing smile on her face.

"Liam Burnett, meet Terri Johnson, formerly Jones, late of Boone, Iowa, now back home," Quinn said, and Terri marveled not for the first time at how easily they'd accepted her. She knew as kids she and Teague had been quickly recognizable as siblings, but she'd never expected it to be so... precious. And she liked that Quinn kept to her choice; she had decided the moment she was certain that Teague was alive that her real last name was worth having again. It was honorable again.

"And this is Case McMillan," Quinn went on.

Liam shifted his gaze to Case, who had also gotten to his feet. The two men shook hands, and Liam said with obvious sincerity, "Thanks for being there, for stepping up for her last night. For saving us from having to tell Teague she was almost back to him, but didn't make it."

Terri sucked in a little breath; she hadn't thought of it like that, what it would have been like for Teague if Case hadn't saved her. If her body had been found and eventually identified as the long missing Terri Johnson. She felt a little jab of horror, imagining herself in that position, certain it would have been unbearable.

"Glad I was there," was all Case said. Which was better than "It was nothing," because it was far from nothing to her.

Liam shifted his attention back to her. "I'll have to show you the files. Teague's search files. He sent out inquiries to agencies across the country every month, with an aged up image he had done—which was pretty spot-on, by the way. If there were any even faint possibilities, he followed up. He never gave up looking for you."

That almost did it. She felt she might burst into tears right here. As if she'd sensed it, Hayley stepped in.

"Put her things in the bedroom, will you, Liam? Then we'll need as much info as you can find that Quinn didn't."

"That'll be a lot," Liam quipped, and Terri liked that he was able to joke with his boss like that. In fact, so far she liked everything about this place, and these people. And their dog. Maybe him especially.

"Brett's on it, too," Quinn added, "so don't go trespassing on that particular turf."

"Oh, well," Liam said, sounding disappointed.

"Just due diligence at this point," Quinn said.

"Got it." Liam took another look at Terri, grinned and gave a wondering shake of his head, then vanished with her bags into the room back in the corner. Seconds later he was running upstairs.

They were back sitting with Hayley and Quinn—and Cutter—when Case said, "This is quite an operation you've got here. Including Igor out there."

"Just don't get him started on Wilbur," Hayley said with a laugh.

Terri thought for a moment, then her eyes widened. "An airplane? You have an airplane, too?"

Quinn grinned, and suddenly the imposing, intimidating demeanor faded and he seemed to be just a guy who liked his toys. "She's a beauty, too."

"I don't want to see your billing rates," Case said.

Terri thought he sounded a little bitter, which puzzled her until she realized that he'd probably had some attorney bills to pay after he lost his legal battle.

"Actually," Quinn said, his tone level, "we don't charge anyone we help."

Terri was looking at Case, and saw his eyes widen. She understood; this was a lovely building in a beautiful setting, they had a helicopter and a plane—Igor and Wilbur, she thought with another inward laugh—and they had at least three other people working here.

"Quinn's sister is a financial genius," Hayley said.

"And we're very particular about who we take on," Quinn said. "So the only thing we ask of our clients is that they in turn, somewhere down the line, help us help someone else if they can."

"What, exactly, are your criteria?" Case asked, sounding fascinated. "I mean, I heard what you told Terri, but is it that simple?"

"Yes. All we require is that you have already fought, if you're able. That the odds, or the size and power of your opponent, are against you. But first and foremost, that you be in the right."

"And who decides that?"

There was no missing the edge in Case's tone this time. But Quinn only smiled. "That's the best part of being privately funded. We decide. After some investigation, of course. You'd be amazed—" Quinn stopped, studied Case for a moment, then went on. "No, you probably wouldn't be amazed at how many people seem like they're in the right, until you dig into the other side."

"No, I wouldn't."

And that was the sound of bitter experience if Terri had ever heard it.

Chapter Twelve

Case recognized Gavin de Marco the moment he walked in the door the canine butler opened, after another distinctive bark of announcement. The newcomer bent to greet the dog with a scratching behind the ears, which Cutter returned with the paw-dancing welcome to a friend.

As Case got to his feet, he thought he would have recognized the man just from photographs, even if he'd never seen him in person, in action, that day in a courtroom. But as he had been that day, the man in person was extraordinary. Case hadn't forgotten a thing, not the man's lean, prowling way of moving, the way he wore his thick black hair a bit long or the gleam of a powerful intelligence in his dark eyes. But most of all he'd never forgotten the sheer presence of the man, the charisma that could quiet a crowded room before anyone there even realized who he was.

And after they realized, that quiet inevitably became tinged with either respect, awe, or a touch of fear.

Case suddenly remembered what Quinn had said about a woman named Katie and a library conference. Gavin de Marco's wife, or girlfriend, was…a librarian? That almost made him smile. But then Gavin was in front of them, and he thought better of it. He also thought he saw a flicker of… something in the man's eyes when Hayley introduced him.

But he quickly focused, as he should, on Terri, who was also now standing, her hands nervously smoothing down her sweater. Case couldn't help but notice the action emphasized the soft curve of her breasts, but knew that hadn't been her intention. Her feminine charms were the furthest thing from her mind right now.

And should be the furthest thing from yours. You're face to face with Gavin freaking de Marco.

"It's true, then," de Marco said as he looked at her, clearly seeing the resemblance the others had.

"Seems that way," Quinn said. "DNA test in progress, but we don't have much doubt."

Quinn had said to Liam, "due diligence." That included verifying she was truly who she appeared to be. Thorough. He should have realized you didn't successfully run an operation like this one without being thorough. *We decide. After some investigation, of course.*

Quinn had apparently briefed Gavin, because he got down to business. "Let me be clear on where things stand," he said to Terri. "You were present at a robbery which has turned into a murder case, but you're hesitant about being a witness due to some actions in your past?"

Terri flushed, but nodded.

"How old were you, then?"

"Seventeen."

De Marco smiled. She blinked. Case saw why; the cool, intimidating, world-famous attorney had suddenly become a warm, welcoming friend.

"Perfect," de Marco said. "I think you can stop worrying about that aspect. But let's talk a little privately."

"Case already knows," Terri put in. "I...trust him."

The famous man looked at him again. "I can see why."

Now Case blinked. That pleased him a lot more than it should have, considering that back in the day they would

have been on opposing sides. He was finding it hard to remember that in most police circles, this man was the enemy.
The apex enemy. But having the approval of a man on the
level of de Marco still mattered.

"And I'd like to talk with you as well. But right now," de
Marco went on, looking back at Terri, "let's not put him in
the position of having to deny knowledge. Quinn?"

"The meeting room's clear. Liam's up in his lair. He's
been at it almost an hour, so he'll probably have everything
you might need." That due diligence again, Case thought.

"And Brett?"

"He's checking into the case."

De Marco nodded, then looked back to Terri. "Join me
upstairs, please." He glanced back at Case, who had that
feeling of once more being thoroughly assessed. "It's easier
to claim confidentiality in an office setting."

As he watched them go he was a little bemused, and not
just by the fact that Cutter didn't even try to go with them,
as if he understood what de Marco had said. More than that,
he'd never had the impression that de Marco gave a damn
about other people's feelings, and yet he was explaining why
he wanted to talk to Terri alone.

He looked back to Quinn, who was watching him with
that level-eyed gaze. "Has he changed, or was I wrong about
him back then?"

"He's changed," Quinn said.

"More like he was changed," Hayley said, and she was
looking at Case rather pointedly. "Betrayal will do that to
you."

Case blinked. "Betrayal?"

"It's a long story, and only his to tell," Quinn said, end-
ing the subject. And Hayley rounded up the dog and took
him outside, grabbing up a tennis ball from a basket by the

rear door, apparently to play. Or maybe to take some of that serious edge off the live-wire animal.

Case was left with the certainty that Hayley's words were aimed specifically at him. Just how much research had they done—on both of them—in the time it had taken he and Terri to get here?

He was once more contemplating the logical course for him, which was to decamp and leave the capable Foxworth people to handle Terri's situation. There was nothing he could do that they likely couldn't do better, so there was no point in hanging around. She was in good hands, and his part in this was done.

He'd do this one on one with de Marco—hell, he'd do that out of sheer curiosity—then he'd get out of here. Get out and go back to…what? His miserable, jobless, not-a-goal-in-sight life? The old shadows tried to rise up again, the gloom that wanted to remind him of his bleak situation and bleaker future.

He attempted to call up the determination not to let them win, not to let them drive him out of this place he loved, but he was having a little trouble finding it. He had no idea how long he'd been pacing around, fighting down the unpleasant memories. He couldn't—

Something cold and damp nudged his hand. A nose. He looked down to see Cutter standing there; he hadn't even noticed they'd come back in. Which told him he'd been lost in this miasma for too long.

Cutter stood looking up at him with those eyes that seemed too intense for a dog. The nudge came again, polite but insistent. And because it was impossible not to, he scratched behind the animal's ears as de Marco had.

He wondered if he also wore the rather bemused look Terri had when she did this. Because, yet again, the moment he stroked the dog's fur he felt that same reassurance. That all would be well, that the qualms and uncertainties didn't matter, that any obstacle would be surpassed.

Hell of a load to put on a dog, McMillan.

A sudden sound turned him around. Some kind of motor starting up. Quinn saw his reaction.

"Backup generator," he explained. "Rafe's doing maintenance on it."

"Is that what he does for you, maintenance?"

Quinn looked at him considering what or how much to tell him. "Among other things. Many other things."

"Him and the dog, huh?" Case said, thinking of what Quinn and Hayley had said about the animal's talents.

"Most of us have skills in a few areas," Quinn said.

The memory practically kicked him. *Army Ranger.* "So if you were a Ranger, what was he?"

"Marines." Again that considering look before he added, "Sniper. According to many, the best since Hathcock."

Case blinked. He'd seen a documentary once on the legendary Carlos Hathcock, and been left in awe. "Heady company."

And now the guy was fixing machinery? As if he'd read his expression, Quinn said, "He works on our equipment because he enjoys it. And because it keeps him from thinking too much."

That, he could understand. Completely. Hadn't he practically rebuilt his truck from the ground up because he didn't want to think about other things?

"You restore that truck you arrived in?"

Case blinked, startled. He hadn't spoken that thought, had he? Was Quinn that good at reading people, and situations?

And what did you expect from the guy who built this operation?

"I…yes."

Quinn only nodded. "Thought so."

"It was my father's," he said, not sure why he felt the need to explain.

"Good reason."

Footsteps on the stairs drew his attention then. He saw Terri's boots first, the ones he'd be willing to bet weren't just for effect but had actually done some hiking. Then her jeans-clad legs as she continued down, then her hips...

He squashed the thought that he'd like to follow her up those stairs just to watch that movement. This was not the moment, the person, the place, or the time in his life to even be thinking such things.

"He'd like you to come up now," she said when she reached the last step.

Something in her voice told him, but he asked anyway. "Feeling better about it all?"

She smiled, and for the first time it was a solid, serene smile. "Yes. He promised he'd be with me every step of the way. That the police want to talk to me as soon as possible, but he'd be there. He's very...comforting."

He wondered if in his entire famous—or infamous—career as a defense lawyer, Gavin de Marco had ever been called comforting. He was still pondering that as he made his way upstairs.

The room was wide open, except for a partitioned off space at the opposite end, where he supposed Liam was holed up doing whatever the resident nerd, as Quinn had called him, did. There was a wall of windows with a view over the meadow, toward the trees. That was where de Marco stood, looking out. But he turned as soon as Case reached the top step.

To his surprise, the famous man crossed over, hand outstretched. "A more proper greeting now," he said. "It's an honor to meet you, Mr. McMillan."

Gavin de Marco saying it was an honor to meet *him*? It

took him a moment to take the offered hand and shake it. And he was off-balance enough to ask, "Is she going to be able to afford you?"

De Marco smiled. "Not an issue. Foxworth will see to it she has everything she needs."

Case wanted to ask how he'd ended up here, like this, doing this, but de Marco went on before he could put the words together.

"Terri told me the details of what happened last night. She would most certainly be dead if not for you, and Foxworth owes you a great deal for that alone. We would stand with anyone who acted so courageously, but when it's done for one of our own…"

"I'm just glad I was there," he said, feeling, as he always had, a little embarrassed by the accolade. He used to brush it off with a "Just doing my job," but he'd lost that easy out.

"But," de Marco went on, "even if that weren't the case, we'd stand with you anyway."

"What do you mean?" Case was puzzled.

"We—and I in particular—would be happy to stand with the man who had the courage to go after Joseph Barton."

Case went very still. Stared at the dark eyes that regarded him steadily. And called himself seven kinds of a fool for not realizing what should have been obvious. That due diligence Quinn had ordered Liam to do hadn't just been about Terri.

It had also been about him.

Chapter Thirteen

Case looked across the table at the man he'd once watched in a courtroom, on a day that seemed eons ago now. And he had the feeling the difference in de Marco wasn't simply that he was no longer in the international spotlight, but rather that the difference in him was why he was no longer in the spotlight. Whatever had happened to make him walk away from the career that had made him world famous had fundamentally changed him.

And if it wasn't for that change he sensed, Case never would have had the nerve to say what he did next. "I would have thought he'd be your kind of client, once."

De Marco smiled. It wasn't a fond smile. "Actually, he did approach me once, some years ago. Took days to get the stink out of my office."

And then, despite himself, Case laughed. And ended up telling him about that day he'd watched him in the courtroom.

"And as a police officer, Mr. McMillan, weren't you upset that the prosecution lost?"

"Case, please. Not after I saw you dismantle that witness. Tinsley was no upstanding member of the community, but he didn't kill that guy."

"No, he didn't, Case. And that you see it that way proves my point."

Case shrugged. "I had this crazy idea back then that the truth mattered."

"And I quit because it does matter."

There was something icy in de Marco's voice on those last words, but Case knew it wasn't directed at him. No, that frost was aimed at whatever had changed de Marco, that had made him walk away from a life many would trade their souls for. Case guessed it was like what he'd felt, multiplied by a factor of a million or so.

Briskly, businesslike now, de Marco went on. "I'd like to ask you something about that, then we'll get to Terri's situation."

"Ask."

"Did you know who—and what—Barton was before you arrested him?"

"Yes."

"And you arrested him anyway."

"I have a thing about drunk drivers who hurt others. And people who think the law doesn't apply to them." He grimaced. "Even ones who have the DA, the mayor and the entire city council in their pocket. Or maybe especially them."

De Marco leaned back in his chair. "Now that you know what the personal cost to you has been, would you do it again?"

Case met the gaze that had intimidated much more important men than he. "In a heartbeat. Sir," he said flatly.

De Marco nodded, as if he'd expected that answer. And when he said, "I think you'd better call me Gavin," Case felt he'd won some sort of prize. Then he moved on, as promised. "I'd like to hear your description of what happened last night."

Last night. Had it really been less than twenty-four hours?

It seemed much longer. But he told the story again. And was surprised when the lawyer didn't ask why he hadn't called the law. But de Marco—it was going to take some getting used to calling him Gavin—did ask something.

"How hard was it, not to call the police?"

"Harder than it should have been," he answered sourly. Then, eyeing the man steadily, he asked, "You sure she won't be in trouble for that old stuff if she comes forward?"

"There will be some formalities, but real trouble? I don't think so." Coming from Gavin de Marco, Case figured that was pretty much bankable. "One last question."

"Shoot."

"How would you handle being on the witness stand yourself?"

Case went still. Very still. "They're not going to call me."

"Because?"

"Because my former employers and the media spent a lot of time convincing a lot of people I'm a liar and a perjurer."

Gavin nodded as if he'd expected as much. Case couldn't imagine what it would take to surprise this guy.

"A media—and some of those employers—owned by Joseph Barton," de Marco said dismissively. "You might want to think about how the story of your heroics last night might change that impression."

"It wasn't heroics—"

He stopped when Gavin held up a hand. "To you, no. To the average citizen, there's no question. Besides, given that… notoriety, it's likely to come out anyway. For the defense, if this man has a halfway decent attorney."

He felt like an idiot. It hadn't really occurred to him that he might get sucked into another public spectacle, enough to remind everyone he was that liar they'd had to get rid of. And that his history might somehow negatively affect a current case, even though all he'd done was try to help.

"I'd say," Gavin went on thoughtfully, "you need someone to stand for you as much, if not more, than Terri."

"Like an attorney?" he asked, his tone a bit acid. "Can't afford one. Last time cleaned me out."

Gavin smiled. "Isn't it lucky, then, that this time you have Foxworth on your side?"

ODD, TERRI THOUGHT. She'd gone upstairs with Gavin tense, and come down much calmer. Case had gone up calm, but come down much more tense. She wanted to ask him about it, but he wouldn't even look at her.

She had, with Cutter for company, unpacked in the Foxworth headquarters bedroom that was much nicer than the motel room she'd been in. The bathroom as well was spacious and spotless, despite apparently being used by anyone who was here. When she'd started, she'd had the uncharacteristic thought—for her, anyway, any other woman would probably have been thinking it all along—that it would be very…interesting, sleeping in here tonight with Case in the very next room.

That other woman would no doubt make sure he didn't stay there.

But her romantic history made her life history seem solid. Although to be fair, once Mr. Gibson had taken a chance on her, her life had stabilized wonderfully. But she doubted a man like Case McMillan would want to take a romantic chance on someone like her.

And the images of what a romantic chance with Case might be like had made her hastily finish her unpacking so that she could get out of that room and quit looking at the bed that was big enough to share even with a man Case's size.

And not long after that, she'd been confronted with the very man who was avoiding her. At least, he was trying to;

it seemed like every time he tried to dodge her, Cutter got in his way.

She wanted to ask what was wrong, what Gavin had said that had him so wound up, but she didn't want to do it in front of everyone. And at the moment, everyone was here. Liam and Gavin were in the corner talking to Quinn, no doubt about whatever he'd found in his searching; the intimidating Rafe was going over something with Hayley, while Cutter acted as if it was his job to watch her like a hawk. Well, her and Case. Cutter again got in Case's way when he started toward the other side of the room from her.

"Bathroom, dog, do you mind?" she heard him mutter. And then had the craziest urge to laugh when the dog looked at him, head tilted, and with what she would have sworn was an eye roll.

Laugh. She truly wanted to laugh. Not quite twenty-four hours ago she'd been a split second from death, and now she was having to stifle a laugh. But the urge faded as she again wondered what on earth Gavin had told Case to make him so tense. She glanced over to where he stood with Quinn and Liam, and wondered if she dared ask.

As if he'd tell you? The man didn't become a household name by blabbing secrets.

Case came back out just as Quinn was gathering everyone around the fireplace. She thought she saw a glint of moisture on his forehead. Concern spiked through her. Was he ill? Then the likely cause hit her; he'd probably splashed cold water on his face to try and stay awake. *The man did babysit you most of last night.*

Maybe that was it. Maybe he was just tired.

Maybe he just wanted to go home and get some rest, and put the silly woman he'd rescued out of his mind.

"All right," Quinn said in a tone that commanded full attention. "Liam's confirmed the basics, that the suspect from last night is still outstanding and as of yet unidentified. I've gotten a text from Brett. He's waiting to hear back from some contacts, and he'll stop by tomorrow morning with whatever he gets. Once we have that, if it's indicated, Gavin will make the approach to the city police. In the meantime, Terri will stay here. Case, you're still staying?"

Terri held her breath, afraid to even look at him. She should feel utterly secure, with all this clearly knowledgeable help at hand, but somewhere in her mind her safety had linked with Case's presence, and that him leaving would shatter her.

"Until this guy goes down," he said, in a gruff, flat voice that made it sound like an act purely of duty.

Which it probably is. Remember that.

Quinn only nodded, as if that was the answer he'd expected. "You carrying?"

"Not at the moment."

"Got a favorite?"

"I'm most used to a Glock 22, but personally I'm partial to the HK VP9, or even better, the .40 cal version."

Rafe smiled. "Happen to have one in the armory. I'll check it out to you."

Terri blinked. Weapons. They meant weapons. Somehow that suddenly made this more real. An abrupt memory, the cold metal of a gun barrel digging into her throat sent a shiver rippling through her, reminding her it had been deathly real all along.

"You'll be her final line of defense, then," Quinn said. Terri felt another chill, fiercer this time. But Case only nodded. Quinn continued. "Be aware, both of you, we'll have all security systems activated, so don't go outside or leave the property without one of us."

He nodded at Liam, who nodded and spoke. "We've got all the usual stuff, door and window triggers, sensors, cameras around the building and in strategic spots outside. And infra-red covering all the possible entrances. On the roof as well."

Who *were* these people?

Her thought must have shown in her face because Liam grinned. "Nobody's gonna sneak up on Foxworth."

"Especially," Hayley said, glancing at her dog, who was still sitting at Terri's feet as if they were attached "—with the distant early warning system here." Their dog was stay-ing with her, too? Hayley went on as if it was a given. "He'll let you know when he needs out, or when you need to be aware of something. I'll show you his food and snacks, al-though one of us should be here in time to do that, morning and evening."

Quinn went on. "Rafe will have overwatch tonight, Liam tomorrow night, then me. We'll continue that rotation as long as necessary." Quinn's stern expression changed sud-denly, a wide grin splitting his face. "At least, until Teague gets home and takes over."

Terri's pulse gave a joyous little skip. *Until Teague gets home...*

She looked over to where Case was standing. He'd been stone-faced ever since he came out of the bathroom. But now, unable to keep her happiness and thanks out of her expres-sion as she looked at him, he gave her the faintest of smiles.

A new determination, born out of the joy that the impos-sible had happened, rose up in her. She'd get a better smile, a grin, even a laugh out of him, somehow.

And then, if she could hang on to her nerve, maybe more.

Chapter Fourteen

Case looked at the phone in his hand curiously. It looked like any other smartphone, except for that extra row of controls and the red button at the top.

"That button activates a closed system, Foxworth only," Quinn had said when he'd given one of the devices to both him and Terri. "It'll flash and sound if we're trying to reach you. And if you need to, just push that button, and you'll be in touch with one or more of us, no matter what time it is. Don't hesitate."

Case had only nodded, but he'd been thinking that Quinn Foxworth reminded him of a SWAT team commander he'd once worked with. Smart, tough, analytical, experienced and determined. Everything a leader should be.

And now here he was, ensconced on the couch with a blanket and pillow, but wide awake. He should be exhausted after last night, but sleep was proving not just elusive but impossible. At first he'd thought it was because the room was warm, and he was trying to sleep wearing everything but his shoes when he usually slept in nothing more than his knit boxers. But peeling off his shirt hadn't helped much, and even though the fire was off now, the building was tight and insulated for the Northwest weather, so it was slow to lose its heat.

He looked at the pistol on the table, full magazine and one in the chamber, two more magazines beside it, and told himself his sleeplessness was because of what Quinn had said. *You'll be her final line of defense, then.* He couldn't be that if he was sound asleep.

But deep down he knew better. There was an obviously more than capable Foxworth man on guard, one with the steely look of warrior. And a clearly alert sentry in Cutter who, after Quinn's command of *Guard*, apparently knew exactly what his job was. The dog actually made rounds, circling the downstairs area, pausing at doors and windows, listening and visibly sniffing. In between he stationed himself at the bedroom door, seemingly dozing, but he wasn't truly sleeping any more than Case.

When he found himself wondering what the dog would do if he tried to get past him, if he tried to just open the door to look in on her, he knew he was over the edge.

Determinedly he pounded the pillow into a new shape, tried to ignore the light of the moon coming through the windows and lay down again. He reached out for the VP40 and slid it under the couch cushion, grips out, where he could grab it in an instant. He'd tested the clip-on holster and found it had minimal drag, so left it in place. He knew he'd be a little rusty, since he no longer had access to the police range and a membership at a private place wasn't in the budget, but if he couldn't take an intruder out with thirteen rounds, he should save the last one for himself.

He hadn't realized he'd finally dozed off until a small sound snapped him awake. He was on his feet, the pistol in his hand, before he had processed why. He heard a tiny gasp. Instinctively spun toward the sound. He let out a long breath and lowered the weapon.

Terri. Probably headed for the bathroom, but now staring at him, wide-eyed. Oddly, now that he knew, his pulse didn't slow after the initial kick. Also oddly, Cutter seemed to be looking at him approvingly, an idea he dismissed for sleep-deprived idiocy.

They were both awash in the silver of moonlight. She was wearing a pair of snug leggings and a loose T-shirt—no fancy nightwear for her. It didn't detract in the least, especially when he could make out the sweet, full shape of her breasts curving the cloth of the shirt.

He saw her gaze flick to his right hand, then back. "Sorry," he muttered, and put the weapon down. "Didn't mean to scare you."

To his surprise she took a few steps toward him. "You didn't," she said, her voice sounding a little odd. "Impressed, yes, but scared, no."

His brow furrowed slightly. Then his pulse kicked up another notch when he realized she was sliding her gaze down over his bare chest to where his jeans rode a little low because he'd undone the top button in his effort to sleep and the zipper had worked its way down an inch or two.

He'd been working out and running steadily and hard for the last year, ever since he'd realized his battle was lost. The four months it had taken for them to batter him into surrender were lost in a miasma of disbelief, pain and bitterness. But after that he'd needed the outlet the workouts gave him.

For the first time he was glad of all that effort for another reason. The way Terri looked at him. And the way she'd sounded when she'd spoken. *Impressed, yes...*

He saw her give a little shake of her head. Probably realizing she was gaping at a guy who had no present, let alone no future. That look might have been appreciative, but it wasn't an invitation. Too bad his body thought it was, and in another moment that fact was going to be obvious and undeniable behind his half-zipped jeans.

"I...couldn't sleep," she said. "Crazy, huh, after last night?"

"Then we both are," he muttered. *Me in more ways than one.*

She smiled, although it was a little wobbly. "Hayley said they had some really good hot chocolate mix. I thought I'd try it. Shall I make two?"

He opened his mouth to say no, don't bother. What came out was, "That'd be nice."

Nice. Sitting over a mug of hot chocolate with the woman who revved him up when he had no business even being in the race? No, stupid was the word for that. And he seemed to be stuck in that mode at the moment.

He watched her walk toward the kitchen, Cutter as usual at her heels. The dog obviously took this guarding thing very seriously.

Something you should emulate, instead of ogling her and letting your imagination run riot.

It had just been too long. That had to be the answer. He'd never been one for casual hookups, and after Jill—and his public disgrace—he'd simply shut down that aspect of his life. It hadn't been easy, but he'd gotten used to it.

At least, until now.

She turned on the light in the kitchen, and he saw her hair was tousled, the long, sandy-colored strands falling past her shoulders in a tumble. He watched her as she opened the cupboard for two mugs. It was a reach for her, and the movement made her breasts sway a little. It almost doubled him over. He sucked in a breath, gritted his teeth, rebuttoned his jeans and ordered himself to settle down. He grabbed up his shirt and tugged it on, not allowing the wish that she'd tell him to take it off again to even form into words in his mind.

An electronic sort of sound from behind him made him turn. It was the Foxworth phone, and the red button was flashing. He grabbed it and answered.

"Status?" The deep, rough voice of Rafe Crawford was unmistakable. Case realized he must have seen the light come on. When Foxworth said overwatch, they truly meant it.

"Code four," he answered automatically in the police parlance for things being under control; he hadn't quite been able to break the habit after a decade of it being second nature.

Of course, there was under control, and then there was under control... The situation might be, he himself, not so much.

"Copy," Rafe said, sounding a bit lighter now. "Figured, or Cutter would have been sounding off."

But he'd checked anyway. Because, Case was beginning to understand, Foxworth left very little to chance, and clearly assumed nothing.

When he put the phone back on the table and straightened up, Terri looked at him questioningly.

"Rafe," he said. "I think he saw the light come on."

She blinked. "He called because the kitchen light came on?"

"I get the feeling they don't leave anything to chance."

Her mouth quirked. That sweet, soft mouth. "I wonder what he'd have done if it had been one of the alarms?"

"Let's just say I wouldn't recommend accidentally setting one off."

She nodded slowly. "He's a little scary."

"Apparently he was a Marine sniper of the prize-winning variety. So a bit scary, yeah."

"You, on the other hand, just make me feel safe."

She smiled slightly, a soft sort of smile that sent his body back into overdrive even as the words she spoke warmed him. And he lowered his gaze because he had to, or he was going to say something unforgivably obtuse.

"You remind me of Teague," she said. "He always made

me feel like that, too. I think that's why I trusted you right away."

Her brother. He reminded her of her brother. Well, that put him thoroughly in his place.

A place he'd damned well better stay in.

Chapter Fifteen

Terri stifled a yawn, then took another long sip of the coffee Hayley had made after her arrival this morning. Case had taken his mug and stood near the kitchen window, looking out. Or maybe that was his excuse for putting the counter and a good few feet between them. She wouldn't blame him.

The hot chocolate—drunk in near silence after her idiotic staring—had worked last night, although it had still taken her a while to fall asleep after that. Her mind had been frenzied again, but this time had been different. Not with thoughts about Teague and reliving the nightmare of those moments in the alley, but the image of Case half-naked, broad chested, ribbed abs and the trail of dark hair arrowing down into his half-zipped jeans, crashing into the unmistakable coolness of his demeanor as he'd downed the hot chocolate and told her rather gruffly she needed to get some sleep.

She had finally slept a bit, but she wasn't sure that was much better, because that vision of him had sparked dreams like she hadn't had since she'd been sixteen and had a crush on one of Teague's fellow Marines she'd met. Of course, Teague had quickly warned her he was a rabbit when it came to women, hopping from one to the other, and that had ended that. She trusted her brother the way she trusted no one else in her life.

After that she had lain awake wondering what he would say about Case. Which reminded her that she would have the chance to find that out very soon, when he came home. Came home, alive and well and no doubt very happy, from what they'd told her. And that joy welling up in her again had finally allowed her to slide into more restful sleep, although by the way she kept wanting to yawn, she needed more.

She apparently wasn't going to get it soon, however, judging by Hayley's rather rapid-fire rundown of the plan for today.

"Brett will be here in about an hour. Liam and Rafe will join us to go over what he has. And Quinn, of course," she added, referring to her husband who was upstairs making some calls. Terri saw pure love glowing in Hayley's face when she spoke of Quinn, and felt a tug of longing inside. She'd never dwelt much on the lack of romance in her life; she'd thought herself immune. But seeing the Foxworths together sparked something that had been buried deeply for a long time.

Or Case had.

She summoned the memory of his sudden coolness last night to chill her own unexpected swell of emotion. She'd probably embarrassed him, gaping at him like that. The man had stayed to help protect her; he deserved better than to have her drooling over his bare torso.

Hayley had been taking some things out of a big white paper bag and arranging them on a large platter. Things that sent out a mouthwatering aroma of sweet, fresh baked goods. Terri's stomach woke up at the scent of cinnamon and fresh pastries. She watched as Hayley stuck a toothpick in a particular pastry, a turnover of some kind—apple, Terri guessed by the color she could see through the slits on top—and then wiped off her hands with one of the napkins she'd gathered.

"Let's go get comfortable," Hayley said, gesturing toward

the seating area around the fireplace. It had come on, the thermostat apparently on a timer, although she'd noticed the place had stayed fairly warm overnight. But she'd also felt the rush of cool air that had come in when Quinn and Hayley had arrived, and doubted if it had broken fifty degrees outside yet. Funny how it felt normal, even after all the time she'd spent in the Heartland. But she'd grown up here, so she supposed the weather would seem normal to her. And she certainly wouldn't miss the humidity she'd left behind, or the tornado outbreaks.

You're just not tough enough for that.

This was not a new thought for her. She'd expected, after learning of Teague's death, that she would never feel anything but pain again. In fact she'd been certain of it, with all the drama a traumatized seventeen-year-old could muster. And it had been true, for a while. She'd wished for a numbness that never came.

But gradually other things crept in. She'd felt relief when her new ID passed inspection several times. A small bit of satisfaction when she'd gotten her GED. An actual spark of hope when Mr. Gibson had given her a chance. And a flash of pride when he'd promoted her to managing the office.

And every time she quashed it, chastising herself for feeling anything at all other than the ache of losing the one constant, the one bright spot she'd ever had in her life. Told herself to toughen up, that without Teague to stand between her and the ugliness of life she would have to do it herself, and she couldn't if she kept letting emotion creep in.

She'd never managed to toughen up enough not to feel.

"Quinn!" Hayley had walked over to the bottom of the stairway and called up to her husband. "You want one of these cinnamon rolls, you'd better get here before Liam does."

Within seconds Terri heard footsteps above, and for some

reason the thought of tough, cool Quinn Foxworth hurrying to grab a bakery treat made her smile. He was tough enough to not be afraid to care. She sighed inwardly. Nope, she was definitely not tough enough.

But now she didn't have to be, did she? The whole reason for it, the thing that had inspired the need to put a barrier up between herself and any feelings, had been turned upside down.

Teague was alive.

Joy bubbled up in her again. She didn't realize she was smiling until Hayley said, "I can only imagine your emotions, after all these years thinking him dead. You must feel almost giddy."

"There's no almost about it," Terri admitted. "In the beginning, after that night I heard…those people talking—" she refused to think of them as parents; they had no right to that title "—I felt as if the ground had crumbled beneath me and I was falling endlessly. When I ran, I didn't care where I was going, only that it was away."

"Too bad you carry stuff like that with you, no matter how far or fast you run," Quinn said.

He had come up behind her, obviously having heard her words. There was no criticism in his voice, only understanding. Only to be expected, given his history. And yet here he was, having built an organization doing amazing things, and with a wife he was clearly crazy about.

Yes, Quinn Foxworth was definitely tough enough. He'd survive, and survive well, wherever you dropped him.

Terri couldn't resist a glance at Case. Because, she told herself, he was cut from the same cloth as Quinn Foxworth. The damage done to him was more recent, so she suspected he hadn't quite leveled off yet, but he would. And then he would rebuild, because he was that kind of man.

Tough enough.

He looked up then, catching her watching him. She wanted to look away, but somehow once she saw those unique eyes of his she couldn't. He gave her a smile that seemed oddly tight, then a slight nod. Then he went back to looking out the kitchen window as if the answers to every mystery were out there. And when they moved into the great room, he stayed there. As if he was distancing himself from everything.

Or maybe just her.

Right now Quinn seemed focused on that cinnamon roll his wife had promised him. She could see why; they weren't just cinnamon-y, they appeared to be stuffed with what looked like cream cheese frosting. He picked up the platter and walked into the great room, putting it on the big coffee table.

"Just think," Hayley said to Terri happily as she grabbed up a stack of napkins and followed, "now you can lay that burden down. Because Teague will be here in a few days."

Terri smiled at the delight in the other woman's voice, warmed inside by the obvious fact that she was happy for her, and for Teague. That meant so much, to know he had friends like these around him.

"The one with the toothpick's reserved, by the way," Hayley said. "It's Brett's favorite."

That only amplified the feeling of warmth. These were good people to have as friends. Teague had, as always, chosen well.

As she followed Hayley, Terri couldn't resist glancing back at Case, who was still by the window and apparently had no intention of joining them. Cutter had walked over to stand in front of him. The dog began nudging him with his nose, as if trying to make him move. Cutter stared up at him for a moment, but Case kept looking outside.

Finally the animal walked around behind him, and out of Terri's line of sight. She was about to look away, telling herself she had to stop staring at him all the time, when Case moved suddenly, sharply, as if startled. His head snapped around to look behind him. And down. She saw him say something too low to hear from the great room, and knew he was talking to Cutter. She wondered what the dog had done.

Terri started to sit on the couch near the warmth of the fireplace, but she caught sight of the neatly stacked pillow and blanket at the other end and stopped herself. Somehow it seemed too…something, to sit where he had slept last night. So she veered to one side and took the individual chair on the other side of the table.

She glanced back, just in time to see Case move again, almost as if he was catching his balance after being pushed. And his gaze still focused downward. Cutter was pushing him? Maybe…herding him?

"He won't give up," Quinn called out, "so you might as well give in."

Terri looked at the other man, a little amazed. He hadn't even glanced that way, yet he spoke as if he knew exactly what was going on.

"He's a herding breed," Hayley explained, as if she, too, knew exactly what was going on. Maybe Cutter made a habit of this. "And as the saying goes, resistance is futile."

And after another minute, Case must have agreed, because he gave in and walked out of the kitchen. Cutter was close on his heels, as if to make sure he didn't try and go back. When he'd taken a seat on the couch, near the neat stack of pillow and blanket, Cutter stood at the edge of the coffee table, looking from her to Case and back. A small sound issued from him, not a bark or a growl but almost a whine, as if he was unhappy with the arrangement.

Quinn and Hayley exchanged a glance, in that way very connected couples had of communicating without saying a word.

"I think that's the best you're going to do at the moment, boy," Hayley said to the dog. "Settle."

With a deep canine sigh, the dog walked over to his bed, circled a couple of times and plopped down. Terri had no idea what the dog was unhappy about, but was glad he'd managed to get the clearly reluctant Case back out here to join them.

Join you, you mean. Be honest.

Teague's oft-repeated instruction echoed in her mind. How many times had her big brother told her to always be honest? She remembered that summer day when she'd finally burst out with the conviction that underlay their entire existence, the day when she'd shouted *You're wrong! Quit lying!* To their mother. It had earned her a backhanded slap and banishment to her room for a week. Worst of all she'd banned Teague from even speaking to her.

Of course, she hadn't counted on Teague's cleverness. So in the middle of the night they met in the bathroom that adjoined their two bedrooms, and both retreated to the room farthest from their parents to talk. She'd protested then that she'd been honest, and look where it had landed her.

"Would you feel better if you'd lied and agreed with her?" he'd asked, without even knowing what the argument had been about.

"No," she admitted. Because the statement she'd erupted at had been yet another condemnation of Teague's plans and her brother himself.

She would never forget the look on his face when she'd explained. "You took that hit for me?" he'd asked.

"I couldn't let her keep lying about you and not say anything."

He'd pulled her into a fierce hug then. "I don't need your protection, sis. But I sure love you for it."

And now, within days, she would get to hug him back. Her big brother. Alive.

Her gaze shifted, once more fastening on the man sitting across from her. Because without him, it might never have happened. He had not only saved her life, he'd cared enough about this total stranger to search out the truth that would soon have them reunited.

And for that alone he would forever hold a piece of her heart.

Chapter Sixteen

Case recognized Brett Dunbar for what he was, despite being in civilian clothes, the moment he walked in. Which was after another announcement by the dog who'd practically forced him to rejoin this party, when he'd been mentally planning his exit. Cutter's bark was yet another different, distinctive one, and again before Case even heard the sound of tires on gravel. The dog must go on alert the moment anyone turned off the road.

How the animal knew who it was just from that sound, or maybe the sound of the vehicle, he had no idea. But he couldn't deny that every time Liam had appeared, it had been the same staccato, two-note bark. And every time Rafe arrived, it was that odd combination of short barks and longer sounds he had no word for. Of course there had been no missing the joyous tremolo that had issued from the dog when Quinn and Hayley had arrived.

He'd asked if they did that often, left their dog to guard people.

"Only when he insists," Hayley had said. And there hadn't been the slightest sign that she'd been joking.

The newcomer had bent to greet the dog familiarly, before he'd even taken off the coat he wore over slacks, a dress shirt—sans tie—and, interestingly, a pair of sturdy boots rather than dressier shoes. Practical, Case thought. Especially here, where there was a lot of open space he might have to trek through. He was tall, looked fit like a runner. His eyes were gray, his hair dark with just a touch of lighter gray at the temples and cropped typically short.

The man started to smile the moment he saw Terri, before Hayley even introduced them.

"I'd believe it even without DNA verification," he said, although he glanced at Quinn and added, "which I assume you're doing?"

Quinn nodded. "Already on the way. But I don't have much doubt how it will come back."

Dunbar looked back at Terri. "You're okay with them asking for the test?"

She smiled back at him. "Of course. I know how it will come back. And I appreciate them protecting my brother."

He didn't say "Right answer," but he might as well have from his approving expression. And then his gaze shifted to Case as Hayley introduced him to the detective.

"I know the name," Dunbar said as they shook hands. "It's a pleasure to meet you."

Case blinked. There hadn't been an ounce of sarcasm in the man's voice. He clearly meant what he'd said. "Not many working cops would want to even be seen with me these days," he said warily.

Dunbar lifted a brow at him. "I can see where you might believe that. So you'd probably be surprised to know just how many, including most I work with, know what really happened, know you were railroaded and admire you for the guts it took to try and hold a man like Joseph Barton accountable for trying to—and succeeding, sadly—to buy invulnerability."

Case stared at him. He couldn't doubt the sincerity not only in his voice but in that steady gaze. For a long moment

Case could only look at him, this man who had succeeded where he had failed, in taking down a much bigger fish. Finally he shook off his astonishment and spoke.

"You're the guy who took out a sitting governor for murder."

"I had the full resources and efforts of Foxworth behind me. And that made all the difference."

Case glanced at Quinn, beginning to think he was still underestimating the power of Foxworth. The big man's expression didn't change, but his wife smiled widely.

"I'm just sorry more on your department didn't stand with you," Dunbar said.

Case looked back at the detective. "They didn't want to crash and burn with me when it all blew—" He broke off, wondering why on earth he was defending them.

Dunbar smiled ruefully. "It's automatic, isn't it? Defending your fellow officers? And yet they didn't defend you."

"Some did," he admitted. "For a while."

"Until they realized Barton was going to walk and you were going to take the hit?"

"They were afraid for their jobs. They had families to support." He gave a sharp shake of his head. "Damn. It really is ingrained."

"It's part of why we survive," Dunbar said. "Those of us who still believe that To Protect and Serve is more than just a motto."

Just hearing the words snapped him back to the matter at hand. His history wasn't important; what was important was keeping Terri safe. Because there was a killer out there who knew she was dangerous to him. He resisted looking at her. He'd noticed the bruise developing under her chin, where the gun barrel had dug into her, and it reminded him powerfully that her life was at stake here.

"Thank you. For everything you said. But right now, we've got some of that protecting to do."

"Yes, we do. A lot, I'm afraid." Case felt a shiver of unease, wondering what it would take for this man to say that.

After a brief consultation with Quinn, they decided to head upstairs, to the meeting room with the table big enough for all seven of them. Cutter had apparently read his owner's mind and headed upstairs while the humans were still talking about it, and judging by the dog bed in one corner he was a regular attendee.

Meeting up here, even with the expansive view out to the meadow and the trees beyond, gave this a more formal, official air. Terri looked wary, probably wondering exactly what was going to be coming at her.

She glanced at him before she started upstairs, and the worry in her eyes completely shattered the fantasy he'd had before, that following her upstairs, her in those snug jeans, would be a painfully arousing experience. Because here he was, doing just that, and he could only focus on her fear of what was coming, and not just in this meeting. That protective urge flared in him again, hot, fierce and intensely personal this time. Enough to quash the attraction he constantly battled around her.

And that had never happened to him before in his life.

With a familiarity that spoke of frequent meetings like this, Dunbar pulled a flash drive out of his inside jacket pocket and plugged it into the laptop that sat open at one end of the table. Liam leaned over and tapped a couple of keys on the device, and a screen on the wall came to life, although still blank. Then he slid a remote control across the table to Dunbar, confirming Case's guess that they'd been through this many times before.

Before he did anything else, Dunbar looked at Terri, who was sitting across from him and next to Case in a seat she'd chosen purposely. She'd moved her chair around the corner of the table to sit beside him.

Get real, McMillan. She moved so she could see the screen.

"May I call you Terri?" Dunbar asked politely.

"Of course," she said instantly, with a smile so warm it would have irked him a little were it not for the wedding band on Dunbar's finger. He had the feeling this was a man who would never betray that vow. Or any other vow or oath he took.

Besides, that was something he had no right to feel. Not now, maybe not ever.

"All right, Terri," the detective said, "keeping in mind that it's just as important to say no if it's not him, the first picture you're going to see is of the man we suspect killed the clerk and attacked you."

She looked as if she appreciated the warning. But Case's brow furrowed. "He's been ID'd already?"

Dunbar nodded. He hit a key on the remote, and the screen loaded a black-and-white picture. It had the slightly blurry factor many such shots had, but it was clear enough—and familiar enough—that Terri visibly shuddered. Instinctively, and unable to stop himself, Case reached for her hand. She didn't just let him take it, she curled her fingers around his as if she welcomed the touch.

Dunbar looked at them. "Just to confirm, Case, is this the man you saw in the alley?"

"It is," he said flatly.

"And Terri, is this the man you saw outside the store, who then came in and committed the robbery and assaulted the clerk, and who later attacked you outside?"

He squeezed Terri's hand before she answered. As if she'd taken strength from that small gesture, she echoed not just his words, but his flat, certain tone.

"It is."

He hit a button on the remote and a second image popped up. Two photos, side by side, both clear, sharp and unmistakably a mug shot. Also the same man from that night. With the same full, weirdly square beard, long hair an entirely different color and a row of tattoos around the neck.

"The same?" Dunbar asked.

"Yes," they said simultaneously.

Dunbar let out an audible breath, set down the remote and leaned back in his chair. Case didn't like the sound, or the body language.

"What?" Terri asked.

Dunbar hesitated. Flicked a glance at Case. And Case reacted as he'd been trained, instinctively. He squeezed Terri's hand once more. "She's tough enough."

She went very still. And when he looked at her, she stared at him as if he'd said something totally unexpected.

"Of course she is," Hayley said quietly. "She's Teague's sister."

"All right then," Dunbar said. "Meet Marcus Zukero. Wanted for a string of robberies on the other side, similar to the one Saturday night. Lone operator, most of the time. Until recently, he's been careful about his targets, making sure there's no one else inside, choosing places without security cameras or making sure he's fully masked. Only the more recent ones involved physical attacks."

"He's escalating," Case said grimly.

Dunbar nodded. He glanced at Terri, whose brow was furrowed. "Don't most convenience stores have cameras?" she asked.

"Yes. We're guessing he cased out the place a couple of days beforehand. Then, that back stockroom was clear. That camera had just been installed back there the day before the robbery, because of some nighttime burglaries in the area."

"So he didn't make sure this place was still clear, and got sloppy with the mask. He's getting careless, too," Case said.

Dunbar nodded again. "He's got a long arrest record, a half-dozen times within the city limits alone. And he's a suspect in a lot more similar cases."

"And he's not in prison right now because?" Quinn asked.

"He's never been convicted."

"Why?" Terri exclaimed.

Case knew the answer. At least, he knew the two possible answers. One, he had an intimate and painful familiarity with, happened with disgusting frequency. The other was simply frightening.

He assessed the mug shot, the look of the man in it, then shifted his gaze to Dunbar. "I'm guessing it's not because he's got power and influence," he said dryly.

"It is not," Dunbar agreed.

Case's jaw tightened. A glance at Quinn and the two other Foxworth men told him they also realized what they were dealing with.

"I'm hoping," Hayley said slowly, "that it's because there were never any witnesses. But I get the feeling that's not it, either."

"No," Dunbar said. "There were witnesses, more than once. Those cases seemed ironclad. But some of the witnesses recanted their stories, or decided it wasn't him they'd seen after all." He paused, looking at Terri with concern clear in his gaze. "A couple of the others simply vanished. One was never found, the other…found too late."

Case felt her stiffen, down to the hand he held in his. And he knew she'd gotten there. And her voice was flat, steady and emotionless when she spoke.

"He killed them."

And Case knew her last illusion about being able to simply walk away from this had been shattered.

Chapter Seventeen

Terri felt more than a little numb. She had spent a while—she didn't know exactly how long—snapping back and forth between the churning fear Dunbar's revelations had brought on, and the reassurance the steady manner of those around her provided. For some reason all she could think of was a metronome, with its hand ticking back and forth relentlessly, from terror to hope and back again.

Quinn had snapped out commands, sending Liam to connect with someone named Ty, whom she gathered was their premiere tech guy out of their headquarters in St. Louis. She had registered that, puzzled because she'd thought this was their headquarters, but Hayley had explained they had five offices all over the country. Which had made Case draw back and stare at Quinn.

She remembered clearly the detective warning her gently that there were a lot of open cases with this guy's name on them, and he couldn't withhold the knowledge of her existence as a witness for long. She remembered he and Rafe looking over what appeared to be a map with several locations marked, which Rafe took a photo of. He'd then glanced at Quinn, who had nodded wordlessly. Equally silent, the tall, rangy man had left the room, to do what, Terri had no idea.

Then Quinn had called Gavin, saying the man still had

contacts from his days as a defense attorney, some of them not particularly savory. He might be able to find someone who knew Zukero.

With each Foxworth action her pulse had kicked up again. She felt a rush of gratitude that they were on her side, but that was followed by a rush of doubt; Zukero had gotten away with so much, so many times...

Eventually she couldn't maintain the constant swing any longer, and she had plummeted into the reeling numbness she was feeling now. She'd only been vaguely aware of going back downstairs, and of Case guiding her to a seat on the couch beside the fire. Only vaguely aware when the warmth hit her that she was chilled. Only vaguely aware that Cutter had been close on their heels, and had taken a seat on the other end of the couch, but slightly more aware this made Case sit down beside her, for which she was grateful.

"It's the aftermath," Case said gently. "You've had a long stretch of pure adrenaline and then crashing. It's only normal to hit the wall."

There was such warmth and understanding in his voice she couldn't help herself and turned toward him. His arm came around her, as if he didn't mind at all that she was leaning on him yet again. His jaw was stubbled this morning, and she resisted the urge to reach up and touch.

How could he have this effect on her, after only...she paused to calculate and was even more stunned. Thirty-six hours? Was that truly it? How was that possible? It felt like an eon. The moment when she'd boarded that plane in Des Moines on Friday seemed like another lifetime. So did the amount of energy and action it had taken to actually make this trip in the first place. But once she'd gratefully—after protests Mr. Gibson had quietly but firmly deflected—accepted her former boss's generous gift, and she'd realized she could afford to make this trip if she was careful about the spending, it was as if she'd been released from a fully stretched slingshot. As if all the inertia she'd felt in the years since Teague's death had been merely a postponement of this launch.

But Teague wasn't dead.

And if it hadn't been for Case McMillan, she might never have known.

She wanted to kiss him.

Be honest. You want to do more than just kiss him. And he's clearly not interested. And why would he be? You're the kind who runs from trouble and pain, and he's the kind who fights it.

No, she hadn't fought. She'd always rationalized it with the simple fact that there was nothing left to fight. That if Teague had been wounded and needed help, or had been missing in action, there would have been something to do, something to battle against. But there wasn't, and it was over.

And she hadn't even had the guts to face the reality.

She thought about what Brett Dunbar had said when he'd met Case…*the guts it took to try and hold a man like Joseph Barton accountable for trying to—and succeeding, sadly— to buy invulnerability.*

Yes, Case was that kind of man. The kind Teague—and now she knew the people he worked with—were.

Teague would understand, why she'd run. Or at the least he'd forgive her, but Teague had always forgiven her. He'd known her weaknesses, and he'd always helped her try and stand taller, stronger. As Case was helping her now. Because he, too, knew her weaknesses, even after only those thirty-six hours?

"It'll be all right." Case's voice was quiet, but certain. "You'll be all right."

"How can you be so sure?"

He gestured toward Quinn. "Because I'm beginning to

see what kind of operation Foxworth really is." She couldn't argue with that. But his next words rattled her. "You'll be safe with them."

Her gaze shot up to his face. "Does that mean…you're leaving?"

"Terri…"

She flushed. "I'm sorry. I'm sure you have a life to get back to. You've already done so much. I have no right to ask for more."

He went very still. "Are you?"

"What?"

"Asking for more."

The heat in her face increased, and she was sure her cheeks were bright red by now. She took a deep breath to steady herself. *You're stronger than you think you are, sis.* Teague's oft-spoken words echoed in her mind as she looked up at the man beside her, into those remarkable green-and-gold eyes. His expression betrayed nothing; he could have been asking about the weather. But something about his very stillness told her he truly wanted, and would wait for, an answer.

"I can see Foxworth is good at this," she said. "But you… you make me feel safer than anyone has in years." Something flickered in his gaze then, as if that hadn't been exactly what he'd wanted to hear. Something that made her add, honestly, "And I'd hate for you to just walk out of my life."

"But you don't need me around anymore."

It hit her then, what he really meant. Some undertone in his voice scraped away the pretense, the denial she'd been working so hard to shore up. And the words came tumbling out.

"But I want you." She realized how that had sounded, if only by the look on his face then. She started to add hastily that she'd meant she wanted him to stay around. "I didn't—"

"Don't."

"What?"

"Just leave it at that. I like that better."

And then, looking up into those eyes that so fascinated her, she saw everything she hadn't even known she wanted to see there. Caring, she'd known that all along, but now it was joined by a warmth—no, heat, definitely heat—that fired an echoing heat within her. Sparks, she thought. This was what they meant when they talked about two people striking sparks together.

Crazy, how heat could also make you shiver.

Or maybe tremble.

BUT I WANT *YOU*.

Case stood on the back patio of the Foxworth building, staring out across the open expanse toward the trees. He'd noticed the more recently planted decorative tree of some sort next, which bore some white-petaled flowers that seemed to be giving off a scent that reminded him of lemons. But it was the open space that drew him, as if he needed the emptiness at the moment.

Too bad it had warmed a bit, with the sun hitting the flagstone under his feet and collecting in the sheltered alcove. He'd been hoping for a blast of chilled air, to cool him down.

...I want you.

The words circled in his head in an endless loop. And no amount of telling himself she hadn't meant it the way he wanted her to seemed to be working.

I have no right to ask for more.

Those were the words he needed to remember. Because they applied to him more than her. He had no business even thinking what he was thinking, let alone asking for it. He was jobless, and resisting the idea that if he didn't leave this place he loved, he was likely to stay that way. He was toxic

here, painted as a lying cop who'd pushed around an innocent man. That Barton was about as helpless as a cornered
wolverine didn't seem to matter. Nor did the fact that the
wolverine was a hell of a lot more innocent than the twisted,
arrogant power broker who bought off everyone from his
victims to judges.

He felt the old anger start to rise, and fought it down. It
was pointless. He couldn't afford to waste any more time
dwelling on the unjustness of it all. He needed to focus on
the simple fact that one day before too long the money would
run out, and if he didn't want to be homeless as well as jobless, he was going to have to do something.

And that something was likely going to include some decisions he didn't want to make.

Hell, it already had. The decision to walk away from the
woman inside, who had looked at him with such trust in her
eyes. And longing? Interest? Hunger?

No, idiot, that was just wishful thinking on your part.

But didn't it just figure, with the way his luck—most of
it bad—was running, that he'd run into the first woman
who had drawn him like this now, when his life was in utter
chaos.

He drew in a deep breath of the clean, fresh air. Tried to
settle his mind. He would do what he had to here, including
help keep her safe, this woman who had already been hurt
so much by life.

And then he'd walk away, so that he wouldn't add anything to that pain. And he'd just think of it as another form
of saving her life.

Chapter Eighteen

Terri had never had a dog, so she wasn't quite sure what she was supposed to do. But it was obvious Cutter wanted her to do…something. The way he nudged her with his nose as she sat on the great room couch, backed away, then repeated the procedure, made it fairly clear. Finally she stood, and he wagged his tail in apparent approval.

What he did next was clear even to her. She didn't think there was anyone who wouldn't recognize the traditional "follow me" movements the dog made, going a few steps, then looking back at her. She wondered what he would do if she resisted, if she didn't move. She was curious enough to try it. Cutter lasted about ten seconds before he trotted back to her, circled behind her and gently bumped the backs of her legs.

She couldn't help it, even amidst all this; she laughed.

"All right, dog, I'm coming."

She'd felt restless anyway, with everyone gone. Detective Dunbar had left, promising to keep his inquiries active and to let them know if anything turned up, and kindly taking the time to reassure her she was in exceptionally capable hands. And she hadn't missed the fact that he'd glanced at Case as he said it, as if including him in the list of protectors.

The Foxworth people were upstairs, making calls, planning, doing whatever it was they did in situations like this. Case wasn't with them. He'd gone outside barely a minute after everyone else had left the room.

Escaped, you mean.

Because there was no doubting the haste with which he'd done it.

Can you blame him? He probably thought he was about to be free of this mess you dragged him into, and then you sucked him back into it by crying on his shoulder.

Because Case McMillan wasn't the kind to walk away from someone crying for his help. In fact, he was probably the kind of man who felt responsible for the life he'd saved. She could even understand that, sort of. How would it feel to risk your own life to save a stranger, only to have that stranger murdered later by the same guy you'd saved her from?

When she realized the dog was leading her to the back door, she stopped in her tracks. Case was out there. She stared at Cutter, for some reason remembering when he'd sprawled on the couch, leaving only the spot right next to her for Case. Then she gave a sharp shake of her head. The dog probably just needed to go out. Although why he hadn't followed Case when he'd gone outside, she didn't know.

But since the Foxworth crew was busy working hard— for her—she figured the least she could do was let their dog out. Except wouldn't she need a leash? Wouldn't he run off if she didn't?

But then she remembered when they'd arrived and he'd come out on his own, and how he opened the front door himself for new arrivals. So apparently he had free rein. She hesitated another moment, but Cutter was practically dancing next to the door. Finally she gave in, walking over and opening the door. The dog darted through, but then stopped, looking back at her, making her wonder yet again if the purpose wasn't to get himself outside, but her.

She gave a low chuckle at her own thoughts and stepped forward, still watching the silly—or very clever—dog.

Then a movement drew her attention away from Cutter. She looked up to see Case, standing a few feet beyond the edge of the patio, turning to glance over his shoulder at her. Something shifted in his expression, but he turned back to looking out over the huge meadow before she could put a name to it.

She wanted to retreat, but he'd seen her now, and it seemed too cowardly so she kept going. By the time she'd taken three steps she'd found her resolve. He didn't deserve to be stuck in this, not after what he'd done. And it was clear Foxworth knew what they were doing. She trusted they would keep her safe, for Teague's sake yes, but also because that was what they did.

She owed him this, at the least. So she walked toward where he was standing. The moment she stepped off the patio she felt a change in the air. Away from the stone and the side of the building the air was suddenly cooler, almost chilly. Wondered why he stood out here instead of in the relative warmth of the patio. But she kept going, afraid if she went back inside now she wouldn't have the nerve to return and do what she had to do.

She came to a halt beside Case. But not too close, because she knew by now how he rattled her. If she could feel his heat, his strength, she would weaken, change her mind. And if he touched her…

He didn't even glance at her. And that made it easier to plunge ahead. "You don't have to stay. I think I can trust these people. They'll take care of everything. For Teague's sake, if nothing else."

"They will," he confirmed.

Her heart sank. She found herself gritting her teeth against a wave of regret. She'd been determined to do this for his sake, but now, faced with the reality of him actually walking out of her life, never to be seen again, she was ready to jettison her convictions.

She told herself again that what he'd said when she'd fumblingly asked him to stay hadn't meant what she'd first thought.

But he'd stopped her when she'd tried to edit her own words.

Just leave it at that. I like that better.

Just leave it at *I want you.*

She shivered despite herself, and it had nothing to do with the chill in the air. She tried to suppress it, because she knew instinctively what would happen if he noticed. She had a gut-level certainty about who this man was. He was cut from the same cloth as those people inside. Not just upholders of the right, and willing to fight to do it if necessary, but…caretakers.

He was cut from the same cloth as her brother.

She'd vowed when she thought Teague dead that she would never again let herself depend on someone else. It simply hurt too much when you lost them. She'd spent the last ten years struggling, fighting to stand on her own, telling herself she was doing it because Teague would have wanted it.

But now, as she fought the urge to lean against this man, she wondered if she had really changed at all, if she'd learned anything, if she'd gained even one iota of strength.

Finally, standing beside him and looking, as he was, out over the meadow, she asked, "Will you leave?"

He looked at her then. "Is that a question or a request?"

She felt her cheeks heat, and wondered when was the last time she'd blushed so much in a day. With an effort she kept her voice neutral. "Whichever you need."

One corner of his mouth—that tempting mouth—twitched upward. "What I need—" his mouth tightened slightly now "—is to stop wanting what I can't have." Her heart leaped as her mind wanted to interpret that as a feeling matching her own. But his voice had been as level as hers, without inflection, and it made her doubt. And there was only one way to find out.

She steeled every bit of nerve she had, reminding herself of that scared girl she had been and how far she'd come. She still fell a little short of asking exactly what he wanted, but vowed she'd get to that, depending on his answer to what she did ask.

"And why can't you have it?"

He turned to face her. No shortage of nerve on his part. "Because I have no right to even ask for it." She saw his jaw tighten, then release. "I've got no job, and not much of a future."

She wanted to burst out with some righteous indignation, because that's what she felt after hearing what the detective had said to him about the case that had cost him his career. But it wouldn't make any difference.

"I'd offer every ounce of moral support I have, because you deserve it, but it wouldn't change the reality of what happened."

"No, it wouldn't."

She bit the inside of her lip, hesitating. She was probably the last person on earth who should be giving advice, but this mattered to her.

He mattered to her.

"If you're certain that future you once had is gone forever, then you have to start building a new one."

Something changed in his expression again. Something lighter came into those changeable eyes, and she almost wondered if he was going to laugh at her. She didn't think so, he was too kind, but—

"I guess you'd know a little something about that. Building a new life."

"A little. I know how hard it is, but I also know sometimes you have no choice."

His mouth twisted wryly. "Clearly you're tougher than me."

She was the one who laughed at that. "Me, tougher than you? Hardly. You're the one who risked your own life to save mine."

"That was just mental and physical training. There are other kinds of tough. I lost a job. You lost the person you loved most in the world. And you rebuilt."

"But it took me two years to even start to try."

"And you were seventeen. Like I said, tougher."

He meant it. Those green-gold eyes fastened on her, and something in that steady gaze practically screamed sincerity to her. He meant it. In his mind, in her circumstances, she was tougher. And he wasn't afraid to admit it. He was wrong, of course, but just the idea that he would think that was…

She didn't have a word for it but knew how it made her feel inside. And suddenly she wished she could take back her words about him being free to leave.

Because Case leaving was the very last thing she wanted.

Chapter Nineteen

He'd made it to his truck. But apparently getting into it was going to be trickier than expected.

He settled his go bag more solidly on his shoulder; he'd never gotten out of the habit of making sure it was with him, and had been thankful for that now. He stared down into a pair of dark, amber-flecked eyes. The eyes of the dog now sitting between him and the driver's door.

"Move it, mutt."

Cutter never even blinked. Nor did his gaze shift. It was like being in a stare down with something wild and unpredictable. Which was just unsettling enough that although he wondered what the dog would do if he tried to push him aside, he couldn't quite work himself up enough to try it. But there was no way to open the door without hitting the dog.

He'd left Terri in a rush, afraid he was going to do something truly stupid. He'd gone inside and grabbed the backpack, made sure he hadn't left even his toothbrush behind, scooped up his jacket and headed out the front door. He hadn't even realized Cutter was on his heels until they were out front and the dog raced toward his truck as if he'd somehow known that's where Case was headed.

As if the dog had sensed he was going to cut and run. And he was. Not because the situation was worse than what he'd faced before. Not because he didn't think he could help keep Terri safe. No, he was going to cut and run because she was getting to him in ways he couldn't afford. Ways he didn't dare even think about. Ways she would regret, once she was a little less scared. Right now she was just grateful to him, and that was overwhelming her common sense. Once she knew she was safe, that it was over, she'd realize he had too much baggage to deal with. And then she'd be stuck in the awkward position of having to tell him to go.

Too bad this darned dog didn't realize it.

"Running into a little interference there?"

He spun around and saw Hayley Foxworth walking toward him. Good, maybe she'd get her blessed dog out of his way.

"Not sure what he's up to, but he's definitely interfering."

"Cutter is…unique." She came to a halt beside him. Case noticed the dog never even looked at her, his supposed owner, but stayed fixated on him. "He has his own ideas about the way things should be. And once he's decided, there's no dissuading him. Trust me—I've tried."

He glanced at her, not sure if she was kidding or serious. "That makes it sound like he's running things around here."

"Sometimes," she said with a smile, "he is."

He looked at Cutter again. That eerily intense gaze still hadn't shifted. He turned back to Hayley. And in a different way, her light green eyes were as compelling as the dog's. Not to mention full of that feminine kind of understanding that warned him she might just have an idea of what he was feeling right now.

"Um…dog?" he suggested, with as much tact as he could manage.

Her smile widened. "Sometimes he is," she repeated. "And sometimes he's the most effective operative we have. He never, ever quits, or gives up on a cause. Foxworth as it is now wouldn't exist without him. He's got a nose for cases that fit our mission. He senses when people need help that we can provide. Among his other particular...talents."

He'd known people who were crazy about their dogs before, but this was more than a little over-the-top. It must have shown in his face, because she laughed this time.

"Oh, I know how it sounds. You remind me of Quinn in the beginning, and I know how hard he fought the idea, how long it took him to trust. But Cutter's track record is undeniable. So, since you know about it, I'll just say Cutter started the investigation that brought down the governor. Ask Brett Dunbar. Who, by the way, also met his wife on that case. That other talent I mentioned."

Case blinked. "What?"

"I told you, if not for that dog, Quinn and I would never have met. And over a dozen other couples wouldn't be together if not for him. Including everybody here, except Rafe."

Case looked down at the dog, who hadn't moved an iota, and was still staring up at him. And in that moment, looking into those dark, gold-flecked eyes, it almost seemed possible. All of it almost seemed possible.

"So," Hayley said, drawing out the syllable, "you might as well give in and come back inside."

He looked at the woman who was obviously an integral part of what seemed to be a sizable operation. He'd already realized she had an uncanny instinct for reading people, and for providing the emotional understanding the tough guys around her were probably a little short on. And for the moment he put aside her absurd claims about the capabilities of the canine at his feet.

"You don't need me."

"We don't, no." Her voice softened. "But Terri does."

For an instant he thought she meant it in relation to the way she'd said her dog had brought couples together. As if she thought he and Terri were…should be… He shoved aside that assumption. And spoke firmly.

"All she needs—" *and wants* "—is to be reunited with her brother."

"And you don't want to be around for that? Help see to it that it happens? That she stays safe until he arrives?"

His jaw tightened. He wanted all those things. Badly.

"That's what I thought. And what he—" she gestured at the dog "—knew. You're part of this, Case. You need to be part of it. And you've earned it, risking your own life to save hers."

"She doesn't—"

"Owe you? We know you don't think of it like that, or we wouldn't want you to stay. But she does trust you. Completely. Do you know why?"

He shrugged awkwardly. "Because of that night, I guess." His mouth twisted. "And because I remind her of her brother," he said, and it came out sounding more than a little sour.

Hayley gave him a smile that seemed out of place with what he'd said. "So that's it."

"What?"

"You think she looks at you like a brother."

He blinked. "That's what she said."

"No, she said you reminded her of him. And for her, that's the highest possible compliment she could give a man." Her smile widened. "I've watched her watching you, Case. And believe me, she doesn't look at you like a brother."

The implication in her words and her tone kicked up his pulse. Could she be right? He'd already noticed how observant Hayley was about people. How she seemed to understand even what wasn't stated.

Cutter moved then, getting back up on his feet and pressing himself against Case's leg. Without thought he reached down to touch the dog's head. The moment he did he experienced that odd sensation again, that was warming and soothing. And a sudden feeling that Hayley was right, that he should stay, at least until this was over and Terri was back with her brother. He'd already left his former career in fragments. He didn't want to leave this unfinished.

He let out a long breath. Then, decision made, he shoved his keys back into his pocket. Hayley smiled, and oddly, her dog gave a small yip that sounded approving.

You're starting to believe the crazy, McMillan.

"I'm guessing you're thinking her life's in an uproar, so she's not thinking straight."

He blinked, startled at the accuracy of her guess. Which sent him back to her comment that Terri didn't look at him like a brother. Was she right about that, too?

Then she gestured at Cutter. "But he's thinking straight."

If not for that dog, Quinn and I would never have met. Over a dozen other couples wouldn't be together if not for him.

Her earlier words echoed in his head. They sounded more foolish than they had when she'd said them. But foolish people did not build an enterprise like the Foxworth Foundation.

"So what am I supposed to do? Just stay put while you do the work?"

"It's what we do. And we can do it better if we know you're helping to keep her safe," Hayley said.

He was torn. He wanted to be out there, hunting. He wanted this guy taken out, and fast. It wasn't a new feeling for him. He'd felt it often when there was a predator like Zukero on the loose. But this time it was different. The city was no longer his to protect, no longer his concern.

But Terri was.

He couldn't quite explain the feeling of responsibility he had. He knew the theories, that saving somebody's life created a bond of sorts. But he'd saved more than one person in his career in uniform. Several, in fact. They'd even pinned some awards on him for it. For all the good it had done when he'd come up hard against the wall of Joseph Barton's purchased power.

Still, even without the badge and the mission, he wanted to go after this killer, fiercely. The only thing he wanted more was to protect Terri.

He couldn't do both.

He shouldn't do either.

Walk away.

Yes, that's what he should do. He shouldn't let Hayley and, of all things, her dog stop him. They didn't need him.

Terri didn't need him.

I want you.

His gaze fastened on the madrone tree on the far edge of the meadow. The distinctive reddish bark stood out, made it the easiest to focus on. He tried to do just that, focus on that tree as if it was the first one of its kind he had ever seen, and clear his mind of everything else.

But the only thing he accomplished was to realize that what he'd thought was a solid foundation had crumbled beneath him; the thing uppermost in his mind was not worry about what he was going to do with the rest of his life.

It was making sure Terri had the chance to live the rest of hers.

Chapter Twenty

Terri watched Case walk across the room toward her. She knew he'd been trying to do the right thing, but it still hurt that he'd almost left. She also knew he thought she was under too much stress to know what she really wanted. After all, a man who'd already murdered multiple people was probably out there looking for her to add to his scorecard. And she probably should be more frightened than she was. But the still new knowledge that Teague was alive buoyed her up above the worry.

She stood beside the fire, glad of its warmth even though the room was already cozy. Case came to a halt a couple of feet away. A safe distance? Is that what he was thinking? She heard Hayley going up the stairs, most likely leaving them the privacy to deal with this.

The question was, what was "this"?

"I was going to leave," Case said, his voice gruff.

"I saw." Her own voice was tight.

"But I need to see this through."

She understood what he meant; she just didn't like it. And that enabled her to keep her voice calmer when she said, "I don't want you to stay because you think you should. You already saved my life once."

"And that's why."

"What? You think you took on some kind of responsibility for me, by saving me?"

He started to answer, stopped, then said only, "In a way."

She had to look away, afraid he'd somehow read what she wasn't saying in her expression. She tried to keep her feelings out of her tone. "If that's the only reason, go."

"It's not the only reason."

Her gaze snapped back to his face, because his voice had sounded exactly as she'd tried to stop her own from sounding. She told herself not to read anything into that. Or into the intensity of the way he was looking at her, those almost exotic eyes boring into her. Not to fool herself into seeing something that wasn't there.

To fool herself that he wanted to stay.

Because he wanted to be with her.

Be honest. You want him to want you, period.

The admission made her want to turn away, to run from this. But then something he'd said came back to her again. *I have no right to even ask...*

If that's what he thought, how he felt, then maybe it was up to her. She swallowed tightly. "What other reason is there?"

"This," he said hoarsely. He crossed the short distance between them in one stride, his hands going to her shoulders. He held her, but not so firmly that she couldn't break free if she wanted.

She didn't want to. All her wanting was tied up in what she knew was coming. And then his mouth came down on hers. Just as she'd been thinking, dreaming about since that night. It was ten times the jolt that night had been. All the terror of those moments in the alley, all the fear of finding out she now likely had a killer hunting her, vanished at the first touch of his lips. She knew they hadn't gone away, it was just that now, that she was getting what she'd longed for so much, they didn't matter. Nothing mattered except the burst of heat and sensation.

It was almost fierce, as if he couldn't help it. There was a hunger in it, and every nerve she had rejoiced in like recognizing like. She'd known it would be like this, with him. She didn't know how, since she'd never experienced anything like it, but she'd known. And all her suddenly enraptured mind could think was, "At last."

That fierceness gentled, his mouth became more coaxing. The first wave of sensation ebbed a little, to be replaced by a warmth that rippled through her, spreading to every part of her, secluded spaces that she hadn't even realized were cold until he warmed them.

She wanted more, and more; she didn't want this to stop, ever. She clutched at him, needing him closer. As if she could ever move such a big, powerful man. Unless he wanted her to. And she couldn't stop herself from taking the fact that he did move closer as an answer to that question.

She heard a soft moan, realized it had come from her. It triggered something in him as well, because she heard a low, almost harsh rumble that sounded as if it had ripped from him involuntarily.

And then it ended. He broke the kiss, let go, pulled back. And then, as if that weren't enough he took a step back. She stared up at him, a little dazed. Why had he stopped? It had been so lusciously sweet, so nerve-searingly wonderful, why had he stopped?

Then she heard footsteps on the stairs. Had he heard them before she had? Was that why he'd stopped, because someone was about to walk in on them? Or had he stopped on his own? Had it…not been as amazing for him as it had been for her?

Are you going to just stand here obsessing about whether he stopped because he wanted to or because he had to?

She realized she didn't want to look at him, for fear the answer she didn't want to know would be clear on his face. Although she'd never been rattled in quite this way before, she'd gained a certain strength over the last decade, and she called on it now. She steadied herself and turned toward the stairs to see Quinn heading toward them, although he was looking at the phone in his hand and not them. Thankfully, since she had the feeling her emotions would definitely be clear on her face.

Quinn didn't bother with preambles. "As we expected, the city police handling the case are very anxious to talk to you."

Terri couldn't stop her grimace. Quinn only smiled at her. "It will be fine," he said reassuringly. "I think you'll find having Gavin de Marco in the room representing your interests will keep things well in check. We've set it up for tomorrow morning."

She glanced at Case. "Will you be there?"

He let out a short, sharp laugh. "I'm the last person you need in the same room with you and them." She frowned as if she didn't understand. So he told her, flatly. "Once they realize who I am, they'll decide you're a liar, too."

"They're going to want to talk to you anyway, since you witnessed the assault in the alley," Quinn said.

"I know, but...don't link us," he said, with a flicker of a glance at Terri. "My rep could cast a shadow on her, in their minds."

"We'll deal with that attitude if and when it happens. But that brings me to a question. The investigator who's handling this is a Jim Coffman. Know him?"

Case looked startled, then almost relieved. "Yeah. He's a decent guy."

Quinn nodded. "Feeling I got," he agreed. "Brett doesn't know him personally, only by reputation as a good investigator."

"He is."

"A friend?"

Case's expression changed. He lowered his gaze, and she heard him suck in a breath. "He…was. One of the few who protested what they were doing. And who reached out, after." He grimaced. "I pretty much shut him down. I didn't want anything to do with the place or the people."

"Understandable," Quinn said.

Terri stared at Case, hurting inside at the pain she'd heard in his voice. Case's life had been blown apart almost as much as hers.

Quinn shifted his gaze back to her. "I don't want you going to the city, where Zukero is most at home, so Detective Coffman will be coming to you."

Case's head came up sharply. "Here?"

Quinn smiled. "No. I don't want them knowing where she's staying either, until we get a better feel for things." Case relaxed visibly. "Gavin has an office in town for occasions when we want people to have to walk past his name on the door."

Case chuckled at that. "It'd get my attention—that's for sure."

It was odd, Terri supposed, that the fact Case approved of the Foxworth plan made her feel better about it herself. She trusted his judgment that much, already. Not simply because he'd saved her life, but because of who he'd obviously been, an incorruptible cop. It had been the job that had let him down, not the other way around.

"So, will you be there?" she asked again. When he hesitated, she added quietly, "With me? Please?"

He let out a breath. Glanced at Quinn, who simply raised a brow, awaiting a decision. A decision that was Case's to make. One side of his mouth—God, that luscious, fire-inducing mouth—twisted upward.

"All right."

He sounded more uncertain than she could have imagined. It was not a trait she would have associated with him. And it made her fully realize what she'd done. At first she'd been thinking only of herself, and that she wanted him there. But she'd also wanted him to stand proudly among those who had let him down, so they'd know they hadn't beaten him. It had been an impulsive idea, maybe one she shouldn't have voiced.

But now that she had and he'd agreed, albeit reluctantly, she was glad. Not only for her own sake, but for his. After what he'd done for her, it was only right that she would want the best for him, wasn't it?

It wasn't until she looked at him again, saw the tension in his jaw and the taut cords of his neck, that she belatedly considered that maybe she didn't have the right to assume she knew what was best for him.

"You...don't have to. If you'd really rather not."

He turned his head, and she struggled to meet that intense gaze. "I said I'd do it."

And Terri realized that for a man like Case McMillan, that was all it took.

Chapter Twenty-One

"It'll be all right," Case said to Terri as they got into the big Foxworth SUV.

He'd been glad of the size of it; at his height the backseat of a smaller one would be cramped. Of course, they'd had to share that seat with Cutter, who had leaped in and taken a spot near the window—Case supposed so he could see or smell things as they passed—leaving just enough room for he and Terri to sit right beside each other. He would have preferred a bit more space between them, because the memory of that kiss was still rocketing around his brain.

His entire body, he corrected himself wryly. Which was aching as much from the need that had sparked as from spending another night sleeping on the couch in the Foxworth great room. With Terri just one door away.

Your own fault, McMillan. You gave in to the urge and set yourself up for all kinds of hell.

She was looking at him now, smiling, as if she hadn't needed his reassurance. "I know," she said, confirming his guess. "Nothing will ever be as bad as thinking my brother was dead. That tidal wave wiped out my life. This is just some heavy surf."

Case watched her, seeing the true person she was. This was no longer the rightfully terrified woman he'd encountered that night. This was the woman who, at seventeen, found the courage to walk out of what was left of that life and build a new one. One that didn't include the gargoyles who had celebrated the death of the person she loved most.

"You really are going to be fine." It wasn't reassurance that time, it was simply expressing his new certainty about the woman before him now. She seemed to hear the difference, and the smile she gave him made him want to kiss her all over again.

And all over.

The sound of an incoming text on the SUV's dash helped him veer off that unhelpful path.

"Gavin," Quinn said as they pulled off the long Foxworth headquarters driveway onto the road. "They've arrived at his office."

Less than five minutes later—Redwood Cove was more village than town—they, too, had arrived. Quinn parallel parked the big vehicle with practiced ease, in front of an all-too-familiar kind of car. Case recognized the plainwrap, as they called it, instantly.

"And there they are," he muttered.

"The office is upstairs," Hayley said as they got out.

They walked past what appeared to be an American vision of an Irish pub into an alcove leading to a stairway. Somehow the idea of the man who'd been one of the most famous lawyers in the world having an office above a pub seemed... appropriate. What surprised Case was the lack of signage. There was no sign out front, or on the wall in the passageway to direct you, not a clue that if you were looking for him you needed to go up those stairs. It seemed you would only find Gavin de Marco if you already knew where to look.

Or if you had Foxworth guiding you.

Maybe he worked only with Foxworth now. Case knew he'd walked away from all the fame and glory and money, but he'd never known why. But to go from defending the highest of high-profile crooks and criminals to helping a foundation that fought for the little guy spoke of a gut-deep change in the man, and he wondered what had brought it on.

There was, however, as Quinn had promised, a sign on the door. The kind of elegant plaque you'd normally see at the kind of office you'd expect Gavin de Marco to occupy. He remembered what Quinn had said about the purpose of this place, and thought that sign and the name would do the trick.

Once they stepped inside, something else solidified that impression with a jolt. One entire wall was glass, and the expansive water view over the small cove and out to the sound would have been enough on its own, but the sight of the seventy mile distant but still massive Mount Rainier was breath stealing. Fourteen-thousand-plus feet of mountain jutting up out of seemingly nowhere did that. He assumed the private part of the office had the same view, and he caught himself nodding; this was the kind of office where he'd expect to find someone on de Marco's level.

"Wow," Terri said, staring just as he was. "This is the first severe clear day where I could see the mountain. I think I'd forgotten just how huge it really is."

"Spoken like a native," Case said. There were mountains all around Puget Sound, but only one was *the* mountain.

Hayley came over and gently touched Terri's arm. "Ready?" Terri drew in a long breath.

"You'll have Gavin with you," Quinn assured her. "And as we talked about, any time you want to call a halt or need a break, you just say so and it'll happen. He'll see to it."

"You'll be here when it's over?" Terri asked, and Case didn't miss the quick, sideways glance she gave him, including him in the question.

"We will," Quinn said.

"Well, I may not be back from the bakery yet," Hayley said, quite cheerfully.

"Those cinnamon rolls?" Terri said, sounding hopeful.

"I'll bring you back two. You've earned it."

The two women smiled at each other, and Case marveled again at Hayley's knack of reading and relating to people.

Gavin's office door opened, and they all turned. A second man was behind him, and Case recognized him as quickly as he had the unmarked police car outside.

"Hey, Hard Case," Coffman said when he saw him, using the nickname Case hadn't heard since he'd left the force.

"Jim," he said, keeping his voice neutral with an effort as the detective walked over to him.

"You sure as hell dropped off the planet. Tried to call you a few times."

"I know," Case said. "I was…in no shape to talk about it. And after I blew you off a few times, I figured you wouldn't want to talk to me, so I didn't call back."

"You figured wrong, buddy." Coffman reached out and gripped his shoulder. "I've been worried about you for a year now. Me and a lot of others." The other man lowered his gaze, as if in shame. And it echoed in his voice when he spoke again. "We should have stood up for you. More than we did, anyway."

"You spoke out," Case said. "I can't tell you how much that meant to me."

"For all the good it did," Coffman said sourly, letting go now.

"I'm sorry I never told you at the time. I know it must have complicated your life."

Coffman shrugged. "Nobody said being a cop would be easy. I just never realized how many of the problems would be coming from the inside." He shifted his gaze to Terri, and with his usual grace, said, "Sorry, Ms. Johnson. Didn't mean to ignore you, but I haven't seen this guy in a long time."

"Don't apologize," she said. "It's good to know he wasn't alone as he thinks he was."

Coffman smiled. "He was not." He looked back at Case. "Every time we're at the Hole In One—" Case nearly winced at the name of the old hangout, where many officers went at end of watch, and where he'd spent more than a few hours himself "—and a story about that slime Barton comes on the news, we all raise a toast to you, for having the guts to even try to take him down."

Case stared at his old colleague, more than a little stunned. He'd thought of himself as a pariah for so long he was having trouble processing that maybe he wasn't as disowned as he'd thought. He felt a light but steady touch on his right arm. Terri's touch, which he would have thought—after that kiss—would have rattled him. But instead it steadied him, lessened the churning in his gut over the stirring up of old, painful memories.

"I've got your statement," Coffman said to him, "but I may have more questions later."

Of course he would. Although he'd put everything he could think of in the document he'd put together at Foxworth, and that Quinn had sent to Gavin. Case suspected they didn't like the idea of him as a witness, not after he was tossed from the department under a dark cloud. But he had seen what he'd seen in the alley, and it would add to Zukero's sentence if he was convicted. Which would happen unless the entire system had crumbled—Terri's testimony should be more than enough to get the job done. The bigger crime had been what she'd witnessed. They could paint Case as what he was, just somebody passing by who got involved.

Right. Like they won't drag up every aspect of your past to discredit you.

He tried not to think about what Zukero's defense attorney might try to do to him on the stand. Time enough to worry about that if and when they caught the guy.

"Shall we?" de Marco, who had considerately not interrupted the reunion, asked, gesturing toward his inner office. Case had the thought that back in the day, this little two-minute interlude would have cost at least fifty bucks if de Marco was charging them his usual rate. Maybe more.

He wondered what he should do now. No meeting involving a complex situation and lawyer was ever short; if he'd learned nothing else from his own experience, he'd learned that. He stared out the big windows toward the waterfront, which looked interesting. Maybe he should take a walk.

You mean take a hike, which you should have done the moment you knew she was going to be okay.

"Mr. McMillan?"

He spun around to see de Marco still in the doorway, looking at him. Maybe the guy had arrived at the same thought, that now that Terri was here and safe, he should take that hike.

"We'll start with all of us, until we reach the actual witness statement. Ready?" de Marco asked, nodding toward the room where he could now see a small conference-type table with a half-dozen chairs. And then, as if he'd read Case's reaction perfectly—which he probably had, you didn't rise to the heights he had without being damned good at reading people—he added, "She's requested you be there."

"And you didn't talk her out of it?" The words were out before he could stop them.

"I didn't even try," de Marco said. "The more people who care about her she has around her right now, the better."

Care about her. Yeah, he did that. A little too much.

But he walked into the room anyway.

Chapter Twenty-Two

Terri found herself wishing Hayley had foregone the trip to the bakery, even for those luscious rolls. She'd never been in a room with four people quite like these, very different yet similar in one aspect, an aspect that was almost overwhelming. And none more so than the man at her right hand; Case might be at loose ends just now, but he was no less a powerful presence than the others.

They were most definitely men. The kind of men who did what had to be done, be it protecting lives or rights.

As Teague had been—no, *is*!

She still delighted in having to correct herself, and wondered how long it would take to get out of the decade-old past-tense habit. However long, she planned to enjoy every step of that particular task.

Gavin, as he'd insisted she call him, opened the meeting by thoughtfully dealing with her biggest worry first. "Detective Coffman is quite aware of your crucial importance to their effort to put Zukero where he belongs. They want you in protective custody."

She met the famous attorney's steady gaze, then looked at Quinn, who gave her a slight nod. Finally she looked up at Case, whose jaw was set and whose tension she could feel radiating from him. Because she'd insisted he be here?

He'd seemed almost glad to see the man who had once been, and maybe still was, his friend. But she'd also wanted him here because, quite simply, he made her feel safer. And she couldn't stop herself from leaning slightly, so that their arms touched. Nothing blatant, just a touch.

Only then did she look at the detective. He was an older man, older than the others in the room anyway, with close-cropped graying hair and dark brown eyes. He had a steady look about him that she liked, but she was under no illusion that he wanted to protect her more than his case against the man they were hunting. That was his job, and she had the feeling he was very good at it.

But she was concerned about more than just putting Zukero away. And she trusted these people her brother worked for. And Case. Above all, she trusted Case, never mind how short a time she'd known him.

"I already am protected," she said simply.

Out of the corner of her eye she saw Quinn and Gavin smile. And she smiled herself when she heard Case mutter under his breath, "Damn straight." And when he looked at her, she saw the determination in his eyes, and she felt safer than she had since she'd walked out of the store that night.

Coffman was looking at Quinn. "You've got quite the reputation around here. You're coordinating this? Foxworth, I mean?"

"We are. Full force. She's family."

Coffman blinked. "Family?"

"Her brother is one of our top operatives."

Coffman looked at Gavin then, and she didn't think she was wrong in thinking the detective a little awestruck. "And you, too?"

"You want Terri, you deal with me," Gavin said simply, unequivocally.

Coffman grimaced. He turned back to Case. "And you're on this as well?"

He repeated Quinn's words, although they had an entirely different effect on her coming from him. "Full force."

Coffman considered this, and she noticed Case never looked away from the man who had once been a colleague and seemed to still want to be a friend. Finally Coffman said, "Okay, I'll sign on to it as long as we have access, but I'll have to clear it with my boss."

Case's head came up as he looked back at his former colleague. "Who is your boss these days?"

"Captain Bristow."

Case's eyes widened. Terri could tell by his tone of voice and his smile that he was joking when he said, "Captain? That reprobate made captain?"

"He did. And amazingly, he's pretty good to work for."

"Always figured you'd replace the old man when he retired."

Coffman laughed. "Not me. I'm not brass material."

"They just didn't want to lose their best detective."

Terri watched this exchange with interest, realizing she was getting a glimpse of who Case had been. But then something about the way Coffman was looking at Case registered, in the moment before he said quietly, "Not after they'd already lost their best cop. The one with more guts than any of us."

Case went very still beside her, his expression a combination of bemused and puzzled. As it had been when detective Dunbar had said something similar. Apparently he'd never realized how many had been on his side, who thought he'd done the right thing. Or he had been too shell-shocked to think of anything except that life as he'd known it was over. She understood that feeling, all too well.

She was still thinking about that when Quinn and Case

left the room. The in-depth interview about the robbery and what had turned out to be a murder was about to begin. At least Gavin was still here, acting as her attorney. And she appreciated the way he quickly got an agreement that her juvenile transgressions of taking already donated clothes and stealing food were not an issue and would not be brought up, since they were long past the statute of limitations for misdemeanors. And she liked the way Coffman smiled and said he guessed she'd already punished herself about those actions quite enough.

She went through it all again, that night when she'd headed for the convenience store mainly for the warmth, had passed a man outside she'd barely glanced at. She went through it step by step, appreciative again when Gavin sensed the memories were crowding her and made sure she got a breather. And for the way he'd warned the detective before they'd started that she would go through this once and only once.

When she'd finished with the part about the robbery, and the vicious beating of the clerk that she'd observed but not known was fatal, she'd needed one of those breathers.

She was surprised when Coffman's questions began; she'd been afraid he was going to jump to what had taken place in the alley. She breathed a little easier as she listened and responded as best she could. There had been a couple of questions she'd been able to answer—description of the tattoos that ringed Zukero's neck, the logo on his hoodie—but most she could not. She had no idea how tall he was except taller than her, what kind of gun it had been other than a black handgun or if he'd had any kind of accent, or in fact anything helpful, except that he'd smelled a bit like marijuana and had a long, scratchy beard.

She was starting to feel like the most oblivious person on the planet when he abruptly shifted to the scene in the alley. Just the question caused a spike in her pulse, but she got through the story by focusing more on Case's part in it. Still, it came out in short, choppy sentences.

"He threw something—he told me later it was his keys— that hit the metal trash can. It made a loud noise. Zukero jerked around to look. That was the first—the only time I felt the pressure of that gun barrel under my chin stop. Case was there in an instant. Slammed the hand with the gun. Zukero shoved me away. I hit the wall. Case put himself between me and him. Me and the gun. Zukero ran."

She was about to say something about how Case seemed torn between staying with her or chasing Zukero, but at the last second stopped herself. It wasn't her place to say it.

Still, after a moment of looking at her, Coffman said quietly, "Sounds like the Hard Case I remember." At her expression, he smiled. "What we used to call him. Because he was so damned upstanding."

"Seems he still is," said Gavin, who hadn't spoken other than to rein in Coffman when he'd asked her to speculate on some things she really didn't know.

"Yes," she agreed firmly, "he is. And he deserved better than he got from your department."

"I won't argue that. But throw in the courts and politicians, too," Coffman said mildly.

"That," Gavin said in a tone that rang with experience, "is a given. Are we done here?"

"This time," Coffman said. "But I may need—"

"To talk to her again. I know the drill, detective. And you have my number if that need arises."

Terri felt relief as he made it clear that any further contact would be through him. And she gave a small, wondering shake of her head that the lawyer so famous even she had heard of him was staunchly in her corner.

Coffman paused with his hand on the doorknob, and looked back at her. "You're lucky to have Case on your side.

He wasn't just a good cop, he's a good man. Don't let what happened distort your view of him."

"It couldn't," she said, liking the man for standing up for his friend despite the current distance between them.

Coffman nodded, and left.

"You're all right?" Gavin asked.

"Yes. Thank you. Will he really need to talk to me again?" she asked.

"Eventually," Gavin said. And there was great empathy in his expression when he added quietly, "If not before then, then certainly in trial preparation."

She blinked. Trial. Testifying. She'd known that, but she'd managed to put it out of her mind for the moment. She suppressed a shiver at the thought of having to see Zukero again, even—or maybe especially—in a courtroom.

But she would do it. She had to do it. Case had risked his life to save her. She couldn't be a coward and refuse.

Chapter Twenty-Three

"Coffman was decent to you?"

Case asked it while watching Terri watch the fire. They had the place to themselves again, with the exception of Cutter, who was so glued to Terri's side that Case had once again ended up sitting next to her because it was the only open spot. At the moment he was regretting he hadn't headed for the chair opposite her, and wondering why he hadn't thought of that before he'd sat down.

"He was," she answered. "Quite polite, in fact. Although perhaps that was more Gavin being there than him."

"He would have been anyway. He's not a bad guy."

"There are good cops. Many of them. Even most, maybe."

Terri turned her gaze from the fireplace to Case. Who tried not to think she was talking about him. And to ignore the fact that when she looked at him he felt just as the hot, dancing flames must feel.

Giving emotions to lifeless things, now, McMillan?

That he himself had felt pretty much lifeless for the last fourteen months was an irony he didn't deny. He'd just developed a very different opinion about how he'd reacted in general to his situation in the last three days.

Three days. Three days and not only his life, but his entire view of his life—and himself—had been turned up-side down.

"You look so...intense. What are you thinking?"

She caught him off guard with the question. That had to be the reason he answered the way he did. Honestly. With words he hadn't said even to himself. "That I'm nowhere near as tough as I used to think I was. I lost a job. You lost your brother. You rebuilt. I'm still...wallowing."

Her expression flickered for a moment when he mentioned her brother, and the loss that was no longer. But otherwise she looked merely thoughtful, considering.

"It's been what, a little over a year for you? Two years after Teague was...reported KIA, I was getting off a bus in Iowa. I was totally lost. I'd just kept moving, as if that could put the pain behind me. It felt as bad as that first moment, as if nothing had changed, or healed, and never would."

He appreciated that she was trying to show she'd been no better off than he was at the same time period, but that didn't change the basics, that the causes of their pain were not very comparable.

And then, as if she'd read his thought, she said gently, "I lost my brother. You lost your future, yourself, maybe your whole concept of self. Is one really worse than the other?"

He just stared at her, lost for words at her seemingly complete understanding and compassion. Perhaps she had an excess of it because it had been so lacking in her life growing up. Except from the one person she loved, and had thought lost forever.

He searched for something, anything to say that would move past this awkwardness, the tightness in his throat and chest. "What happened when you got off that bus?"

She smiled then, widely. "The first person I ran into was one of those good cops."

He hadn't expected that. "Right off the bus?"

She nodded. "He'd just dropped someone off. He must have read my expression, because he took the time to talk to me. And he bought me lunch, even sat with me while I ate it."

Hitting on you? Case's first thought made his jaw tighten.

"He said I reminded him of his daughter, who'd gone through a lost stage, but now was about to graduate college."

Okay, so probably not hitting on her. Case mentally apologized to the unknown officer. He tried to imagine what the lost, betrayed, teenaged Terri must have looked like. Something to spark that protective instinct he himself had, that's for sure.

She went on. "He's the one who aimed me toward the county GED program, and actually introduced me to Mr. Gibson, where I ended up working." Her smile became a soft, knowing one. "He's the kind of cop you were."

He lowered his gaze, not knowing what to say to that, either. "I'm…glad you found someone like that right off."

"There were lot of someones there. Everybody in that little town was kind to me. Well, except for Mrs. Waters, but everybody warned me about her being the town curmudgeon."

He couldn't help the chuckle that escaped. "My dad used to call our next-door neighbor that. I had to go look it up."

"Do you…still have him?"

"Yeah. He's living in Arizona now. Drying out after all the years here, he says."

Terri smiled. "How about your mother?"

His own smile faded. "Never in the picture."

Her brows rose. "Never?"

"She never told my dad she was pregnant, because she planned to dump me anyway. He only found out about me through a friend of a friend. By then I was six months old, and in the system awaiting adoption. He came for me."

Something changed in her expression then, making it a combination of wistfulness and warmth.

Wistfulness because she'd never had that kind of parental love and devotion? That he could believe. Warmth because… she was glad he'd had it? He wasn't sure why he was pouring all this out anyway. He rarely did. Never, in fact. Yet he kept going. Maybe because of that warmth.

"He had to wade through a lot of crap to prove he was my father, and then jump through a lot of hoops, but he won."

"And he raised you himself?"

He nodded. "With a lot of help from his sister. She was essentially my real mother. We wouldn't have made it without Aunt Fay."

She was looking at him wide-eyed now. "And you think my life was tougher?"

It took an effort, but he met her gaze. "It was. First, what happened to me was all before I was even old enough to remember. And second, I have never for one moment doubted both my father and my aunt wanted me, loved me."

Something came into her expression then, something between amazement and a warmth that dwarfed that of the fire. "That you would understand that…" Her voice trailed away, and he thought he saw the sheen of tears in her eyes. Then she blinked rapidly and he knew he'd been right. "They must be so proud of you."

"You mean like real parents would be of you?"

He saw his point register in the shy little smile that curved one corner of her mouth. That mouth he wanted to kiss again. And again. Why the hell did the Foxworths keep leaving them alone here, except for their darned dog who kept getting in the way of his plans to put some distance between them? He knew they were around, keeping watch as Quinn had laid out—and the lethal Rafe was enough to make anyone who'd looked into those cool, assessing eyes feel safe—but they weren't coming inside. He knew it was part of the plan, but it wasn't helping.

Before he could do something stupid like follow through on that wish to kiss her, every part of her, he rushed on. "Yes, they are proud of me." He grimaced. "Even now."

"If they're the people you say they are, probably more now than ever."

It was his turn to stare. "You really have left your parents, and their influence, behind you, haven't you? You haven't let them color your view of…everything."

"I refuse to give them—just her, now, I guess—that much power." Her smile turned rueful. "It took me a while to get there, though. Without Teague to remind me."

"But his lessons took, in the end."

That got him a much better smile. "Yes. And his example. Oh, Case, I can't wait for you to meet him!"

He blinked. She was about to be reunited with the beloved brother she'd thought dead, and she was excited for him to meet him? And more, she expected—wanted—him to be here that long?

"What if they round up Zukero tomorrow? With Coffman, Dunbar and Foxworth all working it, it could happen."

"Are you saying that if they do, there will be no reason for you to stay?"

The coward in him wanted to look away from that steady gaze, to refuse to answer her question. But somehow he couldn't. What was it about this woman that turned him to mush so easily?

"My life's a mess, Terri."

"For now. Do you intend to leave it that way?"

"No, but—"

"Besides, I'm not asking for your life, Case. Just you."

A shiver went through him. And all the logic, all the reasons why letting this go in the direction she seemed to want was beyond foolish, seemed to fall away. Still, because he was who he was, he asked, "Do you mean what that sounds like?"

She stood up then, and he felt a sudden chill, and shivered again. He hadn't realized how much of the warmth had come from her, not the fire. Instinctively he stood as well, still staring at her, waiting for an answer. When it came, it took his breath away.

"What I mean is you only have to sleep out here on this couch if you...want to."

That slight catch in her voice, the tiny bit of roughness that matched what he felt, sent a ripple of need through him. She turned and walked toward the bedroom. He watched her go, seemingly unable to move.

He felt an odd pressure at the back of his knees. Realized it was Cutter, nudging him, as if to make him follow her. Oddly, it broke his immobility. He glanced at the dog, brow furrowed. Cutter looked up at him with an expression that he'd almost call impatience. Odd, he'd never thought of dogs having expressions other than maybe angry and happy.

When he looked up again, Terri was gone, into the room she'd just invited him to. All the reasons why he should stay right here flooded him, but were countered by two undeniable things.

Cutter was still nudging.

And Terri hadn't closed the door.

Chapter Twenty-Four

Terri had almost given up hope when she finally heard Case step through the doorway behind her.

"I need to…clarify something."

As it had from the first time she'd heard it, his deep, slightly rough voice sent a shiver of awareness through her. Her body was already awake and humming, which only amplified it. She'd already unbuttoned the top three buttons of her shirt, and didn't bother to redo them before she turned around to face him.

"Yes?" she said, making her tone barely questioning, and more of an answer to what he hadn't yet asked. She saw his gaze flick down to where the tops of her breasts were revealed by the opened shirt, but immediately return to her face.

"You said sleep." His voice was downright gruff, as if he was having to force the words out. She realized suddenly that there was force involved here. Because he was who he was, because he would never assume, he was forcing himself to make sure she'd meant what he'd thought she meant.

What she had meant.

And suddenly she felt a rush of emotion, a rush that told her she'd judged him correctly. He had to be absolutely sure she wanted this before he took another step. And if he wasn't sure, he would walk away. He'd just put all the power into her hands, and she had no words for how that made her feel.

"I meant sleep…eventually. Unless that's all you want."

He took another step into the room, then stopped again. "I don't want you to regret this."

She smiled at him, letting everything she felt show. "I've never done this with someone I met three days ago, and maybe it's crazy but I have no doubts, and I promise no regrets. No awkward morning after, Case."

She saw his jaw clench, as if he was fighting some internal battle. To say no? Or to say yes?

"I'm not…prepared for this."

Protection. Of course he'd thought of that. She hadn't meant it as a test, but if she had he'd passed with flying colors. Which didn't surprise her in the least.

"Foxworth is." She had already seen the box of condoms in the nightstand drawer. "Or perhaps a prior guest of theirs."

She reached over and pulled open the drawer, dug into the box and tossed him one. He caught it in a reflexive motion, stared at it as if he hadn't been sure that's really what it was.

He muttered something she suspected was an oath under his breath. But it came out in a tone of surrender that told her she'd won. He crossed the room in two long strides, his arms, those strong, protective arms coming around her as his mouth came down on hers in a kiss that made the one that had sparked this need seem like merely a prelude. The spark became a flame, and the flame a blaze as he tasted her, and she understood because she couldn't get enough of the taste of him.

Suddenly taste wasn't enough. She wanted to touch, to stroke, and she yanked at his clothes even as he tugged at hers. And with every move, with every barrier between them removed it grew hotter, until she moaned aloud under the mounting pressure. The sound seemed to galvanize him and then she was on the bed, naked, watching hungrily as he kicked off his boots and shed the last of his own clothes.

He was as beautiful as she'd imagined, taut, strong, broad shouldered and narrow hipped, powerful chest and ridged abdomen. She was in awe. Then her gaze slid downward, to his fierce erection, and she felt a surge of need that left her breathless.

She held up her arms. He came down to the bed in a lithe, supple movement that sent new waves of want and need through her, each one more powerful than the one before. She reached for him, letting out another little moan at the feel of him, satin-smooth skin over taut muscle. His hands slid over her in turn, finding each sensitive spot as if he had a road map.

When she couldn't take any more she reached to guide him home. He stopped her with a hand over hers as her fingers curled around rigid, ready flesh.

"Fair warning," he growled. "It's been a long time—I may be a little…quick."

"Oh, please." Her words sounded like the entreaty they were, and in that moment he broke.

He slid into her, making her gasp with the fullness of it, the utter rightness. Deeper and deeper he went, until she felt as if he was touching the very heart of her. He drew back and she nearly cried out in protest, but then he was back, and in her to the hilt.

He stopped moving, but Terri didn't mind. She was savoring the closeness of him, his heat, his power, him deep inside her, stretching her.

"I…" His voice trailed away.

"What?"

He gave a slight shake of his head, his expression seeming almost embarrassed. "I was going to say… I've missed this, but how can you miss something you've never felt before?"

She couldn't find any words for how that made her feel. So instead she pulled him closer, holding on tighter, as if she couldn't have him close enough. He let out a low groan and began to move again, tentatively at first, until she urged him on and his strokes became long, deep and powerful.

Her entire body tensed, hovering, on the edge of something explosive. Her awareness of this only ratcheted up her tension, and for a moment she forgot to breathe. Or couldn't, because her every sense focused on one thing. Case drove deep one more time and it hit, her body convulsed and wave after wave of fierce, hot sensation swept her. She heard Case let out a near shout that encapsulated what she was feeling. She clutched at him, hanging on, because she felt as if she were in free fall.

She cried out his name, knowing he would be there to catch her. Because from the first moment she'd seen him, in that faint light in the alley, some part of her sensed that this was a man who could move her in ways she'd never known.

She'd been right.

CASE FELT THE odd nudge, but it didn't seem threatening. Which was good, because he didn't want to move. In fact, he didn't want to ever move again. He wanted to stay right here, with Terri in his arms, comfortable, content, and more relaxed than he'd been in over a year. No, longer than that. More like...forever. Because he'd meant what he'd awkwardly blurted out last night, when he'd first sunk into her welcoming warmth. He'd never felt this before. Not like this, not this consuming combination of want, need, and utter conviction this was right. In the first moment she'd opened to him, letting him slide into her sweet, slick heat, he'd known that nothing else mattered. Not his past or hers, not what had brought them together or what might happen tomorrow.

The nudge to his back came again and he opened his

eyes. The room was brighter than he'd expected, and he was a little stunned when he realized it was fully light outside. Working carefully not to awaken the woman who had driven him to such heights, he twisted around to glance behind. He found himself facing Cutter, who was looking back with an expression he could only describe as apologetic. It almost made him laugh. Which, he supposed as he eased out of bed and pulled on the jeans that lay in a heap on the floor—Terri had practically yanked them off him, a memory that sent a ripple of heat through him—was an indicator of his mood. Because clever though he might be, Cutter was still a dog.

Although he had managed to get in here when the door had been closed. The lever-style doorknob, he supposed. The animal certainly seemed smart enough to figure out if he pawed it just right, it would open if it wasn't locked. And locking it had been the last thing on his mind last night, though it probably shouldn't have been.

Cutter walked over to the bedroom door, stopped and looked back at him, waiting. Clearly he needed to go outside. Hayley had told him the doors were locked and secured at night, but openable from the inside when that setting was activated, and had showed him the control panel for that and some other security features of the building. Foxworth didn't skimp, and he'd been grateful for that, because it would make it easier to keep Terri safe.

"Sorry we made you wait so long, buddy," he whispered as they left the bedroom. Then he grinned, because in truth he was not sorry at all. After the way he'd spent last night, *sorry* was the last word that came to mind.

Cutter headed for the door out onto the back patio, so Case followed. When they stepped outside, Cutter took off at a trot into the huge open space beyond. Quinn had told him not to worry about letting the dog out alone. "He knows he's working. He won't wander off." Privately, he'd thought the man a little overconfident about it, betting that if a rabbit broke cover or a deer wandered by, the dog would be gone after it in a flash.

Judging by the lack of overcast he'd bet it would hit at least mid-sixties later, but right now it was still a bit chilly. Or maybe it was the fact that he hadn't pulled his shirt on, which might have been a mistake on his part. But he wasn't sure how urgent the dog's request had been, and it didn't seem wise to chance it.

He noticed the lemony scent of the blooms on that newly planted tree again. He supposed it was a testament to his change in mood that this was the first time he'd truly noticed the mass of wildflowers that practically carpeted the huge meadow. Or maybe not all wild—he noticed some that looked familiar, like Aunt Fay's favorite daffodils, the flowers she called the harbinger of spring when they first appeared. He supposed there must be some that bloomed later, or maybe lasted longer, since it was nearly the end of May.

He walked out to the edge of the patio, while still keeping an eye on Cutter in the distance. Something moved in the grass a few feet away from the dog. Something small. Cutter stood rigidly still, and although he couldn't tell from this distance, Case guessed his nose was probably working madly. Oddly, the dog looked toward him then. Then back to whatever creature had caught his attention. The creature who had apparently reached its threshold of fear and had darted away, stirring the tall grass as it went.

But Cutter didn't move. He didn't give chase.

Wrong again, McMillan.

And he had the crazy thought that the look the dog had given him had been a reminder that the rabbit or whatever lurked wasn't his job just now. Case didn't know if the reminder had been for the dog, or him.

He glanced back toward the building, wondering how long

this was going to take, and if he'd be able to sneak back in and slide into bed beside Terri before she woke up. Because he really wanted to be there when she did.

A sudden movement by the dog snapped his head around. And there it was. Cutter had spotted something and taken off, and Case would be left to explain how he'd lost the Foxworth dog. But Cutter wasn't running for the trees or the heavier brush; he was headed toward the big outbuilding. Then Case heard a familiar, almost rhythmic series of barks, and with a sense of relief, he recognized it. Rafe was coming this way.

The dog reached his quarry, who said something to the animal and bent to scratch behind his ears. Then both headed his way. There was barely a trace of a limp in the man's stride, Case noticed and wondered if the warmer weather helped or he was simply having a good day.

He was still thinking about that when Rafe came to a halt beside him. He had a coffee mug in his hand, although it appeared empty, giving Case a clue about why he was here. His eyes looked a little weary, and Case remembered abruptly that he'd been charged with overwatch last night. So he'd likely been awake all night, on guard.

Unlike you, who was awake almost as much, but having a much better time.

"Have a good night?" the man asked, his tone a little too neutral. On the heels of his thought, if he was the blushing sort, that would have done it.

"Great," he answered, meaning it in every way possible.

"I gathered," Rafe said, but he was smiling as he nodded toward Case's torso. And he belatedly realized that Terri's nails had likely left a mark or two. He remembered savoring the feel of those nails digging in as she convulsed around him. He had to suppress a shiver of reaction and the urge to race back inside and rejoin her.

Then Rafe looked down at the dog. "Still batting a thousand, huh, mutt?"

Cutter let out a soft woof that Case would have sworn sounded satisfied. Sort of a canine version of, "Of course!"

Case realized he was talking about what Hayley had told him about the dog's…other skill. The matchmaking thing. He thought it a bit silly, yet Rafe had said it as if it was a given.

The man's cool demeanor discouraged it, but he said it anyway, "You don't seem like the type who'd buy into that."

The chilly gray eyes regarded him steadily. "I'm not."

"And yet…?"

"And yet," Rafe agreed, his tone wry enough to make Case sure it had been a battle for the man to get to this point.

"So why are you the exception?" he asked, remembering what else Hayley had told him.

The man's gaze now turned practically icy. "He's a smart dog. He knows a lost cause when he sees one."

Feeling he probably should have left well enough alone, Case looked back at Cutter, who was waiting expectantly at the back door.

"No automatic opener here?" That seemed like a safe enough change of subject.

"No. Part of the illusion the humans are in charge."

Relieved at the joke, which he assumed indicated the man hadn't truly taken offense, Case pulled open the door and Cutter trotted in. Case watched him, but his mind was processing the fact that, for all the dangerous people he'd encountered in his years behind the badge, none seemed dangerous in quite the same way as Rafe Crawford.

Chapter Twenty-Five

Terri stirred sleepily, wondering where the heat had gone. That sweet, soothing heat that had been hers all night, that—

Case. He was gone.

She jolted awake. Had she dreamed it all? It wouldn't be the first time since he'd charged into her life that she'd had racy dreams about him.

Racy? Got the understatement hat on today?

She smiled as Mr. Gibson's oft-used phrase ran through her mind. Smiled wider as certainty returned to her waking mind. Last night had indeed been very real. She could still feel the new awareness of her body he had awakened, and even the spots that were a little tender were welcome. And the scent of him, that woodsy, masculine sort of scent, lingered on the pillow beside her. She drew in a deep breath, stretched, feeling decadently luxurious.

Her hand slid over the sheets on his side of the bed. She found herself smiling again just at the phrase. *His side.*

But then the coolness of the sheets registered. He wasn't just gone, he'd been gone for a while. That unsettled her. Had he not just gotten up for a trip to the bathroom?

Doubts flooded her. Had last night not been for him what it had been for her, nothing short of astonishing? It had seemed to be. He'd certainly lacked nothing in the enthusiasm department, or in his obvious desire to send her flying higher than she'd ever soared in her life.

Was it that he didn't trust her when she'd promised him no awkward morning after? Because it was morning, and judging by the light filtering through the shades, it had been for a while.

So maybe that was it. He just wasn't the sleeping in, or lazing around in bed type. Although she could have used some non-lazing around in bed time this morning. When she realized what she really wanted was reassurance, she grimaced. Wasn't that need part of that morning after thing guys hated and that she'd promised him wouldn't happen?

She sat up, running her fingers through her disheveled hair. A shiver of remembered sensation went through her when she thought of Case's hands, his fingers doing the same, tangling in her hair as he'd tilted her head back for another of his breath-stealing, strength-dissolving kisses. Which led to memories of those fingers stroking her, teasing her, arousing a commotion inside her that had exploded just moments after the first time he'd slid into her body.

She'd have thought it was simply the flood after a long drought, but it happened every time. They'd proven that last night, so much that she'd lost track of how many times.

An odd combination of heat and chill rippled through her, and with rather jerky movements she got out of bed and reached for her clothes. What she could find of them, any-way—her shirt and bra were on the foot of the bed, her jeans on the floor, half under the chair beside the small table. Her panties were nowhere visible. She felt a renewed rush of heat as she remembered him yanking them off her, so hard and fast it was a wonder they hadn't ripped. And she wouldn't have cared if they had.

She found his shirt in a tangle on the floor, in the narrow beam of light that was coming through the door open just a couple of inches. Somehow that shirt being there bolstered her. If he'd been going to truly leave, he would have taken it, right? For that matter, he would have closed the door, she was sure of it. Her next step brought her in view of his discarded boots and socks, looking as if they'd been kicked off and aside in a rush.

As they had been. After you practically ripped that shirt off him, just so you could touch him.

The beam of light across the floor widened, and her heart leaped, half expecting it to be Case even though she hadn't heard him approaching. He was, after all, barefoot. The image that came to her then was appealing in a way she never would have expected. It seemed every aspect of the man got to her.

But a canine nose edged the door open just far énough, and Cutter slipped in. He came over and sat at her feet, gazing up at her. She'd swear he looked…satisfied. It even appeared he nodded, although she was sure it was just some doggie quirk.

She reached down to stroke the dog's head, and that strange sort of warmth and comfort she'd noticed before filled her. Okay, maybe he wasn't just an ordinary dog. And when she felt him lean against her leg, she found herself smiling.

And certain.

It would be all right. Long-term who knew, but for right now it would be all right. They would have assessing to do, after this tangle she'd landed in—and dragged him into—was resolved, but that was for then. This was now, and despite that trouble hanging over her head, she'd never felt better.

She bent down to plant a kiss on the dog's head.

"Thank you, o furry one," she said softly, and Cutter answered with a kiss of his own, a quick swipe of his tongue under her chin. Right where the bruise was. Which crazily, felt better this morning. Of course, she hadn't noticed it at all last night. She guessed the nerves could only carry so much sensation, and Case had utilized every bit of her capacity.

She walked out of the bedroom and immediately heard the quiet sounds from the kitchen. A split second later she caught the whiff of fresh coffee and something else, something that made her stomach wake up.

All that exercise last night.

The thought put a smile on her face, and she became almost loopy with happiness as she walked toward the kitchen. The moment she could see, she stopped, enjoying not only the sight of his broad, bare chest, but watching him sip coffee from a mug while he stirred something in a skillet.

The man cooks, too?

As if he'd sensed her presence—she supposed cops had to be extra aware, and being an ex-cop didn't change the knack—he glanced up. And if she'd had any lingering doubts, the look he gave her then would have assuaged them. She walked over to the counter, her stomach now growling as she saw the appetizing pile of scrambled eggs he was stirring in the one skillet, and hash brown potatoes in a second.

"Morning."

"Yep," she said, smiling back. "Late morning at that."

"I'm glad you slept in. But I was starved," he admitted with a sheepish grin.

"I'm not surprised. You…worked hard last night."

He lowered his gaze to the skillets, but she saw one corner of his mouth twitch.

"Speaking of that word…detective Coffman called you Hard Case?"

He gave a half shrug as he stirred. "They hang nicknames on everybody."

"Well, that one certainly fits." She surprised herself at

her own tone; that had sounded almost like a purr. But then she was pretty darned contented this morning. "Perfectly."

His gaze shot back to her. He looked almost embarrassed, but pleased. "If you mean that how it sounded...thanks."

"Oh, I did." She put on her most practical voice. "We're going to have to restock their condom supply."

He let out a laugh, and she detected a touch of relief in it as she kept her promise to keep it light.

"I think there's a big-box store not too far away," she added. "Which is good, because we're gonna need a big box."

Now he was grinning, and there was no mistaking the relief. She was feeling a little relief herself, not just that she'd made him laugh, but that he hadn't turned a hair at the implication they were going to need more condoms.

Cutter, who had been lounging on his bed by the fire— Case must have turned it on, to take the edge off the morning chill—scrambled to his feet, his tail and ears swiveled toward the front of the building. Terri sensed Case's sudden tension. Looked at him in time to see him drop the spatula he'd been using to flip the hash browns and reach behind him. He might have foregone the shirt, but the gun had come with him.

That brought the threat that she'd managed to put out of her mind during the glorious night they'd just spent crashing back into her consciousness. She fought it back, not wanting anything to tarnish the joy she held close. Time enough later to deal, when she had to.

Cutter let out a distinctive bark and headed for the door. Terri blinked, then smiled. "That's... Liam's bark, isn't it?"

Case let out an audible breath that sounded bemused. "Sounds like it." He shook his head. "I know he's smart, but putting a dog in charge of opening the door under these circumstances is not something I'm used to."

Terri laughed. "I doubt many are. He is unique, isn't he?"

Cutter was outside now, and the same bark came again. In the moment before the door shut behind the dog, they heard the sound of tires on the gravel drive.

"Especially," Case said, "if he recognizes the sound of vehicles as well as people."

A moment later the door opened again, and Liam stepped inside, lugging what looked like a laptop case over his shoulder. Cutter was at his side, tail wagging.

"Man, that smells good!"

"Good," Case said. "You can help us eat it." He gestured at the two skillets. "I was…really hungry so I kind of overdid it."

Terri managed not to blush, but barely. "We should invite Rafe, too. You need to let him know you're here, don't you?"

Liam grinned, and reached down to scratch behind Cutter's ears. "I reckon he already knows. He heard my bark. He'll be over to officially hand off, but I gather things were quiet last night?"

Not always.

The blush won this time. Because there had been moments last night where she thought she must have screamed. And that peak moment when Case had shouted her name would forever be in her memory.

"No problems," Case answered, and the slight huskiness in his voice told her his thoughts were similar to hers.

No, no problems at all. I never knew it could be that perfect. That easy. That…amazing.

"Well, you had the best guardian of all of us," Liam said with a final scratch for the dog. "Nobody'll ever sneak up on you without him knowing."

Or guiding?

Case had, in one of the warm, wonderful pauses in their discovery of how perfectly they fit, told her about how the dog had practically herded him toward her when he'd hesitated about coming to her last night.

She reminded herself to hug the furry conspirator the first chance she got.

Chapter Twenty-Six

Case studied Liam as he watched Rafe leave. The taciturn man had indeed shown up shortly after his partner's arrival, confirmed there had been no sign of a threat last night, politely refused to join them for breakfast and gone off to get some sleep.

The young Texan wasn't as good as Rafe at hiding his thoughts. Or perhaps didn't feel it necessary when among, essentially, friends. Because it seemed clear to Case that Liam was worried.

"He seems to be limping a little less today," Case said.

"Yeah," Liam said. "Must be a good day."

"That happen when he was a Marine? Although I gather *was* isn't the right term for it."

"Yeah. They barely saved that leg. And that's what he and Teague say. Once and always."

He was still looking toward the back door, but Case was fairly certain he wasn't seeing it. Then he snapped out of it and gave Case a wry smile. "I worry about him. We all do. He's the damned best at what he does, and he's saved us all at one time or another, but sometimes he gets…"

"Quinn told me what he did, in the Marines. So I can guess what he's seen, and had to do." He could empathize completely; he had his own share of ugly images he could never erase from his mind. And that had been in a supposedly civilized place, not a war zone.

Liam nodded. "I know he lugs around some heavy memories. Really heavy. But he never talks about it."

Terri, who had been preparing plates in the kitchen—"You cooked, I'll serve," she'd told him—had walked over with two plates full of eggs and potatoes in time to hear those words.

"Seems he doesn't talk about anything much," she said.

Liam's mouth twisted wryly. "And believe it or not, he's gotten better lately. A lot better." Then he seemed to shake it off. "He'll be okay. I know it always aches—he's stubborn about taking anything for it. But if he was in a really bad place, Cutter'd be glued to him. Unless you two needed him more, of course."

Case gave a skeptical shake of his head as Terri set down the plates on the counter in front of them and went back for her own. "You all put a lot of faith in a dog."

"Not just a dog. That dog. And he's got our faith and trust because he's earned it, from day one." Liam grinned. "Back when Quinn kidnapped Hayley."

"Kidnapped?" Terri almost yelped, stopping dead in the act of sitting on one of the counter stools.

Case's gaze narrowed. "Hayley told me she wouldn't have met Quinn if not for Cutter. But she neglected to mention that detail."

"It's a fun story. At least it is now," Liam added. "I don't think it was much fun for Hayley in the beginning. Before she was sure we were the good guys." He took a big bite of the eggs. "Hey, these are really good."

"He's a man of many talents." Case's gaze shot to Terri as she spoke, but her gaze stayed fixed on her own plate of food. A little too fixed.

"I'm a little out of practice," he muttered, fighting down the instant response of his body to her suggestive words.

"I don't think so. Not if practice makes perfect." She looked at him, the intensity in her blue eyes leaving him no doubt she intended those words exactly as he hoped. The heat bubbling inside him burst free, and he almost doubled over with the power of it.

Belatedly he noticed Liam eyeing them consideringly. Then the Foxworth man shifted his gaze to Cutter, who was watching them all from his spot on the floor with a rather contented look on his face.

"Another home run, dawg?" Liam drawled out.

Case nearly groaned aloud. "You going to start that, too?"

Liam laughed. "I'm a believer. And a beneficiary. I'd have never connected with my fiancée, Ria, if not for him pushing me. Well, and her being the most incredible woman on the planet."

There was no denying the love that echoed in the man's voice. Case felt a powerful tug inside, immediately followed by a jab of wariness. He envied Liam what he'd clearly found, but wishing for it himself wasn't a place he could allow himself to be, not now.

Maybe you should have thought about that last night, before you went into that bedroom.

Cutter let out a small sound, half whine, half growl, as if he didn't like what Case had just thought, and was warning him against going down that path. Just as the dog had pushed him toward Terri? Great. Now he was thinking the dog was a mind reader?

He gave a sharp shake of his head and focused on eating. The eggs had come out okay, although he was eating more because he knew he needed to than because he wanted to. Liam finished quickly, thanked Case for the food—unnecessary, Case told him, since Foxworth had provided the makings—and carried his plate and fork to the dishwasher. Cutter got up and followed him, sitting down in front of the refrigerator with an expectant look.

"Got the crunchies?" Liam asked the dog, and pulled open the door.

To Case's surprise, he came out with a handful of what appeared to be carrots, the little ones that came in a bag already peeled. Liam tossed one to the dog, who indeed crunched happily. Liam looked over at them.

"They tell you about the carrots? That's his treat of choice, most of the time. Three or four and he's done."

He heard Terri laugh, and it sent a ripple of heat through him again. She sounded so happy, so lighthearted, despite the threat hovering over her. And in that cheerful moment, he dared to think he'd had something to do with that. That the sweetness they'd found last night had given her that. It had certainly brightened his outlook, for now at least.

When Cutter had finished snacking, Liam paused to top off his coffee, then excused himself to go upstairs and dig a little deeper into some other channels about Zukero. Case had the feeling those other channels might be a bit on the shady side, and was for once glad he didn't have to worry about that. Because if information existed out there that could help keep Terri safe, he didn't much care how they got it.

Once he'd vanished upstairs, Case had the feeling it would be a while before they saw him down here again. He was obviously in his element up there amidst all the high-tech gear that took up a large corner of the upper space.

"Wouldn't you just love to hear that whole story? Hayley and Quinn, I mean?" Terri asked.

"And a kidnapping? Yeah, that's got to be quite a story."

He wasn't so sure he wanted to hear about Cutter's part in it. They seemed awfully certain the dog was always right about who he—herded, for lack of a better word, together.

And he'd definitely herded him. Right into Terri's bed.

Maybe you should ask how many of those he'd brought together are still together...

He stifled a sour laugh at himself. Like he had any right to think about permanence right now, let alone actually look for it. Hope for it.

Go after it.

"Why are you looking at me like that?" Terri asked. "Like I'm a puzzle you can't figure out?"

He hadn't realized he'd been studying her quite so intently. "It's not you. It's me." He winced inwardly as the trite breakup phrase came out. He hadn't meant it that way, at all. Not that there was anything to break up. It wasn't like what had leaped to life between them was brought on by anything more than...circumstances.

He was grateful she didn't react to the phrasing. Her only physical reaction was her head tilting slightly. "You?"

"Wishing I had your courage. Maybe I'd have moved past it all by now."

"You think because you were a cop you should be able to handle anything, immediately?"

He shifted uncomfortably. "Well, this at least."

"That would make you not human. And while I'm perfectly willing to admit you're superhuman in some areas..."

And that quickly, with just a pointed look and a sexy smile, she blew all thought of everything except how damned incredible last night had been out of his mind. And if Liam wasn't upstairs right now, he'd be acting the caveman, not Superman, and carrying her back to bed.

Chapter Twenty-Seven

Terri hadn't really thought about what staying here, under the protection of Foxworth, was going to be like. She knew it was for her own good, but she would have preferred more time alone with Case. Not that the Foxworth people—and their dog—were anything less than charming. Especially Cutter, who always seemed to sense when the situation started getting to her. And it was amazing how simply petting him soothed her nerves. It was second only to having Case hold her. Which was like nothing she'd ever known in her life.

Still, knowing someone else was here, even if they hadn't seen Liam since he'd had breakfast with them except for once when he'd come down for more coffee, had cooled things down a bit. Yet the new awareness between them was so powerful she was surprised the air wasn't crackling.

She glanced over toward the far wall that consisted mostly of bookshelves, where Case stood looking at the sizable array of volumes. Somebody at Foxworth either already had quite a collection or was a print book purist. She found herself watching him scan the shelves, and trying to guess what he was thinking by the way he paused to look at a book here, smiled at an apparently familiar title there. That in itself was significant, because it told her he was a reader, as she was. And every thing she found they had in common made her hope stronger, the hope that when this ended, when she was no longer under threat, that they could build something out of this unexpected situation.

And for a while she even pondered fate, which had seemingly thrown this man, who stirred her in ways no man ever had, into her life at precisely the moment she had needed him.

She watched, surreptitiously enjoying the sight of him doing something as simple as picking a book out, carrying it over to set down on the big coffee table—she couldn't wait to sneak a peek at what it was—and then walking into the kitchen and over to the coffee maker that was just finishing up a fresh pot.

Then, much earlier than she would have expected given he'd been up guarding her all night, Rafe opened the back door.

"You didn't sleep long," she said when he came in.

"Don't," he said. She wasn't sure if he meant don't go there, or that he didn't usually sleep long. Judging by the weariness in those gray eyes, she went for the latter. "Liam upstairs?"

Case had gotten out another mug as he answered, "Yes. He's only been out of there once."

"Then he'll have the number off Zukero's birth certificate by now," Rafe said. His tone was the wry one of someone whose life didn't revolve around devices, but there was a kind of pride in it, too.

Case held out the newly filled mug to him. "Guessing you need this."

"You'd know about that," Rafe said as he took it.

Terri watched that exchange, seeing in their expressions and hearing in their voices that there was something more to it than a simple acknowledgment of the need for caffeine, but she had no idea what. Unless…had Rafe guessed? What they'd been up to last night?

She looked away to hide the flush she felt rise to her cheeks as Rafe said, "I got some texts a while ago. Answers to inquiries I made yesterday."

"About Zukero?" The change in Case was so abrupt and strong Terri was surprised she didn't hear a snap.

"That's one of the two topics. Word is he's gone to ground. Hasn't been seen since Monday."

Case set down his own mug, his gaze fastened on the Fox-worth operative. "So he knows."

"That he's looking at murder? Seems like."

"Your sources?"

"A couple of police officers, former military. And some other vets I'm in contact with, on the other side." A shadow darkened his eyes. "Homeless, by choice. But that puts them in touch on the street."

"And they were able to text you?" Terri asked, remembering the days when her life had been so lean a cell phone had been out of the question.

"They help when they can. Gives me the excuse to see that they have phones, in case they need help."

He shrugged, as if that kind of concern was nothing. She was becoming more and more impressed with these people her brother had found.

"No wonder Teague fits right in here," she said quietly.

Rafe met her gaze and held it. "Yes. He does."

She smiled as another little shot of giddiness hit her at the knowledge her brother was alive. Before she could break into a burble, Case saved her by asking, "What was the second topic?"

Rafe's gaze shifted to him. "You."

Case blinked and drew back. "Me?"

Rafe nodded. He pulled out his phone—one like the

phones Quinn had given them—and called something up. Then he set it on the kitchen counter, where they both could see the exchanged texts.

Name Case McMillan ring a bell?

Hard Case? Hell, yeah. Guy tried to take down that scumbag Joe Barton. More guts than I've got.

Didn't go well?

He got so screwed over. All political bullcrap. I swear half the department was ready to walk. Some did. I would have, if I hadn't just made sergeant.

Sounds like you admire him.

I do. Most of us do. He was a damn good cop, and a good guy. You in touch?

Yes.

He okay?

About like you'd expect.

Tell him to reach out. He's got people worried about him.

"Got a couple more just like that, from different people. Consensus is the same. You were a good cop and a good man who got screwed by a crooked system."

Case was staring at the screen. "Somebody…actually quit? Over what happened to me?"

"Several somebodies. You already had a lot of respect and a great reputation. What you tried to accomplish blew you up into legend territory."

Terri couldn't resist reaching out to touch his arm. His head came up sharply and he looked at her. He didn't just look surprised; he looked stunned. Clearly he'd had no idea the kind of support he'd had among his then colleagues. Which told her how stunned he'd been back then, too—he must have withdrawn completely to not be aware.

"I...didn't think of it that way. It was just the right thing to do."

"No matter how influential the offender," Terri said.

"Well, yeah." He shrugged, a bit awkwardly. "I had the stupid idea people would be glad to know the truth about the guy who proclaimed himself the city's savior, while taking tons of money under the table to steer city contracts to his buddies."

"And you wish you had *my* courage?" she asked, quoting his own words back at him. "You've got more than enough of your own, Mr. McMillan. And that it's not still Officer McMillan is their great loss, not yours."

He stared at her for a moment. She saw him swallow, as if his throat was tight.

He glanced at Rafe, who shrugged in turn as he agreed. "She pretty much said it."

Terri almost enjoyed his embarrassed expression, but more powerful was the ache inside at what he'd gone through.

The sound of Liam coming down the stairs ended the moment.

"Good, you're here," he said when he saw Rafe. "I've got a little more."

"You always do," Rafe said. Terri had the feeling he was trying to sound weary, but the slight twitch at the corners of his mouth gave him away.

"What can I say—I'm good," Liam said, with a grin that expressed he was used to his colleague's ways. "Anyway, I couldn't find any residence ownership or rental info under his name, and the address from his last arrest was fake. We know he's usually a lone wolf, but he wasn't the last time he got caught. The guy who was with him on that one—it was another robbery, of a bar in the city—was a James Barry. He's in lockup, had a valid address, but it's now rented to someone else with no connection I could find."

"I thought you said you had something?" Rafe observed dryly.

"Yeah, yeah. It's a process," Liam retorted.

"And elimination is part of it," Case said.

"See, he gets it," Liam said, grinning again. "Anyway, I backtracked on Barry, found they were arrested together twice before in other jurisdictions. Went further, and found a relative of his, apparently his mother's brother." Terri could see by the gleam in the man's eyes that this was the payoff. "Whose name is Bennie Zukero."

"They're cousins?" Terri asked as Case went on alert beside her.

"Looks that way. So here's where we are. We already know Marcus Zukero's parents are still in Los Angeles. Walker checked into that for us." He glanced at Case. "That's Hayley's brother, who runs Foxworth southwest. But from what he found, there's been no contact, and he thinks they're really straight arrow. And no records that I can find indicate otherwise."

"But he could run there. He's still their son," Case said.

"Which guarantees nothing," Terri said before she could stop herself.

Case's gaze shifted to her. And there was something gentle in his eyes and expression when he said, "Point taken."

She looked back at Liam in time to see him exchange a

raised-eyebrow glance with Rafe, who in turn silently inclined his head toward Cutter. Liam's expression changed to a knowing smile and he gave a short nod. Clearly the two men had just had an entire conversation—which somehow involved the dog—without uttering a word.

Suddenly something Liam had said earlier came back to her. *I'd have never connected with my fiancée, Ria, if not for him pushing me.*

Then what Case had said tumbled into her head. *Hayley told me she wouldn't have met Quinn if not for Cutter.* And she remembered the times the dog had seemed to nudge him…closer to her.

She looked down at the dog with renewed curiosity. Were they serious about all that?

"Walker's going to keep an eye out, and he'll let us know if Zukero shows up," Liam said briskly. "As for here, I've got a last known address for the Barrys, down in Tacoma. Quinn's already down at the airport in Bremerton, so he's going to head there."

"To watch, or make contact?" Case's tone had an edge to it.

"He'll scope it out first," Liam assured him. "He knows what he's doing—I promise."

Case let out a low sigh. "I'm sure he does," he said as Liam walked a few feet away to answer his cell which had just rung.

"It just drives you crazy to not be the one out there hunting," Rafe said, and it wasn't a question.

"Yes," Case admitted. Then, after drawing in a slow, audible breath, he added, "But nothing's more important than keeping Terri safe."

And Terri knew she'd never heard anything that had made her believe so strongly that she was exactly that. With Case, she was safe.

Liam ended his call and walked back to them, his expression much less cheerful. He called to Rafe, who'd been headed for the door but immediately turned around.

"That was Quinn."

"He got something in Tacoma?" Case asked instantly.

Liam shook his head. "No. He just talked to Brett. He heard from a contact on the other side, who thinks he saw Zukero."

He sounded awfully grim to her, but if Zukero had been spotted, that was good, wasn't it? She waited for whatever had put that tone in his voice.

"He was driving by and only caught a glimpse, and by the time he got turned around the guy was gone. So we can't be sure."

"What's the punch line?" Case asked. Clearly he'd heard the same thing she had in the other man's voice.

"It was near the ferry landing in Seattle."

She understood now. Zukero could well be on his way here.

Chapter Twenty-Eight

"There are a lot of things near there. Touristy things, places to rob," Terri said.

"Yes." Case couldn't argue that, but that didn't change the bottom line. "But there are also two ferries, either of which would land him at most thirty miles away, possibly half that." He turned back to Liam. "How long ago?"

"Twenty minutes now. And no guarantee Terri's not right about why he was there. With the response time what it is these days, it's easy pickings."

"Besides," Terri added, sounding grateful that the Foxworth man had given her words credence, "he'd have to pay going that way, and aren't there cameras? He'd have to risk being on security video."

It was a long-standing joke in the area that you could get into the city for free, but you had to pay to escape.

"We'll be looking into that," Liam said. "Brett's already on his way to the landing in Bremerton."

"His guy a cop?" Case asked.

"Former. Does some PI work now."

"So Zukero wouldn't know." He wasn't sure if it was good or bad that the man who'd spotted him hadn't been in uniform or a marked police car.

"I'll take the island," Rafe said, referring to the other destination for ferries leaving out of Seattle. "You stay and get on the security video."

That quickly they were rolling, each with their assignment, a task to do, action to take.

Except him.

Rafe had been right. It was driving Case crazy to sit here and let others do the searching, the hunting. But he also knew this Foxworth building was in effect a safe house, and he doubted that between the security systems and Cutter, anyone would ever manage to sneak up on them. And since the goal was to keep Terri safe, that was what he should focus on.

He was just used to being on the front line, not the last fallback.

"McMillan?"

He looked over his shoulder at Rafe, who had the back door open, ready to exit; Liam was already upstairs and no doubt working whatever magic he did with that frightening array of computer equipment.

"Yeah?"

"It's good to know she's got you here."

He left without waiting for a reply. And when the door closed behind him, Cutter let out a little sound that sounded almost like a human "Hmpf." As if he was irked to be left out of the assessment.

"I get it." Terri's soft voice yanked him out of silly thoughts about the dog. He turned back to her. "Your nature is to go get the bad guy." She smiled, but blinked rather quickly, like something was bothering her eyes. "Even when getting the bad guy costs you."

Belatedly he realized she'd been blinking back the moisture pooling in her eyes. As if what had happened to him had hurt her as well. He stared at her for a long, quiet moment. Then, his voice low and rough, he said, "I'd like to take you back to bed right now, but…"

"It doesn't seem right, when everyone else is out there working to keep me safe?"

He let out a breath of relief that she'd understood. "Exactly."

"Well, we can sit out here instead, then, and plan." She gave him a smile that held a touch of mischief and he wondered how much of the marvel she'd become was pure relief that her brother was alive, and how much might be... something else.

"Plan?" he asked, a bit wary.

"What happens when this is over."

It almost came tumbling out, that he wanted to be with her, that he wanted them to build the best lives they could, together, but he couldn't beat down the feeling that he didn't have the right. Not yet. So even as he silently vowed he'd spent enough time—too much time—wallowing in the wreckage and it was time to move on and rebuild his life, he told himself until he did, he didn't have the right to assume she'd want to share it.

"What happens is you see Teague again, and spend wonderful days reveling in the fact that he's alive," he said.

The light that came into her eyes then was a balm to any of his rattled, tangled feelings. This was worth it, no matter how it ended between them.

"And he'll be doing the same," he said, letting that new conviction echo in his voice. "Reveling in the fact that the little sister he never stopped looking for is found at last."

The light doubled. She looked like a kid on Christmas morning, knowing that the gift she'd wanted more than anything was under the tree. And nothing like a woman who'd almost been murdered, and whose assailant was likely hunting her right now. And again he told himself it was worth it. That look on her face, the pure joy of it, was worth anything.

When Hayley arrived—greeted by Cutter with that distinctive bark and an almost puppylike wiggle—bearing some luscious smelling takeout for lunch, Case was suddenly nervous. The woman was clever, observant and read people very, very well. And he suspected how they'd spent the night must be written across his face like a gang tattoo. She did look at them both rather intently, but her only reaction was to smile, look down at her dog and murmur something that sounded like, "Well done."

They shared the meal that tasted as good as it had smelled, and Hayley chatted easily about anything but the current situation, something Case appreciated. After they'd eaten, Hayley turned on the big flat screen and told Terri she wanted to show her a video. When she realized it was of her brother's wedding, she let out a joyous "Oh!"

It seemed so personal Case wasn't sure he should stay and watch, but he didn't want to blatantly walk away, either. But then he saw the expression on Terri's face, the utter bliss in her eyes, and he couldn't move.

So he watched, curious. The bride was lovely, long dark hair caught up at her crown and then tumbling down to her shoulders, her gown a sweep of white trimmed with a cheerful yellow that matched the flowers in the meadow where the ceremony was occurring. The meadow just outside, with the backdrop of towering evergreens. In a few frames he could see Cutter, who wore a bow tie with every evidence of pride. He noticed Terri giggled at the sight of that.

But he focused mainly on the groom, the man whose presumed death had shaped Terri's entire adult life. Teague Johnson was lean, strong looking and moved well, like the former Marine he was. But most of all he saw that he had the same sandy blond hair as Terri's, and in one close up toward the end, he saw the same clear blue eyes, the same straight, perfectly shaped nose. The resemblance was unmistakable.

And by the time it ended Terri was crying, but also smiling so widely it was obvious they were indeed tears of joy.

The quiet hours they had into early afternoon ended abruptly when Quinn arrived, back from Tacoma, a few minutes later Rafe from his own mission, and on his heels detective Dunbar. Liam, hearing the commotion, descended the stairs looking like he had news. The rapid-fire conversation after that reminded Case of the briefings they used to get whenever the detective division was hot on the trail of one of their most wanted.

Quinn noticed Liam's expression and nodded at him to go first.

"He hit again," the tech whiz said quickly. "Where he was spotted by your guy—" he nodded at Dunbar "—at the ferry landing. Held up some tourists with an expensive car waiting in line. They'd gotten out to stretch their legs after driving in from Spokane." The man's expression changed, tightened. "He backhanded their little girl when she wouldn't stop screaming in terror when she saw the gun."

They all went very still.

"She's okay," he went on quickly. "Just scared."

"Nightmare material," Case muttered.

"They gave him what cash they had, but it was only about fifty bucks."

"Stealing cash ain't as easy as it used to be," Dunbar said dryly.

Liam nodded. "The police there think he would have tried for more, maybe somebody else in line, but a couple of truckers noticed what was going on and headed toward them and he ran."

"Typical," Quinn said. "So, he's either out of control, or desperate, to try something that public, in daylight."

"And not one to try using a stolen credit or debit card," Liam said. "Cash only."

After Rafe and Dunbar had reported no luck at the ferry docks on this side, that no one recalled seeing the man in the mug shot, Hayley said, "This could be good, right? If he was only there looking for targets, and not headed over here, then he probably doesn't have any idea she's here."

Case had already reached that conclusion, and admitted that his own tension had eased a little at the realization.

"Yes," Quinn agreed. "He may be hunting her, but not know she's left the area." Then he went ahead with his own report. "I talked to the Barrys' next-door neighbor. Chatty sort. She said there'd been no sign of visitors. Also said that the Barrys were angry at their son's cousin Marcus, thinking he was the one who led their boy astray."

"So they're not likely to help him out," Terri said.

"Not voluntarily." Case's words came out more grimly than he'd intended, making Terri's eyes widen, but he'd worked more than one case where innocent parties were forced into helping the not so innocent.

The discussion went on for a bit, and Case was again amazed at all the potential paths and resources Foxworth had.

Quinn was pacing the floor in front of the fireplace where they'd gathered. He did not look happy. Zukero's image was on the big flat screen, hovering over them in pixels as he hovered over their lives right now. Quinn glanced up at it, and grimaced as he spoke.

"It's frustrating to have to just wait and hope he pops up somewhere, gets spotted and then stays long enough to be grabbed."

"Welcome to my world," Dunbar said dryly.

"Amen," Case said, remembering the feeling all too well.

Dunbar seemed to hesitate, unusual enough that it caught Case's attention. The man didn't seem like an uncertain guy.

Quinn apparently noticed it too, because he said, "What, Brett? Something's whirling in that brain of yours."

"I was just thinking there might be a way to make sure he pops up on the radar and stays long enough to be grabbed."

Quinn stopped his pacing. The two men's gazes locked, as if they both knew they were on the same wavelength. They had worked together a long time now, had apparently found a working balance between Dunbar's official capacity—and restraints—and their relative freedom.

"What?" Terri asked, sounding eager for anything that would end this personal nightmare. Case understood, even as he dreaded it a little, for fear that when the reason he and Terri had come together was done, so would they be.

Quinn kept his gaze on Dunbar. "You're thinking...a trap?"

Dunbar nodded.

"No," Case said flatly. "No way."

He caught Terri's startled look out of the corner of his eye but never looked away from Dunbar and Quinn.

"But why, if it would work?" Terri asked, and she sounded almost excited.

"Because," he said grimly, "there's only one thing that might lure him into that situation." He turned his head to look at her then.

"Case," she began, but he shook his head.

"The only bait he'll take is you."

Chapter Twenty-Nine

Terri hadn't quite thought of it as being bait, but that didn't really change her mind. "I know that," she said. "But if it will work…"

"It's too risky," Case said. "He already almost killed you once."

"And you saved my life. Which," she added rather pointedly, "is one reason you get a say in this."

The other reason is I think I'm crazy in love with you.

The words echoed in her head, but she didn't dare voice them. She couldn't say any of what she was feeling, not in front of the others. That had to wait until they were alone again. So she went with something else that was also true.

"I want this over. For many reasons."

The main one being I want it over so we can begin, without this hanging over us.

That, however, was not something she wanted to say in this roomful of men all focused on protecting her. They'd probably think she was a fool, being so certain this was the man she wanted by her side from here on. Case himself probably would think the same.

So instead she went with another, still quite valid point. "One of those reasons is I don't want Teague to have to deal with me being in trouble when he gets home."

Case blinked and drew back slightly, as if he hadn't thought of that aspect. So she wasn't alone in her tunnel vision. "He won't care about anything but you being alive and here," he said.

"But he'll also feel compelled to protect me."

"I know the feeling."

Case said it under his breath, so quietly she couldn't be sure if she was meant to hear it. But there was no doubting the sincerity of it.

She thought about the philosophies that believed if you saved a life, you were responsible for that life from then on. She didn't want Case with her because he thought he had to be. Not that way. But surely, after what they'd found together, it was more than that? Surely, after the incredible hours they'd spent learning each other, how he'd learned every spot to touch, stroke or kiss that made her moan, and she'd learned nearly as much about him, that was something to build on? Because she wanted to learn more. She wanted to learn everything. She wanted to know this man intimately in every sense of the word, not just the physical, spectacular though that had been.

What she didn't know was if he wanted the same thing. She couldn't believe he was the type to casually walk away, but the circumstances were both unusual and their own kind of pressure.

She couldn't dwell on this now. She had to focus. She looked at Dunbar—funny how when he was here officially she and Case felt it proper to use his last name—who was sitting silently, just watching, like a fisherman who'd made his cast and now waited to see if anyone bit. Quinn was looking thoughtful, perhaps considering all the options. Liam and Rafe were watching their boss, as if waiting only for his command. And she had little doubt that whatever that command was, they'd follow it.

"What kind of trap?" she asked.

When she heard Case suck in a tense breath, she glanced at him. She could sense he was on the edge of a protest, and probably a strong one. He seemed to feel her gaze and turned his head. Or was he shaking it in a firm no? So she went on, made sure her voice was quiet, reasonable. And that her own fear was as hidden as she could make it.

"It can't hurt to listen, can it?" He said nothing, but his jaw tightened. She set her own jaw and looked back at Dunbar. "Although I admit, I'd be afraid to just be out in the open with Zukero around."

"Rightfully so," the detective said.

"I could do it," Hayley said quickly. "Lighter wig, similar clothes, we use your bag, and jacket."

Case went still, but Terri stared at Hayley. She was volunteering to be a target? For her? "But...what if...?"

Hayley smiled. "I've had some training. A lot of it, in fact, in several disciplines. Quinn saw to that."

"Only," her husband said dryly, "when it became obvious you weren't going to stay out of trouble."

Terri felt a spark of envy at what these two had. It was what she wanted for herself. She always had, but just never believed she would. Had never met the man she wanted it with.

She glanced at Case who, for some reason, suddenly looked a bit gobsmacked. He didn't seem to be focused on Hayley, or Quinn or anyone for that matter. He had that dazed kind of expression that suggested he wasn't seeing anything in the room but instead had turned completely inward. If they were anywhere else, anywhere and alone, she'd dig into that, but they weren't and this wasn't the time.

"I'm sure you could handle it," Dunbar said to Hayley, "but I don't think it would work. Terri was up close with Zukero, and there's an obvious height difference. He'd notice."

"What do you think, then?" Quinn asked.

"Something simple. Use all contacts, official and non. Have it put out they're looking for a person of interest in the case. Full description, including what she was last seen wearing. Make sure the slime Zukero hangs out with hears about it, maybe sees a photo."

Quinn shifted back to Terry. "If you decide to go for this, the police investigating the murder would prefer to handle it. And you. It's your choice, if you'd rather they be the ones—"

"Instead of the people my brother trusts and works with?" Terri interrupted, holding the intimidating man's gaze. "The family he found here? No."

Quinn smiled at her last words, and suddenly he wasn't quite so intimidating. He looked back at Dunbar. "I'd want this on our turf. From his record, I'd say he'd be off-balance over here. He's a city rat through and through."

Dunbar nodded thoughtfully. "Good idea. They can drop where they think she might be, that she has family over here, maybe a neighborhood. But unless he's completely oblivious, the name Foxworth is going to make him wary."

"Then we keep the name out of it. And probably—" Quinn gestured at their surroundings "—this place, too."

"The Cedar View house." It was the first time Rafe had spoken.

"My old place?" Dunbar asked. He glanced at Terri and Case. "I used to rent this little cabin," he explained. "When I moved out, Foxworth bought it, for when they needed someplace other than here." He looked back at Rafe. "It would be a good location."

Rafe nodded. "High ground, isolated, no close neighbors to put in danger."

Liam grinned. "My new toys will help, too. That drone's camera is amazing. And with the Foxworth fleet, I can alternate so one's always in the air, watching."

Dunbar looked thoughtful, then nodded. He looked back at Rafe. "You'll be there? If we have to take him down hard?"

"Damn straight."

"You could take some heat if you do have to."

Terri realized they were talking about Rafe's expertise. The sniper expertise Hayley had told her about. Her breath caught when the taciturn man said simply, "For Teague's sister? So be it."

Terri made a quick swipe at her eyes as emotion surged through her. Her brother had truly found his rightful home here. And what he'd found, what he'd built, was spreading to encompass her, even though a week ago they'd never laid eyes on her.

"I don't know what to say, to any of you. You've all been ready to help me from the first moment I got here. Before you were even sure I really was who I said I was."

"We were sure from the get," Hayley said softly. "The resemblance is obvious. The DNA test was a mere formality, for us. And it was no surprise when it came back a sibling match."

They had, Hayley had told her, all their DNA profiles on record. Apparently the Foxworth Foundation dealt with dangerous situations often enough for it to be wise. She didn't like thinking about that, but she was still glad they'd had Teague's to be compared with hers, and that the results had been conclusive. She'd known they would be, of course, but nice for them to have the absolute certainty.

"Then we're on?" Quinn asked, focused on Terri.

"I want this over with," she answered.

"When do we start?" Liam asked, sounding eager to get moving.

Terri almost smiled. But instead she turned to look at the one person who had been utterly silent since he'd made that comment about feeling compelled. "Case? What do you think?"

"Sounds like you've decided." He sounded more than a little stiff.

"I want this over with," she repeated. Then, holding his gaze, she added pointedly, "I have other things I want to focus on, as soon as possible."

She saw him swallow before he said, "Fine." He looked at Quinn. "I'm with her, 24/7, until this is over."

Quinn lifted a brow, whether at the flat decree or Case's fierce tone, Terri didn't know. Despite her worry about the danger of the situation, she herself was delighted with the declaration...up to those last four words. The head of Foxworth glanced at Cutter before saying, almost blandly, "I assumed."

"Then perhaps the story we put out is she has a brother over here," Dunbar said. "Or...a significant other."

Case seemed to stop breathing for a moment. It was strange, the way the detective was looking at them as if he knew, or at least had a good idea, of how they'd spent last night. But she was too busy wishing that significant other part was true to dwell on how he might have guessed. Maybe he was just that good. But then he focused on Case.

"She can put Zukero away for good. You know he won't hesitate to take you out too, to get to her."

Terri's breath caught; she hadn't really thought about that. But Case clearly had, as he said flatly, "I'm aware."

His earlier words rang in her head. *Until this is over. Then what? You walk away?*

No. She couldn't, wouldn't let that happen. She wanted this not just behind her, but behind them.

Because there had to be a "them." There just had to be.

Chapter Thirty

Case turned to pace the other direction across the now empty great room. Normally he would have contributed to the discussion and planning that had just gone on here, but he hadn't been able think.

You've done it before.

It was turning into a chant inside his head as he paced.

It was the truth, of course. He'd worked traps for bad guys before, and he'd protected witnesses before. Each time had been intense, the prolonged high alertness a strain, but it had never...panicked him before.

Yet the idea of Terri being the target did just that.

He was alone now, with nothing to distract his thoughts. Terri was in the bathroom and the others had scattered to prepare for the operation they would put in motion. His job, at least, was simple. Keep Terri safe.

He heard the sound of the shower running, and tried not to think of her in there, naked and glistening as the water streamed over her body. Before he could stop it the thought of joining her had flooded into his mind, and he found his fingernails digging into his palms in his effort to fight the urge. But things had begun, and that was the last thing he needed to be thinking about right now.

Well, the next to last thing.

The very last thing he wanted to think about was his utter, total gratitude when Hayley had volunteered to be the bait. Normally, and despite whatever training she'd gotten, he would rebel against the idea of putting a civilian woman in such a position. But instead, he'd been hit with a blast of relief. Short-lived, admittedly, because he knew Dunbar was right. Hayley had to be around five foot six, while Terri was a good four or five inches shorter. Zukero would know immediately.

He tried to focus on what was coming, the plan they'd lain out, with more meticulousness than he'd seen even in some major law enforcement operations. Between them, the Foxworth team and Dunbar—who was clearly comfortable with and trusted by them—thought of things he hadn't, and he'd always been touted for seeing possibilities others missed. But he couldn't seem to manage it. Because overpowering everything was the knowledge that blast of relief had pounded home.

He loved her.

He'd met her freaking days ago and he loved her.

He stopped pacing and dropped down on the couch, his head in his hands. This was ridiculous.

"When did you become such a total wimp?" he muttered into his hands.

He felt a gentle but definite push against his knee. Startled, because he'd heard nothing, he shot upright.

Cutter.

The dog was right there, and he'd never heard a thing. Talk about out of it…

The moment he made eye contact with him, the animal dropped his chin down to rest on the knee he'd nudged.

"Did the pacing bother you, or was it that you have exclusive rights to whining around here?" he asked.

Cutter just looked at him. Case grimaced.

"Hell, you probably don't ever whine."

Again the dog just looked at him with those dark, gold-flecked eyes that seemed too wise for a mere dog. But then, he suspected there was nothing mere about this animal.

With a wry half smile, he finally reached out to do what the dog apparently wanted. The moment his fingers ran over the soft, thick fur on the dog's head that odd sense of comfort returned. That soothing idea that maybe everything would be fine had suddenly worked its way into his head.

Cutter whined.

Case blinked. "So you do whine?"

He stroked the dog's head again. And the maybe part faded and all seemed possible, that he could rebuild, he could get past it once and for all, that Terri might really want him.

Might even eventually love him back.

Cutter made a low sound, not a whine at all, but something that resembled an approving "Mmm-hmm."

He was doubly glad he hadn't given in to the urge to join Terri in the shower when Quinn and Liam returned, Liam from upstairs again, Quinn from outside, Case presumed from the outbuilding, since he and Rafe had walked out together. They probably would have been just in time to hear some rather juicy sounds. He smothered a smile of pleasure at the memory of hearing Terri cry out his name as she hit the peak he'd worked hard to get her to. By working hard, of course, he meant holding back himself, which had never been a big problem in his life until this blue-eyed, sandy-haired waif dropped into it.

The woman who stirred him as none ever had. And who had, hair still damp from her shower, emerged from the bedroom dressed in jeans and a silky sort of T-shirt that clung in all the right places. Or the wrong ones, for his ability to focus anyway.

And barefoot. Somehow that got to him as much as the shape of her under the blue shirt that matched her eyes.

"I sent the mug shots to all phones," Liam said as she came up to them. "And directions to the Cedar View house to Terri's and Case's."

"Hayley's over there now, checking on what's in stock and what you—and Cutter—might need," Quinn said.

"We're keeping Cutter?" Terri asked.

Case registered how much he liked that simple *we* as Quinn nodded. "He's decided he's on your team. And he's worth more than any alarm system, because once we show him the boundary, he'll warn you if somebody crosses it before they ever hit the actual alarm system. He has a way of knowing if it's one of us, even at a distance, so don't waste time questioning it. And if you have to go out, you take him with you. He knows his job is to protect you first, take the bad guy out second. If necessary he'll find the quarry for you."

Case had seen some excellent police K9s over the years, but this was sounding surreal.

"But it won't be necessary," Quinn assured them. "Now I'm thinking we'll move you tomorrow first thing. Once there we'll go over the property and the house so it's all familiar. Once you're settled in, we'll start the ball rolling."

"Is that as in cannon ball?" Terri asked dryly, making Case marvel anew at her casual nerve. But perhaps he shouldn't be surprised; if her brother fit in with this crew, maybe it was in the genes. Certainly not the ones from their parents, so maybe there was some heroic ancestor.

"Rafe is loading up equipment," Quinn continued. He turned his gaze to Case. "We'll bring out an AR if you're comfortable with that." Case nodded; he was quite familiar with various incarnations of the ubiquitous rifle, and was glad—although no longer surprised—that Foxworth was covering all the possibilities. "Besides Liam's flying toys, the house itself has a full alarm system, not just doors and windows but any possible point of entry, including the roof."

Case didn't have to look at Terri to know she was listening intently. He could practically feel the concentration emanating from her. He was glad she was taking this seriously, and beyond angry that it was necessary.

Quinn went on. "Triggering any of it does not, however, go to the county call center at 911. It comes straight to us via these." He held up his own Foxworth phone. "At least one of us will be there on watch, outside, at all times. And Rafe will be on overwatch most of the time."

Case knew that meant a whole set of problems Terri had probably never had to think about in her life. Then Quinn reached behind him into the large duffel he'd come back in with and pulled out two baseball-style caps. He handed one to Case, one to Terri. When he spoke, his voice had taken on a snap of command that told Case this was important.

"If you have to go outside after dark, you put this on. No exceptions. Understand?"

Terri looked at the man, wide-eyed. Case was studying the cap. He ran a finger over the cloth. Then he looked back at Quinn. "Reflective, for night vision equipment?" he guessed.

"Yes," Quinn said. "The less time Rafe has to spend making sure a target isn't you, the better. A few seconds can make a lot of difference."

"Oh!" Terri exclaimed, now looking at the cap in her hand with a lot more interest. Case was impressed that no sooner had he thought of a problem than Foxworth addressed it.

"Case, you and Cutter will be the last line of defense, but nobody's getting past us." Quinn's mouth quirked. "Unless we want them to, of course."

He didn't say it with braggadocio, or any kind of arrogance, just with quiet confidence. The kind that told Case he was probably right. Still, he'd be glad to be armed. When it came to Terri, he wasn't taking any chances. He'd have protected her anyway, it was just in his nature, but…he loved her, and that changed everything. No matter how crazy it—or he—was.

So now he was looking at an unknown stretch of time playing the part of what, inside, he really wanted to be.

The man in her life.

Chapter Thirty-One

When they arrived the next morning, Terri was a little surprised. She had expected some hidden place in the woods. And there were tall evergreens to the back of the little brown house, but it faced an open view to the east, looking at more trees in the distance, and through occasional gaps a view of the Cascade Mountains. It also sat atop a hill, with the nearest neighbor not so near, and well hidden by the trees.

"Good line of sight from the road."

Case murmured it as he studied the surroundings from the driver's seat of his truck, as if he were thinking out loud. And she realized he was looking at the place from a tactical viewpoint, at how defensible it was.

They pulled to a halt beside the compact SUV that was already there she presumed Hayley's. Cutter's soft yet distinctive bark from the small rear seat in their cab told her she must be right; it was the same bark she'd heard him greet Quinn and Hayley with before. And it made her smile.

"I love how everybody has their own bark, but Quinn and Hayley share one."

"Mmm." Case was still scanning the exterior.

"Hayley told me that they knew Laney was the one for Teague when Cutter started greeting her with Teague's bark."

That got his attention. His brows rose and he glanced back at the dog. "You keep life interesting, don't you, mutt?"

Cutter stretched forward and swiped his tongue lightly across Case's cheek in a doggie kiss. Case didn't quite jump in surprise, but the look on his face was definitely startled. Terri stifled—barely—a delighted giggle.

We're going to need a dog.

The giggle became a sigh as her thoughts once more strayed from the present to the future. She simply had to rein that in. And right now she needed to be more in the present than she'd ever been in her life.

Hayley stepped out of the cabin-like building and waved at them. Quinn's SUV had pulled up beside them, and as he got out he nodded. "Go ahead and take a look at the inside. Liam and I are going to check out all the systems, while Rafe picks his spot. Although I think he's had it since we bought the place from Brett's old landlord, with situations like this in mind."

"You end up protecting witnesses a lot?" Case asked.

"Only occasionally. Sometimes it's just a place for people to stay until they get their feet under them again." Quinn smiled with a certain satisfaction. "And buying it helped out someone who helped one of ours."

"Dunbar?"

Quinn nodded. "He had his own very rough patch, and this is where he started to heal."

Terri thought of the tall, strong detective and wondered what it would take to lay him low. She was glad he was past whatever it had been, if for no other reason that she appreciated the respect he'd shown to Case.

And there she was, back where she'd started again, acting as if she had some permanent claim on the man. Determined to focus now, she followed Hayley. And stopped dead just inside the door, surprised. From the exterior, she had had expectations; this place didn't meet them. The main space was much larger than she'd expected from the outside, or at least felt that way with its tall, vaulted ceiling.

The gray wood floor fit the rougher, outside appearance, along with the large stone fireplace on the far wall. There was a spacious, comfortable looking couch in front of the hearth, and a low, rough-hewn coffee table. To one side was a television; on the other side was a torchiere-style lamp with a reading light attached, which fit with the bookcase on the opposite wall that was almost as full as the one at Foxworth headquarters.

The kitchen she could see into from here was sleek and up-to-date, with a granite-topped island and a couple of bar stools. An open door across the room revealed an equally updated bathroom, and next to that there was an alcove with a desk, some tech gear and a couple of large computer monitors. She assumed the walled-off space served as a bedroom. And there her train of thought threatened to derail once again.

She wasn't used to this. She'd long ago given up fanciful thinking. Her capacity for it had died along with her brother.

But he's not dead!

Maybe that was it. Maybe it had been reborn with the knowledge that what had killed it hadn't really happened at all. Or maybe it had only slept, and it was simply that until now, she'd never met anyone capable of awakening it.

WITH THE FOXWORTH people outside, Case could almost convince himself they were really alone, here in this semi-isolated cabin that backed up to woods and looked out over an expanse of hillside, trees and mountains in the distance that gave him an odd sort of calm. Almost like the weird feeling he got petting Cutter, although that was much harder to explain. Then again, he knew there were therapy dogs used to bring comfort to kids in hospitals, patients in nursing homes and various other people in distress. So maybe it wasn't the dog's effect that was of interest, but he himself. In distress.

He'd been about to call himself pitiful, but realized he would never consider those others in distress pitiful. And he could almost hear Terri protesting if he'd said it out loud.

But right now she was crouched beside Cutter, ruffling his fur and scratching behind his ears. And crooning. A nonstop string of sweetness that made him smile at the pair.

"Yes, you are such a good dog, and so smart I'll bet you're smarter than a lot of people, aren't you, yes, you're such a good boy, and thank you for deciding you needed to be here, on guard."

And then Cutter did what he'd done to Case in the truck, flicking his tongue lightly over her chin in a canine smooch, making her laugh in delight. And then she looked at Case, and he knew immediately she was thinking of that moment outside just as he was.

Something in her eyes made him look away. He needed to concentrate on why they were here.

"Please don't shy away from us," Terri said softly as she straightened up and turned to look directly at him.

She was learning to read him too well. "This," he said, gesturing around the cabin, "and the reason we're here, is not conducive to good decision-making...about that."

She studied him for a moment before saying, still softly, "All right. As long as that goes both ways."

His brow furrowed. Did she mean both of them making decisions? And what if they did, and made opposite decisions? In the end, he didn't even have to ask what she'd meant, because she told him.

"Which means that saying yes to us is just as possible as walking away. Hopefully more possible."

She left him there, staring after her, as she took Cutter

into the kitchen. "I have to see this carrot thing again," she was saying to the dog.

He watched as she opened the fridge and took out a bag of the familiar small peeled pieces. She tossed Cutter one, and he indeed chomped it down with every evidence of gusto.

Case gave a bemused shake of his head, almost grateful for the distraction of the dog. It was easier to think about him than about what Terri had come right out and said.

Saying yes to us.

She wanted that to be more possible than walking away. So did he. He only wished it was that simple.

But it was time to focus on the matter at hand. He began to explore each area of the cabin, noting the position and size of the windows, all of which were alarmed, the location of the also alarmed back door, which was as solid and secured as the front door. The back entry was also adorned with motion sensor lights that looked like they would be blazingly bright, and cameras covering the entire area. He'd already noticed there were no plants or shrubs up next to the house; if anyone managed to get through the alarms outside, they'd be fully exposed. Even the trees behind the place were a good twenty feet away, and those lights would probably reach that far.

Quinn had been right. This place was as secure as a house could be, especially with Cutter as the early warning system. He started to feel a little better. He walked over to the counter, where he'd put down the pistol Rafe had given him back at Foxworth. He picked it up, slid it out of the clip-on holster. He checked the chamber to confirm it was empty, and picked up one of the three magazines Rafe had left him. He slid it in place sharply, then racked the slide back and let it slam closed.

"Why that gun?"

He'd been aware of her watching him. So aware that her question caught him off guard and he answered automatically, as he often had before. "It's striker-fired. No hammer to catch on anything. I like the trigger pull on it." His jaw tensed slightly as he added, "And with no hammer it won't go off accidentally if you drop it."

"That's happened to you?"

"No. My partner, early days. Round hit a bystander. Kid was okay, but he never got over it."

It was a moment before she said quietly, "And apparently neither did you."

"If you mean am I paranoid about it, yeah, a bit."

"Pretty sure that's a good thing."

He glanced at her. She was smiling. That damn approving smile he would crawl over hot shell casings for. And, interestingly, there wasn't a hint of fear in her eyes as she watched him clip the holster with the now ready weapon onto his waistband.

"It doesn't bother you," he said.

She shrugged. "Teague taught me to be wary but not afraid of guns. He said they're like very effective power tools. No better or worse than the person using it."

"I like him already." He meant it as a quip, but something about the way her eyes flashed made him wish he'd kept his mouth shut.

"Good," was all she said, but it didn't relieve him of that unsettled feeling.

The front door opened, and Hayley stepped in. She paused just inside, looking at them rather assessingly. But she said only, "I need to remind Cutter where the boundary of the property is. You might as well come along so you'll know as well. Plus you need to know where Rafe will be, and we'll introduce you to Liam's toys so if you see them buzzing about you'll know."

Terri laughed at that. He was continually amazed at how lighthearted she seemed, what a change finding out her brother was alive had made. He had to take that into account too, didn't he? That maybe she was so giddy with that joy that it was spilling over just now, and later she'd realize that's all it had been?

Later.

That was the key word. Right now the job was keeping her safe, so when that later came, she was able to make that decision for herself.

Chapter Thirty-Two

When they stepped outside he finally found that old focus he used to be able to call up on demand. Cutter didn't dash off as he would have expected, but stayed between Hayley and Terri. When they reached what Hayley said was the boundary of the acre property, she then said something he couldn't quite hear to the dog.

Case noticed a line of shrubs, rhododendrons if he had to guess, and figured that must be the property line. They walked along it, Hayley murmuring to her dog as they went. His ears were up, and his entire posture was alert. And Case thought anyone who underestimated this animal would pay a price.

"I forgot to say, about the alarm inside, they're passive infrared motion sensors, and will ignore anything up to seventy-five pounds moving at ground level. Which," she added with a loving stroke of her dog's head, "includes this guy. So he can move without triggering the alarm, but any human bigger than a child can't. And anybody who decides to risk the alarm is going to be face to fang with him, and they'll lose."

"He's amazing," Terri said, clearly fascinated.

"He knows his job. You can send him to any of us out here by name, just tell him to find. Otherwise he won't leave you.

And if you try to send him and he doesn't go, he probably knows something you don't. Trust him." She pulled out her phone, hit the red button and then spoke. "Liam? You have one of your gnats airborne?"

She gave them a wink as she spoke, and Case guessed "gnats" was a teasing dig at the tech guy.

"Hey! Little respect here," they heard him answer, sounding utterly unoffended.

A moment later Case caught movement on the upper edge of his vision. If he hadn't known, he probably would have written off the glimpse of motion as a bird, so he hoped anybody else would do the same. Once he looked directly, it was obvious what he was seeing; small, smooth and quiet, the device hovered, then rotated in place.

"You're crisp and clear," came Liam's voice over the phone's speaker. "They're equipped with night vision, too, so we're good."

"How long can it fly?" Terri asked.

Liam heard her, because he answered through the phone. "About a half hour on a full charge. But don't worry—there'll always be one aloft. Battery takes about an hour to recharge, add a few minutes to let it cool down first, so I brought three and a spare so there's always a fully charged one. And a couple of backup drones, of course, just in case."

"Of course," Hayley said with a grin.

"And just when do you recharge?" Terri asked.

That got her an approving look from Hayley, and a startled, "Me?" from Liam.

"Quinn will cover when he needs a break," Hayley said. "Whether Liam likes it or not," she added pointedly into the phone.

"Yeah, yeah," they heard him mutter before disconnecting.

"And even I can take a shift or two, thanks to our wizard's patient training. But with the gnats we can see all and yet stay out of sight." The drone ended its hover, heading back toward the trees outside the perimeter. She looked at Terri and smiled. "Normally Teague would be Liam's backup on this. He's pretty good at this tech stuff, too."

"He was always pretty current on computer stuff," she said. "Our father assumed that was the way he'd go." She smiled, a rather bittersweet smile. "He wasn't as furious as the mother was when he joined the Marines, but close."

Hayley looked as if she was about to say something, then changed her mind. Instead she walked on a little farther, then gestured toward the rise that was the beginning of the neighboring, heavily forested hill. "Rafe's spot is up there. If it goes to hell, pay attention to where the firing's coming from." She looked at Case. "I'm assuming you'll be able to differentiate rifle fire from handgun fire?"

He nodded. "Don't want to assume Zukero will be limited to one or the other, though. Or that he'll be alone."

She nodded. "Just know that if you hear more than a single rifle shot from Rafe's hide, there's probably more than one guy coming at you. He does not miss."

Case was sure this was not an exaggeration. There had been a rock-solid core beneath Rafe's laconic exterior, and when the chips were down, he would come through.

Hayley went on. "Now that you have an idea about the boundary outside, let's head back in and we'll go over the camera feeds."

"Oh! Duh," Terri said with a sheepish smile. "I just realized, that's what all the monitors are for, right?"

Hayley smiled. "Yes, one for the front cameras, one for the back. Between them you have a 360-degree view around the house."

"What about inside?" Case asked. It was a legitimate question, even if his reasons were a bit selfish.

"There are cameras inside, but they're only triggered by

someone setting off the other alarm system. We're protecting you, not spying on you." Hayley gave him a sideways look, and he caught the slight smile. "Besides, nothing going on we don't already know. We've had too much experience with Cutter's knack for bringing people together not to recognize it." The smile became wider. "And by the way, when I said I picked up everything you needed, I meant it. There's a lasagna for dinner in the fridge, and a new box in the nightstand."

Hayley was casual, as if she'd had this conversation many times. Which, if what she said about her dog was true, he supposed she had. He wanted to glance at Terri, but he'd swear he could feel her looking at him and he didn't dare. He was glad it took a couple of minutes to get back to the cabin.

When they were back inside and Hayley had activated the outside cameras, the images she'd promised popped up, four to each monitor.

"What's the third screen for?" Terri asked, nodding toward the third, smaller monitor.

"That's hooked to a separate computer, if you actually need to use one, so it doesn't interfere with the security feed."

At that moment Quinn came in from outside. "We're all set. We'll continue coverage as we did back at Foxworth for tonight, while you get used to the normal sounds of the place. There's a bit of wildlife around."

"A bit?" Hayley retorted with a grin. "Woodpeckers? Check. Eagles, check. Raccoons, check. Deer, check. The occasional bear? Check."

"You left out the coyotes and the now and then mountain lion," Quinn said dryly.

Terri was grinning back, while Case shook his head, bemused. "I've spent way too much time in the city."

"So, more than a day, then?" Terri asked, her brows arched upward.

Case felt a burst of that warm, aching sensation again, not

the physical wanting that was always there, but that deeper sort of yearning that had made him realize just how he felt about this woman. Yes, it had been less than a week, but that was long enough to get past the compulsion to continue to protect, if this was a normal situation. That's the way it had always happened before; in uniform he'd helped or even saved somebody in trouble, and felt connected to them until they were safely back on track. Then they went their way and he went his, most times never to encounter each other again.

The thought of that happening with Terri made his mind scream out a harsh *No!*

"Take these, both of you," Quinn said as Case made himself tune back in. He held out what looked like two earbuds. "They're already connected to our system. Case, you'll be used to this, but Terri, if something goes down, you won't have to have the phone in your hand, just close. Range is about fifty feet. And we'll all be live on the same channel."

"Okay," she said, taking the small earpiece.

"Just to make sure we're all on the same page," Quinn continued, "the bottom line is Terri's safety, and we do whatever we have to, to assure that. After that, we want Zukero. But Foxworth has a good reputation around here, so no killing this…jerk just because he deserves it."

Case knew this was directed at him, knew that Quinn had read him well. And that once he and Hayley left the cabin, Case would be the only one likely to or able to do just that. Except maybe Cutter, he added to himself with a glance at the still alert dog at their feet.

He tamped down the admitted urge. "I haven't killed a lot of his ilk who deserved it because they were still only suspects, not convicted. I'll manage again," he said.

Quinn studied him for a moment. "So you still think the system works?"

"The system isn't and never was the problem. It's the people running it."

"Amen," Hayley said.

"All right," Quinn said, accepting his word. Case was a little surprised at how much that meant to him. He'd come to respect this man, and the organization he ran. "Best case scenario, they catch him in the next twenty-four hours and we don't do this at all. Next best, Terri's safe, he gets handed over to Brett who gets to hand him over to that system and he spends the foreseeable future eating prison food. Agreed?"

"Agreed."

"Then we're on. Tomorrow we'll start putting the word out, via Brett's contacts in the city. The official word will be they're looking for her as person of interest, implying witness. Then Rafe's contacts on the street will put out that she's run here, to be with you, Case. Once he's moving, Brett will have the word out to be on watch at the possible travel points. But we can't be sure he'll be spotted, and we don't know if he'll be driving and if so what."

"Good thing it's not summer yet," was all Case said, thinking of the huge increase in traffic to and from.

"Small favors," Hayley said in agreement. "So, we'll still be on watch, but we'll leave you to get used to the place, so you have an idea what's normal." Again that knowing look flashed in her eyes. "Otherwise, get some rest. Recreation. Whatever. Tomorrow it truly begins."

Chapter Thirty-Three

Terri stretched luxuriously in the comfortable bed. It was smaller than the one at the headquarters building but she didn't mind. The last three nights they'd spent here had been glorious, and every time she had awakened to Case's strong, muscled warmth beside her she felt a renewed burst of joy.

Sometimes she was even able to put out of her mind why they were here. It had only been Friday that the process had really begun, that the information had been planted with Foxworth care. And when it did invade her mind she tried to redirect it, wondering what part Teague would normally play in that process, what he'd be doing if he was here and they were helping some stranger. If that didn't work, she simply thought about this, and the last few nights spent with Case beside her, loving her.

Case shifted, and she figured he must be awake now that it was getting light. She heard a faint crinkle, realized it was a foil wrapper and grinned to herself.

"Hayley is quite something," she said. "She truly thought of everything."

Maybe even enough condoms.

A vision of the last time they'd used one, just a couple of hours ago, flowed hotly through her mind. He had urged her to ride him, and the only thing more wonderful than the feel of him so deep inside her was the rough sound of his voice when he'd groaned out her name as he bucked beneath her.

But now he was silent. She wondered if he'd fallen back to sleep. She couldn't blame him, since he'd certainly exerted himself last night. Hard case indeed… She turned her head to look at him.

He was awake. And even in the faint light of dawn she could see he was staring at the ceiling.

"Case?"

He didn't look at her. But at last he did answer her. And when he did, she wished he hadn't.

"I just want you to know, that if this is just because you're so happy about your brother, I get it."

"If…what is?"

"This," he repeated. Then, finally, he looked at her. "So if when Zukero is locked up and Teague is back, you want me to bow out, I'll understand."

Conflicting emotions collided in her gut, knotting it tightly. She wasn't sure if appreciation for his tactfulness, the shock that he would even think that or the hurt at the very thought of him walking away would win. It took her a moment to get it all under control enough to speak, and when she did the effort made her voice cool.

"Are you giving me an out, or yourself?"

She heard the deep breath he sucked in and saw his powerful chest rise. Then he rose up on one elbow and faced her. She braced herself inwardly, afraid of what might be coming. She tried to calm herself. Only an idiot would walk away from what they'd found, and Case was no idiot. He was still off-balance after what had happened to him, having what he'd thought would be his life's work taken away, followed by the crumbling of his home life as well. He'd been betrayed on all sides; it was no wonder he was having trouble getting past that.

"Terri, I—"

Cutter, who had been sprawled on the floor beside them—albeit with his ears up as if he was listening to their conversation—let out an almost musical bark as he leaped to his feet and ran toward the front door.

"Hayley?" Terri guessed.

"Or Quinn."

Before she could go down the path of how much she admired and envied the life and work those two had built, she reached for her shirt, which was tangled with the sheet and blanket and hanging over the side of the bed. As if it had been a signal to him, Case did the same, pulling on the green long-sleeved shirt that brought out the green in his hazel eyes, sadly hiding that broad, strong chest and flat, ridged abdomen she thought she'd kissed every inch of last night.

Not to mention a lot of other luscious inches.

She heard the approach of a vehicle, and was still wrestling with her bra as he got to his feet and zipped his jeans. Before he could walk away she spoke, with a bit of vehemence.

"Fair warning," she said. He stopped, but he didn't look back. "This conversation is not over."

"I assumed," he said, his deep voice a little gruff.

And then he was gone, around the corner of the bedroom alcove. For a moment Terri just sat there, torn between being exasperated, hurt and determined. She heard the knock on the door, then heard it open, and Quinn's voice.

Then, as it had for ten years, determination won the battle. She wasn't going to let him throw them away out of some misguided nobility, and Mr. Case McMillan could just get used to it.

"WE MAY HAVE MOVEMENT."

"Zukero?"

Quinn nodded. "It's thirdhand, but one of Rafe's contacts, a vet in Seattle who hangs out near the Pike Place Market, texted him. Said a guy who knows Zukero told him he'd been around the last couple of days, stealing food and grabbing purses from tourists. Always gone with his loot by the time the police got there. Said Zukero knows they're looking for him."

Case heard Terri's quiet approach, but didn't look. Didn't dare. He just kept his attention on Quinn. Terri didn't speak, was clearly just listening.

"He must have gone through that convenience store money pretty fast if he's down to purse snatches," Case said.

Quinn nodded. "Most interesting point is last time he told the guy he'd see him tomorrow. Meaning today. But he didn't show up."

"Maybe he got arrested," Terri said, sounding hopeful.

Quinn gave her a regretful look. "No, we checked. And anybody who snagged him would let Brett know, now that he's got the word out." Quinn smiled. "I don't think anybody in this state would ignore Brett Dunbar."

"Taking down a sitting governor will do that," Case said wryly. "So maybe he changed his hunting ground?"

"Could be."

"Or…" Case flicked a glance at Terri and let the obvious question fade away.

"Or," Quinn said with a nod.

"You think he's coming?" Terri asked, the hope fading away.

Quinn held her gaze. "Rafe's guy planted the seed, as we asked. That you're over here, hiding from him."

"So he could have been stocking up, gathering cash to get him over here and expenses until he finds her," Case said, his voice flat.

"Could be." Quinn looked back at Terri. "Rafe's guy also

dropped the last name this place is listed under, as who you were running to. And Liam planted the name and address in several online sources. He'll have to look, but if he does he'll find it."

"I'd like to say he's not that smart," Terri said sourly, "but he has gotten away with a lot, and for a long time."

"There's smart, and then there's smart and dangerous," Case said. And this guy was dangerous to one person above all. Now that the wheels were in motion, he was even less happy about this. He wanted it over. But he also had to admit this was likely the best way to put an end to it, and soon. "Maybe once we're sure he's found this place, we should move Terri somewhere else."

"No!" She nearly yelped out the protest. Quinn looked thoughtful, and she went on in a rush. "What if he sees the move? We won't know where he is until he gets close, but he could be in the area, watching before he makes a move, couldn't he? I don't want this to all be for nothing because he gets scared off or thinks I'm not here."

Quinn silently shifted his gaze to Case. With a sigh Case put up his hands in surrender. "Good points, every one," he conceded. "I was just…"

He let it die, not wanting to admit out loud that he was beyond afraid for her, afraid that somehow Zukero would find a hole, a gap in their coverage, would find a way to get to her and finish the job he'd started a week ago.

A week ago.

One short week, and his life had been turned upside down all over again, as it had been just over a year ago. And suddenly something else hit him, about Terri's reaction to the idea she leave and be kept safe somewhere away from the danger. It had been instant and gut level: she would not run.

And if she'd been the one, that year ago, she would have stood her ground, right beside him. She would never run, not like Jill had. He knew it deep down to the bone, no doubt, no hesitation.

And he had no words for the feeling that knowledge gave him.

Chapter Thirty-Four

Sunday was a quiet, peaceful day, at least outwardly. She'd caught him glancing at her warily now and then, as if he was expecting—and dreading—her reopening that conversation as she'd promised.

She would, but she didn't mind letting him stew in it for a while.

Sometimes it's best to let them spend some time worrying about what you're thinking. She smiled inwardly; Mrs. Gibson had been as wise as her husband, although in a different way.

Quinn had told them Foxworth would essentially vanish now, in case Zukero had made his way over here and was watching. They'd be here, but hidden in the trees and using Liam's drones for observation.

Rafe will take care of it if it goes to hell outside. If it comes to that just stay back to give him a clear shot, he'd said, and the businesslike way he said it—and the way Case had nodded as if he'd expected no less—was a bit unnerving. They were all risking a great deal to keep her safe. "If you need us, use the phones. And the earpieces in case you have to move fast."

She marveled anew at their preparedness for a situation like this. A bit on edge, she searched for distraction. She found that Hayley's preparations were just as thorough in the kitchen, and decided to distract herself with a favorite kitchen task. Soon both things she'd hoped for had happened; she was calmer, and at the sweet aroma of her first batch of cookies baking Case had put down his book—the book he'd turned exactly one page in during the last hour—and followed the scent.

"I expected Cutter first," she said, keeping her tone teasingly light.

"His nose was twitching, but obviously he has better willpower than I do," Case said.

"I just love sugar cookies.

He glanced at her makeshift rolling pin, which happened to be an empty wine bottle she'd found in the recycle bin. "Nice repurposing," he said with a small smile.

She smiled back. "It works. They're boring circles because I just used a glass to cut them out. I admit, making these isn't as much fun without the set of animal cookie cutters Mrs. Gibson had, but still…"

He looked at the flat dough she'd rolled out. "Maybe just cut them out with a knife?"

She had to laugh at that. "That would work if the only animal I did was an amoeba. I can't even draw a circle without it being lopsided."

"Nice to know there's something you're not great at."

Her gaze shot to his face, but he was still looking at the cookie dough. Intentionally? To avoid her eyes? Was he regretting the compliment? Afraid she'd dive back into that aborted discussion?

Rein it in, girl. Just because he makes your emotions run riot doesn't mean you have to let your mind follow.

Then, as if he'd only been thinking of the matter at hand—and he was a guy, 100 percent, so it was possible, even probable—he said, "Is there a sharp knife?"

Curious, she said nothing but reached into the drawer where she'd seen one and pulled the small blade out. He took it when she offered, but with barely a glance at her, which she figured confirmed her earlier guess.

He leaned over the bottle-flattened dough and tilted his head slightly. Then he moved the hand with the knife and began to cut. In a matter of seconds, she was looking at a graceful and completely recognizable seagull in flight. She stared at it for a moment, a little astonished.

"Do another."

It sounded a bit peremptory, but he didn't react to that, merely did that thoughtful thing again before he put the knife back to the dough. It became the recognizable shape of one of the big cruise ships that traversed the sound in the summer. Then he glanced at Cutter, smiled a little crookedly and produced a dog, ears and tail up, and bearing a striking resemblance.

"Speaking of being great at things," she declared. "Brilliant, Hard Case." She enveloped him in a hug. Felt him go very still, then hug her back as the oven dinged. "Keep cutting while I take these out."

He did, although he paused to grab a warm cookie first. Cutter had gotten up and joined them, drawn either by the aroma now that they were done, or by Case's glance. *Which could certainly draw you...*

After his first bite, he savored it for a moment then looked at her. "Wow. If I was a nicer guy, I'd say you should share these with the Foxworth folks. But I think I could eat them all myself."

"I'll make more," she said, ridiculously pleased. "But if they're staying out of sight how do we get the cookies to them?"

"Maybe Cutter could deliver them, but he's liking the

smell a bit too much," he said as he tossed a small bit of his cookie to the dog, who caught it and smacked at it hungrily. "Uh-oh, I've corrupted him now."

Terri laughed. She felt a fullness in her chest. She loved this so much, just being with him, doing ordinary things and joking lightheartedly. She wanted more of this, a lot more.

Face it—you want a lifetime of it.

She hurried to think of something else before she ruined her plan to make him wait by blurting that out loud. "Maybe if we give him a whole one, he'd deliver the rest safely." She pulled out the Foxworth phone. "I'll ask them how to do it."

"Make sure you tell them we're code fo—that we're okay first thing."

She gave him a sideways look, wondering how often he had to catch himself, stop talking in police codes. But when she put it on speaker and hit the red button, she said all was well before she said anything else. Liam answered that everything was secure outside as well.

"We need to send you something," Case said. "Will Cutter bring it?"

Liam's voice came through clearly. "Sure he will. Just tell him to find me, and he will. What's he bringing?"

"The best cookies you'll ever taste," Case said before she could answer.

"Whoa!" Liam sounded more excited than sugar cookies warranted, but it made her smile anyway. "Send him fast."

"As soon as they're cool enough to bag," Terri said. "But you have to share."

"Promise. And I'll send him back to you right away."

In the end they attached the baggie full of cookies to Cutter's collar with a zip tie, and stepped outside.

"You'd better tell him," Case said. "Hayley said he knows you're the one he's here for."

"Isn't this crazy? I've never seen a dog like this."

"I think life would be easier with just an ordinary, goofy one."

"Okay. We'll find one," she said, carefully avoiding looking at him as she made a commitment to the future he didn't even believe they had. Yet. She bent down and told Cutter, "Find Liam."

The dog trotted off as if he already knew where his quarry was. He crossed the open space and vanished into the trees. Five minutes later he was back, the baggie still attached but now with a small card in it. Case handed it to her while he cut the bag loose. It was a business card for Quinn Foxworth with "Thanks" written on it. On the back was written an additional "thank you" from Liam, and a "ditto" from Rafe. It made her smile.

It was the kind of Sunday she'd always dreamed about. Slow, relaxed and with someone she loved. Loved more than she'd thought herself capable, especially in a matter of days. She simply could not believe he would just throw this, throw them away. She was tempted to push the issue now, but when it came down to it she couldn't. She wanted this day, this perfect day with a morning spent making love, a day with a sweet, clever dog, home-baked cookies and an evening of quiet sharing by the fire. She wanted it complete, so she could treasure the memory forever. It could wait until morning. Because just in case, she wanted one more night with him to lock away in her mind's treasure chest of memories.

So she quashed the need for a declaration, and instead did everything she could to lure him back to bed.

It didn't take much.

CASE WAS FEELING incredibly calm, given the circumstances. Or maybe just drained. The thought made him grin to himself. Last night had been…well, as incredible as all the nights with her had been. This week had been the most amazing of his life, here, tucked away in this quiet cabin with her. He had wondered how long Foxworth would be willing to keep this going, but Quinn had assured him they'd known it would take time.

As for Case, he had the lazy feeling he'd be happy if this went on endlessly. This morning he was relaxed enough that when he had his jeans and shoes back on and had let Cutter out to do his business, he decided to take a turn in the kitchen. He could whip up a fairly decent omelet, and with the eggs, butter, cheese and fresh chives he found in the fridge, he'd wasted no time getting started as soon as Cutter came back.

It came out well, and Terri's hungry approval as she ate what he'd fixed warmed him. Her hair, still tousled by his fingers, and the fact that she was still wearing his T-shirt also warmed him. Oddly, it wasn't in an exactly sexual way, more in a comfortable way. Or maybe he was just worn out after last night. He had to smother what would no doubt have been a smug, male grin.

Both kinds of hunger sated for the moment, he was lulled. Terri went to get dressed as he moved over to sit in front of the fireplace that had kicked on in the not-quite-spring-yet chill. He picked up his book, a fascinating firsthand World War II recollection, and opened to the page he'd marked. It was the kind of peaceful, warm morning he'd seen few of, and none in the last year. But now…

Maybe Zukero hadn't gotten the word yet. Maybe he was still looking for her on the other side. Maybe—

Didn't you swear off wishful thinking, McMillan?

Even as he thought it, it happened. Terri came back, and stood before him.

"I need to ask you something."

He looked up from the book. His expression turned wary when he saw the determination in her gaze. When she returned his look steadily, he knew. He let the book drop to his lap and waited silently, braced. He knew what was coming. And it did.

"Are you looking for a way out? Is that why you've convinced yourself I don't know what I want, or I'm not thinking straight?"

He drew in a deep breath. "I just know this situation is crazy, you're under a lot of stress and that's not conducive to clear thinking."

She let out a short, sharp laugh. He blinked, startled. "You know my history, more than anyone ever has. Do you really believe that after how my life has gone, I can't think straight under pressure?"

He drew back slightly, his brow furrowing. He hadn't thought of it in quite that way. Cutter, who had been sprawled on the floor, sat up, as if he sensed the sudden tension between the two humans.

"Thinking with a gun to my head is one thing," Terri said. "I'll grant you I didn't handle all that too well, especially after hitting that wall. But now? With time to think and process?"

"Terri—"

"So back to question one," she said, cutting him off. "Are you looking for a way out?"

"No!" It broke from him sharply. Cutter let out a sound that was half whine, half growl, and he took another deep breath to calm down. "I'm trying to give you a way out." He lowered his gaze, unable to meet those bright blue eyes any longer. When he finished it, his voice was low and rough. "I don't want you to feel you owe me."

Movement caught the edge of his vision. Something red. Fast. A split second later it hit his head. His head jerked up, and the red pillow from the couch fell to the floor on his feet. She'd thrown it at him.

"Is that what you think?" she demanded. "You think I'm sleeping with you out of gratitude? To pay you back?"

"I didn't mean—"

"Because that's sure what it sounded like. Which makes me what? What, exactly, are you calling me, Mr. McMillan?"

Crazily, all he could think was that her brother would be very proud of how she'd turned out, given it seemed he was the only good influence she'd had growing up. She—

A buzz from the phone on the table saved him from making a bigger fool out of himself. Grateful, he immediately reached out and hit the red button and turned on the speaker. Quinn's voice came through clearly. And held the snap of command.

"Heads up. We've got company."

Chapter Thirty-Five

Case was on his feet so fast it startled Terri. That he reached to confirm the handgun was in place rattled her.

"Zukero?" His voice mirrored his reaction, short, sharp and definite. Cutter, too, was on his feet, ears up as he stared toward the front door.

"Unknown." Liam's voice this time. "It's a guy on foot. Coming up the hill. Doesn't look like Zukero from above."

There was a pause and they heard Liam mutter something. Case had grabbed up the earpieces Quinn had given them, turned them both on and handed one to her. She slipped it into her ear just as Liam went on.

"He has short hair and is clean-shaven, but he could have done that. I don't see any neck tatts, though." Liam sounded frustrated now. "He's wearing a baseball cap and sunglasses, so I don't have a visual on his face. And if I go down low enough for that, no way he won't see the drone. He's still pretty far down the hill."

Cutter had reached the front door and stood there, on alert, listening. Terri had no idea if he'd heard something outside, or if he was just reacting to the tenor of the familiar voices.

"Hold off on that," came Quinn's voice. "I've got binocs on him. If it is him, he's definitely lost the hair and the full beard. Don't see the tatts either. It's a bright enough day we can't assume the shades are for disguise. And he's still too far away for a positive ID. We'll let him get a little closer." There was a moment's pause, then the voice of command again. "If it is Zukero, we assume he's armed and here with lethal intent."

She heard two clicks over the phone, and Case said, "Copy."

"Rafe, you have a bead on him?" Quinn asked.

"Affirmative."

Terri felt a little shiver as she thought of the tall, lean man with the shadowed gray eyes somewhere up the hill with his weapon, aimed— Her thought was interrupted by the realization of them talking on the one hand about how far away the approaching man was, and on the other casually assuming Rafe could take him out.

He does not miss.

Hayley's flat statement came back to her. Such faith they had in the man.

Like you have in Case?

"Well, that's interesting." Quinn's voice came through her earpiece, thankfully diverting her before she could go down that path, now when she needed to be fully paying attention. "He's carrying a dog."

"Carrying a dog?" Terri asked, frowning.

"Yes. Black-and-white one, small. Maybe a pup. Looks like it might be hurt." Cutter growled, at this point more a sound of warning than threat.

Terri felt a jab of concern. "Maybe he's just someone looking for help with the dog?"

"Up here?" Case said, sounding edgily doubtful.

"I know the only neighbors are down the hill, but…"

"Hold," Quinn said. "We don't want to take out an innocent bystander who might just be trying to help an injured animal."

They heard a distant bark. Cutter shifted restlessly, the growl intensifying, as if he sensed—or heard—the man getting closer to the perimeter he'd been shown. It didn't seem impossible, with a dog this clever.

"Maybe he thinks it lives here, if he found it running loose." Terri thought it sounded reasonable, but also knew she might just be trying to avoid the possibility it really was Zukero, here and hunting her.

A piteous yelp changed the mood instantly. Terri felt the instinctive human response to the sound of a dog in pain.

"We should help him. That dog's definitely hurt," Terri said.

"Or it's Zukero and he's the one hurting him," Case said grimly.

Once more, she hadn't thought of that. Her cold, unfeeling parents hadn't been able to instill that in her, thanks to her brother. But she knew it was not coldness that made Case think that way; it was years of experience with the worst of human nature.

"Possibly," Quinn agreed. "Options are intercept now, or let him keep coming and watch."

"I don't want him getting away," Case said vehemently.

"Agreed." Quinn's response was mild by comparison. "If it is Zukero, he's well disguised. So let's hold back a little longer."

"But the dog," Terri protested.

"I know, and I promise you, if he's hurt it, he'll regret it." Quinn's voice was still mild, but somehow that made the promise even more ominous. "If he keeps coming, he'll be closest to you, Case. Get a look if you can without him seeing you."

"You think he'd recognize me?" Case asked.

"If you took me out as efficiently as you did him, I'd remember," Quinn said.

Case looked almost embarrassed, but pleased at the words. Clearly he had a lot of respect for Foxworth.

Cutter was growling steadily now, and looked up at Case to be sure he was hearing it. She figured it had to be a general warning that someone was approaching, because the dog couldn't possibly know who they were watching for. But she would bet money he knew they were watching for someone specific, or at the least a specific threat.

She knew the moment the man crossed the boundary of the property by Cutter's sudden, fierce string of barks. Case crossed to the front window in two long strides, but stopped at the edge and stole a look through the blinds. He pulled back so quickly it was hard to believe he'd seen much, but he immediately spoke.

"The hat's from a delivery service, and the shirt matches. Couldn't see the logo because of the dog. With the sunglasses, and discounting the hair and beard, I can't tell anything other than he's the right height and build. And no tatts."

"He could have covered them with makeup." It was Hayley's voice, for the first time. Terri knew she had been covering one of the ferry docks, watching for Zukero, but clearly she was monitoring the situation here.

"Or maybe he really is just a delivery guy who found a loose dog," Terri said.

"Possibly. Or maybe hit him."

"Is he really hurt?" Terri asked anxiously.

"No blood I could see, but one foreleg's hanging funny." Case's jaw tightened for a moment before he said, "I could go out and meet him. Then we'll likely know for sure in a hurry."

"Yes," Terri snapped, "because he'll shoot you on sight."

Case's head came up to look at her, and his expression was a little startled. And from the earpiece she heard a short chuckle, although she couldn't tell who it had come from.

"She has a point," Quinn said, sounding as if it might have been him. "On the other hand, if you let him in, Rafe's out of play."

"And he's under the same roof as Terri," Case said flatly.

Terri clenched her teeth and never looked at him. And when she spoke, her voice, with effort, was even. "I'd rather take the risk than maybe hurt an innocent man trying to help an injured dog."

Case frowned, started to speak. "Terri—"

"Please, Quinn," she said, not looking at Case.

She thought she heard a long breath before Quinn's voice came through the earpiece. "If you were anyone else, I'd just say it's your call. But Teague…"

"Would understand," she said. *At least the Teague I grew up with would.*

"Time," Liam said sharply. He's on the walkway to the cabin."

"Let him come," Case said suddenly. "I'll take the door. If," he added with emphasis, "Terri stays hidden, and swears she'll run if she has to."

Has to? A chill enveloped her as she realized he meant if it was Zukero and he couldn't stop him. Which would mean he was hurt. Or worse. She opened her mouth to take it all back but Quinn spoke first.

"Do it. Terri, take Cutter with you. Now."

It was no less than an order. From the man her brother obviously had chosen to work for, admire and respect. No matter her qualms, no matter that she now wished she'd kept her mouth shut, there was only one thing to do.

She started to move. "Cutter," she said as she went, understanding the urge to keep the animal safe. The dog looked at her, then back at Case.

"Go," he said, and there was the same snap of command

in his voice that had been in Quinn's. Then he added just as sharply, "Guard."

As if he'd understood perfectly—had Quinn told him what commands to give the dog?—Cutter gave a short bark and spun on his hindquarters and came after her. The chill came again, and she thought she'd never felt so stupid in her life. They were sending Cutter with her not to protect him, but for him to protect her.

I'd rather take the risk...

Her own words rang hollowly in her mind. Because she realized how blind she'd been. It wouldn't be her taking the risk. It would be Cutter.

And Case.

CASE OPENED THE door to the knock, his right hand behind him, gripping the butt of the holstered HK. The now obviously hurting dog—that foreleg was definitely broken—did look like a puppy close up. He was squirming in the guy's arms. The man was looking down as he tried to hold on to the whimpering creature, and for a moment all Case saw was the top of the black cap, and the bill that was hiding the man's face.

I'd rather take the risk than maybe hurt an innocent man...

Terri's words echoed in his mind. She couldn't know she'd practically quoted the mantra he'd lived by as a cop. He released the holstered pistol and moved his hand forward. He swiped upward at the hat, catching the brim and shoving it back, figuring he could always claim he'd been trying to help with the dog and it was accidental. At the last second he reached out with his little finger and caught the temple of the sunglasses, yanking them upward as well.

"Sorry," he began, in case it was necessary.

The man looked up. Case saw his eyes. Those eyes. Saw

the nose, the reddened jawline as if he had just shaved, hard…and the slight mismatch of color on his neck, where indeed makeup did mask the betraying tattoos.

"You," Zukero hissed.

Case didn't bother with subterfuge. "Howdy, Marcus," he drawled, loudly enough for it to be heard through the earpiece.

Zukero shoved the injured dog at Case. It yelped in pain. Case grabbed it instinctively. Zukero took the chance to push his way inside, slamming the door shut behind him. Case realized in the next instant that the man hadn't been wrestling with the dog, he'd been trying to hold on to both the dog and his gun. Case reacted swiftly. Grabbed at the wrist of Zukero's gun hand, trying to both contain the weapon and not hurt the dog any further. Another pained yelp told him he hadn't been fully successful. He winced more from that than the free fist Zukero slammed up to his jaw.

Case took the extra second to get the dog clear. It cost him. Zukero twisted his hand around. Pulled the trigger.

The shot seemed amplified by the heavy log walls of the cabin. Case's ears rang almost before the searing pain from his left side registered. He hung on, forcing Zukero's hand upward. Zukero pushed at him, hard. Then plowed his free fist into Case's side, near the wound. Pain slammed through him, making the room spin and the ringing in his ears louder. He held on, twisted, caught a foot behind Zukero's knee and brought him down to the floor.

He heard a loud, fierce, menacing snarl. Rather vaguely he thought of the hurt dog, but then his brain registered the truth. It was Cutter, charging, in that moment looking more wolf than dog. Zukero yelled, tried to twist free. Case held on to that gun hand. Then Cutter was on him. Zukero threw up his free hand in an effort to ward off the animal clearly intent on his throat. It was a mistake. Cutter's jaws clamped on to his forearm.

The two wrestled for a moment. Zukero's knee dug into Case's wounded side and pain shot through him again. Through it Case heard running footsteps. And then a thud. Zukero collapsed, half atop Case, Cutter atop Zukero, jaws still clamped tight on his wrist.

And standing above them was Terri, with her makeshift bottle rolling pin in her hands. The bottle she'd clearly just hit Zukero over the head with.

A split second later the front and back doors slammed open. Quinn and Liam were there, weapons drawn.

It was over.

Chapter Thirty-Six

"According to Brett, he left the city two days after we planted the info," Hayley told them as she and Quinn joined Terri and Case around the big coffee table back at Foxworth headquarters. Rafe had departed to his lair in the outbuilding, and Liam hadn't returned yet.

"He found the cabin the next day," Quinn said, "so he must have had the location. He'd apparently been watching from a delivery van parked down the hill. They're so ubiquitous nobody thought anything of it."

"Then he saw Cutter," Hayley put in, "and assumed he was yours, so figured the injured dog would be an in."

"So he what, grabbed the first stray he saw?" Case asked. "That poor puppy?"

"Apparently," Quinn answered. Then added, with a severe expression, "And broke his leg to make it easier to get him to whine so pitifully."

"But he'll be all right?" Terri asked anxiously, for the first time tearing her gaze away from Case, whom she'd been watching carefully for any sign of his own pain. If he was feeling the gouge left in his side, he wasn't letting it show. Rafe, of all people, had quickly doctored the gouge with a kit produced from the Foxworth SUV. And efficiently, said the doctor in the clinic they'd stopped at; there was nothing more for him to do except feel relieved that the police were already involved and he didn't have to go through the reporting procedure.

"Our vet, Dr. Moore, is fixing him up, and says he'll be fine," Hayley reassured her.

Cutter let out a little yip from his spot, as if he recognized the name. "Speaking of dogs," Case said, leaning down—a little gingerly, she noticed—to stroke the dog's head, "you are amazing. From goofball to guerilla fighter in the space of a second."

Hayley smiled widely. "He is amazing."

"When you told me on the phone to let him out I was afraid to," Terri admitted. "Afraid he'd get hurt." She shifted her gaze back to Case. "But you were already hurt, and that trumped everything."

"It was just a—"

"If you say the words *flesh wound* I will cheerfully punch said wound," Terri stated. Case blinked. He lowered his gaze, but he was smiling. And somehow that made her able to admit what had truly been bothering her. "The minute I realized what I'd let you in for I wanted to take it all back. I feel so stupid, thinking it might not be Zukero."

His head came back up. His eyes, those amazing, gold-green eyes, locked on to hers. "Don't. You could have been right."

"But I was wrong."

"You didn't want to risk hurting an innocent person. I would have expected no less, not from you. You know too much about being that person, hurt by a simple mistake."

She was aware of Quinn's and Hayley's presence, but said it anyway. "I think doing the right thing and nearly being destroyed is worse."

"We'll get to that," Quinn said briskly, and she wondered what he meant. But before he could go on, Cutter was on his feet, letting out what she recognized as Liam's bark as he ran toward the door. Terri thought she heard Liam speak from outside, and Cutter rose up and batted at the door control. It swung open, and the young Texan came in with his arms full of black-and-white puppy. The dog had his left foreleg splinted and bandaged, and was looking much happier. Terri couldn't help herself, she leaped to her feet and walked quickly over to greet them.

"You poor baby," she crooned as she patted the dog's head. He swiped his tongue over her wrist, clearly no longer terrified. "You're so sweet."

"Thanks," Liam said, and when she looked up at him he was grinning at her.

"You, too," she said, and patted his cheek as she had the dog's head. "But don't lick me."

"I never trespass," Liam said, nodding over her shoulder toward where Case was sitting. She considered it progress that she didn't blush but grinned back at him instead. "Besides, I'm completely, happily corralled anyway."

He carried the pup—with a fascinated Cutter on his heels—over to where Quinn and Hayley were sitting and watching them. And smiling.

"Dr. Moore says he's probably about five months old," Liam told them. "And a little malnourished, as you can tell. He gave him some food there, and he kept it down okay. He guesses he's been on his own for a month or so, judging by his weight. But otherwise, unless something comes back on the tests he ran, he's okay, and should be fine once the leg is healed. He wants to see him again in a week."

"We'll make sure it happens," Quinn said.

"Good of Foxworth to see to him," Case said.

"It's who they are," Terri said, as she resumed her seat beside him.

"I checked online and local neighborhood sites," Liam said. "Nobody's reported him missing."

"Not sure they'd deserve him back anyway," Hayley said, a bit acerbically.

"So now he just needs a good home," Terri said.

"I think we saw to that, too," Liam said, and he plopped the puppy down, not in Terri's lap or in Case's, but across them both. Before either of them could respond, he'd shifted his attention to Quinn. "I'll head up and finish off the reports."

Quinn nodded. Then Hayley said, "And then go home and stay for a while. Ria's probably been missing you like crazy after the last week."

"And I her," Liam said before he headed up the stairs.

"Now," Quinn said, "we get to deal with the aftermath. I'll call Gavin and give him the update. Terri, he'll be here tomorrow, and we'll go over everything that happens from here. He'll be with you every step of the way through the end of the trial, and Foxworth will be with you until Zukero is locked up." His gaze shifted to Case. "Change your mind about how public you want to be about your part in this?"

Terri, who had been petting the puppy who seemed quite content to be held by both of them, looked up at Case just as he shook his head decidedly. "No," he said. "The less I'm mentioned, the better."

"All right." Quinn left to make his call, and Hayley tactfully headed upstairs to join Liam.

Terri went back to the little bundle of black and white, stroking him as he seemed to quiver in delight. Probably at simply being treated kindly and having a full tummy. And as they sat there, the pup stretched across both their laps, Terri dared to hope Liam might be right, that the good home this little guy had found was with her and Case.

"We never finished that conversation," she said quietly.

"We don't need to."

"Yes, we do. At least, I do."

He shook his head. "You already did." She drew back slightly, puzzled. He gave a half shrug. "You more than proved you can think straight under stressful circumstances." He was suddenly smiling. "And you actually took the bad guy out with a freaking wine bottle rolling pin."

She stared at him. "Does this mean…you'll give us a chance?"

He reached out and touched her cheek gently. "It means now I have to be as brave as you've been. It's time—past time—to put it behind me and move on. I think I just never wanted to…until you." He took in a deep breath. "I know it hasn't even been two weeks, and we'll need more time, more normal time, to find out what we really have, but—"

"I know what we have," Terri said. "Enough to build on."

"And as someone who built a life from nothing, I'd say you'd know." This time he leaned in and kissed her, gently, tenderly, with the kind of warmth she knew deep inside was the kind that would last forever.

THEY'D ALL BEEN keyed up the entire two days since Zukero had gone down, waiting for this moment. But Terri was wound so tight she couldn't stay still, jumping up every few minutes to pace some more. Finally Cutter came over to where she'd again perched on the edge of the couch and plopped his chin on her knee. Case smiled when she reached out automatically to pet him, because he knew what she would feel. Knew the easing of tension, the sense of soothing that the dog somehow was able to transmit. Knew it because he'd felt it himself.

Hayley walked over to where he stood watching from across the living room of her home. "Laney will get him here," she assured him.

"He still doesn't know?" Case asked quietly.

She shook her head. "Laney promised. She would never break it." Then she looked up at him. "This is an amazing wedding present you're giving a man you don't even know."

"I know him better than you might think," he said, thinking of the unsent letters he'd read, and the stories Terri had told him about her beloved big brother.

Cutter warned them, as he always did, his head coming up and a distinctive bark issuing from him. But he didn't leave Terri, Case noted.

When the door opened a tall, pretty, dark haired woman walked in, immediately recognizable from the wedding video they'd seen. Then he saw the man who held the door for her as Quinn greeted them. He instantly recognized not only Terri's brother, but another kind of brother, the under-the-skin kind, from that kind of brotherhood he, Quinn and his crew all shared and he himself had once known. He could see it in the way the man moved, the steady, unwavering look in his eyes.

"Laney, Teague, meet Case McMillan," Quinn said quickly. "You'll want to thank him later, but he's not really why you're here."

The other man's gaze narrowed, but he didn't question Foxworth. The respect he had for the man was clear in his face as he merely said, "Okay."

Case wondered for a brief moment what it must be like to have such faith and trust in your boss. He had no doubt Quinn Foxworth had earned it, from all of them. And even Case could hear the emotion in the usually imperturbable boss of the Foxworth Foundation's voice when he said quietly, "There's someone here who's been waiting a very, very long time to see you."

Hayley stepped over to Teague and took his arm. She said nothing, merely pointed into the living room. Terri's brother turned to look where she'd gestured. To where Terri, her face pale, her eyes wide with stunned joy and glistening with tears, as if she hadn't dared to truly believe until this moment, was slowly getting to her feet. And Case knew that it had all been worth it, everything they'd gone through, for this moment. His chest tightened and his own eyes stung as moisture collected. He didn't even try to fight it.

He shifted his gaze to Teague. He imagined this man, this Marine, had probably weathered sneak attacks with cool aplomb. But now his lips parted, as if he needed more air as he stared in obvious, utter shock.

"Terri?" he said, and his voice nearly broke.

She ran to him then. "Teague," she said, and her voice was both a broken and a joyous thing. She threw her arms around him. That the solid, powerful-looking man staggered under the impact spoke worlds about how shaken he was. But then he was hugging her back, fiercely.

"This time needs to be theirs," Laney said, and Case saw that her cheeks were wet as well, and the love for the man now holding his long-lost sister fairly glowed from her.

"Agreed," Hayley said, emotion making her voice tight, too.

They left the pair there, Teague still clearly stunned, but together with his little sister again at last.

Chapter Thirty-Seven

Quinn led them down the hallway of his and Hayley's home to an office of no small size. A two-sided desk sat in the middle, while cabinets and shelves lined the walls. A moment after they stepped inside Cutter arrived, ears and tail up. As if he'd decided Terri and Teague didn't need him anymore.

Hayley pulled the door shut behind them and Case found himself enveloped in a bear hug. Laney, Teague's Laney. "Thank you," she whispered. "Thank you, thank you, thank you."

He didn't deserve that effusiveness. "Thank Foxworth," he said awkwardly.

"I do," she said, releasing him at last, and stepping back to look at him. "Every day. But Hayley told me how you saved Terri, and got her to them. And saved her again when that horrible man tried to kill her again. And now my Teague is free of the one nightmare that has haunted him for a decade. It wouldn't have happened if not for you."

She spoke as if she was rejoicing as much as her new husband. And why not? She clearly loved the man. And hadn't Case been as elated as she was, just to see the joy bubbling up in Terri when she'd actually seen her brother for the first time?

Because you love her.

Yes, he practically shouted to himself at the hardly new revelation. He did love her.

"Now," Quinn said briskly, "we have another matter to deal with."

Case supposed he should leave. This sounded like Foxworth business. Everybody in this room except him was part of the marvel that was the Foxworth Foundation, even Cutter. Maybe especially Cutter.

He edged toward the door. He'd just leave them to it. He'd—

He stopped, staring down at the dog who was suddenly— how could he move so damn quietly?—between him and the door.

"Move, dog," he muttered.

Cutter merely looked at him, the amber flecks in those dark eyes seeming particularly bright at the moment. Impasse. He may not have known the dog long, but he knew it was futile to argue with him when his canine mind was made up.

And then Hayley was beside him. "That other matter is you," she said quietly, taking his arm and urging him back into the room. He turned because resisting her didn't seem right after all they'd done, but he had no idea what she meant.

Quinn was looking at him intently. One corner of his mouth curved upward, as if he was registering something that had gone as expected. Cutter's move, no doubt. Done without a spoken command. Had he signaled the dog to stop him somehow? Hell, maybe they communicated via telepathy. Nothing would surprise him about this dog anymore.

"How do you feel, today, about what you did back then?" Quinn asked.

His brow furrowed. "I don't regret what I did. It was the right thing to do. I only regret I let the results take me out for so long."

Quinn nodded as if he'd expected that answer. Then, his gaze fixed steadily on Case, he said, "One question." Case looked back at the other man warily. And waited. Quinn asked the question. "Do you want vindication and your job back?"

His first instinct was to laugh at the very idea. But it faded as he realized the man was utterly serious. And how could he laugh when he'd already seen what Foxworth could do?

Vindication and his job back? Once he would have leaped at the slightest chance. Now?

His head was practically spinning with chaotic thoughts. If he got his job back, he would have a life to offer Terri. But he knew that world well enough to know he'd never be completely accepted back, except by those who'd never believed the lies in the first place. And there were enough of the others—mostly in positions of power—to make life miserable.

Hell, there are enough to make life short.

He knew what it would take to restore him. It would take unmasking some very powerful people. And they wouldn't go down easy. And on the job he'd end up having to spend his entire life watching his back. And Terri, if she decided she wanted him, would spend it wondering if this would be the day he didn't come home. Just as she'd thought her brother hadn't.

Vindication and his job…

"Yes, and no," he said.

Quinn smiled. "It may take a while," he warned.

Slowly, he nodded. "I know how deep those poisonous roots go."

"Do you want to lead the digging?"

Case drew back slightly. "Me?"

"You've got the knowledge, and the most at stake. You'll have all Foxworth resources behind you, but you'll be on point. It'll be a lot of work, getting all those i's dotted and t's crossed, completely and unassailably enough to take them down."

He stared at the steady-eyed man opposite him. "Why?" he finally asked. "Why would you care about this?"

"Because," Hayley said as she went to stand beside her husband, "it's what we do. You're an honest, good man who got screwed by those who think they're above such things as being true to an oath or a promise. Those who think they're better than the rest of us, because they've somehow managed, usually crookedly or by pure money, to gain power."

"In other words," Laney put in from where she was watching with interest, the smile at her new husband's joy still on her face, "you're the exact kind of person Foxworth was built to help."

"And," Hayley added, "you have the Cutter seal of approval."

He looked at the dog, who gave a wag of his tail as if in answer. He looked back at Quinn, having a little trouble processing this unexpected turn. "So," the Foxworth man said, "do you want the job?"

Case blinked. "The job?"

"Didn't expect you to do it for nothing," Quinn said. "It would be a special assignment post. And after that, well, we'll know how we work together, and if we're all happy, we'll go from there. Been thinking we could use another hand on board."

A job. Working with people he already knew he could trust with his life. Who were the real thing, not the sham he'd believed in before.

Before.

He could leave that before behind. At last. And start building a new forever. With Terri.

It would take time, for her to be sure it hadn't just been the heat of the moment, and now Foxworth was giving him that time. He knew she wasn't about to leave here, not when she'd only just found Teague again. But now he could stay too, giving up the idea of leaving this part of the country he loved for a new start, because Foxworth wasn't just offering him that new start, they were offering him the chance to take down the people who had come so close to destroying him.

"Oh, and in case you're wondering if this is too big," Quinn said cheerfully, "I figure we'll bring Brett in, if necessary. Tossing his name out at the right moment should tell us some things."

"And Gavin, of course," Hayley added, just as cheerfully.

Catching. All this cheer had to be catching. That's why he felt it welling up inside him.

"Yes," he said, quickly, before he could talk himself out of it. "Absolutely yes."

Quinn's smile widened, and he nodded. "Good. Take a couple of weeks to get settled, and let Terri and Teague get caught up, then we'll start."

"And you might," Hayley suggested wisely, "make sure Terri knows how you feel. If you haven't."

With a little jolt he realized he'd never actually said the words to her. How had Hayley known?

"Had a little practice with this?" he asked, his mouth twisting wryly.

She laughed, and nodded at Cutter. "Thanks to him, yes."

There was paperwork, and Case wasn't sure how much time had passed when the office door opened. He heard Terri's voice and his head snapped around.

"—thought I'd never find a man who could live up to my memory of you, bro. But he found me. Saved me."

"Good enough for me," Teague Johnson said, his voice still sounding a little rough as they stepped into the room.

"I want to do this formally," Terri announced. "Case, this

is my brother. Teague, Case McMillan. Otherwise known as the man I now and will always love."

His heart full with her words and the confidence with which she spoke them, Case turned around to face the man he hoped one day would be his brother-in-law. Teague stepped forward and held out his hand. Case took it, and Teague's fingers tightened. It wasn't a male testing at all, it was so pure a gratitude it practically flowed between them.

"Thank you," he said. "Thank you for my sister's life."

"Neither you, nor she, owe me for that. Anybody would have—"

"No, they wouldn't. Didn't. You did," Terri said fiercely.

Cutter yipped, oddly sounding as if he was agreeing with her words and tone. Case released her brother's hand and turned to look at her.

"And you did the same for me," he said, knowing he would remember forever that image of her standing over Zukero with that makeshift but effective weapon in her hand. He couldn't deny he was glad, that it had been her who had in turn saved him; those scales were balanced now. And she still wanted him.

And suddenly he knew it would all work out. They would—and could now, thanks to Foxworth—take their time, let things level off, and then…then they would start to build. Build a place for them, a relationship, a life.

"Welcome to Foxworth," Quinn said. He was grinning.

Case found himself grinning back. And when Terri hugged him he couldn't stop himself. He kissed her, in front of them all, because nothing in that moment mattered except her. And then he said the words he should have said long ago.

"I love you, Terri."

She grinned up at him impishly. "I know."

He laughed and kissed her again. And he only vaguely heard the noise Cutter made, that sounded for all the world like an approving sigh.

* * * * *

COMING SOON!

We really hope you enjoyed reading this book. If you're looking for more romance be sure to head to the shops when new books are available on

Thursday 1st April

To see which titles are coming soon, please visit

millsandboon.co.uk/nextmonth

MILLS & BOON

LET'S TALK

Romance

For exclusive extracts, competitions
and special offers, find us online:

f facebook.com/millsandboon

𝕏 @MillsandBoon

◎ @MillsandBoonUK

♪ @MillsandBoonUK

Get in touch on 01413 063 232